Praise for J

Bouncing

"Jaime Maddox, Jaime Maddox. She always seems to start out with these feel good lesbian romances. You're reading along, enjoying the fun and light ride, and then—BAM—you get hit with the twisty and suddenly the light ride turns into a twisty, turney awesome mess."—*Danielle Kimerer, Librarian, Reading Public Library (Reading, MA)*

Deadly Medicine

"The tale ran at a good, easy pace...It was one of those books that it is hard to put down, so I didn't...Very, very well done."—*Prism Book Alliance*

Hooked

"[A] compelling, insightful and passionate romantic thriller."—*Lesfic Tumblr*

[Maddox] did an excellent job of portraying the struggles of addiction, not the entire focus of the story, but informative just the same...All the characters are deep, bringing them to life with their complexities. An intricately woven story line adds credibility; life leaps from the pages."—*Lunar Rainbow Reviewz*

By the Author

Agnes

The Common Thread

Bouncing

Deadly Medicine

Hooked

The Scholarship

Love Changes Everything

LOVE CHANGES EVERYTHING

by
Jaime Maddox

2020

LOVE CHANGES EVERYTHING

ISBN 13: 978-1-63555-835-7

This Trade Paperback Original Is Published By
Bold Strokes Books, Inc.
P.O. Box 249
Valley Falls, NY 12185

First Edition: December 2020

Credits

Editor: Shelley Thrasher
Production Design: Stacia Seaman
Cover Design by Tammy Seidick

Acknowledgments

My thanks to everyone at Bold Strokes Books for making the publishing process go so smoothly, especially my editor, Shelley Thrasher. My first reader, Margaret Pawling, has been the first reader since the first book, and I'm grateful for her eagle eye and honest feedback. Thank you, readers, for reading and emailing and making me feel that what I write is worth reading. Finally, to the three people who share every day of my life—Carolyn, Jamison, and Max—you are my heart, my world, my life. XOXO.

To Yankee
Love really does change everything, doesn't it?

CHAPTER ONE

C lear!"

Dr. Samantha Brooks stepped back from the gurney and turned her eyes to the cardiac monitor on the wall, listening for the familiar *thrump* as three hundred and sixty joules of energy coursed through the human body lying before her.

"What's goin' on?"

Dr. Tara Simon slid next to her and looked at the patient. Sam momentarily ignored her and spoke to the X-ray tech. "Shoot a lateral cervical spine, would you, please?" Then she turned to the aide. "Back on the chest."

Sam turned to her colleague and answered her question. "Seventeen-year-old girl, texting and driving, car versus telephone pole. She's been in cardiac arrest since the medics got to the scene. V-fib the whole time, not responding at all. When I opened the cervical collar, her neck seemed a little crunchy. That would explain it."

"It sure would."

They stood silently beside each other, as they'd done many times, watching the action, their bodies still but their minds in crisis mode. Sam knew exactly what Tara was thinking because she'd trained her. Twenty years earlier, they'd been residents together, and Tara had come home with Sam one weekend and fallen in love with the mountains of Northeastern Pennsylvania, and with a colleague who was a native. Like Sam, she took a job in the ER after finishing her residency and had never left.

"You've gone through all the algorithms?"

"Yep." Sam sighed. She'd done everything by the book and considered all the things that could have caused this girl's heart to stop—blood loss, a collapsed lung, blood in the sac around the heart. Brain trauma. Sam had examined her patient for all the clues and come up with nothing except the possible neck injury. She'd run the code and hoped for the best, but there had been no response. It was a stab in the dark, running a code when she didn't know what caused the heart to stop beating in the first place.

Sensing her sadness, Tara rubbed Sam's shoulder as the X-ray tech asked them to step out while she shot the image, and a moment later a line of bones appeared on the computer screen just inside the code room.

"Jesus," Tara said.

Biting her lip, Sam nodded. "Okay, everyone. That's enough," she said to no one in particular, focusing on the broken neck on the screen. "Thank you."

"Any sign out?" Tara asked as they walked from the room.

Sam shook her head. "It was a remarkably uneventful day until twenty minutes ago. The PA is seeing a couple of minor things, and I'm just working on charts."

"Early night. Good for you," Tara said. "Go hug your kids."

"Actually, it's not. Julie wants to see me. In her office."

Tara leaned back and made a face. "Ooh. That can't be good."

"No shit." Sam loved Tara, but sometimes she annoyed the crap out of her.

A nurse approached and began questioning Tara, and Sam took the opportunity to escape. Weaving her way through a maze of corridors, Sam nodded and said hello to a dozen familiar faces before stopping at a large, dark door. As she leaned against it, she nearly fell into the quiet darkness of the hospital chapel.

She knew this place well and mindlessly made her way to a small altar, where a dozen candles flickered, disturbing the stillness. Throwing a dollar into the donation box, she grabbed a candle and lit it, then turned to the bench to pray. The chapel had no statue of Mary, yet Sam blessed herself and talked to her anyway.

She didn't look up when she heard the door open, just sat lost in her thoughts, wondering how many lives would be torn apart by the loss of this one young girl. If only she had been wearing a seat belt,

Sam mused as someone slid onto the bench beside her, interrupting her musings. Turning, she met Tara's concerned gaze. Tara squeezed Sam's hand before folding her own in her lap. "You okay?" she asked.

Sam nodded, and they sat quietly together.

"It's not even about the prayers," Sam said after a while. "I just find this place so peaceful."

"Quietest place in the hospital," Tara whispered, and Sam smiled. "Am I disturbing you?"

"I'm getting old, Tar. It's getting to me, you know?"

Tara scooched closer. "How can it not? She's the same age as our kids, for fuck's sake. Every time they get into a car, I freak out."

Sam didn't cringe at the use of the F-word in the chapel. In the ER, people used it in just about every sentence—sometimes as a noun, sometimes as a verb, sometimes as an adjective. Still, she couldn't help ribbing her friend. "Stop cursing. You're in church."

"You couldn't do a thing to help her, Sam. She was dead at the scene."

Sam nodded. She knew that. It didn't matter. "When I was a student, working in this very same ER, I felt so optimistic about my future. I thought I could make the world a better place."

"And now?"

"I don't know anymore. I just finished rereading Victor Frankl. *Man's Search for Meaning*. I read it in college and found Frankl too dark. Now, I think he's brilliant. Am I just more mature?"

"Our job can be crushing."

"Yes, it can. And every case I see reminds me of not my own vulnerability, but my kids'."

"You can't protect them, right?"

"No. I can't." Sam's pulse pounded a little faster at the thought.

"You're an interesting person, Samantha Brooks."

Sam didn't feel interesting, just tired. She didn't reply. Instead, she leaned back, studying the stained-glass mosaic of a dove in flight. "What makes you say that?"

"After twenty years, you still surprise me."

"Hmm."

"No, seriously. You're Dr. Perfect all the time. You never do anything wrong, the staff loves you, and you've got all your shit together. You save lives and make crazy diagnoses. No one would ever suspect that such things as self-actualization trouble you."

"Don't tell anyone."

"So what's up with Julie?"

Shaking her head, Sam shrugged. "No idea. She showed up an hour ago and asked if she could speak to me *in private*."

"Hey, maybe someone complained about you!" Tara joked. "*Finally.*"

"It's bound to happen eventually," Sam said, and then they were quiet again.

"I pray a lot, Sam. My grandmother was almost a nun."

Intrigued, Sam turned to her. "How does one *almost* become a nun?"

"It was her dream, from the time she was a little girl, and she planned to enter the convent after school. But then her mother became sick. Rheumatoid arthritis. Very quickly, she lost the ability to walk and raise her arms above her head. She was a farmer's wife, with six kids, so that was a problem. My great-grandfather sat my gramma down and asked her if she might find another way to serve the Lord—by taking care of her mother. And the rest is history. Ten years later, her mother died, my grandmother met my grandfather, and they started multiplying." She paused. "I always find that story so compelling. It's humbling to know that my wonderful life is possible only because my great-grandmother was afflicted with one of the most painful conditions known to mankind."

It *was* a powerful story. "You're an interesting person, Tara Simon."

Tara winked in reply.

"Thanks for following me."

"I had to make sure you're okay. If you take the bridge I'd be so fucked."

Sam stood and shook her head. "So much for reverence in this holy place." She winked. "I have to go to my meeting."

"Let me know how it goes," Tara said as she walked to the candle box. "I'll light one for you," she said with a wink.

It was a short trip to her boss's office, and Sam stopped before the door that was always open. After knocking, she waited for the woman behind the desk to meet her gaze. She did so with a warm smile, and at her invitation, Sam strolled in and sat in one of the two institutional-grade, faux-leather armchairs arranged before the desk. The office itself was bland, painted a shade of depressing beige that was due for a touch-up, with a large metal desk at its center. At least it appeared to be metal. The papers and journals and files piled on its surface made it difficult to be certain. A filing cabinet was positioned against a wall, and a surprisingly healthy-looking plant sat on top. Requisite diplomas and certificates were framed and hung on the walls, but the plant was the only sign of life—aside from the woman sitting behind the desk.

Dr. Julie Wilde might have been lacking as an interior decorator, but she was an exceptional department head. She'd been a staff physician when Sam worked in the ER as a college student. Then Julie had been just a few years out of residency but as smart as could be. She had great surgical skills and was kind, and Sam always enjoyed working with her. As a freshly minted director, Julie was the one who'd interviewed Sam almost twenty years ago and hired her for the first and only job Sam had ever had. Julie had helped her make the transition from the structured environment of her residency to the independent practice of an attending physician in the emergency department. Her guidance had helped Sam grow over the years, to be not just a good doctor, but also a colleague to her fellow physicians, a leader to the staff and residents, and a representative to the hospital on a key community committee.

She didn't hesitate to give Sam hell, either, when she needed it, and that's exactly what fueled the fire burning in Sam's chest now. When Julie had stopped in and asked if she could meet with Sam at the end of her shift, Sam knew something was seriously wrong. If Julie's concern was minor, she would have just told her, instead of bothering with the formality of a private meeting. It had been an endless hour since, with Sam worrying about everything from a change in the schedule to getting fired, and a host of smaller problems in between.

"What's up?" she asked without preamble, before taking a breath and forcing herself to relax her rigid posture.

Julie smiled, although she sat tall in her chair, as stiff as Sam, seeming too professional for a casual meeting between department head and subordinate. Yep. Something was up. Something big. "No fooling you. I thought I'd start by asking about your family and that well-deserved vacation you're planning."

"Of course. But you first. How's Amanda?"

Julie's wife, Amanda, had been diagnosed with breast cancer and was still undergoing treatment. Julie sighed. "The chemo's kicking the crap out of her, but once this is over, the doctor says she'll be fine. Fortunately we caught this early, and she's responding to treatment. And thank you for all the food. With my work obligations and her treatment schedule, cooking has been the last thing on our agenda, so you've helped a lot."

"I'm glad she's responding, Julie. And the food is no trouble. I have to cook for my family anyway, so it's just a little extra."

"Speaking of your family...how is everyone?"

"The twins are great. Your invitation to the graduation party is in that big pile of mail you seem to be ignoring." Sam motioned with her head. Then she smiled. "I can't believe it. My babies are graduating high school. I remember being pregnant...Aw, you don't want to hear this nostalgia."

"I don't regret never having children. Amanda and I have been able to live quite an amazing life. We were at Yosemite once." She deepened the timbre of her voice. "Many, many years ago."

They laughed. "Yes. I'm hoping I can keep up! The entire family is certified in CPR, so I'm good there."

"Tell me about your adventure."

"I can't wait for this trip, Julie. It's going to be fun. More than fun. Spectacular. Two weeks to see the Grand Canyon, Death Valley, and Yosemite. I don't think I've had that much time off since maternity leave."

"You've done it the right way, though, Sam. I see a lot of women trying to have it all—a tribe of kids and full-time careers, too. They seem to somehow end up with lots of problems. You told me during your interview that you wanted kids and wanted to work part-time, and you've stuck to it. You could have done a lot more professionally if you wanted to, but you've done something better—raised two remarkable sons."

Sam was touched. She respected Julie, and coming from her, the compliment meant a great deal. "Hard to believe it's been nineteen years. Do I get a toaster for twenty?"

"A blender."

"More practical, with this job," she said as she raised a mock glass.

"Don't even joke, Sam."

Sam winced at her inappropriate comment. One of her colleagues was on an extended leave while rehabbing from drug and alcohol addiction. It made everyone's life more difficult—all of the staff had to pick up extra shifts—and Julie had been forced to hire a temp to fill in the ones they couldn't cover.

Sam thought the temp was a smart enough doc, but he used the "I just started here" excuse a little too often. Reading her mind, Julie asked about him.

"He's not so bad that I have to change my travel plans. Just a little lazy, I think. He moves his tail when he has to."

"That's what I've observed, too. The staff is accepting him, and that's what we need. Vinnie could be out for six months."

Sam drew her breath and weighed her words. "I think we need to be open to the possibility that it could be longer. Let's face it—if he admitted to using six OxyContin a day, how many was he really taking? Plus the booze! He's lucky he's still breathing. When he comes back—he may want to work reduced hours to keep his stress level down."

"I think he needs to work. He has five kids."

"That thinking is what got him into trouble in the first place, Julie. He was always poaching shifts. I only work twenty hours a week, and he was constantly trying to help me out by covering for me. I explained that I don't get PTO because I'm part-time, and that I need my hours to pay my bills…he just joked about me being a kept woman! He hounded me."

"I've been thinking that I should do a policy about switching shifts, just to make it more formal, so people aren't doing it all the time."

"Some people don't know how to plan their lives around their work schedule, and Vinnie is definitely one of them."

"If he doesn't come back, since your boys will be starting college and will be a little more independent, I wonder if you might consider working full-time."

"I haven't thought of it, but I will. Let me get my kids settled first. But I don't need to work more. I *am* a kept woman, you know," she said with a wink. "I'd do it for you, though, just to help out until everything settles with Vinnie."

Julie laughed. "How is Doug?"

"Never better. Being dean of the medical school is the perfect job for him. He gets to travel, hobnobbing with important colleagues and donors, and he teaches a little, oversees research projects. He does everything but actually practice medicine."

Julie sniggered. "You get your hands dirty enough for everyone."

Sam beamed. "It's a tough job, but I'm glad it's mine." She paused. Julie seemed more relaxed after their short conversation. Had Sam just imagined the stress she thought she'd picked up earlier? "So is that why you wanted to see me? To offer me full-time with fabulous benefits?" she finally asked.

"Hmm," she said as she fished a manila file from a pile of them and pushed it Sam's way. It wasn't a patient chart—the hospital had gone paperless years before—but it resembled one. In black marker, on the identification tab, was written a name. Tyler Sheffly. On the upper margin in similar script was his medical-record number and date of birth, which Sam noted. He was eighteen years old, almost the same age as her sons.

"What's this?" she asked, her heart beating faster. While it was possible Julie wanted her to look at the file to review the work of a peer, the circumstances suggested to her that her own work was under the microscope today.

Sliding the file into her lap, Sam pulled a pair of cheaters from her lab-coat pocket and adjusted them on her face. The paper felt cool, mirroring the cold now coursing through her veins.

"You're being deposed in a lawsuit," Julie said, her mouth puckered in sympathy.

"What? I'm being sued? Fuck! Why?" she asked as she began leafing through the contents of the file and found a letter from an attorney's office, a firm with five names. Another from the hospital attorney. Then pages of a medical record that was now thirteen years old.

Julie was silent as Sam read the paperwork. Finally, Sam looked up again and questioned her. "This case is ancient. What's going on?"

"You saw this kid back in 2007. He was five. He technically has until age eighteen, plus two years, to file a lawsuit."

"And they waited."

"They waited."

"Why?"

"After talking to the hospital counsel, I suppose they wanted to give it time to see what kind of complications he had."

"So, they didn't want to rush to judgment?"

She looked over the top of her glasses and met Julie's gaze. "Or they wanted to collect more evidence. Or his parents didn't want to sue, but now that he's an adult, he does. Who knows?"

"So am I being sued, then?"

"Well, as you can see, he just turned eighteen. They have two years to decide. For right now, they're just deposing you, taking your testimony to decide if they're going to pursue legal action."

"How the hell can I give testimony on a patient I treated thirteen years ago?"

"You can basically read the chart to them. Unless you remember the case?"

"How can I…" She'd reached a page in the chart that made her stop. It was a transfer sheet, with the hospital logo at the top and writing beneath. Tyler Sheffly's demographic information was imprinted on top, the stamp a crooked mark smudging the page. Beneath it, written in her own hand, the diagnosis. *Subdural empyema.*

Now her heart pounded harder, the pulse in her throat threatening her air supply.

Only once, in a career that spanned more than twenty years, had she written that diagnosis on a patient's chart. Of course she knew this kid.

"Oh, God. I do remember him, Julie." She looked up and met Julie's gaze. "I remember this case well."

Julie smiled weakly, like an undertaker at a funeral, in a circumstance where the smile seems so out of place. "It's an unusual diagnosis. I thought you might recall the case."

Letting out a huge sigh, Sam thought back. "I do. I just don't understand why I'm being sued. Deposed. Whatever. I'm the one who made the diagnosis. The pediatrician completely missed it."

"Well, she's being sued, not just deposed. Along with the radiologist and the hospital. Since you remember, can you tell me about the case? I'm just curious."

Sam sat back, now actually feeling a little more relaxed since she'd learned what was going on. Staring off into the middle distance, out the window behind Julie's desk, she summoned long-buried details. "He was a cute little boy. Dark, curly hair, big brown eyes. He didn't look sick at all when I first saw him. He just wasn't getting better. The pediatrician sent him in for a workup because it was a Friday night, and—what else could she do? He had a fever—off and on, I think, but nothing in the ER. Sinus symptoms, runny nose, headache. He'd been on an antibiotic from the pediatrician, but it wasn't helping. I don't know why, Julie, but I threw the book at him. Labs, CT scan, IV fluids, IV antibiotics. Because, even though he looked good at that point, the parents impressed me with the history. You know what I mean?"

She nodded. "Gut instinct is an important clinical tool."

"Exactly. I wanted to do a spinal tap, cuz this could have been viral meningitis, but the parents flat-out refused. The mom called the pediatrician on her cell phone from the kid's room—because they know her personally. Handed me the phone to talk to her. Anyway, she and the parents decided against the tap. I made them sign a refusal of care, made them sign out against medical advice, and off they went."

"So how'd the diagnosis of a brain abscess end up on the chart?"

Sam laughed. "The angels were with me, Julie. Or, more importantly, with him. It was my weekend on—Friday, Saturday, Sunday-evening shifts. Sunday night, the kid comes back. Symptoms are worse now. Fever won't come down. He looks sick. I started another IV, got a dose of antibiotics going, and sat there trying to figure out what the heck was going on. The parents still refused the spinal tap, wanted me to call the pediatrician and get the kid admitted quickly so they wouldn't have to wait in the ER. Apparently, she wasn't answering her cell phone. I refused. Something wasn't right, you know? I didn't want this little boy—who was just a few months younger than my own sons—going upstairs without a diagnosis. At least not without the pediatrician coming in to see him.

"I forget now how it all happened, but somehow, the pediatrician called in admitting orders. I was stuck in the middle there, trying to be the advocate for my patient, while his parents were trying to run the show, and the pediatrician had no idea what was going on. She'd seen him once days earlier, and by that time, I'd seen him twice. And suddenly, they're wheeling the kid out of the ER and upstairs for admission.

"Then, fate stepped in. Just as I was standing there trying to reason with the parents, the radiologist called to give me a report on another patient. It was the same guy who'd read Tyler's CT two nights before. While I had him on the phone, I asked him if this kid might benefit from another imaging study. You know, like a CT with contrast, maybe. I don't know what I was thinking, I was just grasping for something because I was worried.

"So he pulls up the imaging study and says he'd take another look, and then the next thing he says is something like, 'Oh, shit. He's got a subdural empyema.'"

Julie laughed. "I bet there were a few other choice words, too."

"That would be a good bet." Sam would have laughed, except there was nothing funny about the situation.

"So what did you do then?"

"I talked to the pediatrician, and called CHOP, and arranged the transfer. Then I ran, literally ran, to the peds floor to explain the situation to the parents. Of course—you're getting an idea about these parents by now, right?"

Julie nodded, a smile tilting up one corner of her mouth.

"They were not the least bit concerned about the diagnosis. I think they were pissed that I wanted to transfer their child to Philadelphia instead of letting someone treat him in Wilkes-Barre."

"But they went?"

"Yes. By that point the pediatrician was petrified that she'd misdiagnosed a brain abscess and her patient was probably going to die. She refused to admit him. I left as the parents were arguing with her on the phone. I didn't stick around for the transfer, just made sure the orders were there and the nurses understood what was happening. I spoke with the pediatrician a few weeks later about another patient, and she told me he was doing well. He'd had emergency surgery and was expected to make a full recovery."

"Interesting case," Julie observed. "Although full recovery after brain surgery is sort of subjective, isn't it?"

"For sure. If he's anything less than a genius, they can argue it's because of the infection. If it had been diagnosed sooner…" She let the implication hang.

"I can see why you'd remember the case. Not something you see every day."

"Not something you see *ever.* But more than that. You know I believe in angels. I have an angel on my stethoscope, to guide me. A little ER angel was definitely at work that night. If all the pieces hadn't come together perfectly, that little boy would have died. If I hadn't been the doctor here when he came back, he might have fallen through the cracks. It was just obvious to me that something had gone wrong. He was so much sicker than he had been two days before, and there was no diagnosis. It seemed like it was just meant to be—I was here, the radiologist called and saw the infection on the CT..." What should have been a happy memory, a victorious moment when she'd saved a life, was anything but. Suddenly, she felt drained.

"So why the hell are they suing?"

Julie shook her head. "I don't know. I'm sorry you have to go through this...especially now. I mean, there's no good time to be sued, but right now is sort of a high time for you, with your sons graduating. I hate to see this taint your summer. Especially since it seems you did everything you could for this patient. You saved his life."

Sam thought so, too, but it was nice to hear Julie say it. It reaffirmed her belief in herself, but she was still troubled. This legal entanglement was not going to be pleasant, even if she'd done everything right.

"What happens now?"

"You get to have a copy of his chart to review. Treat this confidentially. Lock it in a closet or something at home, so his privacy is protected. Because the case is so old, it's going to fall under Pennsylvania's umbrella policy. The hospital attorney won't be defending you. It'll be someone who works for the Commonwealth. His name is," Julie paused to look at a piece of paper, then handed it to her as he continued, "Harry Johnson. You have a meeting with him next week."

Sam glanced at the paper, a printout of an email.

"All the details are there." Julie winked. "And since you have that cushy part-time schedule, it was easy to arrange the meeting for a time when you're off."

Sam rolled her eyes. She was used to the playful harassment of her colleagues, who teased her about spending half her life getting an education that she barely used. "Okay, so I meet with Harry, and I read from the chart, and then what?"

"He's going to prepare you to meet with Tyler's lawyer, ask you questions, tell you what to say and what not to say. Get you used to sitting in front of a bunch of strangers. He'll probably videotape you, just so you're comfortable with that."

"So this is not a hearing? Just a meeting?"

"That's about it. Maybe a practice run."

"What should I wear?"

"Be presentable. It's not court, but you want to seem professional."

Sam shifted, folded her hands in her lap, and looked at her friend. "Fuck."

CHAPTER TWO

Sam slid four eggs onto rolls, then onto a plate, and carried it to her kitchen table. She watched with joy as her sons scooped up the sandwiches and devoured them.

"Let's talk about our day," she said, sipping her coffee.

"Accounting test," Charlie said between bites. Even if his mouth wasn't full of food, he wouldn't have been any more talkative. Getting information out of her eighteen-year-old twins was like removing a sliver from under a fingernail using only her teeth. Difficult and painful.

"Spanish," Danny added.

"It's winding down, guys. Pretty soon you'll be walking across the stage."

"I can't wait," Danny said.

"Who's driving this week?" They shared her old SUV but typically went everywhere together, so it didn't matter. The only issue that came up with the car was whose turn it was to drive. They'd compromised by alternating weeks.

"Wroagahng," Charlie said through a mouthful of food.

Sam glared at him as he swallowed.

"Sorry. My turn."

"And what are your plans for after school?"

"Lifeguard meeting," Danny said.

"The pool opens on Memorial Weekend?" Sam knew exactly when the pool opened, but she wanted to hear it from them. She wanted them to *communicate* with her, to share the small details of their lives.

They were honor students, Eagle Scouts, accomplished young men, but they couldn't talk with their mother. It was so frustrating.

They nodded.

"Okay," Sam said, trying her best not to let her feelings show. When had parenting become so difficult? When had those precious little boys who had adored her begun to treat her as an afterthought? "Your father left for Philadelphia this morning. He has a conference, so he won't be home until very late. I have a meeting this morning, then work at three. You guys are on your own until late tonight."

"Hmm," Danny said.

"Whatever you're thinking of, forget it. I don't want any phone calls from the police, or the fire department, or the school, or the coroner. Okay?"

"Yes, ma'am," they said in unison.

Smiling sweetly, Sam sipped her coffee. "Perfect."

"What's your meeting about?" Charlie asked, in a rare display of interest in something that didn't directly relate to him.

Out of the corner of her eye, she noted Danny watching as well. Listening.

Sam sighed. Being a teenager was hard enough without dealing with the worries of your parents. Sam knew that all too well. For their entire life, she'd done her best to keep them sheltered from the things they were powerless to fix—her work worries, her mother's health issues, her occasional spats with their father. But they were older now, and maybe it was time to share a little. "I'm being sued. Maybe. I have to talk to a lawyer today."

"What?" Charlie demanded.

"Why?" Danny asked.

Hiding her smile, she told them a diluted and redacted version of the events of thirteen years earlier.

"There is no way you would ever do anything wrong to hurt a little kid. Are these people crazy?"

"I love that you think so highly of me," she told Charlie. "You're sweet. Thank you. But even good doctors can make mistakes."

"Did you?" Danny asked.

"Make a mistake?"

When he nodded, Sam shook her head. "No."

Leaning forward, Charlie put his hand on hers. Danny topped his.
"Then you have nothing to worry about."

Sam swallowed tears. A minute earlier, she'd hated them. Now, she'd fallen in love all over again.

"Go to school," she said.

She stood and kissed both on the tops of their heads. "Please put your dishes in the dishwasher, and drive safely, and have a wonderful day."

"You, too," Danny said.

"I love you both," Sam replied as she turned to leave.

"We love you, too."

"I second that."

Like a mother duck, she followed them to the door and then watched from the window until the car disappeared. Grabbing her fanny pack, Sam put in her AirPods and turned on some meditation music. After she locked the back door behind her, she walked through her yard and to the base of the mountain that shadowed her house.

The day promised to be gorgeous, and already the sun was shining across the mountain range behind her, warming her back as she began climbing.

As a kid in an era with little technology, Sam had often wondered how many steps it took to climb to her favorite lookout spot. She'd tried counting but always gave up after a while. Now, her watch counted for her, and she was always pleased by the results when she glanced at her wrist. She pushed herself, too, trying not just for steps, but for time. At almost fifty, she considered exercise more important than ever.

Today, though, she wasn't climbing for the exercise. Today was all about the view.

Since she'd first struggled up the Knob with her father as a little girl, it had been one of her favorite places. It was undisturbed, where wild animals roamed and watched her cautiously from a safe distance. It was a peaceful place that fostered deep thoughts, and it was here that Sam made some of the most important decisions of her life. Sometimes she came up here to cry, where no one could see her and question her feelings. Once, she'd had a spectacular first kiss up here, and another time, when she was at a crossroads in her life, she'd stumbled upon a mother bear and two cubs. At that moment, Sam knew the direction she was supposed to take. When she finally became pregnant, she knew before the first ultrasound was done that she was carrying twins.

It was quiet on the mountain, and the view went on for miles, showing the curves of the Susquehanna River as it sliced through the Wyoming Valley. Although she couldn't see the buildings, she knew just the location where the hospital was located, where her kids went to school, where her Bapcia had lived, and where her parents were buried.

Standing still, she closed her eyes, breathing in the fresh mountain air. She counted her breaths, imagined herself growing roots to anchor her in the rock on which she stood. Then she reached up, imagined herself a tree, branches soaring toward the sky, each leaf absorbing the sun that gave it life. In her mind, rain clouds opened above, and the sky poured into her, each drop of rain coursing through her body and back into the earth.

When she finished her meditation, Sam assumed a yoga pose and began a series of movements to stretch and strengthen her muscles. After she finished, she sat, staring into the nothingness of the distant sky.

"This has always been the place I've come to for answers," she said to the heavens. "But now, I don't even know what the questions are."

Perhaps Tara was right—she was already missing her sons, worried about what her life would be like when they were away in college. But under the microscope, Sam knew the problem was even deeper than that. What would her purpose be? As a child she had goals—to climb the mountain, to make the softball team, to get into college, then medical school, then residency. She had allowed herself no period of rest or reflection, just that journey of thousands of steps, putting one foot in front of the other.

Then she'd climbed this mountain when her life had been at a crossroads, wondering what she should do next. She'd been about to finish her residency, and her marriage was in trouble. Should she stay with her husband and have a child, or leave him and travel her own path? She'd spoken to her father, long dead, and asked him for a sign, and then, off the normal trail she hiked, she'd found the mother bear and her twin cubs.

Sam stayed with Doug and had her boys, her purpose clear. She gave the best of herself to them, for eighteen years. Not that she didn't take time for herself—she did. Spa days were a repeat event on her calendar, as were her yoga class and golf league. She occasionally got away without her children—mostly to conferences, but occasionally just for fun. Sam had had a wonderful mother, who adored her grandchildren and was a huge help with them right up until the end. And Doug was a great dad, too.

Her boys had turned out just how she'd always hoped they would—kind, thoughtful, intelligent young men.

Independent young men, who no longer needed her.

Sam would figure it out. She knew she would. She always did. But now, she had to deal with this lawsuit thing, too.

She stood and began making her way back home. At the place in the trail where she'd spotted the bears, she stopped, as usual, and looked for them. They were grown now, and she often wondered about them. That day had been the first time she'd seen a bear on the mountain, and she'd never seen another since, her personal proof they'd been a sign from above.

As she walked, she pondered her wardrobe, wondering what to wear for the meeting with Harry Johnson, the lawyer. She'd decided on elegant rather than professional, to boost her spirits, but truthfully, her wardrobe was limited. She wore scrubs at work and jeans at home. Sweats to yoga class, golf clothing to the links. Her occasions to dress up were limited, and her wardrobe reflected that fact.

Her cell phone rang just as she reached the base of the mountain. Lori. She tapped her AirPod and answered. "Hey, friend. How's it going?"

"Okay on my end. But my ESP told me to call you. What's up?"

"Your ESP is right on, as usual," Sam said. "What should I wear to a deposition?"

"Oh, no," she said, in the sweet way that always told Sam she cared. "What happened?"

Sam told her the story.

"It sounds like you did everything right. Why do these lawyers have to sue the good doctors?"

Sam sighed. "Because they can, I guess."

"One day, when we all stop practicing critical care and just do Botox in the office, they'll see. There won't be anyone to take out the ruptured appendixes or put the stents in blocked arteries. People will die."

Sam agreed, and she knew Lori spoke from experience. As a cardiologist, she'd been in the hot seat a number of times when patients had complications. Sam hadn't reached out to her primarily because she knew how much talking about it bothered her friend, and she didn't want to drag Lori down with her own drama.

"I remember when I got sued over the guy whose artery ruptured during an angioplasty. Sam, it's so crazy. I do the same thing, every time. Wash my hands, don my sterile gown and gloves, thread the wire into the coronaries. It's always the same. So why did that artery rupture, when a thousand before didn't? And why, Sam, why is that my fault? It is a known complication of the procedure."

Sam sighed. She had no answer to Lori's question. "I feel old, Lor."

"You are. Your kids are graduating high school. You're old."

"Thanks for that. But you'll always be older."

"Ha, ha. Seven days. What you need is a change of scenery. Move to Florida, practice here. I feel so young and vibrant when I'm in the sunshine."

"You're not going to look young for long. All that sun is going to kill your beautiful skin."

"That's why God invented plastic surgeons."

Sam smiled. She felt so much better after talking to her friend. "Have you heard from Jim?" Jim had left Sam a message, but she hadn't yet returned his call. She liked to talk to her friends every week, but between her schedule and theirs, sometimes it was hard.

"Yes. Did you hear his news?"

The excitement in Lori's voice told her it was something good. "No. What's up?"

"He was nominated for some great award, for cancer research."

Sam felt a smile form. Jim, who was so brilliant, had chosen such a great field to utilize his talents. "I didn't hear. I owe him a call."

"We're invited to some ceremony in Las Vegas."

"I'm in."

"You better be," Lori said.

"Really, I'm in. So, how's He-Man?" Sam asked, and Lori laughed. She'd been married and divorced three times and now dated a series of men who all looked the same—young, wild, and built like superheroes. Sam still marveled at the changes in Lori, from the shy young woman who'd been her studious lab partner in college to a motorcycle-riding cardiologist living on the beach in Florida.

"His name is Carlos."

"And he's a bouncer?"

"No. That was Brian. This one's a bounty hunter."

"You're living the dream, Lor."

"Someone has to, because you certainly aren't. You're working too hard. And not just in the ER. At life. It's not meant to be taken seriously, Sam. Just have fun, because pretty soon a balloon is going to rupture your artery, or a cancer is going to invade your brain, or something else bad is going to whack you."

Sam couldn't argue. "Maybe I'll come visit."

"Maybe, schmaybe. Just do it. When you send those cubs to college, get your butt on a plane and come see me."

"I am going to seriously think about that."

"Uh! I don't know why I love you so much, but I do."

"Thanks for calling, Lor."

After showering, Sam sat at her vanity and finished her hair and makeup before selecting something to wear. Lori hadn't answered her question about what to wear, but it didn't matter. Sam imagined her friend in six-inch heels with silk pants of an African print and a matching scarf. Fingering the contents of the suit section of her closet, she chose a white linen jacket, then coordinated it with teal pants and a multicolored silk shell. While she checked herself in the mirror, she nodded approval. Sophisticated, but not too businesslike. Comfortable. And she looked good. Fifty was still a year away, but she could still pull herself together when she had to.

The meeting was in Kingston, a fifteen-minute ride from her house, but she gave herself half an hour. Being early gave her a sense of control in a situation where she felt totally helpless. To lift her spirits, she drove the Mercedes. It was thirty years old and not her everyday car, but this was one of those occasions when it should come out of the garage. It had been her dad's car, and if ever she needed his arms around her, it was now.

Had he ever been sued? Probably not. She'd never heard her parents talk about it, and he'd practiced medicine at a time when lawsuits against physicians weren't so prevalent. How would he have handled it? Probably with dignity and class, just how she was planning to.

She saw plenty of parking at the Saxton Pavilion yet Sam chose a spot far away from other cars, then locked the doors. Carrying a small briefcase containing the file Julie had given her, as well as a few scholarly articles on subdural empyema, Sam made her way into the building.

It took only a moment to orient herself, and she made her way quickly to the appropriate suite. Taking a deep breath to calm her nerves, she opened the door to the legal office and entered a small lobby. A woman looked up at her from behind a desk and offered a bright smile.

"Good-morning, I'm Dr. Samantha Brooks. I'm here—"

"Good morning, Dr. Brooks. We've been expecting you. Do you need to use the bathroom, or would you like something to drink?"

"No, thanks. I'm fine."

The woman pointed down the hallway. "See the open door at the end? That's where you need to go."

Sam nodded. "Perfect," she said, although she felt anything but. Shaky legs carried her down that hall, past half a dozen doors, most of them closed. What awaited her through that door? Would it be as stressful as she'd been imagining over the past five days? Or was this really just a formality? Either way, she'd be happy when this day ended.

Sam knocked on the frame of the open door and looked into the room. A woman sat alone at a long conference table, dozens of papers spread out before her as she seemed to be studying them. Her head was bent, and dark, wavy hair fell loosely past her shoulders. At Sam's knock, she looked up.

For the second time in her life, she was knocked senseless by Kirby Fielding. "Kirby?" Sam asked the question, although she had no doubt who sat before her. She'd never taken a photo of Kirby—she'd never had a reason to. She'd always thought they'd have the summer, that they had plenty of time to do silly things like pose for photos. They hadn't, though, but her image—the deep-brown eyes and angled jaw, the mouth that always seemed to be suppressing a smile—had been burned into Sam's brain. It had been a lifetime since she'd seen her, but nothing about Kirby had changed.

Sam braced herself against the door frame as a wave of emotion slammed her. Her knees felt weak, and she was breathless. She'd always imagined what this would be like—meeting Kirby again. But Teddy had told her that Kirby had moved back to Harrisburg, and Sam knew the odds were slim that their paths would cross. Even in the age of Google, Sam hadn't bothered to look for Kirby. The truth was, she didn't think she could handle it.

Chapter Three

1993

Samantha Burkhart pulled her Mercedes into the last empty parking place she found, far away from the other cars in the lot near the sports fields at Hillside Park in Nanticoke. No sense chancing a dent from another car when she saw so many empty spots.

Using the remote, she opened the trunk and pulled out a duffel bag containing everything she'd need for her summer softball tryouts—clothes, shoes, glove, visor, bat. She reviewed her mental checklist, then hoisted the bag and jogged toward the bathrooms, pointing the remote over her shoulder as she went. When she didn't hear the familiar chirp of the car's lock, she turned her head to look back and ran into a brick wall.

The force of the impact dropped her to the ground, and when she sat up a moment later, she was shocked to realize she hadn't hit a wall at all, that she'd hit a very solidly built young woman who looked as perplexed as Sam felt. Sam was dazed, and it took a moment for her vision to clear. Her chest didn't seem capable of expanding to allow in a breath. Even so, her ego had suffered the most serious injury. How could she have been so stupid?

Before she could apologize, the other woman did. "Wow! I'm really sorry. I wasn't watching where I was going."

Sam couldn't help laughing. In a few weeks, she'd be sitting for the final exam in her statistics class. What was the probability that two women walking in different directions would have their attention diverted elsewhere at the exact moment their paths intersected? She shared the irony. "I wasn't either. What are the odds?"

"I don't know about odds, but I'm happy I can blame you for this. Because, honestly, I feel like an idiot."

Sam grinned at her as she rubbed the back of her head. "Likewise," she replied. The dizziness returned for just a moment before clearing. Her breaths seemed to come easier, too. "I don't think it's all that bad. Nothing broken. How about you?"

The woman sat and squinted at Sam. "Are you a twin by chance, or am I seeing double?"

Sam rose to her knees, moving a little closer to her. "Are you serious?" She'd taken first-aid and CPR as part of her training for her job in the emergency department at the local hospital, and she knew that double vision was not a good sign in someone with a head injury. Holding up a finger, she moved it in front of the woman's face. "How many fingers do you see?" Sam asked.

The woman studied her for a moment before turning her attention to the finger Sam held in front of her. "Five. Well, actually, four and a thumb. The thumb doesn't count as a finger, does it?"

Sam leaned back and shot her best fake disgusted look. "Are you always so lame, or did the head injury cause it?"

Her retort provoked a chuckle as the woman gracefully rose to her feet and extended her hand to help Sam. She accepted it, shocked by the strength of the grip, by the ease with which she was lifted, then pulled to within a foot of the other woman's face. "I suspect it's an innate character flaw."

For a second, Sam was dizzy again, and her breath caught in her throat. Did *she* have a concussion? Big onyx eyes stared down from a few inches above hers, taking her in. A few dark strands escaped a ponytail and framed a face of sculpted cheekbones and an angular jaw line. Her full mouth was perched on the edge of a smile.

Sam sucked in a breath. They stood, staring, and for a second the preposterous notion that the woman might just close the gap between them and kiss her caused Sam's mouth to go dry.

And then, the woman frowned, looking away as she patted her face. "Shit. My glasses." Her gaze shot to the ground where she'd fallen, and there, just a few feet away, sat sporty-looking sunglasses, resting upside down on the lenses. She squatted and plucked them from the ground, then turned them to inspect them.

Sam could see the scratches from where she stood, and she pushed her own glasses up a little farther on her nose and silently thanked the gods they were still on her face. "Ouch," she said.

A sigh escaped the woman's lips, leaving them in a pout that Sam found adorable. "Yeah, they're wrecked. But I guess that's why I have a hat."

She smiled at the positive attitude and held out her hand. "I'm Sam Burkhart." The introduction seemed formal, yet Sam felt the need to introduce herself and to know more about this girl. Holding her breath, she waited, and in an instant, a hand was extended, a smile offered.

"Kirby Fielding," she said, softly, almost as if it was a question. *Who are you, Sam Burkhart?* Sam felt as if Kirby was reading her, probing with her eyes. Her gaze was gentle but her grip firm, and it pulled Sam back to reality.

Sam wanted to ask the same question, to keep talking, but Kirby Fielding had scooped up her bag and was already heading toward the softball fields. Sam had to choose between ending the conversation and running after Kirby. Sam chose to run.

After a few steps, she glanced over her shoulder. "Hey, are you following me?"

"Yes," Sam admitted, and though she thought she should have felt embarrassed, inexplicably, she wasn't.

"I have that problem with cute girls," Kirby said as she turned her gaze back to the sidewalk.

Speechless, Sam uttered the only reasonable retort she could think of. "Oh." Even that seemed strained, too much of a response for this girl who was clearly, unquestionably, flirting with her.

No one had ever flirted with Sam before. Not like this, anyway. She was attractive, she knew, and she often caught guys—and sometimes even girls—checking her out. Her focus had been on school, though, and the one relationship she'd had was with someone even more studious than she.

Turning, Kirby looked at Sam again. "What? No comeback? I'm disappointed."

"Oh, I think you'll recover," she said, and they both laughed as Kirby waited for Sam to catch up.

"You must be new to the league," Sam said after they'd walked a dozen yards. Lame, she told herself.

"Yes. I played in college last year, so that took up most of my free time."

"I would imagine. Where do you go to school?" she asked.

"Wilkes. I did anyway. I'm all graduated now."

"Oh, no. A grown-up in the league. Yikes."

"Don't worry. I'm unbelievably immature."

"Then you'll fit right in." They were silent for a few steps before Sam continued. "Wilkes is a good school," she said, just for something to say, wondering why she was trying so hard to make conversation.

"It was a great time. College was the best seven years of my life."

Sam felt her eyes and her mouth fly open as she looked at Kirby.

"Kidding."

Shaking her head, she turned. They had reached the bathrooms, and Sam still had to change her clothes. She was disappointed that their conversation was coming to a close. "Good luck, Kirby Fielding. I hope you make the cut."

Kirby chuckled. It was summer league. If she was good enough to play in college, she'd make it.

Sam scooted inside the bathroom and changed from jeans and a designer T-shirt to battered sweats and the jersey from a prior softball team. She eyed the floor and decided against sitting, so she walked back outside and had a seat in the bleachers before changing her socks and shoes.

Then she leaned back and just took it all in. The brilliant blue sky, dotted with only a few billowing clouds. Scattered trees, sporting a spotty pattern of leaves. Grass lush and full from early spring rain. A majestic mountain range bordering the distant skyline. The dirt-covered infield, the battered backstop, dozens of girls laughing and talking, hugging people they hadn't seen since the prior summer. It was magical, being on the softball field, something she never tired of. Sam felt the blood coursing through her and took a deep breath, then closed her eyes and melted into the bleachers. "Ah," she said as she opened them again.

After staying there a few moments, she grabbed her bag and headed toward the crowd, searching out familiar faces. Most of the women who played in this league were like her—under thirty, done with school but not quite tired of the game. Since this was her fourth year in the league, she knew almost everyone and thought of most of them as friends.

She gave a dozen hellos before spotting one of her favorite familiar faces and headed in her direction. "Hi, Teddy," she said, and hugged her friend in greeting.

"What's up?" Theodora Watkins asked.

They'd been friends since their freshman year of high school, when they both played on the softball team, and had somehow ended up on the same team every year in summer league. Teddy was funny, irresponsible, irreverent—a perfect foil for Sam. While Sam tended to take life just a little too seriously sometimes, Teddy never did. She was the youngest of five children, neglected by her exhausted parents and corrupted by older siblings. She cheated on tests, bought her class projects and papers from more industrious classmates, skipped classes, drank her weight in alcohol, smoked marijuana daily, and in general broke rules for the sake of it.

The only thing Sam had ever known her to take seriously was softball, and until a knee injury on the ski slopes, she'd been quite the player. Now a brace slowed her down and limited her range, but she still had a shotgun for a right arm and was the best shortstop in this league. Sam played second, and they had an effortless rhythm on the field that made the game not just fun, but exciting to play.

"It looks like I'm not going to have enough credits to graduate. Can you believe that? I'm so pissed. I was really looking forward to getting a job and moving into my own place."

Sam knew Teddy well enough to joke about it. "Oh, what's the hurry? Milk your parents for as long as you can."

Teddy grinned mischievously. "What a brilliant idea. I should have thought of it myself. Ready to warm up?" she asked as she tossed a ball to Sam.

Snatching it with her bare hand, Sam dropped her bag, pulled out her glove, and trotted out to the grass behind the bases, where they began gently tossing the ball, stretching and loosening up between throws. This wasn't truly a tryout for Sam and Teddy. Rules had been established when the league was organized years earlier, and they guaranteed returning players roster spots. The tryouts were for the vacancies left by players who "retired" or moved out of town. All the veterans came to tryouts, anyway, because most of them knew someone who was trying out, and everyone wanted to scope out the competition.

Kirby Fielding was definitely competition. She'd played in college, so she must have talent, Sam thought. Plus, she was huge. Sam was above average height, but Kirby had towered over her. And she was solid. Her shoulders were broad, her biceps bulging when she had pulled Sam up from the ground. She could probably hit the cover off the ball and nail the catcher with a strike from the outfield. Sam wondered what position she played and said a silent prayer it wasn't second base.

She didn't have more time to think about it, as the league commissioner blew her whistle and the forty or so women gathered began walking toward the infield, where she waited for them. "Welcome back, veterans, and welcome to everyone who's new. I'm Karen Chapman, the commissioner this year." After a short speech of welcome and a few words about sportsmanship, alcohol consumption, and the need to report injuries *immediately*, she introduced the four women who would be player coaches for the season. Finally, she read the names of the new players and announced the agenda for the practice.

When she finished, the veterans and some of the rookies took the field, and the remainder of the newcomers grabbed bats and helmets and readied themselves for batting practice. As Sam assumed her place at second base with five other women, she noticed the batter in the box.

Kirby Fielding.

From behind the screen in front of the pitcher's rubber, the pitcher, Heather Maloney, another of her high school teammates, prepared to toss the first pitch of the season. Sam stood behind the bag at second, putting a little distance between herself and the other fielders, hoping to avoid a collision on the crowded infield. Then she watched the first pitch float toward the plate, connect with the bat, and fly far down the left-field line and over the fence. Heather turned and followed the ball with her gaze and then shook her head in disgust, as a chorus of "oohs" rang out from the fielders. The next pitch was much lower in the strike zone, and Kirby lined that one over the third basewoman's head. Heather tried to mix it up, pitching the next ball to the outside part of the plate. Kirby adjusted, throwing her bat out and looping the ball into right field. Twenty pitches, twenty swings, twenty probable hits. It was amazing to watch her work magic with her bat. Kirby was really good.

After she'd thrown the last pitch to Kirby, Heather walked back toward second and handed Sam a ball. "Wanna pitch?" she asked, shaking her head.

"She's good," Sam said. "Don't let her get to you."

Heather puckered. "I feel washed up."

"You're twenty-two, Heather-Feather. Life has just begun."

"I'm not sure I can face that kind of humiliation again. We should get beer. That will help."

"I have a paper due tomorrow," Sam explained.

"Too bad."

"Maybe she'll be on your team."

"What if they're all that good?" Heather scrunched her face in worry as she looked at the line of rookies loosening up behind the backstop.

"Maybe we both need to retire."

Heather walked back toward the mound as Kirby joined the crowd at the shortstop position. The first pitch Heather threw to the next batter was hit up the middle, and Sam watched as Kirby gracefully extended her left arm, scooped up the ball, spun, and fired it to first base. It looked like she could play defense as well as she hit.

No one that followed her compared, and it was no surprise to anyone when the first coach to pick selected Kirby. The other first-round picks were predictable as well—veterans who were consistently the best players in the league. Teddy was selected in the second round, and Sam was picked in the sixth, which was where she batted in the lineup, so she figured that was about right. What wasn't right was her team. She'd been separated from Teddy and was now part of a double-play combination that included Kirby Fielding.

Even though Kirby was good—better than Teddy, in fact—Sam was sad to break up her long-standing partnership with her old friend. She wasn't so sure of Kirby, either. She might be just a little too good for this league. She'd make everyone else, including Sam, look bad. As they sat in the bleachers, Sam beside Teddy, she focused on the woman a dozen yards away, who was huddled with some players she obviously knew. Kirby was a striking figure and a great player, and Sam had to stop herself from staring.

After the teams were announced, Karen Chapman bid them good night, and the parade to the parking lot began. After saying good-bye to Teddy, Sam walked silently, her mind beginning to shift from softball back to real life. It was early May, and she'd be graduating from college in four weeks. Even if she totally blew every final exam, she'd still pass. At this point, nothing could stop her trek across the stage. Unlike Teddy, she'd taken her education seriously, and in a few months she'd be heading to Philadelphia for medical school.

Before then, she had two papers due and four final exams to complete. Even though her acceptance was verified and her first year's tuition paid—by several government-sponsored loans and a small but generous gift from her grandmother—Sam was certain her medical school would not be pleased if her grades suddenly tanked.

And she wasn't the person to blow off anything so important as two papers and her final exams. No, she'd grab a shower and something to eat, study for a few hours, and keep up the hard work until she signed her name on that last blue book and officially ended her college career.

"Hey, do you have any idea where we are? Is there any place to eat around here?"

Sam turned to see Kirby beside her, and an unexpected flutter coursed through her. She laughed it off. "Never been to Nanticoke before, huh?"

"Nope. I've been sheltered." Kirby's smile was a little crooked, and Sam already knew it was holding in her laughter.

"There's a Burger King down the road. You probably drove right past it on your way to the park."

"Ugh. No other suggestions?"

Kirby's grimace caused Sam to laugh, and on cue, her stomach groaned. She was starved. Not a morning person, she had started scheduling her classes for the afternoon so she could sleep in and stay up late to study. It had been a miracle that she'd gotten out of her last class and avoided traffic on Interstate 81 to make it to practice on time. She'd had absolutely no chance to stop for a bite. The apple she'd snacked on in the car had been the only food she'd put in her stomach since a very late breakfast. She needed to eat. And, for reasons she wasn't quite sure of, she wanted to prolong her time with Kirby.

"Well...I was thinking of getting something myself. Would you like to join me?" It was sort of the truth. She had been considering it for the three seconds since Kirby had suggested it. And she was famished. Maybe it would be a nice chance to get to know her new teammate.

"As long as it's not BK..." She left the sentence dangle there, waiting for Sam to catch it.

"Oh, I can do better than that."

"Okay then. Should we drive together?"

Since Stookey's Barbeque was just a softball's throw from her house, Sam shook her head. "No. It would be better if you follow me." They'd reached the parking lot, and Sam nodded toward the last car at the back of the lot, still by itself even with all those other cars there. "I'm the red Mercedes."

"It'll be a challenge to keep you in sight, but I'll give it my best shot."

"I'll pull over and wait for you if I lose sight of you in my mirror. But try to keep up." Sam winked, and Kirby grinned.

After depositing her bag in the trunk, Sam waited at the edge of the lot until Kirby waved from a white Jeep. Then she zigzagged through town, across the bridge into West Nanticoke, and pulled to a stop at the edge of the parking lot at Stookey's. Along the way, her eyes ventured to the mirror, each time finding the white Jeep. The sight of it made her giddy.

Kirby pulled in beside her and met Sam behind her car, and as they walked, she waved at the twenty empty parking spaces between their cars and the restaurant. "Is something wrong with all these parking places? Is that why we parked in another zip code?"

"Exercise is good for you. Keep walking."

"Ah! Stookey's Barbeque!" she exclaimed as they approached the building.

"Yes! Have you heard of it?" The idea made Sam proud. West Nanticoke wasn't known for much, but Stookey's was a landmark.

"Negative on that."

"Well, you'll be here every Tuesday once you taste it. You won't be able to stay away. Even if practice is rained out, you'll come here to eat. You'll come in the off season for their food."

Kirby chuckled. "Well, I like to eat, so you might be right."

They entered and disturbed the staff, who were sitting at a table talking. Kirby looked around at the aged, empty tables. "You're sure about this?" she whispered.

"You have my word," Sam whispered conspiratorially.

Sam stepped up to the counter and turned to Kirby. "One or two?" she asked.

"One or two what?"

"Sandwiches."

Kirby looked perplexed. "I haven't even looked at the menu."

"Ignore the menu. I'll order for you. Just tell me, one or two?"

"Two." She grinned.

Sam turned and placed the order, then pulled out her wallet, and before Kirby could object, she handed the cashier money for the food.

Kirby touched Sam's arm. "That's not necessary. I'm an adult, remember? I have a job."

"I have a job, too," Sam replied as she pocketed the change and headed to the cooler to grab a drink. She motioned to Kirby to do the same. "Your choice."

Drinks in hand, Sam led them to the table in the corner. From there they had an unparalleled view of the traffic on Route 11 through the plate-glass windows that ran from table height to ceiling. They sat on opposite sides of the small wooden table, settling into their wooden mission chairs to study each other.

"So you work, huh? I had you pegged for a student. What do you do?" Kirby asked.

Sam's reply was quick. "I *am* a student. For a few more weeks, anyway. I graduate at the end of the month. But I work as a tech in the ER."

Raising her eyebrows, Kirby dipped her chin. "Impressive. Does that involve blood?"

"Gallons of it. It's amazing." Sam couldn't suppress the smile that spread across her face. Her job really was wonderful, and she loved it.

Kirby studied her for a moment to gauge the comment, and a sudden warmth infused Sam. Kirby looked, not just at her, but seemed to actually see her. Sam knew she was attractive and caught the occasional eye, but Kirby didn't seem attracted. She seemed fascinated. "You're serious. You like blood?" she asked, apparently delighted by the fact.

Sam shrugged. "I'm not a vampire or anything. I don't *crave* it.

But it usually comes with all the fun things I like to do at work, like taking care of the trauma patients."

"What do you actually do? What's your job description?"

Sam's shoulders sank a little as she admitted she really didn't get to do much with patients, mostly just assist the doctors and nurses—set up for suturing and clean up everyone else's messes. "But I can see it all. And the doctors and the nurses and medics are all really nice, and they teach me a lot. I get to look at X-rays and CT scans, and I get to watch them insert tubes and do sutures and set fractures. It's pretty cool."

"It sounds cool. Where do you go to school?"

"Scranton."

"Good school. What's your major?"

"Bio. Pre-med."

"Oh. Are you going to medical school then, or taking some time off?" Sam knew that was the polite way of asking if she'd been accepted. It was a brutal process, trying to get into med school. Sam knew a number of kids just as qualified as she who were wait-listed and looking at graduate programs so they could reapply the following year. She, however, would be following her dream and studying medicine.

"As long as I make it through finals, I'll be heading to med school in the fall."

"That's really wonderful. You must be excited."

Sam thought about it. That wasn't the typical response to the news. Most people were happy for her but talked about the hard work and long hours, or the many years of training she'd have to put in, the debt she'd incur. Some people thought she was crazy to pursue medicine. No one had ever acknowledged how excited she was to begin the next chapter of her life.

"It is exciting. I—"

The waitress brought their food, and both of them dug into huge sandwiches stuffed with sweetly flavored beef.

"Mm," Kirby said as she took her first bite. "This is divine."

Sam smiled and wiped her mouth. She was about to take another bite when she realized she should pace herself. She'd ordered only one sandwich, and if she matched Kirby bite for bite, she'd be finished way too soon. Then she'd have food envy as she watched her new friend eat.

And besides, they'd talked about nothing except her, so she still knew virtually nothing about Kirby.

"If you played softball at Wilkes, you must know my friend Teddy," Sam said.

"Everyone knows Teddy," Kirby said in an especially flat tone.

"She does make an impression," Sam said, then waited for Kirby to respond. When she didn't, Sam changed the subject. Everyone knew Teddy, but not everyone liked her.

"What do you do?" she said as she sipped her chocolate milk. "Now that you're an adult?" Sam leaned back and watched Kirby, thinking for a moment how differently her evening had turned out from what she'd anticipated. Not that she still wouldn't work when she got home, but for now, she was enjoying herself just sitting and talking.

Kirby held up a finger while she chewed, and after she swallowed and sipped her Coke, she answered. "Banking." Then she took another huge bite, rendering her mute to follow-up questions. And Sam had questions. What did a banker do? Why did she choose that field? What bank? How did she manage to look so good in a baseball cap? Instead, she took another bite, this one smaller, before resuming her interrogation.

Kirby laughed at the rapid-fire demand for information but answered everything between her bites. She had started at an entry-level management position with a large regional bank, and at the moment she was handling commercial-loan applications. She loved her job but hated the dress code. Her ideal job would require her to wear shorts and sneakers every day, even in winter. Her schedule almost never included weekends. The baseball-cap thing was just good luck. "And I was forced to make the hat work after I destroyed my sunglasses."

"My condolences on the glasses." Sam frowned. "They looked outrageously expensive. Fortunately, mine stayed on my face, because I look terrible in hats. I'm glad they're not a part of the league dress code. Just shirts. I only wear a hat if the sun is right in my eyes. But it sounds like your job is going well. Other than the sneakers." Sam paused. "Wow, that was a run-on sentence."

Kirby nodded as she chewed. "Compromises."

Sam looked at her, confused at the comment.

"On the job. It's a compromise. I hate the dress code, but there are other benefits."

"I guess that's life, right? I have to work weekends sometimes. This coming weekend, in fact. I do the overnight, so that way I can study for a couple of hours if it gets really slow. That's sort of a compromise."

"I guess weekends are a requirement in the ER, huh?"

"Yeah, but I don't mind." Her father had been a pediatrician, and he'd worked all kinds of crazy hours. Evenings, late nights, weekends, holidays. It seemed normal to her. Plus, in the ER, the weekends could be wild. "People get drunk and stupid and end up in the ER."

Kirby eyed her. "And you don't pity them at all, do you?"

Sam shrugged. "I'm taking advantage of their bad judgment to gain experience."

"You sound like a future politician instead of a future physician. Are there many female doctors at your hospital?"

Shaking her head, Sam frowned. "Not too many. A few family docs, a pediatrician, a neurologist. My favorite is Julie Wilde, who's an ER doctor. I don't get to work with her often, but she's amazing. She's smart and tough as nails, great at procedures like IVs."

Kirby sat back and seemed to be weighing her words. "She sounds like a good role model."

"Absolutely. I always trade for shifts when she's working, if I can, so I can spend more time with her. She even wrote my letter of recommendation for med school." Sam nodded toward the last bite of Kirby's second sandwich. "So, I guess the food was okay, huh?"

Kirby rubbed her stomach, and her look of delight caused Sam to smile. "It was great, but I still have room for dessert."

Sam shook her head. "Not here. We can get a pack of cookies at the gas station or an ice cream at the ice cream stand. That's about it."

"Nothing else?"

"Not in West Nanticoke."

"Small town, huh?"

"Oh, yeah."

"I thought we might have just been on the outskirts or something."

"Sadly, no. A hundred years ago it was a booming coal town, with a general store and a dry goods, a school, a few churches, and, of course, hundreds of families. In 1972 the town had a huge flood from Hurricane Agnes. Many of the homes were lost, and people just moved away."

"Ah, Agnes. I've heard about her. So why are you still here?"

Sam turned her head and looked out the window, up to the mountain, and pointed. "I live up there."

Kirby followed her gaze. From where they sat it just looked like the side of a mountain, with no homes visible. "Are you part goat? Do you live in a cave?"

Sam rubbed her hands together excitedly. "Possibly part goat. I love to climb things. And there are great caves to explore up there."

Kirby leaned back and frowned. "You're kidding, right?"

Sam laughed. "No, actually, I'm not. Where are you from, anyway? Mars?"

"Harrisburg. We had some Agnes flooding, too, but I was just a baby back then. I've only heard stories and seen pictures."

"Yeah. Me, too. No personal memories."

"Do you live with your parents?"

Sam nodded. "My mom."

"Siblings?"

"No. Just me. How about you? What's your family like?" Deflecting was a good plan. Too much sharing never turned out well.

"Big family. My parents felt the need to preserve the intellectual class by creating their own basketball team."

"Can I get you anything else?" The waitress suddenly appeared, startling them.

"Not for me," Sam said as she looked to Kirby.

"I'm okay as well," she said.

When she'd disappeared behind the counter, Sam winked mischievously. "You still want ice cream, though, don't you?"

"Absolutely."

"Come on, then. I'll drive."

They walked the length of the parking lot in silence, and Sam realized she'd hardly stopped talking since they'd walked in the opposite direction almost an hour earlier. The silence made her nervous, and she wasn't sure why. "Your car will be safe. Or you could drive. Whatever."

"And pass up a chance for a ride in your Mercedes? No way."

"Well, it is a privilege. I don't usually let people in my car." She pressed the remote, and the lights blinked and the car chirped. "Please wipe your feet."

Kirby laughed as she opened the passenger door and was buckling her seat belt as Sam slid into her own seat. "No kidding. This is a really nice car," she said as she ran her fingers across the wood inlays of the dash.

Sam swallowed emotion and kept her retort light. "I know. Don't touch anything," she said as she playfully slapped Kirby's hand.

Kirby pulled her hand back into her lap. "Sorry."

"Don't let it happen again," Sam said as she backed the car out of the parking lot and then headed toward the ice-cream stand. Just to make Kirby laugh, she pushed hard on the gas pedal, and the car's powerful engine revved as it lurched forward. Sam turned to her and smiled when she laughed, even as she took her foot off the gas. It was a thirty-five-mile zone.

A minute later they reached their destination, and as they pulled in, they had their choice of spots in the parking lot. Sam parked on the edge of the lot anyway. Kirby looked at her as if she might comment but held her tongue. Instead, she shook her head. "Looks like another popular place."

"How can you screw up ice cream?" Sam asked as she got out of the car and they walked toward the counter of Maureen's. She ordered a soft chocolate cone with sprinkles, Kirby had the same, and she ordered a sundae for the road. This time, Kirby paid.

"If I'd known you were a banker, I would have let you buy dinner, too," Sam said.

"I try to hold that information back as long as I can."

"Smart," Sam said as she imagined Kirby, wearing battered sweatpants and a T-shirt, all dressed up for work. In heels, she'd be six feet tall.

They sat at a picnic table beside Harvey's Creek eating their cones, and Sam explained the geography of the town. The creek was at the base of her mountain, and she'd traveled through the woods, then walked across the stream to get ice cream during the summer days of her childhood. "The walk home was a bitch."

"I'll bet," Kirby said as she looked up. "It's very flat where I grew up. I rode my bike everywhere," she said, then talked a bit about Harrisburg, what her childhood was like there. She was the eldest of five children, and her parents, both accountants, were still happily married after twenty-five years. Her brothers were still in college, and her youngest sister was in high school. They vacationed every summer in Ocean City, Maryland, and when their children were out of school, her parents planned to buy a condo there. Her grandfather, Kirby's favorite person, had a vintage Corvette and babied it as much as Sam did her car.

The server brought the sundae just as they were finishing their cones, and they headed to Sam's car. A minute later they were back at Kirby's. Sam was sad to see the night end. "I had a nice time, Kirby. It's going to be a fun season with you on my team."

Kirby handed her the bag with the sundae, and after Kirby assured her she'd find her way home, Sam followed her out of the parking lot. A few feet up the road she made an elbow turn and headed up the mountain to home, feeling great, inexplicably happy, and not for a moment wondering why.

CHAPTER FOUR

Placing a set of surgical instruments into a plastic bag, Sam sealed it shut and placed it into the autoclave, then turned the machine on. Her shift had started at eleven, and there had been a major trauma shortly after, but mostly the night had been a slow one. The lead nurse—her boss for the shift—had asked her to make sure the suture cart was fully stocked, and Sam had done that and prepped a half dozen suture kits, when the nurse opened the door to the stock room and looked at her.

"You have a visitor," she said.

"What?"

"Someone's here to see you. Did you finish the cart?"

"Yeah. And I made extra kits."

"Thanks, Sam. That was really nice. If you'd like, you can take your break now and go see your friend."

"Who is it?" Sam asked, baffled. Other than her mom, whose shift occasionally coincided with hers, no one ever visited her at the hospital.

"I don't know her name. Tall girl, dark hair. I left her in the lounge."

Kirby, Sam thought excitedly. But why would she be at the hospital? Sam washed her hands and walked quickly to the break room, talking herself out of the idea that it could be Kirby, all the while hoping it was.

Pushing open the door, Sam looked in and met Kirby's eyes. The smile erupted on her face, but she tried to rein it in as she stood in the hallway with her hand against the door. "They told me I had a visitor. I've never had a visitor at work. I was afraid it might be a stalker." Sam's heartbeat was racing as she tried to steady her nerves.

She walked into the room, and Kirby reached out both hands. One held a tall Styrofoam cup and the other a white paper bag.

"I'm stalking with gifts."

"It smells like coffee," Sam said as she took the cup and removed the lid.

"I figured you could use it if you have to stay up all night."

Sam hated coffee, but she wasn't about to tell Kirby that and admit just how uncool she was. "Thank you. You're very sweet."

Kirby blushed and handed Sam the bag. "I have doughnuts, too. But," she made a face, "I'm not sure how fresh they are."

Sam opened the bag and peeked inside. "No mold," she said, and then she motioned toward the table. "Have a seat. I'm on break now so I have a few minutes, if you can stay?" Please stay, she thought. Please.

"Yeah. I'd love to."

Trying to regain control, Sam focused on the simple tasks of setting a modest table. She took the two cleanest-looking napkins from the drawer and then sat beside Kirby. Pulling the doughnuts from the bag, she put one on each napkin and pushed the furthest in Kirby's direction. Then she opened three cups of creamer and half a dozen packs of sugar and dumped them into the coffee. Forcing herself to take a sip, she wondered once again how people drank the stuff.

After a bite of the doughnut, which was surprisingly good, Sam pushed the coffee toward Kirby. "Have some. I'll never finish it all."

Kirby shook her head and made a face as she chewed. "I can't stand coffee."

Sam burst out laughing. "I can't either."

Kirby joined her. "Then why are you drinking it?"

"Because you bought it for me."

"What would you rather be drinking right now?"

"Tea," Sam confessed with a sigh.

"Me, too!" Kirby said as she tilted her head and smiled.

"Hold on," Sam said, relieved. Jumping up from the chair, she filled two mugs with water and placed them in the microwave.

"So how'd you know I was going to be here?" Sam asked as she waited for the water to heat.

"Well, it wasn't hard. You told me you work here, and that you work the overnight shift, and that you were working this weekend."

Sam pursed her lips as she thought back to their conversation at Stookey's. "Maybe I should be more cautious. If you really were a stalker, I'd be in trouble."

"Good point," Kirby said.

"What are you doing out in the middle of the night?"

"I was at a party, and I had to drive right by the hospital on the way home, and that made me think of you, and I decided to stop. But first I went to the all-night diner for the food."

While they waited, Sam pulled a beat-up plastic bag filled with assorted flavors of tea bags and a honey-filled bear from the cupboard. "This is just like a fancy restaurant, without the velvet-lined box for the tea bags."

"But the ambiance is so much better," Kirby said as she looked around. Sam frowned at the sight of the dingy white walls and sagging couch, the posters about universal precautions against body-fluid exposure.

"We have our own private dining room," she said with a hint of sarcasm.

"I like the company." Kirby's eyes met hers, and Sam felt anxious again, found it difficult to hold Kirby's gaze yet impossible to pull away. Kirby smiled, which eased Sam's tension, and then the microwave buzzer saved her from further torture.

They were quiet as they took care of fixing their drinks, and Sam snuck another peek at Kirby. With her hair down, and a light coat of makeup, she was stunning, and Sam wondered why Kirby had really stopped at the hospital. Although she was happy to see her, the visit was so out of the blue, Sam really didn't know what to think of it.

Sipping her tea, she sighed. "Ah. So much better than coffee."

Kirby raised her mug and Sam met her in a toast. When Kirby didn't speak, Sam did. "To new friends who bring middle-of-the-night doughnuts for my tea."

"I do cookies, too. But I'll have to plan that. It's hard to find a bakery open at this hour."

"Don't you bake?" Sam asked. The kitchen was one of her favorite places, baking a great way to relax.

"Actually, yes. So next time, I'll bake you cookies."

"Chocolate chip?" Sam asked.

"Of course."

They chewed and sipped, and Sam tried to discreetly study Kirby. For some reason, she couldn't stop staring at her. Kirby's evening look was totally different from her softball look. The hair, of course, was different, and so very elegant. She wore a lightweight sweater and faded jeans with loafers, a combination she managed to make stunning. Sam felt a little giddy as she thought about Kirby at the hospital, stopping in at one in the morning just to bring her food.

"I like your outfit. It's casual yet beautiful," Sam said as Kirby caught her staring.

"You think so? I was at a birthday party for one of my old roommates, and I thought I should go a little dressier, but I just didn't have the energy. After spending the week in suits and heels, the last thing I want to do on weekends is get all dressed up."

Sam sighed. "I hear you," she said as she pointed to her scrubs. "I love scrubs. I'd wear them every day if I could. Where was the party?"

"At the Woodlands," she replied, referring to one of the most popular local night spots. Sam had been there a few times, but it really was a little fancier than she preferred, and much more expensive than she could afford. Although her mom supported her financially, Sam tried not to take advantage. For socializing with friends, she tried to limit her budget to the money she made at the hospital.

"Nice." Sam nodded, wondering where Kirby lived that brought her past the hospital on her way home.

"Yeah, but it's a bit much. Most of the girls are staying overnight, they've got booze for their suites, and I predict someone's going to get arrested," she said, shaking her head.

"Yikes," Sam said. "Or, worse, they end up here. We saw someone once who broke his neck diving into a hot tub at the hotel."

Kirby's eyebrows shot up. "He dove into the hot tub?"

Sam shrugged. "A lot of alcohol was involved."

"I can imagine."

Sam sipped again.

"Has anything cool happened tonight?" Kirby asked.

"A head-on collision on the parkway. The guy they brought here went to the OR. He broke a few ribs and had blood in his abdomen, so they're doing exploratory surgery to find out what's wrong."

"Will he make it?" Kirby asked, clearly alarmed.

Sam nodded. "He was awake when he came in, and he had a good blood pressure, so he'll probably be okay."

"It must be hard when people die, huh?"

As much as Sam joked about the cases she saw—a defense mechanism she'd learned from everyone else in the ER—it *was* hard. She often found herself praying in tense situations and always lit a candle in the hospital chapel when a patient didn't make it.

"Yes, it is," she said, but didn't elaborate, not wanting to turn their light mood dark.

"Have you ever delivered a baby?"

Sam laughed and patted Kirby's hand. "I'm just a peon, Kirby. But I was in the ER once when a baby was delivered. That was chaos. Like a visit from the pope."

Kirby looked at her with a confused expression.

"People running in every direction, hospital dignitaries in the ER, and lots of prayers."

"Hmm. Did everything turn out okay? Was the baby all right?"

"Yes. It was all good. It was a girl, and Dr. Wilde, my favorite ER doctor, suggested they name the baby Julie, after her. It was their fifth daughter, so they did."

"You're kidding. Really?" Kirby asked.

"Yeah. Isn't that so cool?"

"That really is."

"I thought so, too," Sam said, and smiled at Kirby, who was covering a yawn with the back of her hand. "Aren't you a night owl?"

"Actually, no." She paused, probably reconsidering her answer. "I guess everyone stays up late in college, though."

The comment intrigued Sam. "But you're out of college now."

"Yeah," Kirby said with a sigh. "It's weird. I've met some friends since I started my job, but most of the people I hang out with are college friends. Classmates, friends from the dorms, softball teammates. So, I feel like I'm still in college. Plus, my apartment's on-campus."

That answered her earlier question, and Sam wondered why Kirby had really stopped at the hospital. It wasn't on the way home from the Woodlands. Interesting. Then she wondered what Kirby's apartment was like. The Wilkes University campus had grown over the years, making inroads into residential areas, so the campus and the South Wilkes-Barre community were indistinguishable, a patchwork of beautiful old homes and modern college buildings.

"Convenient," she replied, without asking either question. She wasn't sure she wanted to know the answers.

"It is. How about you? Do you like the night shift?"

Sam sighed. "Not so much the hours as the action. I really am happy to have a little caffeine. It's getting to be bedtime for me."

"How do you do it? I'd fall asleep in my chair," Kirby confessed.

Chuckling, Sam told her about the routine she followed to get ready for spending the night in the hospital.

"So you'll sleep all day tomorrow?" she asked, then looked at her watch. "Today? Saturday?"

"As long as I can. Hopefully, I'll study a little tonight. It usually slows down about four or so, and I'll have some free time."

Kirby seemed to be thinking of something as she pursed her lips.

"What?" Sam asked.

"Do you want to have dinner with me before work? Tonight?"

The idea of seeing Kirby so soon was exciting, and Sam grew warm at the thought. It was a tempting offer. Sam wanted to see Kirby again, but she didn't want to push it before an overnight shift. "I don't think I can do dinner early, but I could meet you at eight, maybe. Then I'll just come straight to work."

Kirby seemed to debate for a second. "Okay. That'll work. Pizza?"

"No Burger King?" Sam asked, remembering the face Kirby had made when Sam suggested it before they went to Stookey's.

"Ugh!"

They agreed on the Pizza Hut nearby.

"There's a BK across the street, if you change your mind."

"Not going to happen."

"What do you have against that place?"

"Oh, man. It involved stupidity and alcohol and a French fry that came out my nose."

"Oh, wow. Maybe I don't want to know."

Shaking her head, Kirby frowned. "Trust me, you don't."

"All we do together is eat," Sam said, and Kirby laughed.

"Barbeque, doughnuts, pizza. Everything healthy."

"Don't forget ice cream. I used to hang out at Pizza Hut with my high school softball buddies. Fun times. There are a few players in the league who I went to high school with, like Teddy."

Sam noticed that Kirby completely avoided the topic of Teddy. "Oh, yeah? Who else?"

Sam mentioned some names, and Kirby nodded, and they talked about the players they both knew.

"What are your plans for the weekend?" Sam asked. "Other than stalking me?" She pursed her lips as she suppressed a smile.

Kirby yawned. "I'm playing in a golf tournament. In just a few hours, in fact."

"Maybe you should go, and I should get back to work."

"Code blue. ER, five minutes," the operator announced overhead.

Sam stood. "Talk about timing!"

"Is that you?" Kirby asked.

"Yeah. Gotta run."

Sam reached for Kirby's mug, but Kirby took hers instead. "You go. I'll take care of this."

Suddenly Sam felt a little woozy. For the first time in memory, she didn't want to go to the code. She wanted to stay right where she was, hanging out with Kirby. "Thanks. See you later," she said as she started to leave. Then she stopped. "Can I call you when I get up?"

"I've been hoping you'd call me for days. I was forced to take matters into my own hands and show up here uninvited."

Elated, Sam laughed. "I promise I'll phone you tonight. Thanks again," she said as she smiled at Kirby, lingering for just a moment before she dashed back to the ER, feeling a high greater than the caffeine could account for.

CHAPTER FIVE

A few days later, Sam pulled into Teddy's driveway and stopped before the large Tudor-style house. She honked the horn, and seconds later, Teddy bounded around the corner with the energy of a dog who'd just escaped the confines of the backyard. Sam laughed at the thought but didn't share it.

"Can you believe my frickin' parents took away my frickin' car? I mean, really? What is the point here? They own a frickin' car dealership. It's not like they need it or anything. How am I supposed to get to school? What about work?"

Nodding in sympathy, Sam backed out of the driveway and headed toward the softball field. "What did they say?"

"Oh, they're just pissed because I'm not graduating and gave me the BS speech about enabling me." While Sam silently agreed with the Watkinses' decision, she wondered only why they'd waited so long to start disciplining their daughter. Instead of rubbing it in, though, Sam did what any friend would do and offered to help.

"Well, you know I can take you to the games. How about school?"

For a few minutes they discussed their schedules. This was the last week of classes for both of them: Sam at the University of Scranton and Teddy at Wilkes. Their final exams were the next week, so their schedules jibed. And Sam didn't mind studying at the Wilkes University library if it made her friend's life a bit easier. She'd have to make an adjustment or two, but basically she could serve as Teddy's taxi for a little while.

A moment later they pulled into the softball field. Teddy's team wasn't practicing, but she was helping Karen Chapman set up the schedule for games and playoffs, and they were meeting at the field. As they walked from the parking lot, Sam was pleasantly surprised to see Kirby. Over pizza on Saturday night she'd mentioned that she liked to get to the field early, and Kirby said she'd try to as well. Sam breathed deeply at the sight of her. Kirby seemed to take her breath away, and she forced Sam to watch her footing.

She was just off balance, thinking about Kirby constantly. A hundred times over the course of the days since she'd last seen her, Sam found herself daydreaming of Kirby. Her smooth, quick swing as she hit a softball. The concentration on her face as she tracked a ground ball. Her quick wit. Her voracious appetite. Her black eyes and flouncy ponytail. Kirby's laughter, and her own, which just erupted from her when Kirby was around. And this general sense of happiness she'd felt since Kirby arrived in the ER to see her four days ago.

Oh, yes. She'd thought about Kirby. In spite of classes to attend and papers to be written, lab journals to be submitted, she'd thought of Kirby. She'd thought of calling, but she feared the disruption to her routine that Kirby seemed to cause. And she kept wondering why. Kirby was just her teammate, right? A new friend.

So why did Sam feel so obsessed by her?

Why did Sam's mouth seem to go dry as she thought of that moment Kirby had grasped her hand and pulled her to her feet, when their faces had been mere inches apart and she'd thought Kirby might kiss her? Sam had never experienced anything like it, and she thought in a hundred years she would still recall that moment. And the same fluttering feeling she'd felt at the hospital, when she was about to leave Kirby in the break room. And how they'd lingered in the parking lot after pizza, saying good night for half an hour before Sam finally forced herself into her car just in time to make it to work before her shift started.

It was the weirdest idea she'd ever had, but Sam suddenly realized she had a *crush* on Kirby. Sam, who had only ever dated one person in her short life. One person who was a guy. Sam had a crush on Kirby, who was most definitely a girl.

The idea shocked her, and for a moment the thought of running entered Sam's mind. But then Kirby smiled, and Sam melted and thought that having a crush on a girl like Kirby seemed entirely normal.

"Hey, Teddy. Hey, Sam," Kirby said.

Sam watched the interplay between the two, looking for a clue as to why Kirby hadn't seemed to want to talk about Teddy. They didn't say anything, but a flash of something that looked like anger appeared briefly on Teddy's face, before it faded back to neutral.

"Hi, Kirby," Teddy said. Then she looked at Sam. "Catch up with you later," she said and jogged away.

Kirby and Sam continued to the softball field alone, walking quietly beside each other, the subject of Teddy dropped. Sam had known Teddy for eight years, and she was sure there was a story there. But with Teddy, there was always some drama, so it didn't really surprise her. She'd find out the details on the ride home.

"I had a great time talking with you the other night," Kirby said after a moment, her tone more serious than Sam expected of her. Everyone was surprising her today. She adjusted her own attitude before replying, then turned to look at Kirby when she spoke.

Just doing that caused Sam's spirit to soar. "Yeah. I felt like we could have talked all night."

"Wanna do it again?" Kirby asked, and the hopeful look on her face was delightfully endearing. But Sam's last paper was due the next day, and although it was about finished, she needed to proofread and print it before handing it in.

"After the game on Saturday?" she offered in compromise, hoping Kirby would say yes.

Kirby nodded. "I'd like that."

"Do you want Stookey's again, or are you up for a little more adventure?"

Kirby paused and turned to look at her, seemingly intrigued by the mysterious question. "What do you have in mind?"

"Spelunking."

"You think I don't know what that means."

"I know you don't know what that means."

"Well, you are absolutely, one hundred percent correct."

Sam grinned. "Exploring caves. I want to take you for a hike on my mountain." She'd hiked the previous day, and as she stood on her favorite rock, looking out at the river, she'd thought of how amazing it would be to share the view with Kirby.

Kirby's face transformed at the thought, and a radiant smile appeared before morphing into a frown. "Are there bats?"

Shaking her head, Sam looked around. "Nothing more dangerous than you'll see at practice today. If you're quiet, you might see some deer foraging. Squirrels. Maybe some turkeys, or a snake, or even a porcupine."

Kirby stopped. "Wait. Are you trying to talk me into this, or out of it?"

Sam looked at her and their eyes locked. Her heart fluttered and her mouth suddenly dried, forcing a swallow. Her answer was the most honest one she could give. "I don't know." She should try to talk Kirby out of it. She should try to talk herself out of it. She was heading into a dangerous and strange situation, one in which she felt completely off-kilter. Yet Sam knew that what she was feeling for Kirby was not something usual or common, either. It wasn't something she'd ever felt before. And even if something was strange about her affinity for Kirby, Sam couldn't stop seeing her. She simply didn't want to. She just wanted to keep feeling the way she did when she was with Kirby. Every minute of every day for the rest of her life, she wanted to feel this way.

She saw Kirby swallow, too, and what might have been an awkward moment became something silly, and they both laughed, shaking their heads as they glanced away. "Looks like we're *really* early," Kirby said as the empty softball field came into view.

"Practice isn't mandatory. It could just be us," she said, and Sam found herself liking that idea. Actually, since most of the players worked, and some had family obligations, those who were able to attend practice usually showed up a minute before the scheduled starting time and bolted after. Sam loved the field, though, and always stretched out her time here, coming early and staying late. Even if it was just a few extra minutes away from whatever paper or project she had to prepare, this was a wonderful respite from whatever was happening in her real life.

At the field they sat quietly and changed shoes, and Kirby threw a ball to herself while she waited for Sam. After assuming a position just past the infield dirt, they began tossing the ball back and forth. Then Sam began throwing ground balls, mixing in a few pop flies to make it interesting. And, just as Sam predicted, a few minutes before starting time, the coach arrived with the equipment, and a trove of players jogged to the field.

A total of eight of them showed up, and they all assumed a preferred position, but they rotated as players left the field for batting practice. Sam was the first to hit, and when she finished, Kirby was in the on-deck circle, so it wasn't until they'd both finished their swings that they found themselves together on the infield. Sam was anxious to see how she'd play beside Kirby. With Teddy, there had always been a natural chemistry, and they sensed each other well on the field. Sam knew she felt a connection to Kirby as well, and she was eager to discover how that played out.

Her wait was short-lived. The first pitch was hit in the hole between short and third, and Kirby easily fielded it and came up firing to second. There were no base runners, but Sam imagined if there was one, she would have been out. The next ball was up the middle, on the third-base side of the bag, and Kirby went that way, put her glove down, and, without removing the ball, flicked it to Sam at second.

"Show-off." Sam chided her, but she was impressed with the play. After a few hits to the outfield, Sam had a chance to field a grounder at second, and she easily tossed it to Kirby for a pretend force-out.

They'd do fine together, Sam realized. No worries. Her on-field chemistry was as easy as it was with Teddy.

After practice, they were the last to leave, and they walked together toward the parking lot. "Is there anything I should bring Saturday?" Kirby asked.

"A small backpack, a bottle of water. Hiking boots."

"Hiking boots?"

The look of horror on Kirby's face was priceless. Sam shrugged. "Okay, sneakers," she said softly, meeting Kirby's gaze.

"That, I can manage."

They lingered at Sam's car for another twenty minutes, but the setting sun left a chill in the air, and Sam retreated to the shelter of her car while she waited for Teddy. A moment later, she appeared, walking beside Karen, engrossed in conversation. The angry Teddy she'd brought to the field earlier had disappeared, and Sam couldn't help but wonder why.

"Brrr," she said as she closed the car door and splayed her fingers before the heat vents. "It feels like winter."

Sam backed up the car and headed toward Teddy's. "You must be getting sick. The temperature is perfectly fine. So, spill. What's up with you and Kirby?"

Teddy shook her head, then sucked in a breath. "That story would require beer. Bottles and bottles of beer."

"Hmm," Sam replied. "Sounds interesting."

Teddy sighed. "Okay, look. You can't go to the same school and play on the same team for three years without having some drama."

Sam nodded. Although she wanted to know more, she knew she wouldn't learn anything else until Teddy was ready.

Without further discussion of Kirby, Sam dropped Teddy off and headed home. Her house, a small ranch on Tilbury Terrace, sat back from the street, out of the harsh glare of the streetlight but instead illuminated by dozens of artistically arranged accent lights. A floodlight sensed the motion of her car and illuminated the macadam as she turned into the driveway. As always, she parked in the right bay, beside her mom's car, in what would always be known as her father's side of the garage. After closing the door and locking the house, she walked into the breezeway.

"I'm home," she shouted into the quiet house, then waited for a response. When she heard none, the tension in her body settled in her gut. "Mom?" she asked, as she walked toward the living room, her steps tentative.

Cushions were arranged neatly on the couch, and a magazine sat squarely on an end table next to the television remote. But otherwise, the room was empty.

"Mom?" she asked again, heading toward the kitchen. The light above the stove burned perpetually, casting a soft glow over the spotless kitchen. A cookie jar sat on the island, but the table and the counters were clean, without even a dish in the sink. A light glowed through the sliding doors at the far end of the room.

Slowly walking that way, Sam forced herself to breathe, willed her tight chest to expand and suck in air. Ever since her father's death eight years ago, she'd had these panic attacks when her mother didn't answer. Tunnel vision focused on the room beyond the doors, and when she reached them, she lifted her hand and spread anchoring fingers on cool glass. An involuntary sigh escaped when she saw her mom sitting in a cozy chair, reading. Brandy, her Yorkshire terrier, sat on the floor beside her. Suddenly, he heard her, and his little ears shot straight into the air as he raised his head and flew toward her, barking excitedly as he scratched at the glass.

Sliding back the door, Sam bent down and picked him up. "Hello, you little cutie," she said as he welcomed her home with kisses.

She greeted her mom cheerfully, the trepidation she'd felt a moment earlier beginning to ease. The room was painted a vibrant yellow and furnished with overstuffed wicker furniture, and she sat across from her mom on the couch, the dog resting happily beside her.

"Hi, Lovey," her mom said. It was her typical greeting, and it always made Sam smile. "How was your day?"

"It was good," Sam said as she sank into the cushions and rubbed Brandy's head, just the way he liked it.

"What was so good about it?" Irene Burkhart curled her legs underneath her, removed her reading glasses, and appraised her. Sam stared right back, seeing a vision of herself in forty years. Other than the long, lean frame she'd inherited from her dad, she was cast from a mold of her mom. The blond hair, green eyes, and full mouth Sam saw in the mirror were the same ones she'd been looking at across the dinner table her entire life.

"Hmm," Sam murmured, and before she could filter, she blurted it out. The thing that had been on her mind for days. The girl she couldn't stop thinking about. "I made a new friend," she said, holding her breath after the words left her mouth. That shouldn't have been an anxiety-provoking revelation, but it was, and Sam was anxious for her mother's response.

"How nice! I suspect you'll be making a few new friends in the coming months. What's her name? Or is it a him? You modern girls have as many male friends as females, don't you?"

Sam pondered the question. She did have a quite a few guy friends. "I guess you're right. But this one is a her, and her name is Kirby. She's the shortstop on my team. The new Teddy."

Irene frowned. "Well, she can't possibly be a worse influence on you than the old Teddy." She paused in an exaggerated frown, and then the frown deepened further still as she tilted her head. "Can she?"

Laughing, Sam replied. "I think I'm immune to moral corruption." But was she? It was true that she'd always followed the rules and done what she was supposed to, but these new feelings for Kirby were definitely not written in the traditional moral code.

A belly laugh erupted from her mom, and Sam joined her. "You might be right. Since you were a baby, you've always seemed to follow your own path. You have a well-aligned moral compass. Still, a mom's job is to worry."

"And you do it well," Sam said, trying to steer her thoughts away from the one thing and one person that seemed to overwhelm them lately.

Irene shot her a dirty look. "I hope you never have to raise a teenager without your husband around to help."

"I hope not, too," Sam replied, with a sudden heaviness in her heart that had nothing to do with Kirby. Then, to lighten the mood, she continued. "But I think you hit the kid jackpot. I've gone pretty easy on you."

Truthfully, not much about the past eight years of their life had been easy, but Sam had worked hard to be successful. She'd studied and devoted herself to making good grades, spent time with her friends in pre-med or from softball, and worked. Even if Sam had been inclined, she wouldn't have had time to get into trouble. Why was she looking for it now?

"You're right," Irene said as she rested her chin in her palm. "I am pretty lucky."

"Aw, shucks," Sam said playfully with a wave of her hand. "Hey! Tell me one good thing about your day."

Irene smiled. "That's easy. I'm looking at her."

"That doesn't count. I was your good thing yesterday."

"Every day, Lovey. Let's talk about the next few while we have a minute. This is the last week of class, huh?"

"Can you believe it, Mom? I feel like I just started, and I'm a few days away from being done. No work this weekend. My first game is Saturday, and then I'm hiking with Kirby after the game. No plans for Sunday except studying. How about you?"

"This is my weekend on call. I'll try to be home for dinner on Sunday night if you can join me at Bapcia's."

As the director of nursing at the hospital, Irene worked clinical shifts only on the rarest of occasions. But every few weeks, she was the administrator on call for the weekend, and that was a busy job. Fridays, she'd stay at the hospital until nine or ten at night, because the moment she left, someone would call her. It was easier, and more productive, if she just remained in the building. On Saturdays and Sundays, she'd usually go into the hospital at six, to solve all the problems that had bloomed overnight, and stay until late in the evening. Sunday-evening dinner at Sam's grandmother's was one of their traditions, though, and she always tried to make it home for that.

"I'm not sure about Sunday dinner, Mom. I have my first final on Monday, and it's biochem. Do you mind if I skip?"

"Will you stop and see Bapcia after mass? She misses you when she doesn't see you."

Sam had attended the Catholic grade school in Nanticoke, a few blocks from her grandmother's house, and had walked there every day on her lunch break to eat with her. For nine years, rain or shine, they'd had a midday date. When Sam got to high school, she missed their time together and made a practice of having dinner with her at least once a week. When she started driving, Sam would take her grocery shopping and to the mall, or out for lunch. Theirs was a special relationship, something Sam would miss when she went away to school.

"How about tomorrow? What will you eat? Do you want to put something in the Crock-Pot or just eat out?"

"I'll figure it out." Since her father died, she and her mom spent a lot of time together in the kitchen. Her mom worked during the day, so when she came home, she and Sam would unwind and share their stories as they put together meals, then discuss the news or the day ahead as they cleaned up. The hour or two of quiet time was like a balm to them both, easing their stresses and strengthening the bond that had grown so strong in the years since her father's death.

"And I don't want to be a nag, but if you're having someone over, make sure you straighten your room."

The idea of Kirby in her room made Sam's mouth go dry, and she cleared her throat. "I don't think she'll be in my room." Shit! What if Kirby wanted to see it? They'd be alone there, and the thought made Sam feel so jittery that she had to stand. She walked toward the bookshelf and pretended to study the titles. "We're going hiking, and maybe we'll have something to eat. It's really no big deal. But...I'll still make my bed anyway."

"It's not a bad habit. In a few months..."

"Yeah..." As excited as Sam was, moving was still a scary proposition, one she didn't want to deal with now. She changed the subject. "Oh, by the way, I volunteered to drive Teddy to school. Her parents took her car away because she doesn't have enough credits to graduate."

Irene shook her head.

"See how lucky you are with me?" Sam said, hoping her mother agreed. What would Irene think if she knew Sam's thoughts? The idea frightened her.

Irene shook her head again, but Sam heard a soft chuckle.

"On that note, I'm out of here. I've got work to do."

"I'm just going to read out here. The weather is so nice tonight."

Sam thought for a moment. It was a pleasant evening, and the temperature in the sunroom was very comfortable—a perfect place to get her work done. She wouldn't have many more nights like this one. Once she left for Philly, this would never really be home again. "I think I'll join you."

Sam quickly showered, grabbed her backpack, and rejoined her mom. With a pile of pillows against her back, she put a lap desk across her legs and began editing her paper. It was a short work, only two thousand words, but the topic—the hemoglobin molecule—was not holding her attention. Her mind drifted again and again to softball practice and to her new teammate.

She found Kirby intriguing, and she wasn't sure why. She met new people every day, she mused, so why did some of them captivate her, and others didn't? They could talk and talk, that was certain, and she enjoyed Kirby's humor. Maybe she just needed a friend. Her best college friend, Lori Sugarman, a pre-med student heading to medical school as well, was preparing to leave any day for the Air Force, and she'd been too busy in these past months to hang out much. That was probably it, Sam thought. She already missed Lori, and Kirby would be a fun summer friend to spend time with before she left for Philly.

After finding no gross inaccuracies in her grammar or spelling on her paper, Sam placed the pages in a folder and tucked it into her backpack. Pulling out her to-do list, she checked that project off. The rest of the items were more arduous. Biochemistry. Genetics. Latin. Statistics. Four classes, four finals to get through, and then she was done.

She'd be busy, but nothing she wasn't used to. This week was different, though, because when it was over, she'd be going on a hike with Kirby. The thought thrilled her and scared her at the same time.

CHAPTER SIX

Sam walked out of the Loyola Hall of Science on the campus of the University of Scranton on the last day of class and shouted at the cloudless blue ski. Her two best college friends, Lori Sugarman and Jim Fanucci, joined her. Students on their way into the building, most of them underclassman, eyed them enviously.

"It's our last day of class, *ever!*" Jim said. "Let's go for a drink. On me!" Sam met Lori's gaze, and they both nodded. Jim's family owned a small restaurant and bar a few miles away, in Old Forge, the self-proclaimed pizza capital of the world. They'd spent many great times there over the years, most before they were old enough to drink *legally*. Jim's older brother, Frankie, managed the place and knew they were all good kids, so he looked the other way when the barkeeps served Jim and his friends.

Now they were all legal, and just the formality of final exams stood between them and their diplomas. It was an event worth celebrating.

Francesco's was dark when they walked in, but a radio was playing in the kitchen, and they stopped by to say hello to Jim's Nonna and mom, who did all the cooking. The two women greeted the group enthusiastically, offered congratulations, and then sent them back out to the restaurant to wait for the day's specials, which they were busy preparing.

As Jim worked some magic behind the bar, Lori and Sam relaxed side by side in a tall booth lined with crimson vinyl, watching him. "Not too strong, Jim. We have to drive," Sam suggested.

Lori wiggled an eyebrow at her. "I'm sure Mrs. Fanucci would find a place for you to stay if you can't drive home."

"Ha-ha-ha," Sam said sarcastically and shot Lori an elbow. It was a long-standing joke between them—Jim's family's oblivion to his obvious gayness. Jim and Sam had been friends since the first day of college, and since that very evening, when he first brought her to Francesco's, his family had been doing everything they could to foster the romance only they saw blooming between the two of them.

Lori smiled. "At least you'd have nice in-laws. And amazing food."

Suddenly, Sam grew serious. "Is that enough, do you think? Or do you need passion? You're passionate, right? With Chip?"

Lori's bravado faltered. "I guess it's passionate. He's more into it than I am. I'd be happy with good food and a nice mother-in-law. Why?"

Sam shrugged. She wasn't sure why. Actually, she was. She just wasn't sure how to articulate what she was feeling, what she was thinking, the doubts that were beginning to push to the forefront of her thoughts. Sam had spent more time in the past days thinking of such things than she had in her entire life.

She'd been dating the same guy for years, and she suddenly was wondering why. Did she ever really have an attraction to him? There was certainly no passion. He was a nice, solid guy who Sam liked as a friend, but should there be more? Shouldn't she feel the same excitement to see him that she did when she was with Kirby? As hard as she contemplated, Sam could never remember a time when Doug had that effect on her. It was like Kirby had some witchy powers and had put her under a spell.

Her lack of enthusiasm for Doug, coupled with the nonstop thoughts of Kirby that filled her mind lately, had Sam as confused as she'd ever been.

Jim brought their drinks, and she was spared having to answer Lori's question.

"Well, ladies. We did it!" He raised a glass and they joined him, a series of clinks punctuating their cheers. "To bright futures, and designer sunglasses to make them bearable."

They laughed and tasted the fruity mixture that foamed with what seemed to be sorbet. "Mm," Sam said.

Jim beamed. "Isn't it great? I tasted it at the competition's bar down the road, and I think I've perfected it."

"I think you're right," Sam said. "What's it called?"

"Well, there's cranberry juice, vodka, limoncello, and orange sorbet in it. I'm calling it Italian Ice."

"Creative," Lori said, and Sam nodded.

"Clever," Sam added.

"Sometimes," Jim said wistfully, as if he were on his third drink instead of his first, "I think it would be nice to just stay here and tend bar for the rest of my life. I could marry someone who cooks, and we'd do what my parents and grandparents did."

"What's stopping you?" Sam asked, her philosophical flame fanned by the ambiance of the quiet bar and the company of two great friends.

Placing his hands in a bridge beneath his chin, he stared across the table at them. "I don't know. Fear, I think. Some people fear the unknown and would say stay here because it's safe. I fear the opposite. What if I never leave here, and I'm stuck with this?"

Sam puckered her lips. "I'm confused. I thought you just said you wanted to stay here for the rest of your life?"

Lori laughed, Jim sighed dramatically, and Sam shook her head, blinked, and looked at him. "Okay. Let me try harder." She squinted and peered into Jim's eyes. "What the fuck are you talking about?"

Lori and Jim laughed hysterically. It was only on the rarest of occasions that Sam used the f-bomb, but it seemed fitting now.

"Urg! I mean, I want to choose my own destiny. If I come back to Old Forge and tend bar, I want it to be my choice, not because it's what's expected."

"So, you're going to spend a hundred grand and four years of your life to get a medical degree so you can mix frozen drinks at your family's bar?"

"I know it sounds pretty bizarre."

As Sam sipped the last of the drink, she looked regretfully at the empty glass. It was a great drink, the Italian Ice, and it had softened the edges of the anxiety she'd been feeling earlier.

"Jim, you have to do what makes you happy. We all do. If this is what you want in the end, I'll support you." But would Lori and Jim support her if she told them her thoughts?

"Me, too," Lori said.

"I love you guys," Jim said.

Sam looked at her two best friends and wished she knew the answer to her secret question. She hoped they'd always be as close, even though she knew the path they were starting down together was going to diverge very quickly. Who knew where they'd end up?

Nonna interrupted them, pushing a cart heavy with food. A huge plate of bruschetta was followed by a family-sized platter of stuffed shells, a loaf of bread, and a jug of house wine.

"*Grazi*," Sam said, and Nonna beamed, then said something in Italian as she walked away. Whatever it was, it made Jim laugh.

"You're not going to tell us, are you?" Sam asked.

"Not a chance," he replied as he began filling wineglasses.

Lori looked at her watch. "This is technically lunch, guys."

"Yeah. It's kind of early. Maybe water, instead of wine?"

Jim jumped up and went to the bar, then returned with a pitcher of water and three glasses. "Good idea," he said as he poured.

"In a few weeks, we'll be walking across that stage and getting our diplomas. We did it," Sam said, as she raised a glass of water.

"And then, we're off to the bright lights of the big city," Jim added.

Lori touched her glass to the others. "To my new roomies." They'd leased a three-bedroom house and would be sharing the rent for the next year. "May Jim always remember to put the toilet seat back down."

Sam laughed so hard she spilled her water.

"Should we talk about the apartment?"

"We have to," Lori said. "It's a little more than two months until moving day. After finals, we have to sit down and make a list of what we need, and we can all decide what we're going to bring to furnish the place."

"My Bapcia is going to crochet us an afghan for the couch," Sam said and pointed a finger at them. "Don't laugh. We have to use it, or her heart will be broken."

"I only hope we have a couch to put it on," Lori said wistfully.

"We'll figure this out. The flea market, yard sales, the newspaper. Whatever we can't buy used, we'll buy new. And in a few years, we'll look back on this time of poverty and laugh about our struggles and sacrifices," Jim proclaimed with a dramatic sigh.

Later, on the way home, Sam thought about the things Jim had said. Where would she be in four years? She loved working in the ER, but did that mean she should do that forever? She wasn't so sure she had the physical skills to be a great surgeon, or the patience to do pediatrics, as her father had. Histology in college had bored her, so she wasn't even considering a career in pathology. As for the other specialties, who knew? She really had no experience with anything else. Maybe she'd just have to wait and see.

The day was bright and cloudless, and after a few hours in the classroom, and another in a darkened restaurant, Sam longed to be outside. After arriving home, she threw her backpack onto her bed and changed into shorts and a T-shirt, then took the dog into the yard to play. When he lost interest in fetching a stick, she headed to the garage, where she pulled a plastic bin of gardening supplies from the shelf.

After tying Brandy's leash to a stake under his favorite tree, Sam assessed the work that lay before her. It was still too early to plant, but she could do some clean-up and prepare the beds for flowers. First, she used a miniature rake to remove the debris that had accumulated during the winter—fallen tree limbs and leaves, the stalks of a few dead plants, even some stray garbage. She'd just finished the first bed and moved on to the second when her mom's car pulled into the driveway.

Brandy stood and barked, and Sam freed him from his leash before turning to greet her. Irene picked him up and kissed him before kissing Sam.

"This is a nice surprise. I thought you wouldn't be home until later," Sam said.

"It's a wonderful surprise! The CEO's wife had a minor surgical procedure today, and they're holding her until tonight for observation. Since he's there anyway, he offered to take the beeper for the night."

"Lucky you! And there's a further bit of luck in the kitchen. Jim sent us pizza. Are you hungry?"

"How sweet of him! In a while," she said as she nodded toward the flowerbed. "Let me change, and I'll join you."

Sam piled the organic debris into the wheelbarrow and moved farther along the garden. The narrow space of earth between their driveway and the neighbors' property was one giant swath of landscaping that stretched several hundred feet. It took an effort to tend it, but Sam found the work relaxing. When she worked beside her mom, it was even more enjoyable.

A few minutes after she'd disappeared, Irene returned. Gone was the navy-blue suit and dress pumps, replaced by ragged sweatpants and an equally abused long-sleeved tee.

"Tell me one good thing about your day, Lovey," Irene said as she began to pull weeds.

She thought of her friends, leaving Loyola Hall together for the last time. Then she thought of their lunch. "I have really good friends."

"I hope you all still speak after living together."

Sam pulled herself to an upright position on her knees and sighed. "I am a little worried about it. Our life—my life—is sort of…calm. No noise, no mess, no drama. How will I handle living with two other people?"

"And only one bathroom." Her mother turned pointedly toward her and frowned.

"I don't hog the bathroom."

"Hmpf," Irene murmured.

"You made me this way."

"And I fear the world isn't ready for you."

"I've been asking myself today if I'm ready for the world."

Irene sat up tall, her pose matching Sam's. The Lion's Pose. In this case, The Lioness. "You are."

"It's scary, you know? What if I'm not smart enough?"

"Lovey, you're brilliant."

Sam sighed, whispered. "I've never been away from home before."

Irene looked at her, the love in her eyes spilling out. "I bet that's a scary thought. But think of the positives. You'll have a little freedom to come and go. And you'll be only two hours away. You could technically commute."

Sam chuckled. "I just might. I bet Lori will go insane without Chip. We can carpool."

"It's a shame he doesn't want to pursue his education," Irene added as she stood and carried some debris to the wheelbarrow.

"I guess college isn't for everyone."

"But, Sam, surely you understand how lopsided their relationship is going to be, with her as a physician and him as a…a…whatever he is."

Chip worked for his father, who owned rental properties and commercial real estate. Chip literally did whatever was needed to maintain them, from plumbing to weed-whacking. "His family has more money than the Nanticoke National Bank. If the relationship is lopsided, it's because Lori's family is poor, and she exists on financial aid."

"What about intellect? Conversation? Goals? He's beneath her."

"Mom!"

"Sam, please. You know I'm right."

Sam often wondered what Lori saw in Chip. He was funny and made her laugh, but other than that, Sam had trouble talking to him about anything other than sports. But maybe that was enough. It didn't matter, though. I was Lori's life, and she loved him.

"She loves him, Mom."

"That doesn't make them a good match. In order to be happy, you need to have love, but also respect for each other's family and traditions, and for who you are as people. How can you respect that when you don't know anything about it? That's why Catholics should marry Catholics, and Jews should stick with Jews, and whites should marry whites. Professionals, Sam, should marry professionals."

"You're racist, Mom. And prejudiced."

"Samantha, that is not true! Every one of us is a child of God and deserves respect. I have taken care of patients of every faith and skin color, and I have treated every one of them with dignity and kindness. I just think the world works better when we stick to our own."

Sam had a sudden thought, and before she could stifle it, the question was out of her mouth. "What about gay people, Mom?"

Irene visibly tensed beside her. "What about them?"

"Are they God's children?"

"The Bible is clear about this, Sam. It's not my judgment. It's God's."

"And what is God's judgment?"

"Homosexuals are an abomination. They'll all burn in hell." Her voice was little more than a whisper, as if she feared provoking the Almighty by speaking of such a despicable topic.

Sam felt suddenly sick, nauseated, and she couldn't say anything as she fought tears. Her mother didn't notice as she continued to work beside her.

Stifling her emotions, Sam sat quietly and soon found herself lost in her own thoughts. Between finals, and a move to Philadelphia, and thoughts of Kirby, she had plenty of them to drown in. Even still, Kirby came to the forefront of her mind again and again. Sam supposed she could cancel their hike and avoid Kirby. That would solve the problem, wouldn't it? But Sam *wanted* to be with Kirby. She wanted to talk with her, and hike with her, and throw a ball with her. She wanted to stare into Kirby's dark-brown eyes and see the way Kirby looked at her. She wanted to feel the way she felt with Kirby, that high she'd never experienced before with another human being. She wanted all those things. She just didn't want to know what it all meant.

They worked until dark, then ate a salad and pizza, and Sam mostly stayed in her own head. Her mother didn't seem to mind the lack of conversation. Teddy called and asked her if she wanted to go out to celebrate their last night of class, and Sam was about to turn her down when she realized she needed a distraction.

Half an hour after her phone rang, she was at Teddy's and, in another fifteen minutes, at the Station in Wilkes-Barre. The bar and nightclub complex was built in a former railway station, and the decor suitably matched, but Sam hardly noticed. She sipped a wine and danced, talked to high school friends and college classmates. Around midnight, when stifling yawns became challenging, she began a hunt for Teddy. She suspected Teddy would tell her to go home, and Sam wouldn't be afraid to leave her. Half the population of the bar went to the same college, and Sam was sure Teddy could find a couch to crash on.

Her search took her onto the long porch, and she immediately saw a familiar face in the crowd. Kirby seemed to sense her and turned to offer a warm smile. Sam hesitated for a moment, not wanting to *want* to talk to her, but knowing she was powerless to resist. She walked over to the spot where Kirby stood beside a woman who looked like she'd stepped off a magazine cover. Not at all the kind of super-athletic friend she imagined Kirby hung with.

"Hi, Sam!" Kirby said. "I can't believe you're here. I didn't know you hang out in Wilkes-Barre. Have you been here all night? What are you drinking? Can I buy you a drink?"

"Which question should I answer first?" Sam laughed at the run-on sentence but caught herself when she noticed the frosty look Sam's companion had shot her way. Uneasy, she held out her hand. "Hi. I'm Sam."

"Trisha," the girl said, with a nod and a half smile.

Kirby didn't seem to notice and continued talking to Sam. "Are you excited about tomorrow?" She looked at Trisha. "Tomorrow's our first softball game. Or is it today? Saturday. Our game is Saturday."

"Yes. Our game is in a few hours. I need to get home."

"Oh, I should go, too."

"Are you okay?" Sam asked. She didn't know Kirby well, and she wasn't sloppy but just seemed a little off kilter. And she was in a bar, which meant she'd probably had a few drinks.

"She was until you got here," Trisha said under her breath, and both she and Kirby looked at her.

"Huh?" Sam asked.

"Oh, nothing, nothing!" Kirby said. "I'm fine. Just tired. Can I walk you to your car?"

"Oh, do. I'll wait right here for you," Trisha said sarcastically.

Kirby shook her head. "Actually, I do need to go. But it was nice talking to you, Trisha."

Kirby began walking, and Sam followed. "What was that about? Did I miss something important?" she asked when they were a few feet away.

"I'm not sure, but thanks for saving me from it."

Sam looked at Kirby, and in the dim light of the bar, she thought she detected a blush creeping up from the collar of her shirt to the back of her bare neck.

"I have to find Teddy," Sam said as she stopped and looked around.

"Teddy? She's here somewhere."

They found her at a table with a bunch of friends, and as expected, she declined the offer of a ride home. Kirby's Jeep was parked near Sam's car, so they walked together. "I wish I'd caught up with you earlier in the night," Kirby said.

"We didn't even get there until ten."

"That explains it."

"I'm happy we don't have an early morning. Ten o'clock will be here soon enough," Sam said through another yawn.

"Am I boring you?"

Sam blinked. Nothing could be further from the truth. Seeing Kirby had turned the entire night around. She'd been rather miserable and thought Teddy would help cheer her. And she had. They'd danced and laughed, and had a great time. But seeing Kirby had taken the night to a whole new level. She couldn't let Kirby know that, though.

"Yes, I'm afraid so. You're going to have to try harder to amuse me tomorrow."

"Today."

Sam nodded and yawned again. "I should go."

"Yes. Me, too."

"How far is your place?"

"On-campus. I could walk."

"Maybe I should drive you, and you get your car in the morning."

"Sam, I'm not drunk."

Sam studied Kirby for a moment. Her speech wasn't slurred, and her gait was steady. It was that first impression, though—the pressured speech as Kirby greeted her.

"You just seemed..."

"Excited. I was excited to see you."

Sam's breath caught in her throat. What exactly was Kirby saying? That she was as attracted to Sam as Sam was to her? It was a scary thought.

"I guess I did save you from Trisha."

Kirby made a slight bow. "And I'm grateful."

Sam leaned against her car. "I suspect we could talk all night."

"But it's probably not a great idea."

"Go home," Sam said, although she really didn't want to.

"You first."

Resigned, Sam tilted her head. "On three? Last one out of the parking lot is a rotten egg."

Kirby smirked. "A rotten egg? Are we seven?"

Sam did feel like a little kid around Kirby. "One," she said as she ran around the back of her car and hopped in. She took a moment to glance over and saw Kirby already backing up. She shrugged and raised her hands in defeat, then watched as Kirby blew her a kiss and drove away.

CHAPTER SEVEN

On Saturday morning, Teddy was waiting when Sam pulled into the driveway.

"I can't believe you're conscious."

"Years of practice," Teddy retorted. "But I am so ready to move out of my parents' frickin' house," she complained as she landed on the front seat. "They actually lectured me about staying out all night. I'm frickin' twenty-two years old."

Sam had no reply that would help, so she was quiet for a moment before she changed the subject. "So this is weird," she said.

"What?"

"Playing against each other. You look funny in a jersey that doesn't match mine!"

"I know. And frickin' Ashley can't even catch an underhand toss to second base. She only plays there because she sucks and can't play anywhere else."

Reaching across the divide, Sam smacked Teddy on the shoulder. "Hey, I'm insulted," she whined.

"You know what I mean!"

"I happen to think second base is an important position."

Teddy waved dismissively. "Oh, stop it! I'm not talking about you."

Sam offered a toothless grin. "You miss me."

"Of course I do. How's your team? You like your hotshot short-stop?"

"No one compares to you."

Teddy reached out and punched her gently on the arm. "You remember that."

At the field they went toward separate benches, and Sam was happy to see Kirby kneeling in the grass behind theirs, stretching. Sitting beside her, Sam began her own routine.

"You don't usually stretch," Sam said, based on the first two times they played together.

"Neither do you."

"I start slowly. That's my warm-up."

"I see. Well, when I play at the crack of dawn like this, I have to stretch. My muscles are still asleep."

"Yes. The alarm had cruel timing this morning. Nine o'clock seemed awfully early."

"I hear you."

They were in a hurdlers' stretch, and Sam's muscles practically squeaked. "I don't know how I'm going to make this hike," she said. "I'm so out of shape."

"Want to reschedule?" Kirby asked.

The thought was disturbing. Since they'd made the plan, she'd been counting the hours until this moment, until she saw Kirby again and had a chance to talk with her, to giggle at something silly Kirby said, to make her laugh in return. And the prospect of canceling sucked all the air from her lungs. Shaking her head, she answered. "No. Absolutely not. We are hiking. Today."

"Well, o-k-a-y, then. We're hiking. Today."

They warmed up their arms by throwing the ball to each other and took the field first as the home team for this game. After watching a few pitches, the first batter hit the ball in the hole between second and third, and Kirby reached down to backhand the ball, came up throwing, and got the runner at first by a step. She met Sam's eye and lifted her pointer finger. One out. The first out of the game, and the year, and her new softball double-play combination. Sam was happy she'd gotten that out of the way.

The game was a good one, with great defensive plays on both sides, timely hitting, and the winning run scored in the bottom of the last inning.

After congratulating each other, both teams settled in to watch the second game, and they stayed until it was over. Teddy had plans for after the game, so she didn't need a ride, and Sam and Kirby walked out to the parking lot together. It was one of the few quiet times they'd shared since the night before, but Sam was almost too nervous to talk. What if Kirby didn't like the hike? What if she didn't like Sam? More worrisome—what if she did? The thought made her jittery.

"Follow me," Sam said as they reached the cars.

"K."

It was a five-minute ride to her house, and she directed Kirby to park her Jeep behind her car in the driveway. Her mom was at work, but Sam was never sure when she'd return.

"So you live with your parents?" Kirby asked.

"My mom," Sam said, without further explanation. It was just too hard, still, to talk about her father, and it made everyone feel awkward when she did. If she continued to hang out with Kirby, Sam knew she'd tell that story eventually, but she refused to ruin this beautiful day with talk of her dead father. "And a ferocious beast."

Kirby eyed her suspiciously. "Yeah?"

"My dog, Brandy. I have to warn you…he's never killed anyone, but he will try to smother you with kisses."

Kirby nodded. "I consider myself warned."

Sam opened the door from the garage, and Brandy launched at her, landing halfway up her thigh. He didn't even bother barking at Kirby as Sam scooped him up and he slathered her with kisses. Sam turned toward Kirby so she could pet him, and only then did he flatter her with his attention.

Kirby offered him her hand, and he licked it, which made her giggle, a sound Sam found infectious. She giggled right back.

"Are you hungry?" she asked as they began walking toward the kitchen.

"Maybe. What do you have to eat?" Kirby asked.

"Finicky, are you?" she asked as she passed the dog to Kirby's arms.

"Another big word. And it's not even Latin," she said as she nuzzled him. "I almost have a dog," she said, more to Brandy then to her. "He's a ferocious German shepherd named Phoenix, almost bigger than me. But he's not as friendly."

"Brandy loves women, but not men so much. And I'm studying

for my Latin final, so you are in for a treat today. I know cool words."
She paused as she poked her head in the refrigerator. "I have a few cuts
of Old Forge pizza. A pot-roast sandwich, or lunch meat, or PB&J, a
frozen burrito. We're like a restaurant here."

"What will you have?"

They went for the pot-roast sandwiches, which Sam heated in the
microwave, and they washed them down with sun tea Sam's mom had
steeping on the counter. When they were done, they both changed into
jeans and sneakers and headed off toward the backyard.

Sam's sunroom was in the back of the house, and beyond that
a patio extended for several yards before giving way to an expanse
of lawn that stretched all the way to the base of the mountain. They
walked side by side, talking about the game, until they came to a path,
partially obscured by the vegetation growing wild in this part of the
yard. They split, with Sam in the lead, and walked for a few minutes to
a switchback before Sam paused to check on Kirby. "You good?" she
asked as she turned to look at her.

"Never better," she said as she kept walking, passing Sam with a
gentle punch on the arm.

Sam chuckled and fell in behind her, not worried about Kirby
getting lost. She knew this mountain well, and besides, if they stayed
on the trail, it would eventually lead them where they needed to go.

From behind, Sam couldn't help admiring Kirby's physique. The
jeans looked like they were tailored for her, hugging her thighs and her
butt. Her shirt stretched across her back and showed off the muscles of
her shoulders and arms. It was an impressive sight.

"Do you lift weights?" Sam asked, and couldn't believe she'd let
her thoughts take the shape of a question.

"I used to, when I played in college. But what do I need to be
strong for now? I'd rather just do aerobics and stay toned, not big."

"So you used to be bigger?" Sam couldn't imagine what she'd
looked like then.

"Yeah. Like twenty pounds heavier."

"Wow. That's a lot."

"It came off pretty easily. I just stopped lifting."

After a half hour of climbing, they reached a clearing, and Kirby
turned, clearly appreciating the vista of the mountains, divided from
north to south by the Susquehanna River.

"Wow," Kirby said as she turned in a circle, taking it all in.

Sam felt the high of adrenaline, but another unique lift as well. It was a wondrous feeling to share this view—her mountain, her river, her valley—with Kirby.

She reached for her water bottle and pulled it from the mesh on her backpack, took a drink, and offered it to Kirby, who thanked her and took a few sips. It wasn't a hot day, but beads of sweat had formed in the small of her back and on her forehead. They'd worked hard on the walk.

A few steps below them, a boulder protruded from the earth. It was an obvious spot to rest and enjoy the view, and Kirby didn't hesitate to climb down and sit. Sam quickly followed.

They relaxed in companionable silence for a few moments, looking out. Then Sam closed her eyes and breathed deeply, tilting her face to the sun and inhaling the earthy scent of the forest. She felt herself melting into the rock on which she sat. A calm washed over her.

"I feel so small. Insignificant." Kirby whispered, as if trying to preserve the peace they enjoyed.

"Yes," Sam replied, for Kirby had stated it perfectly, and she couldn't add anything.

She heard Kirby sigh and turned to meet her eyes. Instead of the view, Kirby was looking at her. Before she could question, Kirby spoke.

"So, about last night."

The day was bright, and Kirby's eyes were masked by her sunglasses, but Sam sought them anyway. She already loved that connection. "Trisha was a little…odd."

Kirby looked away, back toward the river, and when she spoke, her voice was soft. "Trisha was sort of hitting on me. But not without cause, because the last time I saw her, I was hitting on her. But that was before I met you." Sam could see Kirby swallow, and she felt her own mouth go dry as she grasped what Kirby was telling her. Turning her head, she studied Sam for a moment before deciding to go on. "I'm gay," she said, and a hint of a smile formed at the corners of her mouth, as if she was barely containing her happiness.

Sam wasn't surprised at all. They'd been flirting, sort of. And Kirby did seem to hang out with all the girls. No, it wasn't a surprise. What was surprising was her own feelings. At that moment, it seemed like the most natural thing in the world to be gay, although Kirby's naked truth caused a slight tremor of fear to invade her peace. Pulling in a deep breath, she nodded. "I know."

As she stared at Kirby, Sam's fears melted away. She wasn't sure how Kirby felt about her, but she couldn't deny her own feelings. Since the moment Sam had seen Kirby, sitting on the ground after they'd knocked each other over, she'd been infatuated with her. Everything she did, everywhere she went, everyone she talked to magically reminded her of Kirby. And then one thought led to another as she wondered what Kirby was doing, where she was, who she was with. It was a powerful force, this attraction. She'd had many friends in her life, and even a boyfriend, but no one she'd ever connected with like the woman beside her.

Sam reached out, and then she was surprised to see her fingers at Kirby's face. And then, she realized, at that moment, to not touch her would have been more surprising. Her gaze followed her fingers along Kirby's hairline, along her jaw and to her lips. She lifted Kirby's sunglasses and looked to Kirby's eyes, saw them shutter as her pupils dilated. They both leaned in, just slightly, and then Sam closed the gap, and her mouth found the softness of Kirby's.

It was nothing more than a physical link between them, the bridge completing the connection they already had. Yet, at the same time, it was everything, sucking the air from Sam, sending her spinning, as Kirby gently nibbled on her lip, as their tongues tentatively found each other's.

Too soon they pulled apart, breathless, trembling, but their eyes held.

Wow, Sam thought. *I'm gay, too.* This one moment, this one kiss, this one girl—it explained so much to her. Things about herself she'd never dug deeply into, feelings and ideas and plans that didn't seem to run exactly along the course she always thought they should. In the span of a few heartbeats, she was revealed to herself.

She needed a moment—or maybe a year or two—to let this new reality sink in. But she didn't have that, for Kirby was still staring at her, and as much as she wanted time to work through these new feelings, this attraction, for the first time in her life, she wanted to rip someone's clothes off.

Levity seemed like a safe place. "So, about this kiss," Sam said with a chuckle as she watched Kirby pull back a fraction of an inch. A blink seemed to break the trance, and her expression became blank.

"I've never kissed a girl," Sam confessed.

"I know," Kirby said with a nod.

"That bad?" Sam asked.

With a look of wonder on her face, Kirby sighed. "That good."

Sam's lips curled up into a satisfying grin. "Yes. Yes, it was."

Turning from Kirby, Sam looked again out at the river and the mountains. "I need to digest this situation."

"That's understandable. For me—well, I know what I want and who I want. I guess you're still figuring that out."

"You're not upset?" Sam asked, turning to her again.

"It's kind of what I expected. I asked around about you, you know," she said with a wink.

"You asked? About me? Who? What?" The idea petrified Sam.

"Oh, everyone I know on the softball team. Teddy."

"What did they say? What did Teddy say?" Sam felt breathless again, but this time fear was stealing her oxygen. She was the subject of gossip. Did her friends and teammates suspect what was going on?

"Nothing, really. No one can say for sure if someone else might play on our team. But they consider you a definite *wannabe*."

Sam was shocked, not just at the label, but that people she knew were discussing her. "Teddy said that?"

"No. Teddy is your knight. She's a fierce protector."

"What did she say?"

"She heard I was asking about you, and she called me the other day and told me that if I had questions about you, I should ask you instead of starting rumors."

"Ouch."

"Nothing I can't handle. Besides, she was right."

"So you decided to come out to me?"

Kirby nodded. "I figured it might be a conversation starter."

"I'll say."

"She also said…you have a boyfriend."

Sam felt the words like a punch to the throat, felt the pressure to explain. "I do, sort of. It's not serious." She sighed.

Kirby nodded and bit her lip, giving her time to form her thoughts, but Sam didn't know what else to say. Kirby knocked Sam in the ribs with her elbow, and Sam feigned pain from the gentle tap. "Since when have you been at a loss for words?"

"I honestly don't know what I'm feeling. I…really care about my boyfriend, Doug. He's a nice guy. He's been an inspiration to me, really, because he's so smart and accomplished. We've always been great friends. But there's never been any passion, you know? No desire." Sam waved her finger back and forth from her to Kirby. "No… *this*. We were both in the pre-med club in high school, and he asked me to prom, and I went, because it was just easy. And we've been dating since. *For five years!* Because it's easy. Never anything exciting. It's rather boring, actually."

"Is that what you're looking for? Excitement?" Kirby didn't look pleased, so Sam was quick to reassure her.

"No, no. Yes! Not in the way you're thinking. I wasn't looking for excitement, but you just…excite me." She shrugged and smiled, pausing as she stared at Kirby, trying to read something in her poker face. But while Kirby stared at her, Sam wasn't sure what she was thinking. "I don't know what it all means, Kirby. I've never been so happy to be with someone. So anxious to see someone. I think of you from the moment I open my eyes in the morning until the minute I close them at night. I don't even escape you in my sleep. I dream of you."

Kirby smiled, but her smile was sad. "It sounds like you have a decision to make."

CHAPTER EIGHT

It was the longest walk home in history, Sam so distracted she'd slipped twice on loose rocks on the trail. They hadn't said anything else, just that Sam needed time. But what did that mean? Would Kirby try to kiss her again when they said good-bye? Sam would probably skip softball practice this week, because of her exam schedule. She'd next see Kirby in a week, at their upcoming game. What then? Another hike? More food? More kissing? What did Sam need time for? She already knew her feelings for Kirby were real; that one kiss answered all the questions she'd had about her obsession.

Sam wasn't very experienced in the matter, but that kiss was amazing. It had awakened a part of her she'd been able to deny, at least doubt. While others she knew practically obsessed over sex, she never had, never saw the appeal. Biologically, she understood its function. Socially, she understood the importance of marriage and family. But sexually—she'd never understood sexual attraction. Not until Kirby.

This question was Sam's to answer, and Kirby seemed prepared to give her time to make sense of her feelings.

They'd agreed not to call. Tuesday was their next practice, and if Sam went, they'd see each other then, check in with each other. But they'd agreed there'd be no flirting, no teasing, none of the banter that had paved the path to the place where they now found themselves. They'd take a step back and give it a few weeks, and then—well, they'd see.

"Do you need to use the bathroom before you go?" Sam asked.

"No, thanks. I'll just leave you to your studies. First final Monday?"

Sam nodded. "Biochem."

"Sounds like fun." They skipped the house and walked around the side to Kirby's car. Sam kept a deliberate distance between them.

"Well..." Kirby said sadly.

Sam held up her hand, and a harmless wave breezed through her fingertips. "See you soon."

When Kirby's Jeep disappeared around the corner, Sam retreated to the kitchen, poured herself a glass of water, and flopped into a chaise lounge on the patio. Brandy joined her.

Mindlessly, she rubbed his little head as she stared into the cloudless sky. She was gay. Wasn't she? She'd kissed a girl, and it had been amazing, so that was the obvious conclusion, wasn't it? Or was she bi? She'd heard of that, although she didn't actually know anyone who was bisexual. How did that work, exactly?

She didn't know anyone who was gay, either. She had an idea about Teddy, but they'd never discussed the topic. She was the super-jock who never dated, who seemed too busy having fun to be tied down. But, seriously, the last time she'd seen Teddy with a guy, they were dancing at their senior prom. That was four years ago. And Jim... well, Sam was sure it was only a matter of time before he figured it out. Otherwise, her references were limited. There were two women who lived together in a big white house in town, and when she'd become aware of the concept of homosexuality, Lola and Peg had come to mind.

But this was different. This was her. She'd never been gaga over a guy, but that was just because she had plans, right? One day, when she had time for something other than studying, she'd catch up with the rest of the world in the romance department.

Another thought occurred to her. She couldn't be gay, because she wanted kids. Her high school job had been babysitting, and her favorite family times were spent with her mom's sister and her huge family. She had half a dozen cousins, some of them still in diapers, and they all adored her as much as she loved them.

What had she been thinking? She couldn't be gay. She was too... girly. Right?

This was nothing! A harmless, immature crush, and it would stop here. She didn't have anything to think about. She was straight.

So why could she not stop thinking of Kirby? Why did she only want to be with her? Why had Kirby's kiss caused her to practically melt into the rock?

It was nearly seven o'clock when she finally wandered in from the patio, where she'd sat studying the curves of her mountain after walking Kirby to her car. After she finished her shower, her mom was checking the mail in the living room, one eye on a Lifetime movie as she sorted envelopes.

"Hi, Lovey. How was your game?"

Padding over, she curled up on the chair and began combing her wet hair with her fingers while she thought of the kiss. Everything inside her dissolved as she remembered the touch of Kirby's lips, and she could hardly find her voice.

"Good. We won. Mom, how did you know Daddy was the one for you?" she asked, remembering her mom's prediction from the night before about homosexuals and hell.

Sensing an important moment, her mom clicked off the television, set aside the mail, and shifted on the couch so she could see Sam. "What's going on?"

"I'm just thinking about things…"

They were quiet for a moment. "Lovey, you're about to graduate college. Start medical school. Move away from home for the first time. You have a lot to think about."

"You're right. But, honestly, don't you think I should be more, I don't know—boy crazy?"

Irene laughed. "I was thirty-five when I met your father. Never married, never really serious about anyone until I met him. I knew I wanted a career, and I always figured the husband and family would come later. And I was right. I think you're just like me. You're driven, focused on your education. One day, when you meet the right man, you'll know it."

Was that true? Had she just been too sheltered to notice a nice man? Or, what if the issue was something else altogether? What if it wasn't a man who'd make her happy? What if it was a woman?

She had a dozen reasons to not ask her mom that question, so she went back to the first, the one that had caused her mother to turn off the television in the middle of a Lifetime movie. "How did you know with Daddy?"

Her mom's response echoed in her thoughts as she tossed and turned in her bed hours later. "I thought of him all the time. I waited by the phone for his calls, canceled plans with everyone else so I could be with him. My face nearly cracked from smiling and laughing all the time."

How could this happen? When? Had she been a lesbian her whole life and just buried that fact? Had she simply been hiding from the truth in the cubicles of her high school and college libraries? Or had she been too busy with her academic agenda to get serious with any of the intelligent young men with whom she worked and studied?

Staring into the darkness, she looked back on her life, searching for signs. She was athletic. Did that mean anything? Was this genetic? One of her grandmother's sisters on her dad's side had never married. As a young high school graduate, she'd moved to New York City and worked as a seamstress in a factory and stayed there for years, returning to Nanticoke when her ailing mother needed help. Sam had vague memories of Chochie Mary as a spunky woman who didn't take any crap from anyone. Sam's grandfather, who was pathetically dependent on her grandmother, was one of her favorite targets. Had Mary been gay?

Sam remembered her, suddenly stricken with emotion. Mary and her sister, Sam's grandmother, had passed away within months of each other, a few years after Sam's father. So many people had died, lost to her forever. What would happen to the rest of them if she told them this?

The impact of that revelation would be devastating. She couldn't—wouldn't think about it now.

God, she was a mess!

Climbing out of bed, Sam tiptoed through the dark house and did something she very rarely did—poured herself a drink. Wine, since that was all her mother kept in the house. A big glass of cabernet.

On the couch, she sank into the overstuffed cushions and pulled an afghan around her legs, beginning to think again. She examined every friendship she'd ever had for clues of a hidden lesbian connection.

Lori? Their attraction was magnetic, but she couldn't honestly say it was anything other than friendly. Lori was the sister she'd never had. A confidante and playmate. But kiss her? Never.

What about Heather, her friend and teammate from high school? Like Lori, Heather was smart and studious, but again, Sam couldn't say she felt any attraction. Together they'd completed school projects and worked on committees, studied and cheered on their school teams, but they were friends. That's what friends do.

Teddy? No way. Nor any of the other girls she'd played softball with in high school. They were all teammates and pals. They hung out sometimes, but mostly they did things—hiking trips deep into the woods, kayaking the Susquehanna River, biking.

Then she thought of Jacquie, the non-athlete who went out for the team just because it would look good on her resume. While her athletic skills were lacking, her personality was huge. Sam had never known her well, but after a few softball practices their junior year, she found herself talking to Jacquie, found herself calling her on the phone for no reason, just to talk. She'd never done that before with a friend.

That was also when she started dating Doug, and even though they were going to prom together, she found herself shopping with Jacquie, planning with her, discussing it all as if they'd been best friends forever. Their friendship was a shooting star, streaming across a few months of their lives, and then it crashed. Sam had worked that summer in the ER, and the one memorable time she shared with Jacquie was at a party at a classmate's lake house, where Jacquie was too drunk to walk straight and confessed to Sam she'd lost her virginity with the football player who'd taken her to prom.

Trying to remember how she'd felt back then, Sam thought she'd probably had a crush on Jacquie. Although she really didn't call her after that party, Sam responded to Jacquie's revelation by sleeping with Doug, and she'd spent much of the rest of the summer with him. But she remembered thinking of her, and she vividly recalled her sudden animosity toward the football player Jacquie started dating.

But she liked boys, didn't she? Many of her friends were boys. Boys were great. They were fun. They were athletic. They just weren't…appealing.

Thinking of Doug was no help. Their relationship was built on the common bond they shared—their studies. They liked each other, and laughed at each other's jokes, and were comfortable together. But what she'd told Kirby on the mountain was true. He didn't excite her.

When her friends talked about sex, it seemed as if they really enjoyed it. They looked forward to it. Sam could never say that about sex with Doug. She'd always thought she was different, perhaps a little too Catholic. When she was married, and the burden of sin was lifted from her, she figured she might enjoy it more. Look forward to it.

Now, though, she wasn't sure her religious beliefs had anything to do with it. Kissing Kirby had made her lust in a way she'd never experienced before, and Kirby was a woman, and no Catholic doctrine supported that, either. In fact, the church would never sanction a relationship with Kirby.

After a while, she sat and finally just thought of Kirby. She couldn't deny the happiness that filled her. The kiss was erotic, the most sensual experience of Sam's life.

She might have been attracted to Jacquie at one time. She probably was. But she knew with crystal clarity how she felt about Kirby and what she had to do if she wanted to explore those feelings further.

And, no matter what it meant, Sam had no doubt that exploring these feelings was exactly what she wanted to do.

She picked up the phone and dialed. It was late, but she had to make the call. It couldn't wait any longer.

A man answered on the first ring.

"Hi," he said. "What's going on?"

He was probably busy studying for his own finals, but she somehow felt dismissed. It didn't matter, though. She'd been dismissing him for more than five years.

Douglas Brooks, the boy who'd been her high school sweetheart, the one she'd dated through four years of college, didn't excite her, and she knew now that he never would.

But he'd been a good friend, a positive influence, and she needed to settle things with him so she could move on to whatever lay ahead for her. Whatever…the thought quickened her pulse.

She cut him off as he began to tell her about his grueling schedule. There was no point in dragging this out.

"Doug, I need to tell you something. Can you stop for a second?"

"What?" he asked, seemingly surprised that she'd cut into the middle of his thoughts.

"I want to take a break," she said, immediately bashing herself in the forehead as punishment for her cowardice. No amount of time would change anything. But why hurt him? Why not just let him off gently?

"What? You're breaking up with me? Why? Is there someone else?" he asked with more passion than she'd ever heard before.

"No, of course not," she lied. And then she told him about how she'd worked and studied for five years and never dated anyone except him. She had one last summer before her real work began in medical school, and she wanted to relax and enjoy it. "And besides, Doug—you're too busy. You're so accomplished, and ambitious—you really don't have time for me."

"Ouch."

"I'm not trying to be hurtful, but it's true. Let's talk when I get to Philly in the fall, and we'll see how things are going for both of us, okay?"

He seemed to understand, and Sam was relieved, but her thoughts lingered on Douglas for only a few seconds. She closed her eyes, and with her mind finally at peace, she thought of Kirby as she drifted off to sleep.

CHAPTER NINE

Sam's Sunday morning was a lazy one. After attending the last mass of the morning at eleven thirty, she picked up her grandmother and took her to lunch, then picked up Teddy and headed to the Wilkes University Library. A week of punishment had done nothing to improve Teddy's temperament.

"How can I possibly pass my finals when I don't even have a frickin' car to get me to exams? What am I supposed to do, take the bus?"

"You know I can drop you off on my way to Scranton."

"It beats the bus, but still. I'll be living at the library."

"It's finals week, Ted. You're supposed to live at the library."

"Hmm. That's a good point."

They drove in silence for a few minutes, and then Teddy spoke again. "Sam, how's Doug? You never talk about him."

Sam grew warm, blushing as anxiety coursed through her. Could Teddy know?

"He's good. I think. I'm not really sure. We broke up."

"What? You've been together forever."

"Yeah, well. It was time, then," Sam said dismissively, hoping Teddy wouldn't probe.

"I didn't know."

"It's not really important. I mean, he's been in Philly for the past two years, so I hardly saw him anyway."

"That's true, I guess. I don't think I've seen him since he left for medical school."

"He's Mr. Academic, you know? Doing research with one of his professors, too busy for anything else."

"Is that why you broke up?"

"No. It was just time. I realized I'm not in love with him, so why delay the inevitable?"

"So are you seeing someone else, then?"

Was she? Sam wondered. She hadn't spoken with Kirby, but that's what she wanted. To be with Kirby. And she was pretty sure Kirby felt the same.

"Not really. But I'm thinking about it."

"Hmm?" Teddy said suggestively. "Anyone I know?"

"I'll let you know when I know." Sam took a deep breath and followed the advice Teddy had given Kirby. "Teddy, can I ask you a question?"

"Yes, but I probably won't answer it truthfully."

Sam burst out laughing. "Do you already know the question?"

"I have a feeling I do."

Sam looked at Teddy, saw her staring out the passenger window. Teddy's obvious discomfort was predictable, but Sam wasn't about to let it stop her. "Are you gay?"

"Yep. That's the one."

She spoke into the glass, her arms crossed defensively. Sam softened her tone as she continued probing.

"You saw that coming, huh?"

"You've been hanging out with Kirby, Sam." The statement was almost a sigh.

"What does that mean?"

"I mean…Wait. You really don't know?" Teddy shifted away from the window and turned to look at her.

"I'm confused," Sam said, taking a peek at Teddy before turning her eyes back to the road.

"Hmm. I figured she would have said something by now," Teddy said. "But maybe she's not as big a jerk as I thought she was."

Sam sighed. "Teddy? What are you talking about?"

"Kirby. We used to date."

The words whacked Sam. It didn't surprise her that Teddy liked girls—she'd suspected that. But that one of those girls was the very same one who now had so totally captivated Sam—that was shocking.

Never once had Teddy brought Kirby to a party, or a bar, or on a hike. As far as she could remember, Sam was pretty sure she'd never heard the name Kirby until the first day of softball just a couple of weeks ago. "You dated Kirby?"

"Yep. For like a long time. That's why she stayed in Wilkes-Barre after she graduated. I was planning to live with her last fall. And then... she broke up with me. Just like that." Teddy snapped her fingers to emphasize her point.

Sam took a moment to process Teddy's words. Teddy was gay. Teddy had been in a serious relationship with Kirby, so significant they were planning to live together. And for some reason unclear to Teddy, Kirby had ditched her. What Teddy hadn't talked about, but was now obvious, was the animosity she felt toward Kirby.

She'd intended to talk to Teddy about her own feelings for Kirby. Knowing their history, how could she do that now?

"I'm sorry, Teddy." Sam felt a mixture of sadness and frustration.

"Oh, don't worry about it. It's no biggie. I just wanted you to know, because—well, it seems like you're getting pretty cozy with her. She's been asking about you, you know?"

Sam nodded. It was now or never. "She told me," Sam said, smiling. "She said you're my knight, protecting my honor."

Teddy was quiet, so Sam looked over and saw her blushing. "Thank you."

"You're welcome."

"How did you know?" Sam paused for a second, then clarified her question. "That you're gay?"

"Is this a trick question?"

Sam turned to look at her, confused. "No. It's not."

Teddy shifted in her seat. Her tone was soft but edged with impatience. "It's pretty simple. I like girls. I don't like boys."

Sam took a deep breath to fortify her nerves. "I see," she said, then paused. "I think I'm gay, too."

Even without moving her eyes from the road, Sam could see Teddy shaking her head. "I don't think you are."

"Really?"

"Well, you've had a lot of chances, Sam. All those parties I invited you to, with the softball team. Didn't you ever notice no guys were ever around?"

"I did. I just thought it was a team thing."

"No, no, no. Not a team thing. A chick thing. But as much time as you've spent with all your softball teams, and mine—you've never really caught on. It's like you're oblivious. Or straight."

For a moment Sam thought about the parties Teddy mentioned. So many girls were there, talking, laughing, drinking, most in groups, but some coupled off, oblivious to everyone else around them. She shook her head at the memory as the truth hit her. "I am so stupid."

Teddy's voice was deep, flat. "Yeah. You kind of are."

"I have a crush on Kirby, Ted."

"She's easy to crush on. But she's a heartbreaker. Be careful."

"I've never been with a woman before."

Teddy chuckled, and Sam turned again to look at her. "No kidding."

"You're not a very nice person. You know that?"

"That's true. I'm somewhat self-centered. But in this one instance, I am looking out for you. If you want to walk on the wild side and sleep with a woman, Kirby is perfect. She's great in bed, and she won't let you get too attached to her. You can have a summer fling before you head off in the fall to begin the rest of your life."

Sam digested Teddy's words. Was that really what this was about? A fling, to ease her boredom? To satisfy a curiosity? Sam didn't think so. Her naïveté about the softball team was due to her focus, she suspected. Dating had never been on her mind. Besides, she was dating Doug, and even if it was a bland and passionless relationship—it was perfect for her. It didn't interfere with her personal objectives. And perhaps she had some strange, subconscious motive to hang around Teddy and her friends to fulfill a secret longing to be around women.

"Thanks for talking to me, Teddy. You're a true friend." She thought about Lori and Jim. Her relationship with them was much deeper than her friendship with Teddy. They were like-minded and academic, ambitious, on the same path. Teddy, though, just liked her for who she was, because she liked to hang out and walk in the woods, ride bikes, and throw a ball. "In fact, I think you're the best friend I've ever had."

Teddy blushed. "Hey. Don't get mushy with me, okay?"

Sam nodded. "Sorry."

It seemed as if every Wilkes University student was at the library, and Sam had to circle several blocks before she found a parking spot.

The library itself was crowded, too, but Sam was able to find an open cubicle, where she settled in with her biochemistry book and the thick notebook in which she'd scribed her professor's words. Teddy went in another direction, and soon Sam was able to lose herself in her work. After a while, she stood to stretch and sip some water from the fountain. Hours later, when her stomach started to grumble, she decided to call it a day. She'd surprise her family and go to Bapcia's house to eat, then head home to put in a few more hours before bed.

When she couldn't find Teddy in the library, she went outside, where a bunch of students were gathered on benches. Teddy was among them.

"I'm going to hang out for a while," she answered when Sam offered her a ride home.

Suspecting home was an uncomfortable place for her, Sam didn't argue, but she did shoot her a stern look. "Study!"

The walk to the car was refreshing after five hours inside. The day was sunny and warm and the sky bright, and all around the campus the greenery had come back to life. Her car was facing her, and as she approached it, she saw a yellow piece of paper tucked underneath the windshield wiper. Hoisting her backpack up onto her shoulder, she reached over and plucked the note from the glass.

> *If you're hungry, I have food. I won't promise it'll be*
> *good. I also have beer, which might bring you cheer. If not,*
> *at the worst, it'll help to quench your thirst.*
>   *Kirby*

Sam laughed, but her heart pounded with excitement. The poem was followed by an address. Kirby lived on this street. Sam looked up, searching the house before her for numbers. It was an old structure, one that had probably once been a single home but now housed several student apartments. The address was next to the front door. "Oh, wow." Looking in the driveway, she saw the white Jeep and smiled.

"It's fate," she said to herself. Opening the car door, she sighed, and after throwing her backpack onto the back seat, she approached Kirby's door.

"Hi," Kirby said a moment after Sam rang the doorbell.

Wearing a loose-fitting T-shirt and running shorts, and with her hair in a sloppy bun, escaping in every direction, she looked adorable. Sexy, even, and Sam had to clear her throat before she answered.

"Hi."

"How's it going?" Kirby looked concerned, and Sam swore that just having Kirby's eyes on her warmed her.

Sam shrugged. "It's biochemistry. My mind is fried."

"Understandable. Do you need a break? Are you hungry?"

"Starving. Do you really have food? Or was that just a ploy to see me?" She studied Kirby as she awaited the reply and wasn't sure which answer she hoped for.

Kirby chewed her lip, an adorable expression of self-doubt on her face. "I actually went out and bought food as an excuse to see you."

"Cunning." So much for giving it time. Could it be that Kirby was struggling with this situation as much as Sam was?

Shrugging, she pursed her lips.

"Are you going to invite me in, then?"

Stepping back, Kirby nodded and spread her arm before her. "Right this way."

Sam entered a brightly lit vestibule, and from there, Kirby led her a few feet to her door. After opening it, they emerged into a surprisingly modern kitchen, with faux wood tiles and stainless-steel appliances.

"Nice place, Kirby. I expected it to be…older."

"The building is a hundred years old, but the apartments were all built a few years ago. It's great. Small, but perfect for one."

Sam wondered if this was the apartment Teddy had planned to move into but decided not to ask.

"Can I get you a beer?" Kirby asked.

Sam pursed her lips. If anything was going to happen with them, Kirby needed to know the truth about her. She was a total nerd, into reading and exercising and not into partying much at all. "I don't drink much. It's not a religious thing or anything like that…I do drink on occasion. It's just not a habit."

Kirby nodded. "That's cool. I don't either. Can I get you something else, then? I have Snapple, Coke, Sprite, water. Pickle juice. Milk. You name it."

"Snapple is perfect, but I might chase it with the pickle juice."

"I won't drink it all, then. And you're hungry, right? I bought chicken to grill, and I have everything we need for a salad."

Sam smiled. "Sounds perfect. What can I do to help?"

"If you can throw the salad together, I'll put the chicken on the grill."

Pulling the food from the fridge, Kirby nodded toward a cabinet. "My biggest bowl is in there. I'll be back in just a minute."

"No problem."

Sam wiped down Kirby's counter, washed the vegetables, and began slicing everything for the salad. She'd just finished when Kirby reappeared. "Would you like to eat on my porch? I have a table out there, and it's a nice evening."

"That would be great," Sam said, and after Kirby loaded a tray with everything they needed, Sam followed her through the house and out the back door. A square picnic table was tucked into the corner of the porch, and a grill sat just beyond the stairs, tendrils of smoke floating out from beneath the cover.

After placing her burden on the table, Kirby hurried to the grill and tended to the chicken. "It's fine. Just a little barbeque-sauce dripping, I think."

Sam set out the dishes and flatware, filled their salad bowls, and then sat back and studied the view while she waited for Kirby to finish with the chicken. A picket fence enclosed a patch of grass in a neat if plain-looking yard. The back sides of adjoining properties were adorned with strings of lights and school flags, laundry, and garbage. Clearly, students inhabited this block. Then there was Kirby, her wavy dark hair pulled up, exposing her neck, looking as sexy as could be. Sam saw her in profile and tried not to stare, but it was difficult to resist. She'd thought of Kirby so much, it was hard to believe she was sitting on her porch, watching her cook dinner. Hard to believe that just twenty-four hours before, they'd kissed.

Thinking of that kiss caused Sam to fidget, and she took a sip of her drink just to have something to do with her hands. God, she was pathetic.

"I think it's ready," Kirby announced, and Sam watched her again as she loaded a platter with barbequed chicken and brought it to the table. They loaded their plates and dug in.

"Mm," Sam said when she tasted her first bite. "This is really good. The sauce is excellent."

"It's my secret recipe."

"Really?"

"Yes. Heinz."

"Good choice."

"The salad is great, too."

"I make a lot of salads. I try to eat healthy."

"What's your favorite food? Like, I mean, death-row last meal."

"Well, if I was going to the chair, I'd forgo the rabbit food and do something decadent. Lump crab," she said as she chewed. "For an appetizer. Then, I think, a big, juicy steak. Macaroni and cheese, for comfort. And a very big glass of wine, to ease my nerves."

"Good choices. How about dessert?"

"Oh, ice cream. No question there." Sam nibbled a carrot and frowned. "Compared to death-row fantasy food, this salad suddenly sucks."

"Well, yes, but it will have a better ending."

Sam laughed so hard she began choking, and tears streamed from her eyes as she fought to control her breathing.

Kirby watched her closely, wearing a look of concern. "I thought I was going to have to do the Heimlich," she said once Sam was clearly out of danger.

"Don't make me laugh when I'm eating. Apparently, I'm a lightweight."

"Noted. So, biochem tomorrow? Are you ready?"

"Surprisingly, I think I am. After that, it'll be much easier."

"That's good. Get the hard one out of the way first."

"I agree," Sam replied. "I'd just be worried about this all week."

"And when do you finish? When's the final final?"

"Friday morning."

"Wow. And that's it. You'll be a college graduate."

Sam leaned back and looked at Kirby, thinking again about that reality. Her hard work was about to pay off. She was going to graduate. It was a thrilling thought, but she had to keep her excitement in check for just a few more days so she could concentrate on learning enough details to pass her last four exams.

"It's hard to believe," Sam confessed, almost awed by her reality.

"What's next for you? I mean, obviously medical school, but when is that?"

"I move into my apartment August first."

Kirby whistled. "That's just around the corner. And where's that? Philly?"

"Yes. I'll be living with two friends in an apartment in Manayunk."

"You'll be a big-city girl, huh?"

Sam shrugged. It was a long way from West Nanticoke, Pennsylvania, to Philadelphia, in many ways. Sam was a small-town girl, about to embark on a great adventure, but she knew she would always be the same person she was now. A simple person, living a simple life. After learning what she needed to, finishing medical school and residency, she'd come home to practice, probably in the same hospital where she now worked in the ER.

"You can take the girl out of the mountains...but she'll probably find her way back."

"So that's your plan? To come back here when you finish school?"

Her gaze wandered as she tried to articulate her thoughts, and she focused on the laundry drying on the railing of the balcony of the house behind Kirby's. Daydreaming with Lori and Jim, it was easy to see herself returning to the mountains to live and practice medicine. Jim came from a huge Italian family, and their life was focused on the restaurant. He was sure he'd hang out his shingle in Old Forge, on the same street where he grew up. Lori was planning a future with Chip, and he was strongly rooted in the area. As soon as she fulfilled her military obligation, she'd be back.

Sam also had a family she adored, but more than that—she felt a pull to the region that was hard to resist. The people were good, hard-working men and women who cared about the weeds in their front lawn and what their neighbors' children were doing after dark. There was plenty to do—especially for someone like Sam, who enjoyed the outdoors. The cost of living was reasonable, so she'd be able to work less and spend time with the children she planned to have one day. And they'd be safe playing in the same streets and parks she'd played in when she was a young girl.

Yes, she was convinced she'd come back to Northeast Pennsylvania to live, but how could she explain that to someone like Kirby, who was probably just passing through on her way to something better? It seemed impossible, that explanation, but Kirby made her want to try.

"I do. I love this area. I love to sit by the river and think, and get lost in the woods. I love the softball fields where I play with my friends, the winding country roads to bike, the mountains to ski. It's a great place."

Kirby nodded. "It is. I can see why you'd want to come back here."

Sam looked at her and nodded toward the laundry drying on the porch rail. "How can you beat the view?"

Kirby nodded. "If you walk to that spot over there," she pointed, "and look that way," she pointed in the opposite direction, "you can see a tree."

Sam craned her neck but saw only the brick and mortar of the adjacent building.

Kirby pointed to the building with the laundry, her voice soaked with a kindness Sam hadn't seen before. "They're students. I guess they can't afford the dryer. They hang their clothes out all year round."

Sam opened her eyes wide. "So does my mother! I mean, she's out there in the snow, hanging out the delicates so the dryer doesn't ruin them. Sometimes our laundry is actually frozen solid. If it fell on her she'd die of head trauma."

Kirby laughed. "It must be a local thing. I'm kind of a dryer girl myself."

"Oh. Me, too. A clothesline in the yard is not one of the reasons I want to come back here after med school."

The mood was relaxed, and since they were on the subject—sort of—Sam decided to bring up Teddy. "Why did you decide to stick around after graduation? I mean, other than the view?"

Kirby pursed her lips and began stacking their dishes, and for a moment Sam thought her question would go unanswered. Then she frowned and looked up at Sam. "A girl."

"Hmm," Sam said. "It doesn't sound like that story has a happy ending."

"Like you, I was a good student. I majored in finance, which is pretty tough. This girl I was dating was fun—and I liked that because she made me relax a little. Sometimes, I get too hung up on details. Unfortunately, she was never serious. Not about school, or our relationship or anything. She just…I needed to move on."

Feeling suddenly uncomfortable, Sam nodded. "That's sad." Should she tell Kirby what Teddy had told her or just drop it? It wasn't technically lying if she didn't confess that she knew, but it still felt awkward. Sam couldn't play those kinds of games well, and she didn't want that sort of deceit drowning the seed of friendship—or something more—growing between them.

"Was it Teddy?" she asked softly.

Kirby looked surprised at the question. "I know this is kind of new to you, but it's an unwritten rule that you should never out anyone. So I really can't tell you."

"Teddy told me you dated."

"What?" Kirby asked, and Sam wasn't sure if the look on her face was surprise again, or anger.

"Today, actually. I asked, and she told me."

Kirby put her head in her hands, then ran them through her hair and finally linked them on top of her head. "I didn't put it together that you were *the* Sam, until Teddy started talking to you at the first practice. And by then, it was too late. I was smitten."

Sam's eyebrow shot up. "Smitten?"

"Totally."

Smitten was too benign a word as far as Sam was concerned. Obsessed, infatuated, mesmerized. These were the terms she'd use to describe her attraction to Kirby. It had started the moment they met, and this lovely dinner had only served to water the seeds already blossoming in Sam's heart.

"So, Ms. Smitten. I have news. I broke up with my boyfriend last night and was wondering if you'd like to go on a date with me?"

Kirby became still as her eyes searched Sam's. "You broke up with him? Just like that?"

Suddenly, tears sprang to Sam's eyes, and she glanced away as she collected herself. When she looked back, Kirby was still there, gazing at her with a gentle expression of concern that tore through Sam's heart. "I feel like it was never real. Does that make sense?" When Kirby nodded, Sam continued. "But I didn't know any better. Not until you."

"Maybe that's enough for now, Sam. I mean, are you ready to jump into another relationship? And, with a girl? I mean, there's no rush."

"Well, I do have a busy week. But Friday? Would you like to go out and celebrate with me?"

Kirby tilted her head, and a soft smile appeared, once again unraveling Sam. "I'd love that."

CHAPTER TEN

Miserable weather threatened to ruin the mood on Sam's last day of college, but even the thunderstorms and rain that flooded the streets of Scranton couldn't diminish her happiness when she signed her name on the last blue book. Latin was finished, and so was the semester, and the year, and her time at the University of Scranton.

Once again she joined Jim and Lori at the bar, and this time, they were more nostalgic as they talked about the four years they'd shared in the Loyola Hall of Science—their teachers, their classes, the MCATs, their classmates. Dozens of their peers were heading to medical school, many of them in Philly. The list of people they'd invite to dinner was short, but they laughed as they eliminated people one by one.

"The truth is," Sam said as she looked at them quite soberly, "you are two of my favorite people in the world. I'm so lucky we all found each other and that we're going on this big adventure together. If I never see another Scranton alum, I'll be okay. As long as I have you two, I'll be happy."

"I was going to say that. You stole my speech," Jim whined.

"I was going to say that, too. You're always copying off me," Lori chimed in.

"That's how I got through college, Lori. I copied off you. Both of you," Jim confessed as he downed his newest creation, The Graduate. It wasn't his typical fruity drink. This one was full of gin, and Sam hated it.

"Ha! I wish I had half of your brain, Jim. You make it look so easy." Jim had gone to Scranton on a full scholarship after earning valedictorian honors at Scranton Prep. He was the first of his family to attend college, and he'd once confided in Sam that if he hadn't had the scholarship, his father probably wouldn't have paid for him to go. Why waste money on an education when a good job is waiting for you in the family business?

The pizza was great, but what a waste of a brilliant mind that would have been. And they would never have met each other.

"What are you and Chip doing to celebrate?" Sam asked.

"Oh, he's taking me to the lake, and then he's going to drive me to Philly for my swearing-in. We're going to stay in a *hotel*!"

"Oooh! Fancy! Are you sure you don't want us to come?" Jim asked coyly.

"To the hotel? With me and Chip? Uh, no."

Sam was blushing, glad for the darkness in the corner of Francesco's dining room. Calm down, she told herself. It was a harmless barb, but she'd been questioning her relationship with Lori lately. And Teddy. They were important women in her life, and it was important for her to know if she harbored some secret crush before she moved in with Lori and Jim in a few short months.

"I wish I could be there, Lor," Jim confessed.

"I swear to tell the truth, the whole truth, blah, blah, blah," she said. "It's no biggie. But I will be so mad if you two don't come to my college graduation."

They all laughed. "What day is it?" Sam asked. "My calendar is very full."

"I'll try to make it, but you know I'm very busy, too," Jim added.

Sam and her friends talked a while longer, about a trip they planned to Philly to check out their schools, and the apartment, and their summer plans. The party broke up as Nonna came to check on them. They'd try to get together before their commencement ceremony, but Sam wasn't sure if it would work out. They were suddenly busy people. "Why don't we go to Chip's place at Crystal Lake? They're never there. We can go mid-week, hang out, swim. What do you think?"

"Sounds good to me," Jim said.

They made a tentative date, and Jim walked them to the door, with pizza to go. They hugged and promised to talk soon. On the street where their cars were parked, Lori and Sam hugged again. "We did it, pal," Lori said.

"Woooey!" Sam said as they broke apart. Their friendship had started by accident, in their first biology lab as freshmen. After that, they were together by choice, scheduling as many classes with each other as they possibly could. They'd studied together, coordinated on projects, taken the same MCAT class. Lori had picked Sam up when her spirits were down, and Sam had done the same in return when Lori needed it. Sam brought Lori and Jim together, and it was a perfect fit. He was irresistible, and twice as smart as both of them combined, and could always figure out the most complex lab experiments. After the first few weeks of their triumvirate, they were inseparable. They still were.

Suddenly Jim came running out the door. "One more hug!" he screamed.

They formed a circle and had a group hug. "Hey, stud muffin. Thanks for everything."

"Anytime. I can't wait to go to the lake."

Lori walked her to her car and surprised Sam with a tiny kiss, one that did nothing for Sam but reassure her that she was not attracted. They headed their separate ways with a bounce in their step. The drive home was surreal. She'd finished college. She was going on a date with Kirby Fielding. Even though Interstate 81 was jammed with rigs and the normal Friday afternoon traffic, on this day, they didn't bother her. The rain persisted, the overcast sky blocking her view of mountains on either side of the Wyoming Valley. As she crossed the Susquehanna River, she felt as if she were floating across on the wave of fog that made visibility impossible.

At home, she wasn't sure what to do with herself. A nervous anxiety overtook her, and she glanced at the clock, counting the minutes until she saw Kirby. By four o'clock she thought she should go for a run, just to relieve her stress. She hated running. Looking out from the sunroom to the fog-shrouded mountain, she decided to take a short hike, and half an hour later, breathless but much calmer, she sat on her favorite rock and gazed out over the river. The rain had slowed, but fog hovered over the water as far as she could see. Today, that wasn't very far. It was still beautiful, though, and the fog acted as a buffer, quieting everything, calming nature. Calming her.

They'd agreed to meet at seven, but instead of going out to dinner, Kirby had suggested they eat at her place, followed by a video. While the sky was now quiet, the storms were expected to pick up again, and flash flooding was predicted. It seemed smarter to stay in.

More dangerous, too.

Kirby's clothing stood a near-perfect chance of staying in place if they were out at a restaurant. Sam wasn't so sure she'd keep her hands to herself if they were alone at Kirby's. *When* they were alone. The thought both excited and terrified her. Now that she'd figured this out, understood what desire truly felt like, she was eager to discover what wonders awaited her with Kirby. At the same time, she was embarrassingly inexperienced, and even though Kirby knew that, it still set Sam on edge.

But why was she thinking this anyway? It was their first date! Sex should be the last thing on her mind, yet all week long, as she'd turned the pages in her textbooks and made notes in the margins, highlighted and outlined and memorized and calculated, she'd paused to think of that first kiss. And the second. And the third and fourth.

After their chicken dinner on Sunday, they'd kissed at the door to Kirby's apartment. This one had been deeper, a real zinger that left Sam nearly panting—and thinking of nothing else that night. Fortunately, most of her studying for the biochem final was done. On Monday, she'd gone back to the library—at Wilkes, of course—and she'd met Kirby for a study break and pizza at Januzzi's. After they ordered, they'd gone into the bathroom to wash their hands and ended up wrapped around each other in the stall.

Sam couldn't believe she'd done that, in near-public, but the kiss had been earth-shattering. They all were.

Now it was Friday afternoon, and in just over two hours, she would be all alone with Kirby, in the privacy of her apartment, where they could kiss until their lips fell off. They could do whatever they wanted, and that was a scary realization.

The clouds moving overhead seemed to turn angry, and Sam thought she could hear thunder in the distance. Standing, she wiped the dirt from her pants and began the hike down the mountain. She'd almost reached the bottom when the sky opened up, and lightning flashed in the northern sky. Sprinting the last two hundred yards home, she found herself soaked to the skin and breathless, but as happy as she remembered feeling in a long, long time.

"Lovey, what on earth were you doing out in the rain?" her mother demanded when she stepped into the kitchen wearing just her T-shirt and underwear.

"Oh, hi. I didn't know you were home."

"Well, it's five o'clock, so it's not that surprising."

"Good point. And to answer your question, I went for a little hike. Just to relax."

"I would think you're relaxed, now that finals are over." Irene looked at her for a moment. "Congratulations, Lovey."

"Thanks," Sam said. She'd been so anxious about her date, she'd totally forgotten the other significant event of the day.

"How does it feel?"

How could Sam explain what she was feeling? Graduating college was nothing compared to these all new sensations flooding her system. All her feelings for Kirby.

"I…I feel like I'm a new person." It was as honest an answer as she could give.

"Hmm. What does that mean?" Her mom leaned against the island, studying her.

"I feel like all the mysteries of the universe have been explained to me." Oh, Samantha, you are going straight to hell, she told herself.

"I guess that's the wonder of a Jesuit education," Irene retorted.

"I'm going out to celebrate. I have to get ready."

"What? You can't go out in this! The forecast is for this heavy rain all night, and flash flooding. Roads are going to be closed. You might not make it home."

"Well, I can just sleep over with someone."

"Who are you going out with? Lori?"

No lies, she told herself. "No. She's out with her boyfriend. I'm going out with softball friends."

"Teddy, I suppose?" she said, and her tone wasn't friendly. What had Teddy done to her mom, anyway?

"No. I don't think she'll be there. It's some new friends. My friend Kirby will be there."

"You're going out in a flood with people you hardly know? Why?"

"Mom! I know them. They're students at Wilkes, and they play softball. They're graduating, too. We're celebrating!"

Closing her eyes, Irene began to recite the Hail Mary.

"Mom, you're being ridiculous."

She opened her eyes. "What else is new? You know, Samantha, you never behaved like this when you were dating Doug. I hope there isn't some new boy in the picture who's going to distract you from your goals."

Sam bit her lip as she pondered a response. When she'd told her mother about the breakup, Irene hadn't seemed surprised. And she was uncharacteristically accepting of Sam's announcement. Apparently, she'd been biding her time, waiting to let Sam know her feelings.

"Mom, this has nothing to do with Doug. Or any guy. I'm going out with friends, to celebrate a great accomplishment in all our lives. There's nothing wrong with that."

As a healing balm, Sam wrapped her arms around her mom and kissed her cheek. "I love you. And you know I'm not going to do anything stupid."

"Just go."

An hour later, the weather was worse, and her mother gave her a stern look as she left the living room to head out for the night. There was a ton of Friday-night traffic, despite the weather, which just slowed everyone down. The two most direct routes to Kirby's house were the roads that flooded often, so she took the interstate, then zigzagged through the Heights in Wilkes-Barre before finally reaching Kirby's street—where she couldn't find any parking.

Fortunately, she wore her raincoat, and an umbrella deflected most of the rain, but her feet were still soaked by the time Kirby answered the door. "Oh, man, this is crazy. Where did you dock your boat?"

"Don't laugh. I don't know how I'm going to make it home tonight. The news says Route 11 in Plymouth is closed, and so is the Sans Souci Highway. If they close any roads west of your street, I'm stranded."

"I wouldn't mind," Kirby said with a wink that caused a fluttering low in Sam's belly and a blush to heat her face.

From a hall closet Kirby produced two fluffy towels, presented them to Sam, and then took her coat to hang in the vestibule.

"You're cute," Kirby said when she returned.

"You're pretty cute, yourself," Sam said. They stood staring for a moment, and then they both took a step forward. Sam looked up while Kirby bent her head forward, and once again their lips met.

Perhaps because they were both so conscious of where they stood, in Kirby's apartment, and where this kiss could lead, they pulled back simultaneously after a few breathless seconds.

"So, congratulations," Kirby said with a dazzling smile.

Sam's smile was a reflex, but she knew it matched Kirby's. For some reason, now that she was with Kirby, now that the anticipation was over, the reality of her graduation was hitting her. "Thank you."

"Step this way into my combined kitchen/dining room and prepare to celebrate."

Sam followed her and found a table adorned with candles, flowers, and a small bottle of champagne chilling in an ice bucket. The odor of something delightful filled the air, and Sam noticed the oven light was on.

"I know you don't drink much, so I bought only a split," Kirby explained as she reached for the bottle. "Just enough to toast."

"How sweet!" Sam wasn't sure what it was about Kirby, but she always knew just the right thing to do. To offer food, or encouragement, or just enough champagne for a congratulatory toast.

"Would you like to do the honors?" Kirby asked.

Sam waved her off. "It's all yours. Then she leaned in to smell the bouquet of cut flowers—daisies and carnations, with a few roses and sparkling, glittery adornments. Sam had felt happy since meeting Kirby at the door, but after seeing all the trouble she'd taken to make this night special, Sam was overwhelmed. "These are beautiful, Kirby. Thank you." Sam waved to the champagne, the flowers. "All of this... it's just—amazing."

"You're amazing. And you're welcome."

After peeling the foil, Kirby pulled and twisted, and the cork emerged with a satisfying pop. Most of the contents of the bottle fit into the two glasses Kirby had set out, and after she put the bottle down, they raised the glasses until they met in the air between them. "Happy graduation, Sam."

Before tasting the bubbly, Sam kissed her again, and the effect was as powerful as any wine she'd ever tasted. Intoxicating.

"So, how was your exam?"

"Easy. Latin roots of English words. It was just a vocabulary test, and compared to my other exams, it was a breeze."

Kirby pulled a small plate of grapes from the counter and motioned for Sam to sit. "Now what happens? When's your commencement?"

"Well, I assume I passed. Actually," she wrinkled her nose, "I think it's mathematically impossible to fail any of my classes. The finals aren't weighed that heavily. So, I'll graduate on Memorial Day weekend."

Sam sipped her champagne and then set the glass down. She hadn't eaten since lunch with Lori and Jim. It was now after six, and even one glass of bubbly on an empty stomach could ruin her evening.

"And what about the summer? Any plans?"

"Work here and there. Have some fun. I'm going to enjoy my freedom for a little while, because when I get to Philly, I think my social life is over."

Nodding, Kirby sipped her champagne. "It sounds awful. You're not going to have much free time in the coming months. Or, perhaps, ever again."

Sam swallowed. It was a sobering thought. "You're right. I'm going to be crazy busy."

Kirby raised her glass again, nodding toward Sam's. "Well, then here's to your last days of freedom. Enjoy them. And remember that your hard work will be worth it. You're one step closer to your dream coming true."

Sam studied her as she sipped the wine, thinking she felt more attracted to Kirby every time she saw her. Tonight, she wore jeans and a blue, Bengal-striped dress shirt, untucked. Her feet were bare, and her hair was in a sloppy ponytail. Diamond studs, which Sam suspected were real, dotted both earlobes.

"Are you hungry? Shall we start?" Kirby asked.

Sam didn't want to pressure Kirby if she wasn't ready to eat. "Yeah, if you're hungry."

Kirby slumped. "I'm famished. I left work early to get everything, in a hurricane, so I was late, and I didn't really have lunch."

"Can I help?"

Shaking her head, Kirby opened the fridge and pulled out a plate. "Nope. It's under control."

Sam watched as she poured two glasses of water and then peeled back the plastic wrap from a small plate. With a wave of her hand, she presented it to Sam. "Lump crab, chilled with a spicy remoulade."

Sam let out a whoop. "Oh! I love crab!"

Kirby sat beside her, and they shared the plate. "Did you make this dressing?" Sam moaned between bites. It was flavored with a little heat, and Sam detected some citrus as well.

Sam nodded. "It wasn't hard. I got the recipe at the library."

"Well, my compliments to you, Madame Chef."

After they finished, Kirby excused herself. "I'm going to light the grill. I moved it to the porch so I won't drown."

Taking advantage of Kirby's absence, Sam poked her head in the oven. Two small footballs, wrapped in foil, were baking on the bottom shelf. A cake pan covered in foil was centered on the top. Pulling on an oven mitt, Sam slid out the rack and peeled back the covering. Macaroni and cheese bubbled beneath the foil.

Smiling, Sam replaced the foil and slid it back just as she heard Kirby's footsteps in the hall.

"So, *the last supper*, huh?"

"No fooling you," Kirby said with a smirk. "Not that I was trying. I just figured I couldn't go wrong with a menu you've chosen for your last meal."

Sam stood rigidly tall. "Wait. Do you know something I don't?"

Kirby blushed as she looked away for a moment, her mouth open, as she seemed to debate answering. Then she turned back to Sam. "I'm trying to seduce you."

Sam felt herself blush. Her pulse raced, and she grew instantly wet. "I don't think you have to try very hard," Sam whispered as her voice deserted her.

Kirby stepped forward and kissed her softly on the lips. "Don't ruin my fun. I've made dinner, I bought dessert..."

"Ice cream?" Sam asked as she kissed Kirby's neck. At that point, though, it didn't really matter if Kirby had fried some weeds from the garden and served them on paper plates.

"But of course," she replied as she pulled away from Sam and turned to the oven. Removing the macaroni, she looked at Sam. "Be right back. Medium on the steak, right?"

"Medium is perfect."

Kirby disappeared with two steaks and was back in a minute,

setting the kitchen timer. Sam took advantage of the opportunity and closed the space between them, wrapping her arms around Kirby, kissing her neck where it met her collar.

Sam felt Kirby relax against her as she hummed in obvious pleasure. The feeling was entirely mutual. Sam was so turned on, she thought she'd explode. But more than that, she felt spoiled. Like she mattered to Kirby, like Kirby really cared about her. That was impossible, right? They'd known each other for such a very short time, how could that be?

Yet, Sam felt the same. She wanted to do things for Kirby, to take her places she loved and show her family pictures. She longed to make her feel special, because, inexplicably, she was.

"This is amazing, Kirby. Thank you."

Kirby turned in her arms and rested her forehead against Sam's as they wrapped their arms around each other, felt each other's body. Sam's breath was heavy, but so was Kirby's, and after fighting her inclination to resist for a few seconds, she gave up, turned her mouth to Kirby's, and found her soft lips waiting. Wet, warm, inviting, they pulled Sam in even farther. They merged, seeking and giving, until the oven timer startled them apart.

"Wow," Sam murmured as she looked at Kirby. "I'm dizzy."

"Me, too," Kirby said as she nuzzled Sam's neck.

The beeping of the timer seemed to grow louder as they ignored it. Finally, Sam pushed Kirby away. "The steaks are burning."

"Right!" Kirby said, breathless. "Let me flip them. Would you mind taking the potatoes out of the oven? They're more than done."

Kirby was back in a minute, setting a table with unmatched dishes and loading it with food and condiments. Then she pushed Sam, kissing her neck as they moved across the room, and helped her onto the chair before leaving to retrieve the steaks.

And then they were eating. Everything was perfectly cooked, expertly seasoned, and Sam couldn't help moaning as she nibbled the mac and cheese. "Wow. How did you learn to cook so well?"

"I'm the oldest. My parents always needed help. Cooking, cleaning, babysitting."

Babysitting. Kids. How would that work, with two women?

Sam sat back and studied Kirby as she chewed her steak. Seeming to sense her, Kirby looked up.

"You okay?" she asked as she wiped her mouth.

Sam continued to study her. "Something you said. Do you want kids?"

Sighing, she looked down at the water glass on the table, where her finger circled the rim. Finally, she met Sam's gaze. "I'm not sure. I've always known I was gay, and I never really thought it was possible to have kids. But now, women are having children together, with sperm donors and turkey basters. Suddenly, it *is* possible. So I suppose it's a conversation I'm going to have with my partner and see how she feels about it. How about you?"

"Definitely. I wonder if that might be why I've always dated men. I thought I needed a man to have kids. But I've always hated being an only child and thought of the big family I'd have one day. I even named my imaginary children."

Kirby looked amused. "Really? You've named them? Just how many are there?"

"Five. Sam, after my dad. That can be a boy or a girl. Danny and Charlie. They can also be either sex. Then Eddie. That would have to be a boy."

"You could do Edie," Kirby suggested as she took a bite of mac and cheese.

"Definitely not the same. Eddie is firm. Has to be a boy."

"Okay, that's four."

"Then there's Lindsey, after the *Bionic Woman*. Probably a very early crush, now that I understand things a little better."

"I get that." Kirby nodded. "Is there room for negotiation, or is this decision firm?"

Sam pursed her lips. "Well, a variety of names have come in and out of favor over the years. But then I thought...perhaps I should let the...other parent pick a name. To be fair."

"That's a nice gesture."

Sam smiled. "I think ice cream would be a nice gesture."

Leaning back, Kirby pointed at the empty plates before them. "I can't believe you're still hungry."

"Oh, don't worry. I'll make room for ice cream. But maybe we should clean up first."

"Great idea."

They chatted as they put away the extra food and condiments, then loaded the dishwasher. After they finished, Kirby pulled back the blind and peeked into the night. Sam stepped beside her and ducked her head to see around her. A shaft of light pierced the darkness and illuminated the fat drops of rain falling in sheets.

"The forecast did call for rain," Sam said.

"That's an understatement. Good thing I have a VCR, huh?"

Kirby walked to the freezer and paused, looking at Sam. "It's funny how we always seem to want what other people have."

"What do you mean?"

"I've often fantasized about being an only child," she said as she pulled the ice cream from the freezer.

"Really?" Sam found it hard to believe, when all she'd ever wanted was a sibling.

"Five kids is a lot," Kirby said with a dour tone that told Sam she was serious. She looked up from her work and met Sam's gaze, as if to punctuate that thought.

"Are you suggesting I'm crazy to want so many?" Sam asked, her tone gentle.

Kirby was silent for a moment as she spooned big scoops into their bowls, then looked at Sam again. "I'm just saying that we want what other people have, but that's not necessarily a good thing."

"What's so bad about a big family?"

Kirby returned the ice cream to the freezer and grabbed whipped cream from the fridge, then put it on the table between them and their Neapolitan.

"I'd turn that around on you and ask what's so bad about being an only child. You have your parents' total attention. You don't have to wait in line for the bathroom. You get all the presents at Christmas. You get an extra cookie. You actually get all the cookies. You can watch what you want on television. You don't have to wear your older sister's hand-me-downs. How's that for starters?" she asked as she dug into the ice cream and topped it with whipped cream before she licked it seductively off the spoon.

"Well, as one of five children, I'd bet you were never lonely. You always had someone to play with. You didn't have your parents' complete attention, which meant you could have some freedom to do what you wanted to do without them analyzing your every move." Sam took a bite and smiled. "How's that for a counter?"

"You came up with only three things."

"Three big things."

Kirby ate in silence, and Sam wondered if she was pondering what they'd talked about or thinking of a clever response. Finally, she spoke again. "I think my point is proved. We want what other people have."

"Why do you think that is?"

"It's our nature."

Sam shook her head. "I refuse to accept that explanation. We have choices. Our capacity for reason separates us from other life forms, and we can choose to be who we want to be."

"Then you should embrace the fact that you're an only child."

"Oh, be quiet," Sam said as whipped cream foamed into her bowl. She directed the nozzle at Kirby, threatening to spray her.

"Ready for that movie? Then you don't have to talk to me for two hours."

CHAPTER ELEVEN

I rented three," Kirby said a few minutes later in the living room. Holding up the first so Sam could see the name, she pointed at the title. *"Aladdin."*

"Hmmm," Sam answered. "I like that song. 'A Whole New World.' It's kind of romantic. But what are the other options?"

"My Cousin Vinny?" She held the box for Sam to see.

"Hmmm, hmmm. Excellent cast."

"Fried Green Tomatoes?" she said as she presented that one.

"Ahhh! That one's so sweet."

"Or, here's one more. *A League of Their Own.* I *bought* the video."

Sam clapped. "I love that movie! Madonna's great. And so is Rosie O'Donnell."

"What about Geena Davis? Ahhh..."

"Wait a minute. Are you fawning over Geena Davis while you're on a date with me?"

Kirby puckered. "I wasn't fawning. I was admiring her."

"She is a cutie. Sold. Let's watch it."

Kirby popped the movie into the player and then sat beside Sam on the couch. A foot of blue fabric separated their thighs, and Sam's gaze was drawn to the space, until she heard the opening bars of the soundtrack. She glanced at the television and then back to the space, to Kirby's thigh, where her hand rested. Her fingers were splayed but quiet, and Sam wondered at how still Kirby was sitting, considering how wound up she felt.

"I need to use the restroom," she said suddenly, as she jumped to her feet.

"Oh, sure," Kirby said. "You know where it is, right?"

Sam nodded.

"I'll pause the movie."

Sam hurried down the hallway and closed the bathroom door behind her, leaning against it as she slapped her hand to her forehead. "Get a grip, Sam!"

She splashed some water on her face and studied herself in the mirror. She looked great. Her hair was pulled back and held in place by a green band that matched her eyes and her shirt. A few freckles dusted her cheeks, but a light layer of powder covered most of them. She'd worn a lacy blue bra with matching panties, to give her some extra confidence. And, just in case this night ended with some of her clothes off, the ones she had left would look really, really good.

Okay, so what was she so nervous about? They'd already kissed. They hadn't slept together, but it wasn't like she was totally inexperienced. She'd been with Doug. And she'd never wanted to be with him, not really. She'd wanted to have sex, to experience it, to know what all the fuss was about. But she'd never felt passion. Now, though? Just the thought of Kirby made her insides go to mush. So why the nerves? If something happened with Kirby, it was because she wanted it to. Because they both wanted it. And if not, if they didn't sleep together—their time together would still be amazing.

Flipping off the light switch, she headed back to the living room, where Kirby was watching a news alert on television. "The roads are really bad, Sam."

Sam nodded. She'd made a decision, and she wasn't backing down. "Can I use your phone?"

"Sure. Is everything okay?" Kirby asked as she handed her a phone attached to a long cord.

Giving her a wink, she nodded. "Everything is great."

Her fingers flew across the numbers, and she placed the phone to her ear as Kirby watched her closely.

"Hi, Mom," she said when she heard the voice on the other end. "So, as usual, you were right. They're closing roads all over. I'm just going to stay here tonight, so don't worry about me, okay?"

For once, she heard no lecture, just a *have fun* and *good night* and *I love you*. "Good night, Mom. I love you, too."

Sam never took her eyes from Kirby's, not until she handed her the phone and Kirby was forced to find a place to put it. After setting it on the floor, she turned to find Sam right next to her on the couch.

"I want to spend the night with you."

Kirby nodded. "That's what I hear."

Sam sighed for dramatic effect. "I mean, *I want to spend the night with you. I want to…*" Sam hesitated, and Kirby cut her some slack.

"I would love for you to stay with me tonight. Do you want to get some jammies on, and we can cuddle up on the couch and finish the movie?"

They changed in turns, with Sam putting on one of Kirby's T-shirts and shorts, and Kirby emerging a few minutes later wearing something similar.

Sam was sitting cross-legged on the couch, and this time, Kirby beckoned her closer, and Sam didn't hesitate to close the gap. Sam snuggled against her, and they both put their feet up on the coffee table. Sam spent the entire course of the movie monitoring Kirby's pulse and respirations while trying to slow her own.

When the credits rolled, they didn't move, and Kirby used the remote to rewind the video. Then, without saying a word, she turned toward Sam and kissed the top of her head.

Every cell in Sam's body came alive at the tenderness of the contact, at the intimacy. Gasping, she clutched Kirby's shirt as she traced the corner of her eye, then made her way slowly toward Sam's ear. Sam arched, giving herself, wanting Kirby to have access to her skin, craving the heat of her mouth.

Instead of more, though, Kirby pulled away, looked at Sam. "Let's go to bed."

Amazed that her legs could carry her, she followed Kirby to her bedroom and onto the bed. They stretched out side by side in the middle, facing each other. The hall light cast shadows, enough for Sam at the moment, and she mirrored Kirby's pose, resting her head on her forearm an inch away from Kirby's. The only noise was the soft whisper of their breaths and the drumbeat of raindrops somewhere outside the window.

Sam closed the space this time, her lips sought Kirby's, she wrapped herself around Kirby and clung to her. As was always the case with them, the kiss instantly exploded from something soft and tender to hot and demanding, and this time Sam didn't want to control it. Her body seemed to be thinking for itself, and she decided to surrender to it, allow this passion to take her someplace new and exciting. She trusted Kirby, and she wanted her. Whatever happened, it would be okay.

Her fingers found the edge of Kirby's shirt and then the space beneath, warm from the night and from their bodies, and then she felt the softness of Kirby's skin. Stopping the kiss, she gently traced a finger along Kirby's spine, floating along each bone from the bottom to the top, feeling Kirby's breasts, then her hips press against hers and seem to writhe with her.

Her fingers traced the waist of Kirby's shorts, around the front to her hip bone, where, with her thumb, she stroked a hollow spot that seemed to drive Kirby crazy.

"What are you doing to me?" Kirby asked.

Sam had no words. She just kissed Kirby again and slid her fingers closer to her center.

Suddenly Kirby's hand was on hers, halting her progress.

"Sam, this is so fast. Are you sure?"

She was, and after so many years of feeling *nothing,* it was amazing to feel so alive.

"I'm sure. I've waited forever." Placing a tender kiss on Kirby's mouth, she gently stroked the soft flesh of her belly. "But you know this is my first time, right? So I'm not exactly certain what I'm doing."

"It's perfect. Amazing." Kirby smiled around the kiss, then pulled back. "But maybe since I'm a little more experienced, I should show you the ropes."

Sam kissed her hard as desire pounded in her ears, her chest, her center. "If that means you're going to touch me, then please, please, show me the ropes."

Kirby shifted slightly, and suddenly Sam lay beneath her, Kirby's hands on her belly, tracing circles as they kissed, moving slowly up until Kirby found the hard peak of Sam's nipple.

Sucking in a breath, Sam quivered and let it out on a soft moan. "Kirby, ohhhh…"

Kirby stopped, sat up, took off her shirt. The streaking light was behind her, but Sam saw the outline of her breasts and reached up to touch them, using the pads of her fingers to slide along the delicate flesh. Her touch elicited a hiss, and Kirby swooped down to kiss her again.

When she retreated, it was to pull Sam up and her shirt off, and as soon as she was exposed, Kirby began kissing her again, this time on her neck. While her mouth searched and explored, Kirby's hands found her breasts, and her belly, and then, in an instant, Kirby's fingers slipped into the waistband of the panties she'd so carefully chosen for this moment and then were inside her.

Sam was in motion, arching her back and her hips, pulling Kirby closer with her arms, kissing the top of her head. But then Kirby pulled out of reach, sliding that amazing mouth down to the place where her fingers were doing such delightful things. With her hips in the air, Kirby had no difficulty slipping the underwear down, and then she began to kiss her, on the wet folds of her sex, on the throbbing clit that seemed ready to explode.

In a combination of perfectly choreographed motions, Kirby sucked and probed and stroked, and Sam met every thrust, moving her hips in every direction, seeking the contact that would give her release. And then, suddenly, before she thought she was ready, the sensations focused, and she came, in a big, wet explosion that caused her to cry out Kirby's name.

Never had she imagined it could be like that. She'd had orgasms, by herself mostly, wonderful releases of stress that gave her pleasure, but this had been in a different realm. This orgasm shook her entire body, curled her toes, stole her breath. She was numb, limp, and paralyzed as she collapsed onto Kirby's bed.

It was a struggle to open her eyes, but she did when she felt Kirby move from between her legs, and what she saw only added to her bliss: Kirby pulling a blanket over them and then crawling up beside her once again. She curled on her side, next to Sam, her face near Sam's shoulder, her hand seeking Sam's beneath the blanket. She entwined their fingers and then grew still, and the only sense that seemed intact was sound. Her own ragged breathing gradually eased, and she found the strength to turn her head and face Kirby.

Of course Kirby was watching her, and as their eyes met, Kirby's seemed to sparkle. It wasn't quite happiness—more like delight, or perhaps even pride.

"You look kind of cocky right now," Sam told her. Even her tongue felt heavy, and speaking was an effort.

"Hmmm. Well, I'm not bragging or anything, but I think I have the right to be a little arrogant."

Sam licked her dry lips. "You do. Wow. You really do."

A slow, sexy smile spread across Kirby's face, and it recharged Sam. She rolled onto her side, facing Kirby. "I know you wanted to show me the ropes, but I'm not sure if I caught everything."

"Hmm. Should I show you again?"

At her words, Sam grew wet again, but that wasn't what she had in mind. "Oh, no. Not yet, anyway. I need to practice a little before I have more instruction."

Kirby's pronounced swallow told Sam she was equally excited, and she slid closer, until their mouths met. Sam had been expecting Kirby to go very slowly, but she hadn't. In retrospect, Sam thought that was probably the better plan, because she wasn't sure how her nerves would have stood the anticipation if Kirby had taken any more time with foreplay.

Now, Sam decided the same course of action was best. If she took the slow route, she might have a heart attack right here on top of Kirby and never know what it was like to make love to her.

Nudging her onto her back, Sam trailed her left hand down the front of Kirby's body, lightly skimming her breast and belly until she reached Kirby's wet core. Kirby shifted, spread her legs, and Sam traced a finger from front to back along the wet folds. Then she slid a finger inside, just one, and smiled as Kirby's belly contracted. Sam leaned in and kissed her softly, in rhythm with the finger tapping inside her.

Without speaking, she slid down her torso and positioned herself between Kirby's thighs. At the touch of her fingers, Kirby spread her legs, and Sam touched her, switching to her dominant right hand. Swallowing, she closed her eyes and took a fortifying breath. She was really here, naked, in Kirby's bed, doing the things that had driven her to madness as she'd thought of them in the past weeks. She studied the glistening flesh, ran her finger across the short, stubby hairs guarding Kirby's sex, found the engorged clit with her mouth. She couldn't wait but didn't rush, taking long strokes with her tongue, nibbling with her teeth and her lips, caressing with a finger. Her other fingers found their way inside, first one and then another, but she didn't move them as she concentrated on Kirby's throbbing clit. When Kirby arched against her, she moved her fingers, pushed them deep inside, and the moan that escaped Kirby's mouth told Sam she should do that again. And she did, thrusting her fingers in and out, bending to caress Kirby deep inside, while her mouth did the same with her clit. Her taste—salty, sweet, earthy—drove Sam crazy with lust, and of all the thoughts she could have at that moment, she focused on the chemistry of sexual attraction, the power of smells in the primitive mating rituals of animals. This was primitive, as simple as could be, just two naked women driving each other wild. It was absolutely perfect.

Kirby's moans grew louder, and she moved her hands to hold Sam's head. Then, an instant later, with a bucking, thrashing motion and a rumbling moan, she orgasmed.

Sam didn't want to move, and she didn't, instead staying where she was, studying Kirby's anatomy with her eyes and her fingers until Kirby called her back to her arms.

"So, first time, you say?" Kirby said with a pucker.

Sam chuckled. "You're a good teacher."

"Sam, that was incredible."

"Yes."

"I mean, it really was."

"Yes."

"Is that all you have to say?"

Suddenly, Sam was overcome with emotion, and unexpected tears seeped from her eyes. If she'd had any doubts before about the meaning of her attraction to Kirby—and there were doubts—the force of the explosive orgasm Kirby gave her, and the passion with which she'd made love to Kirby had just blown them all from her mind. Being with Kirby was the most perfect, comfortable, natural connection she'd ever experienced. From the moment Kirby had met her at the door—was that just a few hours ago?—they'd worked together fluidly—cooking, sharing, talking, and then, finally, making love. Sure, she'd been nervous, but not because of anything Kirby did, or didn't do. That was all her.

Now those nerves were calmed, and Sam simply felt peaceful. These were not tears of sadness.

Kirby didn't know that, though, and she turned to Sam with an expression of horror. "What is it?" she asked as she circled Sam in her arms and pulled her in.

"I…I…I…" She sobbed as Kirby planted kisses on her forehead, in her hair.

"I…I…I…" She tried again as Kirby murmured comforting sounds and held her tightly.

"I…I'm…just…happy," she finally managed to say.

Kirby pulled her in closer, with Sam almost on top of her as she lay back on the pillows, and didn't say anything else. Sam refused to think, but instead she simply felt Kirby beside her and gradually relaxed, her tears stopping.

After a few minutes, Sam turned to her. "Sorry about the waterworks."

Kirby just shook her head. "It's okay. I understand."

"When did you know you were gay?" Sam asked, tilting her head to see Kirby's face. Her hair had found its way from the strap that held it and now cascaded around her, the disorder somewhat fitting the moment.

"Always. I wasn't conscious of it until one of my friends came out to me, and then it all made sense. But I always liked to be around girls. I'm almost…uncomfortable with men."

"Really?" Kirby's story was so different from Sam's. She'd never felt uncomfortable around members of the opposite sex. She'd just not clicked romantically.

"So, what about you? Any schoolgirl crushes? Before me, I mean, because I think—technically speaking—you're still a schoolgirl."

Sam thought of medical school. "And I will be, for a while. I've been thinking about this. Day and night, since I met you. Because you were so obviously flirting with me from the first time we met."

Kirby smiled and shrugged but didn't say anything.

"And I liked it. I liked you. I wanted to call you and see you and be with you, and I didn't understand that urge. And when I started to put it together, I realized I probably did have a crush, in high school."

"What was her name?"

"Jacquie."

"And nothing happened?"

Sam shook her head at the ridiculous notion. "What? No. I had no idea it was a crush! I just loved to be with her. It all makes sense now, though."

"So you really think you're gay? Or do you think you might be bi?"

Sam recalled the excitement she'd felt in the past weeks, being with Kirby. Of the passion of the last half hour. She didn't need to compare it to what she'd felt for Doug and for every other man she'd ever met. She'd already done that. There was no contest. She'd just simply never felt attracted to a man, ever.

"After this," Sam said, motioning down their entwined bodies toward the bottom of the bed, "I think I really like girls."

"That good, huh?"

"You know, you're very cocky."

Kirby began kissing her again, and Sam's longing stirred as the kisses grew deeper. Then, Kirby's hands began exploring, and all rational thoughts left her mind as she allowed herself to completely and totally let go.

CHAPTER TWELVE

Eventually, they retrieved drinks from the kitchen, then hurried back to bed and talked quietly about the attraction they'd both been fighting. When Sam yawned for the twentieth time, Kirby closed the bedroom door nearly all the way, so just a sliver of light found its way through. They slept entwined until Kirby's alarm clock rattled them back to reality in the morning. They showered together, soaping each other's bodies more enthusiastically than necessary, and couldn't resist the temptation to go back to bed, barely taking time to towel off before tumbling together onto the sheets.

That made Sam very late for the softball game, because miraculously, the field was dry enough to play, and she had to hurry home to change into her team shirt and sweat pants before she drove to the field.

Some streets were littered with the storm's damage, tree branches and trash blown by wind and water, but the roads that led her home were open, and the ride was easy. Physically easy. Emotionally, it was a little harder.

Sam practiced her poker face as she drove, rehearsed aloud what she'd say to her mother about her night with Kirby. Would her mom, the person who knew her so well, see something dramatically different about her? Sam had to use her words minimally, because Irene would take whatever Sam gave her and run with it.

Her worries were for naught. As she rounded the bend at the top of Tilbury Terrace, she was stopped by a white utility truck from the electric company. Its lights were flashing, and it was parked haphazardly across the road. A worker directed her around a fallen tree and then past a dozen neighbors gawking at the spectacle. She knew them all by name, and every one of them waved to her.

At the edge of her driveway, her mother stood chatting with two neighbors, and as Sam clicked the remote control that should have opened her garage door, she realized the electricity had been cut by the downed line. Stopping the car, she greeted the trio. "No power, huh?"

"I've never seen a storm like that," said Mrs. Diamond, one neighbor. "It's good that your mother has a sister who could take her in. I'm all alone," she said sadly, as the other neighbor, Mrs. Rule, rolled her eyes.

"It was ten at night, Mary Lou. It was time for bed anyway."

Anxious to avoid their drama, Sam excused herself. "Nice to see you all. I have to get ready for my softball game."

Sam parked in front of her garage, beside her Chochie Dolores's Ford LTD. Before she could ask, her mom nodded toward the car. "Dick Bilus drove me to Bapcia's house last night. I couldn't get the garage door open without power."

"Wow. Some storm, huh?" Sam said, relieved her mother's attention was so obviously diverted to a topic other than Sam's evening.

"Well, fortunately we don't have much damage. Just some small branches in the back. Maybe you can pick those up after your game."

"Sure," she said, trying not to sound too agreeable, lest she attract her mother's attention.

"We probably won't have power for a while, so Dolores and I are taking Bapcia to Atlantic City for the night. Can you find a friend to stay with? Or you can come with us. But I don't want you staying alone here with no power."

"Oh, I'd love to come with you guys. Can you wait until later this afternoon to take off? I accidentally took Jim's car keys and have to run them back to him after my game. He can't drive without his keys." And the lies begin, she thought. But that little lie, Sam knew, would buy her another day and a half of freedom. Time she could come and go and do what she wanted with Kirby without her mom around to take notes and start putting the pieces together.

"That's ridiculous. How can he not have an extra set of keys? And no, we're not waiting. By the time we get there, it'll be time to come home."

Sam tried to hide her delight. "I understand. And don't worry. I'll find someplace to crash tonight, if the power's still out."

Suddenly, her mother's mood softened. "You should have left me a number, so I could call you. I have no idea about these new friends of yours, and then there's an emergency. I had half a mind to call Suzanne, but I didn't want to say anything to get Teddy into any more trouble than she's already in."

Sam swallowed, trying to quell the sudden trepidation she felt about her mother reaching out to Teddy's mom, Suzanne. Would she have told her mother Kirby was gay? Revealed her as the heartbreaker who ruined her daughter's senior year of college? Insinuated something about Sam? Fuck!

"Who did you stay with, anyway?"

"My friend Kirby. She has a big place." That was sort of true.

"Well, you should have left her number."

"Sorry, Mom. If I ever stay with her again, I'll leave you the number. I promise."

"I should get you one of those car phones, so I can reach you in an emergency. Or better yet, you can reach me. Or the police. All of the doctors have them now."

"And when I'm a doctor, I'll have one, too. But why would I need a portable phone now? Why does anyone?" The last thing Sam wanted was her mother calling her to check on her when she was up to something entirely improper to discuss with one's mother. "But I really have to run."

"Okay. Have a great game. Be safe. I'll call when I get there, and if the power's back on, I'll leave a message on the machine. We're staying at the Claridge. And don't forget mass tomorrow. I don't want to hear about you from Father Timko."

Sam nodded, barely resisting the urge to jump up and down. She'd have another night with Kirby, this time without the fear of her mother dropping in on them. Even though she didn't know where Kirby lived, if she had to, she'd have somehow found her the night before. But tonight, with her mother's attention divided between her own eighty-year-old mother and a bank of slot machines, Sam was safe.

"Okay. I love you," her mother was saying as she tuned back in.

Already running late, Sam didn't bother watching to make sure Irene was really leaving. Instead, she ran into the house and changed her clothes in about six seconds. A minute later, she was back in her car, happy to see Dolores's car missing, and in five minutes she was parked at the softball field.

Feeling absolutely giddy, she jogged past Kirby's Jeep and toward the field. She couldn't wait to tell Kirby. When they'd kissed good-bye a little earlier, Sam had been plotting an excuse to see her again. Mostly a homebody, a nerd who actually liked studying, she didn't go out often. The exception was always softball, and she was sure if she'd told her mother there was a team party, Irene wouldn't have questioned it. Now, though, she could save that excuse. After the night she'd had with Kirby, she wanted more. And that was going to require a good amount of subterfuge.

Sam had made it with just a few minutes to spare, and she joined Kirby on the field. "You're never going to believe our luck," she said in greeting.

"Yeah?" Kirby asked as she tossed her the ball and they began walking toward the outfield grass.

"We lost power at my house. My mom is going to Atlantic City for the night."

A smile exploded, lighting Kirby's face. "So, your place tonight?"

Tilting her head, Sam thought about that for a moment. She'd never considered the possibility, and she'd had chances. Her mother routinely had call at the hospital and made these trips to the casino with her mother and sister a few times a year, but Kirby had never wanted to have Doug stay over. Friends had stayed once or twice, but on those occasions when her mother wasn't home, she typically took advantage of the solitude and hung out in the sunroom, reading or watching television. Now, though, she could think of nothing she'd like better than having Kirby in her space, watching TV or playing Ping-Pong, or maybe a board game. Just hanging out. Sleeping beside her, or maybe not sleeping too much at all.

"Well, I don't want to stay home if there's no power. But if they fix the line…" She raised an eyebrow suggestively.

"I can think of a few things we can do that don't require power." Kirby grinned.

"Maybe we should go back to my house after the game, and you can show me."

Kirby swallowed. "If not, we'll just crash at my place again."

"I really love your place," Sam said dryly as her mind flashed back to the night before at Kirby's apartment.

The games were the typical good battles, and their team won in extra innings, on a combination of a walk by Sam, followed by a long single by Kirby that drove her home. They were both famished after the game and stopped at Stookey's for sandwiches before heading to Sam's. The utility truck was still parked at the top of the hill, and Sam stopped when she recognized the man in the hard hat.

"Hi, Mr. Burns."

"Sam, how are you?" He bent his tall frame down and poked his head into the window for a kiss on the cheek.

"Great. Finished school, ready to graduate. How about you? How's Dave?"

Dave Burns had been her alphabetical partner for her entire grade-school career. No one ever came between Burkhart and Burns, not in line for recess or in the arrangement of desks in the classroom. They were friends outside of school as well. Dave loved exploring the mountains as much as Sam did, or riding bikes, or building rafts to sail the Susquehanna. Lately, they'd been kayaking. Mr. Burns owned an old truck and several kayaks, and even without Dave on hand, Sam borrowed them to float down the Susquehanna.

"Congratulations! Dave's all done, too. He finished exams yesterday, and he's graduating next week. He landed a job with an engineering firm in Allentown."

"I'm so happy for him. Tell him to come over to see me when he gets home, okay?"

"Will do. And we should have the power back up in an hour or so."

"Thank you. One more thing. Can I borrow the kayaks? And the truck? Or could you give me a lift to the river?" Sam had an entire day and a half to fill with Kirby, and as much as she wanted to get her naked, she wanted to do some other things as well.

"Of course. But you're not thinking of going out on the river alone, are you?"

Shaking her head, Sam pointed to the Jeep behind her. "No. I want to take my friend Kirby out."

"Of course, but can I suggest you wait a few days? The river is probably running fast after this rain."

Wow. Sam's brain must have been in some post-orgasmic haze because she should have thought of that. "Good point. Maybe I'll put it off until next weekend. Thanks, Mr. Burns. And thanks for taking care of the power."

Sam pulled away, happy that she'd get to take Kirby out on the river, and even happier her mother hadn't talked to Mr. Burns before leaving for Atlantic City. If Irene had stayed home, she'd have altogether different plans for the rest of her day. Whatever they were, they wouldn't be as much fun as what she planned to do with Kirby.

Sam pulled into the driveway with Kirby right behind her, happy to see her aunt's car hadn't reoccupied the spot it had earlier. She let them in with the key hidden in the rock in the garden. They barely had the door closed behind them when Sam pushed Kirby against it and kissed her. Kirby's response was instantaneous, as she pulled Sam closer with both arms—one on Sam's back and the other in her hair.

They pulled away seconds later, breathless.

"I can't believe this, Kirby, but I want to take you to bed again." Sam was amazed by the lust Kirby inspired in her, thrilled to discover this new side of herself.

"Is the coast clear?" Kirby asked as she nibbled Sam's neck.

Sam wasn't sure enough blood was flowing to her brain to form a coherent response, but she murmured a "yes" as she took Kirby's hand and pulled her toward her bedroom, the dog dancing in circles around their feet as they kissed their way down the hall. The door was open, but she closed it behind them, leaving the dog whimpering on the other side, then pushed Kirby backward onto her bed. In a moment of clarity she was thankful she'd insisted on moving her canopy-covered twin bed to the attic and replacing it with a queen-size model, but the thought left her mind a moment later when she found herself with her hands on Kirby's waist.

Her softball pants slid easily over her hips, the underwear inside them, and in an instant, Sam was inside Kirby, with a finger stroking the hot wetness of her center as her mouth devoured her. She licked and sucked and fucked as Kirby matched her every movement, and in what seemed like seconds, Kirby was groaning and exploding into Sam's mouth.

Sam rested her head and began to laugh as she considered the position in which she found herself. On her bed, fully clothed, with her head between the legs of a half-naked woman she'd just brought to a screaming orgasm.

"What's so funny?" Kirby demanded as she laughed with her.

Sam crawled up beside her. "This," she said with her hand. "What you do to me. It's like I'm a different person than I was just a few weeks ago."

"Maybe you're just you now."

What an amazing observation. Sam marveled at how wonderful it felt to simply be herself, perhaps for the first time since her childhood, before sexuality came into play. Before she had to conform, or rationalize, or hide behind books, unable to explore this absolutely incredible part of her identity.

"Yoo-hoo, Samantha? Are you here?"

"What the fuck?" Kirby said as she sat up.

Sam was already off the bed, examining herself in the mirror. Looking at Sam, she pointed to her boom box. "REM is on the CD player. Just press play and put your clothes on. I'll take care of this."

"Who is it?"

"The neighbor. She has a key. My mother probably told her to check on me."

Sam opened the bedroom door an inch and squeezed through, closing it immediately behind her. And not a second too soon, as Mrs. Rule was heading down the hallway in her direction. If Sam's room had been the first bedroom instead of the last, she'd have a very interesting situation on her hands.

"Hi, Sam! I just wanted to see how you're holding up without the power."

Sam looked past her and noticed the dog, sitting on the step before the sunken living room, eating the dog treat Mrs. Rule must have given him. Good watchdog, she thought. Thanks.

"Good, good. My friend and I are just hanging out, listening to some music."

"Music? With no power?"

"Oh, yes. It's a boom box. Battery-operated."

"Of course. I just wanted to make sure you're okay. Your mother asked me to check, and I'm going to take care of the dog while she's away. You know we all have to look out for each other."

"That's very nice of you, Mrs. Rule. I think I'm going to go to my friend's tonight. Mr. Burns says they should have the power on soon, but I'd rather not be alone, just in case."

"You're welcome to stay with me and Nick, anytime. When the electricity comes back on, we're going to make some Jiffy Pop and rent a video. James Bond."

The scary part of this conversation, Sam realized, was that Mrs. Rule was serious. And a few weeks earlier, before Kirby had blown into her life and tossed everything upside down, she might have considered spending her Saturday night with Helen and Nick Rule, eating popcorn and watching a James Bond movie.

Now, though, she had much more interesting things planned for the evening.

"Maybe another time."

"Okay, then. I'm heading next door. And, Sam, keep your fridge closed to keep the cold in."

"Good thinking."

"Where's your friend? I'd love to meet her. Is she going to be a doctor, too? Such hard work it is. But you should know that. You remember your father, always on call and running off at all hours. What's her name?"

Sam didn't know where to begin responding to Mrs. Rule, but just then her bedroom door opened behind her, and Kirby, fully dressed, emerged. The notes of REM singing "Radio Song" drifted out with her, and Sam released a breath when she realized that Kirby didn't look at all like she'd just had a mind-blowing orgasm. She saw no evidence to suggest what they'd been up to behind her bedroom door.

"Hiya! You must be Sam's friend. I'm Helen Rule, and I live in the next house over. I was just making sure you girls are getting along okay without power."

Kirby smiled. "How sweet. We were listening to some music and stretching. It's good to stretch after the game, to keep your muscles loose. Then you don't cramp up or get injured."

"Oh! I knew it. You're going to be a doctor, too."

"No, no. Not me. But I've had enough injuries to know what to do to stay healthy."

"Really? You're so young. What kind of injuries have you had?"

Sam shot Kirby the evil eye and discreetly slashed her hand across her throat. If encouraged, Mrs. Rule would ramble on all day. She was truly a kind and lovely woman, but with her children grown and living in distant cities, she was prone to spells of loneliness that precipitated lengthy conversations at the mailbox and spontaneous knocks on the front door. Or, in this case, no knock at all.

"You know, broken bones, and sprains and…"

"Oh, at last!"

The conversation halted as the lights flickered and then glowed brightly from the hallway fixture.

"What a relief! I was worried about the house, but now that the power's back, we're going to head up to Wilkes-Barre to another softball game."

"Whereabouts?"

"Kirby, I'll follow you. Okay?" Sam asked as she began walking toward the door, waiting as Mrs. Rule slowly followed.

"Do you need to pack?" Kirby asked.

"Oh, yes. I nearly forgot!" Turning to Mrs. Rule, she smiled. Her pulse had returned to normal after the fright of near discovery, and she was suddenly grateful to have someone so kind looking out for her. She gave Mrs. Rule a hug and thanked her before rushing back to her room to pack a few things for a night at Kirby's. After that close call, she couldn't stay with Kirby in her mother's house. No way.

It took only a few minutes to put an overnight bag together, and when she came back to the hallway, she found they hadn't made much progress in the journey to the front door. Mrs. Rule was bragging about her son's exploits on the baseball diamond, and, to her credit, Kirby appeared genuinely interested.

"That's really something to be proud of. Not everyone can say they were drafted by the Pittsburg Pirates."

"Well, it was fun for him, but I'm glad he's settled down now. He has a good job with the post office."

"I hate to interrupt, but if we want to see that game, we better hit the road."

"I won't keep you a moment longer, then. It was nice to meet you, Colby."

They didn't bother to correct Mrs. Rule as Sam escorted her out the door. This time, it was Sam who backed against the door, collapsing against it with a sigh. Relief, fear, and sexual frustration all coursed through her, mingled with a tinge of *what the fuck were you thinking?* She wasn't sure if she should laugh or cry.

Peeking through her left eye, she found Kirby watching her. "It could have been worse," Kirby said lightly.

Sam was well aware of that. If her bedroom were the first door in the hallway, it could have been so much worse. If Mrs. Rule hadn't announced herself, if that had been her mother, if they had been on the couch instead of in her bed. The possibilities of worse were infinite, but that didn't diminish the effects of the close call. Having a sexual relationship with Kirby was not going to be easy.

How much better would it have been if she'd been caught with Doug, with any guy in her bed? Her mother would have undoubtedly scolded her without ever actually addressing the fact that her daughter was having sex in her house. And that would have been that. They'd had the sex talk, and she was sure her mother suspected she slept with Doug. Why wouldn't her very normal college-age daughter be sleeping with her boyfriend?

The problem was, apparently, Sam wasn't a normal college-age girl. She had no desire to sleep with Doug, yet an overwhelming desire to rip Kirby's clothes off and make love to her again, in spite of the close call. And if—when—her mother discovered that secret, her world would be turned upside down. Sam wasn't certain if it could ever be righted, not with the chains of her conservative, Roman Catholic family pulling it hard in the other direction.

"I don't know if I should laugh or cry," she said through all her emotions.

"It happens to everyone, Sam. And honestly, she doesn't suspect a thing. We're just two friends, hanging out and listening to music."

"I know. You're right—it could have been so much worse. And that's what I'm afraid of. Because, eventually, we're going to get caught."

"I'm sorry, Sam." Kirby shrugged, but her words and her gesture did little to quell Sam's nerves.

Opening her other eye, Sam studied Kirby. "Do your parents know? I'm going to let the dog out," she said as she motioned for Kirby to follow her to the back of the house.

Shrugging again, she spoke. "I think they do. I mean, I've never said, and they never asked. But at some point, everyone stopped asking me if I had a boyfriend. And they always ask me if I'd like to bring a *friend* to family events. So, probably."

"And they're okay with that?"

"It's my life," Kirby said. "And they love me. So, yes, I think they are."

They walked through the sunroom and onto the patio and watched the dog run the length of the yard to his favorite tree.

Sam nodded. That made sense, right? Except in her family. Her life wasn't hers. It was a gift from God, intended to be lived in service to Him and all of mankind. In her family, sexuality wasn't a preference, or even a matter of personal freedom. There was just one sexuality, and everything else—homosexuality, bisexuality, transsexuality—they were all abominations, sins against God himself.

Sam couldn't bear to think about it. Not now. One day, maybe after she was away at school, then she could think about having that talk with her mom. But this was definitely not the time.

Sam looked at the storm damage—fallen branches and leaves, mostly. She should rake up the debris. She should probably empty the dishwasher and perhaps check the washer and dryer for unfinished laundry. Yet she simply didn't have the energy. "Let's get out of here," she said, swallowing the great big surge of bile threatening to erupt from her stomach.

Chapter Thirteen

The house was still standing and relatively intact when Sam arrived home late the next afternoon. The yard was a mess, and it took her two hours to rake and bag the detritus the storm had deposited on the lawn. The work was mindless, and it allowed Sam time to think.

That probably wasn't what she needed.

Since she'd met Kirby, she'd been thinking too much. Mostly about Kirby. Her hair, her smile, her laugh, her body. Then her kiss. After that kiss, she'd thought about her sexuality, but not so much in terms of what that meant to her, just simply what it was. It was obvious to her that she had this attraction to Kirby, and it was almost a relief to understand it. She'd always been a little quirky, but now that hazy conception of herself was so much more clearly defined. And all that was good.

But it was also very, very bad. She couldn't be gay. Even if she was, or thought she was, or was bi, or whatever, it wasn't what was expected of her. It wasn't socially acceptable. And it was definitely not appropriate in her family.

When the yard was presentable, she showered and retreated to the sunroom with the dog, where the fading light gave the room a spooky aura. Turning on the reading lamp, she stood before the bookshelf, hoping for inspiration. Her mom was a voracious reader and always had a title Sam could choose when she needed to escape. And at the moment, getting lost in a work of fiction seemed like a great plan.

An hour later, engrossed in *The Pelican Brief*, Sam heard the garage door open. She stood and met her mother in the kitchen, and based on the smile on Irene's face, Sam knew it had been a successful trip.

"How'd it go?" Sam asked.

"Well, let me tell you…" she said as she poured herself a glass of iced tea and walked back into the sunroom, where she told Sam about her excitement at the casino. Sam was right, of course—her mom came home with a few hundred of the Claridge's dollars.

Soon after that, she went to bed and thought of Kirby. They'd spent two nights in bed together, and Sam was still marveling at the fact. How easily she folded herself into Kirby, how cozy it was to be wrapped in her arms, how soft her skin and hair. How exciting her touch. How truly wonderful it was to just be with her. Sam managed to bury the doubts and worries she'd had earlier about her sexuality, and instead she told herself the truth. Soon, she'd be going to Philadelphia and none of it would matter, because she wouldn't have time to for anything but school. She'd deal with her sexuality later.

A weight lifted from her, Sam thought again of their weekend together. They'd made love countless times in two days, and each time, just when she thought it couldn't get better, it did. In the short span of forty-eight hours, they'd grown more comfortable with each other and began taking their time instead of making love at the frenzied pace that marked their first few encounters. When Sam had left Kirby's that evening, she'd felt good. Relaxed, happy, sated. Now, thinking of their passion, of Kirby's touch, of kissing her and stroking her, Sam had the urge to touch herself. She laughed. An orgasm by her own hand would never, ever be satisfying again.

Instead of trying, she opted to call Kirby instead. Lying back on her pillows, she dialed and closed her eyes as she waited to hear her voice.

"Hi," Kirby said after half a ring.

"Did you know it was me?"

"Caller ID."

"Fancy."

"That's me. Fancy Pants."

"What are you up to, Fancy Pants?"

"I'm trying to catch up on laundry. I've been distracted all weekend."

Sam felt a pang of guilt and decided against sharing the detail that her mother laundered her clothing. Instead, she focused on the reaction she'd caused. "I was distracted as well, and I know you're going to find this hard to believe, but if you were here, I could be again."

"Again? Really?"

"Is this type of response common among people you know?"

Kirby hesitated and Sam laughed. "I'm not asking for details. I mean, just. Wow. It was wow."

"Not that I've had much experience in situations such as yours, but I would say that when people...join the team...they do tend to enjoy themselves. They spend a good amount of time...practicing."

"Hmmm. After all the practicing I did over the weekend, I still need to work on my game."

"Well, I think your game is...phenomenal. But, hey, it's important to keep in shape, keep up your skills."

"Do you want to maybe throw the ball around tomorrow after work?"

Kirby hesitated. "Wait. Do you mean *throw the ball around* or *practice?*"

Sam smiled as she rolled onto her side and buried herself in the pillows. "You know what, K? It doesn't matter. I'd pretty much just like to see you again."

"You know what, S? I feel the same way."

"Go finish your laundry. Call me tomorrow."

"Good night, Sam."

Sam pulled the blankets up and turned off the lamp, finding it hard to believe when the sunlight streaming in through partially opened blinds awoke her the next morning. It was just before eight, which meant her mother had already left for work, but Kirby hadn't. Reaching for her phone, she dialed the number she already knew by heart.

"I just wanted to say good morning," Sam said.

"Well, it just got better."

"That's sweet. How was your sleep?"

"Great. I apparently didn't get enough sleep the past few nights, so I was kind of tired." Her voice was soft, her tone playful, and the banter melted Sam.

"You party animal. Up all night." A flood of arousal hit Sam out of nowhere, and she put her hand into her pajama pants and felt her wetness.

"Hmm. That's me."

"So, I think I'm going to want to practice today," she said teasingly, in the sultriest voice she could muster.

"Samantha, can you please hang up? I need to make a call."

Sam pulled her hand from her pants and sat upright. Shit, shit, shit. She thought her mother had left for work, and she'd let her guard down.

"Yes, of course, Mom. Kirby, I'll call you later, okay?"

"Sure thing."

Sam disconnected the phone and debated what to do. Talking to her mom was the last thing she wanted to do, but probably the smartest. If she pranced into the kitchen like everything was normal, maybe her mother would believe that. Just how much of the call had she heard? Probably all of it. Did it matter? They'd been speaking in a sort of code, the words innocent but full of innuendo. Had Irene heard the undertones of flirtation and seduction?

Sam pulled herself out of bed and dragged herself into the bathroom, where she brushed her hair and her teeth. Her mother was having coffee and reading the newspaper when she walked into the kitchen a few minutes later.

"Morning," Sam said as she walked by and put the kettle on for tea, then popped two slices of bread into the toaster oven.

"Who were you talking to so early in the morning?"

"Oh, that was Kirby."

"You're very friendly with this Kirby all of a sudden."

Sam took a deep breath and let it out before speaking. Best not to deny it—that would only make her mother more suspicious. "Yeah, I guess so. We sort of clicked. What's going with you? No work today?"

"I took a personal day. I needed it after my weekend with those two."

Sam understood. Her mother, her aunt, and her grandmother were all quite opinionated, and the three of them in the same car, and the same hotel room, even the same casino for thirty-six hours, would have exhausted most people.

"At least you won."

"That's true. Do you have some time to sit and talk? I've been putting off a few things because I didn't want to bother you during finals."

"Of course. Let me get my toast and tea."

When she'd prepared everything, she sat beside her mother, who had a notepad and pen before her. Sam could see a list written in her mother's small, neat script.

"Okay. Hit me with it."

Her mother eyed her over the top of her glasses, a stern look she'd been using since Sam was a little girl. Then she focused on her list. "First of all, your cousin's wedding. When I sent back the RSVP, you were dating Doug, so he's invited. How's that going? Any chance of a reconciliation?"

Sam shook her head, and in spite of the circumstances, she was happy with her reply. "None whatsoever."

Her mom eyed her over the top of her glasses. "That sounds pretty conclusive."

Sam wasn't going to sugarcoat it. "It is. Next?" she said as she bit her toast.

"Your graduation party. We should send out the invitations this week. I think the end-of-July date is perfect. It gives the family six weeks to recover from Nancy's wedding."

Sam knew her mother had her heart set on a big party, and she wasn't going to win this argument, even if she would have preferred just a small celebration. "Okay. I'll get to work on the invitations. Did you buy them already?"

"They're on Dad's desk." He'd been dead for eight years, and he still had his own desk. It sometimes irked Sam, the inclusion of her father in what otherwise would have been a benign conversation. Because just his name sometimes stressed her. It wasn't hard enough that she was graduating from his alma mater, and he wasn't there to see it. That she was following in his footsteps, going to medical school, and she couldn't talk to him about it was hard, and it made her sad, and the best way to cope was to bury her feelings, which she could never, ever do when her mother said things like *the invitations are on Dad's desk.* She closed her eyes and bit her lip and moved on.

"I'll take care of them. Is there a guest list?"

"Yes. Next to the invitations. And you know where the address book is. You'll have to buy stamps when you take them to mail."

"Okay. Anything else on your list?" she asked, trying to lighten things.

Irene sat back. "Actually, there is." She paused and leaned back, smiled gently at Sam, and clasped both of Sam's hands. "We have to talk about the Mercedes, Lovey."

Sam sucked in a breath as she panicked. "What about it?"

"Do you really think it's wise to take that car to Philadelphia? Imagine how devastated you'd be if someone stole it, or if you crashed it on the Schuylkill."

The car was ten years old and not really worth much money. But to Sam, it was priceless. It had been her father's car, the gift he bought himself after the last mortgage payment was finally made on their house. The car itself had barely been paid for when he died, of a heart attack whose deceptive signs he'd mistaken for bursitis in his left elbow. She treasured it as a link to him, and as she sat there thinking about it, she knew her mom was right. If something happened to it, she'd be crushed.

"What do you propose?" she asked softly, fearful of her mother's response.

"Let's throw a dust cover on it and put it in the garage. It'll be waiting for you every time you come home. And for now, I'll buy you a little car. Something reliable and good on gas."

For as difficult as her mom was at times, she was a saint at others, like this one. Sam had never even considered transportation, but her mother had. And, as usual, her reasoning was spot-on. She'd rather sell that car than have it stolen, or destroyed. But keeping it? Saving it for one day in the future when she could drive it again? That would be an incredible gift. "Thank you," Sam whispered, choked with tears.

"Lovey, I know how much you miss him. I know how hard it was for you to go to Scranton, knowing he studied there before you, and how difficult it's going be in Philly. But he loved you so much, and he was so proud of you. He would be proud now, just like I am. You're a good girl, and I love you very much."

Silent tears streamed down Sam's face, and she wiped them with the hem of her T-shirt, leaned into her mom, and rested her head on her shoulder. She stayed there for a moment before picking it back up. "I need to go back to bed. I'm exhausted."

"Well, that's what happens to party animals when you're up all night."

Her mother was obviously joking, but even the mention of the conversation Irene had overhead filled Sam with trepidation. Trying to make light of it, she joked back. "Well, I have to get it out of my system, right? In a few months, it's going to be all business for me."

The earlier stern look reappeared on Irene's face. "I certainly hope so."

Sam had decided she would swap out her spring and summer wardrobe for the fall and winter clothing hanging in her closet, and the task always kept her busy for a few hours. As she tried things on and decided what to donate to charity, she realized she'd lost a little weight. How had that happened? She'd always been thin, and she ate whatever she wanted from the caloric perspective. She ate healthy by choice, because she didn't want to fall over at her desk one day like her father had.

Her mom knocked and walked in just as she was assessing herself in the mirror.

"Have you lost weight?"

"I guess so. I've been hanging out in sweatpants for the past few weeks, so I hadn't noticed, but my summer clothes look huge."

"I'd hardly say huge, Samantha. But that's why I came in. There's an ad in the paper for a spring sale at Koral's. Do you want to pick out something to wear to your graduation? And we can have lunch. I don't feel like cooking."

Alarm bells immediately rang in Sam's brain. Her mother loved to cook. "Are you feeling okay?"

Irene waved a dismissive hand. "I'm almost sixty years old. I'm allowed to be tired."

"Fair enough. And in answer to your question, I'd love to shop. And eat."

"Let's go then."

Sam offered to drive, because she loved to, and she suddenly realized she wouldn't have the luxury of the Mercedes for long. She followed the Susquehanna River north to Kingston, then turned on Market Street and headed toward Koral's, one of her favorite local clothing retailers. They stopped at the traffic light near Ertley Toyota. "How hungry are you?" her mom asked.

"Famished," Sam admitted.

"Then we'll look at a car after lunch."

"A Toyota?"

"Don't say it like that. Toyota is a perfectly wonderful car. Highly rated."

Sam didn't mean to be a snob, and she knew she'd be very happy with anything that ran reliably as she made her way around uncertain roads in a new city. It was the loss of her car that bothered her. Even if her mother offered her a brand-new Mercedes, it wouldn't mean as much to her as her dad's old car did.

"Sorry. Sure, we can look at cars. I'm supposed to practice with Kirby later, but other than that I have no plans."

"What is it about Kirby that has you so enthralled?" The tone of her mother's voice, which had the ability to cut at times or soothe at others, but was almost always expressive of some opinion, seemed neutral, as if she was trying to be open-minded. Or was she being sneaky, so that Sam let her guard down and revealed too much?

Sam swallowed and fought her anxiety. Being defensive wouldn't help, and as tempting as a snarky retort was, she instead tried to answer truthfully. What was it about Kirby? The physical attraction, of course—but she couldn't tell her mom that.

Instead, she told her what she'd been thinking lately as she'd tried to figure out her feelings and attraction.

"Remember when I was little, and Eva Jones used to come over for coffee? She'd bring Robin. You wanted so badly for Robin and me to click, because you and Eva were such great friends. But we never did. We couldn't even color in harmony. We had absolutely no connection. And that only grew worse as we got older and began forming our own opinions about things."

"Oh, God bless Eva with that girl. She's nothing but trouble."

"That's beside the point. I tried to have a connection to Robin, but it just wasn't there. But Teddy—we are spot-on. Jim and Lori—perfect fits. Kirby's like that, I think. She's got a wicked sense of humor, and she loves sports. She's intelligent. She's considerate and kind."

"She did offer you her couch on the night of the storm."

"And she made me dinner," Sam said, and regretted the words the moment they left her tongue.

The temperature in the car cooled by fifty degrees in an instant. "She cooked for you? That's sort of a friendly gesture for someone you just met."

Sam didn't want to look like she was backpedaling or get stuck in a lie. Better to minimize. "Well, I'm exaggerating. On the night of the storm, she didn't want to go out to eat because of the weather, so she cooked. And she offered me some."

"I thought you went out with friends that night."

Sam sucked in a breath. "We did. But after we ate."

"So, she didn't want to leave the house because of the weather, but then you left the house anyway. After dinner."

Sam felt like she was on the witness stand, and she couldn't keep her cool any longer. She snapped. "Mom! What's the big deal here? She cooked and I ate. Is that a crime?"

"Hmm. No crime. Just a little peculiar. But forget I mentioned it. Let's get some lunch and find you a beautiful outfit for your graduation. What are you thinking of? A sundress?"

Sam was typically cool under pressure. Nothing fazed her. But at that moment, she would have liked the strongest cocktail ever made to wash down some Jell-O shots. Her mother's words barely registered through the ringing in her ears. "Yes, a sundress."

They parked the car and found plenty of empty tables in the café, and a moment later the server seated them and took their drink order. "What looks good to you?" her mother asked.

"I think I'll have a burger and fries. I need to fatten up." Even as she said it, the thought of food turned her stomach, and after they ordered, she excused herself and went to the ladies' room. Using a hand towel, she wet her face and leaned against the wall, taking some deep breaths.

Suddenly, a woman emerged from a stall. "You okay, hon?" she asked.

"Yes, just hungry, I think."

"Pregnant, are you?" she asked, and Sam burst out laughing. The irony of that statement was simply hysterical. If she'd become pregnant the last time she'd had sex with Doug, which was over the Christmas holiday, she'd be as big as a barn and not a bit worried about the subject that was most troubling her these days.

"Well, I'm glad to make you laugh, then."

"Thank you for being so kind," Sam said as she held the door and followed the woman back out. Somehow, she managed to down most of the burger, then lost herself in the racks in the women's section, where she found several dresses that looked perfect for her graduation. Sam normally hated shopping, but on this occasion, she was excited. Graduation. Wow.

"What if it rains?" she asked suddenly.

"With all the technology we have, with these computers and all, you'd think they could predict the weather more than a couple of days in advance."

"Heather Feather the Weather Girl says that one day, you'll be able to just type in the word weather on the computer, and it will tell you the forecast." Heather was about to earn her degree as a meteorologist. She'd lived up to her name, but because of the competition in the field, she'd earned a double major in computers. She always told Sam they were the future, but Sam couldn't see it. Solitaire, sure, and word-processing. But the weather? It would never happen.

"How's Heather? Do you see her?"

"She's playing in the summer league, but not on my team."

"Invite her over. She's a nice girl. Maybe you should get another dress. Something with sleeves, just in case it's cold."

"You don't have to twist my arm," Sam said as she carried several dresses to the changing room. After assessing the first and discarding it, she emerged wearing the second, a cornflower blue with pale yellow and white sunflowers. "Too casual?" she asked. It might work for her graduation party, but probably not the ceremony itself.

"Why not get it for the party? Dresses are buy-one, get-one-half-off."

"That's a good idea," she said. "Then I don't have to do this again for another four years."

Irene, who loved to shop and had converted the fourth bedroom into a walk-in closet, shook her head. "Maybe we can pick out something for your medical-school graduation now, too."

Sam laughed. "That's tempting, Mom." After another hour of raiding racks and trying on dress and shoe combinations, she had four new dresses. They'd decided they'd return two after the weather declared itself.

When they finished, Sam drove half a block to the car dealership and pulled into the lot. "Mom, how are we going to pay for a car?"

They weren't poor. Her father had no debt when he died, and they had some savings, and life insurance. But they'd lived for the past eight years on her mother's nursing salary, which wasn't quite what his had been. A good chunk of what her father left had paid her college tuition, and the last thing she wanted was her mother making any more sacrifices for her.

"Lovey, it's not a lot of money. I need you to be safe. That's worth a fortune to me."

"Okay, we'll look, but I'm not ready to make a decision."

Yet that's exactly what she did. It was nearing the end of the month, and the salesman had a quota to meet, and he offered them a deal they couldn't refuse. An hour later they'd signed the paperwork that made Sam the owner of a brand-new Toyota Corolla. It was much smaller than her car and had none of the little touches, but it did come with an alarm and a sunroof, and a stereo that played CDs. The salesman's disappointment that they weren't trading in the Mercedes was obvious as he wrote up the sales contract, but other than that, it was a smooth transaction.

It was mid-afternoon by the time they got home, and after Sam put away her clothes, she got to work on the party invitations. Her mother had them custom printed, and Sam had to admit they looked fantastic. The paper was a thick bond, off-white, with a big, purple U OF S at the top. The details were printed in black, except for her name, which was also in purple. It reminded Sam of a wedding invitation, and she supposed it was a little over the top for the occasion, but that was okay. It was a big day, and celebrating it made her mother very happy.

When the envelopes were stuffed, all two hundred of them, she decided she needed a break. She walked into the living room and stopped when she saw her mom on the couch.

This had been happening to her since her father died, the overreaction to finding her mother asleep. It was probably caused by the story her dad's nurse had told them about finding him that day. She'd tried to ring him on the intercom, and when he didn't answer, she walked into his office to summon him. He was leaning back in the chair behind his desk, his eyes closed, and she thought he was asleep.

Every time Sam found her mother asleep—which happened more and more as Irene got older and Sam stayed out later—she heard those words in her mind. *I thought he was asleep.*

Sam swallowed hard and followed the routine that seemed to work best. Placing her hand on the hallway credenza to stabilize herself, she took some deep breaths as she studied her mother's chest, watching for movement. It took a few seconds, but then she saw it, just a hint of expansion as her mother inhaled. Letting out her own breath, she walked through the house and let herself out through the sunroom.

The yard had mostly dried, with a few puddles in low places, and Sam picked up some small branches she'd missed on her first pass. The trail was a mess, with mud and gravel in mounds and other places totally washed out. Wide channels had been carved into the dirt by the force of running water, and Sam had to watch each step she took to avoid stepping in one and breaking an ankle.

The climb took twice as long as usual, but the view was as spectacular as ever. The river was high and looked angry, flowing fast through the bends of West Nanticoke. The sky was a cloudless blue, and the rain seemed to have awakened trees all around, painting the mountainsides green. Birds chirped above, but otherwise, here above the rest of the world, it was quiet.

She lay on her back on the rock, looking up at the blue sky, and sighed. Her relationship with Kirby was only weeks old, and already she was having difficulty navigating it.

Why did her mother have to be so...meticulous? The same attention to detail that produced a stunning graduation invitation had caused her to note the oddity of Kirby cooking Sam dinner. Her mother was brilliant and thoughtful. Reflective. Sam supposed this trait recently had to do with the fact that she spent so much time alone, but Irene's observations were usually accurate about medicine, and politics, and her daughter.

Sam was a different person since she'd met Kirby. Sam wouldn't say she was in love with Kirby, but she was certainly infatuated. And Irene, in her omniscient manner, hadn't missed it. Her observations left Sam swaying, as if caught between several forces: Her mother, her attraction to Kirby and all that that meant about her identity, and Kirby herself.

Caution. She would need to exercise extreme caution moving forward. In a few months, she'd be out of her mother's house and out of focus of that watchful eye, freer to fully discover herself. She'd have time to figure out what she needed to tell her mother, if anything. Really, did she have to come out? Couldn't she just be a spinster, like her grandmother's sister? If she never married, but had a *roommate,* did she have to define that relationship? Whose business was it anyway? She'd spent her high school and college careers buried in books and work and avoiding men, even Doug, and she was sure she could use those same excuses for another ten years. She could simply be too busy to get married. After that—well, no one knew better the stresses of a physician's life than her mom. If she told her one day that marriage and a family weren't part of her plan, she'd have a demanding career as an excuse.

She just had to get through one summer. A little more than two months, and she'd be in Philadelphia, with the freedom she needed to figure everything out.

After picking her way down the mountain, she found her mom resting in the garden behind the house, Brandy sprawled in the grass beside her lounge chair. A magnolia tree, hand-planted by a young Sam one Mother's Day years ago, offered them shade. Both of them turned to her as she approached, and Brandy ran to her, his little butt wiggling ferociously.

He jumped beside her on the other chaise when she sat down, and she stroked the soft fur of his neck.

"How's the trail?" her mom asked, shielding her eyes with a forearm over her head as she looked at Sam.

"Battered."

"Not surprising with the force of that storm. What are your plans for the evening?"

"I'm going to softball," she said, purposefully not mentioning Kirby's name.

It didn't matter. Her mother brought it up. "Is this a team practice, or are you just playing with Kirby?"

"Just me and Kirby," Sam said softly, trying to keep the frustration out of her voice.

"How does that work, Samantha? Don't you need other players to catch the ball when you hit it?" Sam wasn't sure of her mother's tone. It wasn't quite anger she heard. More challenging, perhaps, as if she'd caught Sam in a lie and was trying to ferret out the truth.

"We're not hitting. We're doing some work around second base— tossing to each other for force outs and double plays. It's stuff I used to do with Teddy sort of naturally, because we played together for so long." She didn't mention that she and Kirby had a similar connection on the field. That would ruin her excuse for spending time with her.

Dismissing Sam's explanation, Irene continued the questions, now clearly angry. "Are you having dinner with her? Will you be coming home?"

They hadn't talked about it, but Sam figured she and Kirby would grab something to eat. "Probably yes to both questions," Sam said, trying to keep her voice calm. "Do you want me to pick up Stookey's for you before I leave?"

"I think so. I'm really wiped today. I don't feel like cooking."

"Okay. I'll go grab you a sandwich now."

"Get one for the dog, too."

CHAPTER FOURTEEN

Twenty minutes later she was on the road, and in another fifteen she was parked in front of Kirby's apartment. To her delight, Kirby's Jeep was already there.

"Hi," Kirby said as she opened the door. Sam folded into her arms, her troubles slipping away as Kirby's arms wrapped around her. The hug was warm, and comforting, but as Kirby's hands snaked under her shirt, it quickly became heated. The first touch of their lips was sizzling, and Sam wasn't sure how her wobbly legs carried her to the bedroom, but as soon as they were near the bed, they fell into it. They undressed themselves and each other, touched and kissed and licked and sucked until they finally fell onto the pillow together, panting and sated.

"Can I ask you a question?" Kirby asked a little while later.

"Is it about food?"

"Mm. Yes, as a matter of fact."

"Perfect. I brought Stookey's."

"You're sweet. Thank you. That solves that problem."

"What's your question?"

"What do I have to do to score some food?"

Relieved, Sam sat up, looking around. "I have a bag here somewhere."

"The hallway," Kirby reminded her.

Sam stood and pulled on her T-shirt, then found the food she'd abandoned on the floor. "Where would you like to eat?" she called out to Kirby, who was still in the bedroom.

"The kitchen, I guess," she said as she emerged, still naked. "Or would you like to go over to the park? It's really nice outside. We can take our gloves and throw the ball around."

Sam didn't have to think twice. "The park sounds great," she said, dropping the bag again as she approached Kirby. Wrapping her arms around her, she kissed her lips softly. "But you should probably put some clothes on."

"I don't know what it is about you that makes me want to be naked all the time."

"That's funny. I'm having the same problem." Sam patted Kirby's butt and walked back toward the bedroom, and a minute later they were dressed. Kirby produced two bottles of Snapple from the fridge, and they walked the few blocks to the park beside the Susquehanna, talking about the lovely architecture in South Wilkes-Barre. Wilkes University was buying up much of the neighborhood and restoring some of the decaying properties, repurposing old homes into administrative buildings. The effect was a tasteful blend of historical and modern, aesthetic and functional.

At River Street they crossed and found the park almost empty. With finals past, the dorm students had gone home, and it was too late in the day for staff and faculty to be at the park. Someone was playing with their dog, and an older woman was reading on a bench, but otherwise, they had the place to themselves.

They sat on the ground beneath a tree, and Kirby leaned against it with her food in her lap, while Sam sat opposite her, with her legs crossed. Kirby moaned at the first bite of the sandwich, and Sam's laugh broke the ice.

"Oh, man. This is so good."

"You're pretty easy, you know that?"

"It's even good cold." Kirby grinned, and Sam laughed as she munched a potato chip. When she finished, Sam put her trash in the food bag and lay down on the grass. It was early in the evening, but the day was warm and the cloudless sky still bright. Sam listened to the birds and could hear the faint rumble of the Susquehanna if she concentrated. While the grass was cool against her back, the sun warmed her front. Her earlier stress seemed to ooze from her and into the earth beneath her, and she felt peaceful.

"How was your day?" Kirby asked, and Sam opened her eyes and rolled onto her side.

"Are you reading my mind? I was just thinking about what a crappy day I've had." She lowered her voice. "Tremendous sex aside. But I feel better now, out here with you, enjoying the sunshine and the birds."

Kirby finished her food and placed her hands in her lap. "Well, I'm glad it's gotten better. Why was it so crappy?"

Sam looked at Kirby, resting against the tree. Kirby was beginning to be an important person in her life. No matter what happened between them in the fall after she went to school, Kirby would hold a special place in her heart. She'd opened Sam's eyes to a part of her she'd never known, and every moment they'd shared had been magical.

But she was more than that—in addition to the crazy physical attraction, she really liked Kirby. All the things she'd told her mother were true. Kirby was funny and smart and sweet and kind. Kirby had never been anything but honest and forthright with her, yet still Sam hesitated to really open up to her. Why? The only person she'd ever really talked to was Doug, and after she'd purged her feelings all those years ago, she'd sealed up those emotions and rarely discussed them. Yet her dad was a big part of her, and if she wanted her relationship with Kirby to grow—and she did—then she needed to trust her.

"Well, I got a new car."

"What? Wait, why? Is something wrong with your Benz?"

Sam shook her head. "No, it's fine. It's just that my mom doesn't think I should drive it to Philly. It could get stolen, or I could be in an accident."

Kirby nodded. "That seems pretty smart. What did you buy?"

"A Toyota. Corolla. Blue with light-gray interior," Sam said softly.

"You don't seem happy," Kirby said, tilting her head to look at Sam full-on.

"The Mercedes is really special to me, and even though I know my mom is right, she sort of hit me with this out of nowhere. I haven't had a chance to digest it yet."

"What's so special about the Mercedes?"

Sam breathed softly as she spoke. "It was my dad's."

Kirby nodded and studied her, not saying anything. "He died, a few years ago. So driving that car is kind of…" Sam swallowed tears. "I don't know. It keeps him close to me."

Kirby leaned a little closer but still gave Sam her space. "It's really cool that you have his car. Do you have to sell it? Can you afford to hang on to it, until you're back from Philly?"

Sam nodded as she wiped her nose on her sleeve. "That's what we're thinking. If I still drive it once in a while, the motor won't freeze up or something awful like that. And my mom has space in the garage."

"It must be hard, though, to give it up."

Still nodding, Sam tried a smile. "I'm sorry. I feel like a baby."

"No."

"I don't usually talk about him."

"Do you want to?"

Sam looked up to the sky. "It's funny, because I talk *to* him, all the time. And I've been talking a lot lately. Graduation, going to medical school, making out with a girl…" She let the sentence dangle.

"You have a lot to discuss."

"Kirby, how'd you get to be so poised? You sometimes seem so much older, so much more mature than everyone else our age."

"Oldest child, I guess. Forced into a leadership position by virtue of birth order."

"Thank you for being a good friend."

She winked and smiled, and they were quiet for a while, enjoying the antics of a squirrel playing in the tree beside them. "Wanna throw the ball around?" she asked a few minutes later.

Before Sam could answer, someone interrupted them. "Hi, Kirby. How's it going?" Sam looked up to find two women standing a few feet away. One held a lead, and the dog on the end of it jumped and danced, trying to reach Kirby.

"Hi, guys. Hi, Phoenix," Kirby said in dog-voice as she moved in their direction and began petting the shepherd.

"What's up?" the one holding the lead asked. Even as she spoke to Kirby, Sam could see her gaze shifting, moving toward her. Sam stood and closed the gap between them.

"Hi. I'm Sam," she said, hoping she didn't look like she'd been crying.

"Sam, this is Kathy," Kirby said as she indicated the woman with the dog, "and Cheryl. And Phoenix."

Sam knelt and offered the dog her hand, and he sniffed her, wagging his tail. "I think he smells my dog," she said as Phoenix literally shook all over.

"What kind of dog do you have?" Kathy asked.

"A Yorkie. His whole body is about the size of this guy's head."

"I bet he's adorable."

Sam smiled proudly. "He is. He's a sweet little guy. I asked my parents for a St. Bernard and got a rat instead."

They all laughed. "Much easier to walk a Yorkie, I'd say."

"Are you kidding?" Sam asked. "I have to carry him. He is one pampered little pooch."

"Well, we'd love to meet him some time. Phoenix is huge, but he's a teddy bear. He'd play very nicely with your little rat."

"I bet he would. You're a sweetheart, aren't you, Phoenix?" Sam asked.

"Are you a student here?" Cheryl queried.

"No. Scranton. At least for a few more days. I graduate this weekend."

"Congratulations."

"Thanks. It's pretty exciting."

"Kathy and Cheryl used to be my landladies. And I was their dog sitter," Kirby said when she had a chance.

"You're still the dog sitter," Cheryl said as she pointed at Kirby.

"Of course. How could I resist his guy?" she said as she scratched the dog behind his ears.

"So, what's new? We haven't seen you in ages," Kathy said.

"You know. Work. Softball. Keeping busy." Kirby shrugged and continued to direct all her attention toward the dog. Was Sam imagining it, or was Kirby avoiding eye contact with the humans?

"When are we getting together? What are you doing this weekend? If you don't have plans, why don't you come over? We're having a few friends. Sam can bring her rat, and we'll have a few beers."

"Ah, I think with graduation, Sam probably has her plate full this weekend," Kirby said, without much enthusiasm. "But I might be able to make it."

"Too bad, Sam. But if your plans change, you're welcome. Kirby, we'll see you Monday at one. We'll be there until dark," Kathy informed them.

"Sounds great," Kirby said, finally looking up. "I'll look forward to it."

"Nice to meet you," Sam said as they turned to leave.

"Likewise."

"Kirby, behave yourself."

Finally, Kirby smiled, and Sam studied her for a moment. "You okay? You seem out of sorts."

Kirby plopped down in the grass and pulled a blade from the expansive lawn, then began playing with it. "That was really uncomfortable."

Sam sat across from her. "I can see that. What's wrong?"

"I'm not sure what to tell people about us. I mean, there is something to tell, right?"

Sam's pulse kicked up a notch, concerned about the direction this conversation was taking. "I think there is. Do you?"

Kirby nodded. "Yes. And all my friends think so, too. And they're asking about us, but I don't know what to tell them."

Now Sam's breath caught. "What do you mean? They're asking about me?"

"It's just the softball team, Sam. You and I have been spending a lot of time together, and people are wondering what's going on."

"What have you told them?" Sam asked, trying to keep the panic out of her voice.

"Nothing. But as you can see from our little encounter with Kathy and Cheryl, the questions aren't easy to dodge. These are my friends, people I've been hanging out with for five years. They're curious, and concerned, too, I think."

"Concerned about what?"

Kirby paused, seeming to consider her response. "I suppose it's a combination of things. I'm not around, so they want to be sure I'm okay. They don't know much about you, so they're a little cautious. They do know that you've always dated guys, so they want to be sure I'm not doing something stupid like getting involved with a straight girl."

Fuck, Sam thought. Why couldn't people mind their own business? Why did her relationship with Kirby concern anyone but the two of them?

"If we're together, it would really help me if I could tell people. Do you feel comfortable with that?"

Sam's mouth grew dry. She'd told Teddy she thought she was gay, but Teddy was her friend—a little quirky, and irresponsible at times, but totally trustworthy. Would she feel comfortable with Kirby sharing this very private piece of information with *her* friends? With people she didn't even know? The thought nauseated her.

"I…don't know. Can you give me a little time to think about it?" Sam asked. Her smile felt forced, and she shifted position, suddenly feeling uncomfortable.

Kirby paused, then almost sighed her response. "Sure. Of course. But can I ask you another question?"

Sam didn't want to answer another question. She'd been interrogated enough. First her mom, and now Kirby. Their peaceful time had already soured, and she suddenly needed to go for a run, which would require so much effort she couldn't think. Instead, she sucked in a deep breath and faced Kirby. "Okay," she replied cautiously.

"If I did tell people, what would you want me to say? How would you define what we're doing here?"

Sam's angst increased. "Do we have to define it? I mean, aren't we sort of still figuring this out?"

Kirby exhaled a deep sigh. "I don't know what we're doing. I guess I thought if we slept together just once, and it was really awful, I could say this experiment was a failure and move on. You're not gay. But we've slept together, and it's amazing. We continue to sleep together. Does that mean you're gay? Does it mean we're dating because we keep seeing each other? It's really confusing. And even if I'm not going to tell anyone about us, *I'd* like to know your thoughts, where we stand. Know where *I* stand."

Sam could see the anguish on Kirby's face, and it saddened her that she was the cause. Yet that didn't make it any easier for her. "Know that I'm really attracted to you. And I'm trying to figure out what that means in terms of who I am." She paused. "And I want to keep on seeing you."

"In secret."

Sam sighed. "Yes."

"Even from other lesbians."

"Is that so wrong? I mean, three days ago, I'd never even slept with a woman. Three weeks ago, I didn't even know I wanted to. It's all happening so fast, my head is spinning."

Kirby nodded, her reply barely audible. "Okay."

Sam looked at Kirby and saw on her face, in her eyes, a mix of raw emotion that scared her. Sadness? Fear? Something other than the light in her eyes that had been there since they met. They were quiet, and before Sam could figure out how to respond, Kirby changed the subject.

"Well, since we're talking about this...I'm wondering about this weekend. Your graduation. I'd love to go, if you want me to. But if we're trying to keep things...quiet...maybe it would be better if I didn't."

Sam felt numb. What next? Inviting Kirby to graduation had never occurred to her, and if it had, she would have immediately dismissed the thought. The questions that would raise were beyond Sam's ability to answer, the potential problems catastrophic.

"Yeah, um. It's probably best that you don't. I couldn't possibly explain that to my mother. She's already questioning why I'm spending so much time with you, and I'm worried. Not that she would ever suspect anything like this, but I don't know. It's better if we stay off her radar."

Kirby sighed and looked up at the sky. "This is so weird, Sam. I've never dated anyone who still lived with their parents, so I haven't had to deal with all the secrecy and subterfuge. It's...crazy. I feel like I'm twelve years old."

Suddenly Sam wished she was twelve again. Life had been so easy then. Her father was alive, throwing a softball and studying her spelling words with her, working and providing financial security for their family. She'd had no worries, no troubles more than homework and deciding what to wear to school each day. Who she dated or slept with, and what that meant about her and her future, was not an issue.

Fast-forward ten years, and she had troubles galore.

CHAPTER FIFTEEN

"You're home early," her mom said when she walked through the door.

"Yeah," she said, with a perky lilt to her voice opposite of what she really felt. Her afternoon with Kirby had not ended well, and Sam didn't know what she could do to change the sour mood that had come over them. Well, she did, actually. She could come out of the closet and tell all Kirby's friends, and all her family, and probably the rest of the planet, too, that she was gay. Then she and Kirby could go about their lives as they wished and not have to hide or pretend, and everything in Kirby's world would be perfect.

But not in hers. Sam's world would explode.

"Your friend Jim called," her mom said. "He said it was very important that you call him back."

Welcoming the distraction, Kirby walked into the sunroom and grabbed the phone. As she lay back against the pillows of the couch, she dialed his number.

"Samantha, I have wonderful news!" he said in a voice a few octaves above average. He paused, then asked, "Do you want to hear it?"

Sam laughed. "Of course."

"My Uncle Louis is in ICU! He's going to die any minute."

"Jim, I'm sorry," Sam said, trying to remember who Louis was.

"Oh, don't be! He's ninety-seven, and he's been living in a nursing home. Remember, he fell a few months ago and broke his hip? Anyway, he was never the same after Aunt Gracie died, so we've kind of been expecting this. He had a heart attack, and he's not supposed to live more than a few days."

"Well, then, I guess that is good news," Sam said.

"No, silly! That's not the good news. The good news is about Uncle Louis's house. He has lots of stuff in it. His son, Marco, came in from Michigan today, and the doctors convinced him to pull the plug, so he wants to get all the estate business done before he goes back. They're planning to sell everything in the house for pennies, just to get rid of it. But here's where it gets really good. Little Gracie, his daughter, is my godmother, and my parents always helped out Uncle Louis, so they're going to give me whatever I want so I can furnish our apartment!"

"Wow! That isn't good news, Jim. That's great news. What does he have that we need?" Sam asked, suddenly perking up. They only had two months to completely furnish their apartment, and they hadn't even started.

"Everything, from the kitchen table to the bathroom towels. We can even have all the religious statues and the velvet Elvis painting. We're set."

"Is it nice? No offense, but we do want to be comfortable in our place."

"Well...the table is 1950s Formica, but who cares? It's sturdy, and it'll do the trick. The couch is brand new. Aunt Gracie died on the old couch, so he had to get rid of it. He had this one only about six months before the hip thing."

Sam pumped her fist. This was great! "So, when can we pick up everything?"

"Well..." he said. "They have to wait until he's actually dead to sell the house, but they want to start clearing out the place right away. Like, next week."

"At least Lori will be around then. What day?" Sam asked. "Monday is a holiday. How's Tuesday?" Sam would just have to skip practice, and though that meant she wouldn't see Kirby, this was far more important.

"Tuesday's perfect."

"It is kind of fast," Sam said, chewing her lip. "What will we do with everything until we move?"

"Well, Samantha," he said dramatically, "that's the problem. Any ideas?"

Sam supposed they could bring everything to her house and store it in the garage. It was only two months until moving day, and with the summer weather, she and her mother could park in the driveway. After she shared her thoughts with him, they brainstormed and finally came up with a plan. Sam would rent a truck, drive it to Louis's house, and they'd load it with help from Jim's family. She'd solicit her cousins to see if they could help unload at her house.

"I'll have to check with Irene," she said, "so don't book anything just yet. I guess if she doesn't agree, we'll have to see if Lori has any ideas about where we can store everything."

"Wait...do you think your mom will say no?"

"I don't know. I don't think so, but it will be an inconvenience. I at least have to ask her."

"Call me as soon as you talk to her," he said. "And are we still on for the lake?"

"I'm in," Sam replied. They were going to have a graduation celebration at Chip's lake house, just the three of them.

Much to Sam's relief, her mother was excited. "Would you like me to take the day off and help you guys go through everything?"

Sam shook her head. "No. That's okay. Jim's family will be there. And maybe Lori and Chip. You save your time off for moving us in. But if we can get the cousins to help unload here, that would be perfect."

"I'll talk to Dolores."

Sam hung out with her mom for a little while before she showered and headed to bed. In spite of the great news about the apartment, Sam was troubled about her evening with Kirby. And Kirby was too much a part of her now for her to drift peacefully off to sleep without first reaching out. After she was sure her mother was also in bed, she picked up the phone and dialed Kirby's number.

"Did I wake you?" Sam asked.

"Hmm, maybe. I might have been sleeping."

"I'm sorry. I just didn't want to go to bed angry. I need a little time to process all of this. Can you understand and be patient with me for a little while?"

"Sam, I'm not mad. Maybe a little sad. Confused myself, sometimes, about where I'm going and what my future holds."

That got Sam's attention. "What does that mean? What are you confused about?"

Kirby cleared her throat. "It's nothing major. We'll talk when we're together, okay?"

"But you're all right?" Sam asked, suddenly worried. She'd been so preoccupied with her own fears and feelings, she'd never really considered Kirby's perspective.

"Yes, I'm fine. Tired. I'll talk to you tomorrow."

"Okay."

"Sam?" Kirby asked just as she was about to disconnect.

"Yeah?"

"I'm really glad you called."

Sam was smiling as she hung up and still happy when she awakened in the morning. After checking that her mother had actually gone to work, she called Kirby again.

"What's up?" Sam asked when Kirby answered her office extension.

"Yes, Ms. Burkhart, I do have that information for you. Would it be okay if I call you after the meeting I'm in?"

Sam smiled. "Of course, Ms. Fielding. I shall look forward to that."

When Kirby called her back, Sam told her about the news from Jim, and they agreed to get dinner after practice. As she ate breakfast, she finished addressing her graduation invitations, then took them to the post office. Afterward, she went to lunch with her grandmother, and they picked up some flowers at the nursery. She arrived early for practice, and so did Kirby, and they sat beside each other on the bench, just talking, until their teammates arrived. When it ended, they drove to Austie's and had burgers, lingering until closing.

Sam spent the next morning planting flowers and mulching, getting the yard ready for summer. She'd purposely purchased some extra flowers and mulch, and when she finished her own beds, she spent an hour at Kirby's reworking one in front of the house that had been neglected and starting a new one near Kirby's back porch that would give her a reason to smile when she sat out there. She and Jim spent a sunny afternoon on the boat at Chip's lake house, and they talked well into the evening.

Sam didn't do well with idle time, and when one of the other ER techs asked her to cover a shift, she jumped at the chance, just to occupy her day. The house was clean, the gardens done, the clothes changed out. She didn't have any more classes or finals, but instead of feeling free, she felt bored and anxious.

"You have a call," one of the nurses informed her as she was restocking the code cart after a cardiac arrest. With a flutter in her chest, she picked up the extension, already knowing who it was. No one ever called her at work.

"Hello, working girl. Do they give you a lunch break?"

"Hi...it depends. If it's not busy, I can take one. If it is, I just shovel take-out Chinese into my mouth with one hand while I'm doing CPR with the other."

"You're kidding, right? Because otherwise, that sounds really gross."

"Which part?"

Sam could hear the laughter in Kirby's voice. "I don't know what I see in you."

In moments of self-doubt, Sam wondered the same thing. Obviously, she knew she had some great qualities. But why would Kirby want to sneak around with her when so many other girls were ready to scream their sexuality at gay-pride parades? It was obviously important to Kirby to be honest about who she was, and Sam struggled with even letting other lesbians know the truth. What was the compromise? She fell back on the mantra that was suddenly sustaining her: *This will all be so much better in August.*

"I'm not going to dignify that comment with a response."

"Do you want to have lunch with me? I'm at Abe's and can pick you up a hot dog and fries."

On cue, Sam's stomach growled. "There's a little patio behind the ER with some picnic tables. I can be outside in five minutes." Sam had been near the ambulance doors when the crew brought in their patient and had glimpsed a beautiful day. Spending twenty minutes of it outside would be heavenly.

"It'll take me ten."

"See you then," she said.

Closing the last drawer of the code cart, Sam sealed it with a sticker and wheeled it back to the corner where it was stored, then snuck out the back door of the ER and headed toward the chapel. She was transformed the moment she stepped through the doors and wondered, not for the first time, how it was so quiet and peaceful in this sanctuary when just outside, life and death were waging a bloody, noisy war.

The light was muted, and twenty flickering candles danced before a generic altar. On the right, a statue of Jesus, his hands raised in blessing, dominated an alcove. In the rear of the chapel, from another, St. Francis watched over her. Picking a candle from the box and a stick from another, Sam lit it, blessed herself, and knelt to pray for the soul of the man who'd died in the ER a few minutes ago. She was tempted to linger, just to talk out her thoughts in this peaceful place, but she didn't have much time. At any moment, catastrophe could strike, and her hot dog with Kirby would be canceled.

Back in the ER, Sam found the charge nurse and sought permission to take her lunch break. "I'll be out back."

A handful of people occupied four tables, and Sam chose the empty one, sitting with her face to the sun, soaking up its warmth and energy. Closing her eyes, she raised her face to the sky and relaxed. She could hear cars in the distance, and the voices around her became murmurs, until one whispered in her ear.

"Your neck looks very kissable right now," Kirby said.

Opening her eyes, she saw Kirby's a few inches away. "Mm. Your mouth looks very kissable."

"What time do you get out of here?"

Sam made a pouting face. "I'm working a double."

Kirby pouted, too. "How about tomorrow? One of my clients gave me Red Barons tickets."

Sam's mood improved. The Red Barons, the Phillies' AAA minor-league affiliate, played at a stadium just south of Scranton, twenty minutes away. Watching the team was one of her favorite summer pastimes, and over the years, she'd seen quite a few players who went on to play in Philadelphia. "I love the Barons."

"Wanna go with me? I have two front-row tickets," Kirby asked as she spread hot dogs and French fries before them and pushed a soda cup toward Sam.

"Absolutely! I haven't seen them play yet this year."

"Then you're in luck," Kirby said as she smothered a fry in ketchup and inhaled it.

"Wanna go to Old Forge for pizza before the game? Jim's restaurant is literally two miles from the stadium."

"Oh, yeah. Do you think we can get a table on a Friday night?"

"Leave it to me." Sam winked.

"Hello, girls."

Sam looked up to find her mom staring at them with that unreadable gaze.

"I thought I'd have lunch with my daughter today, but they told me you already had a lunch date. Can I join you?"

"Of course," Sam said as she scooched over on the bench seat, her mind spinning. Was that what her colleagues called this, *a date*? It was just lunch.

"Mom, this is my friend, Kirby. Kirby, this is my mom, Irene Burkhart."

"How do you do?" Irene asked, quite formally. They exchanged pleasantries, and a cloud moved to block the sun. It grew chilly in the May afternoon, and Sam shivered.

"What brings you by the hospital, Kirby? Are you having an emergency?"

"Thankfully, no. I had a meeting with a client just down the road, and he offered me tickets for the baseball game tomorrow. I wanted to check with Sam to see if she'd like to go."

"And you brought lunch, too. How thoughtful," Irene said as she opened the wrapper of a deli sandwich. "I guess Samantha won't need this sandwich I brought from the cafeteria."

"Thanks. I'll save it for later. I'm working a double."

Irene ignored her and focused on Kirby. "Sam tells me you're a banker. That sounds like an important job."

Sam sat up straighter, on alert, trying to signal Kirby with her eyes. Her mother was fishing, and she didn't want Kirby to swallow a hook.

"Not really. It's entry level, but it's a start."

Sam tried not to smile as she bit into her hot dog. Kirby was poised and showed none of the trepidation Sam felt. Displaying the same calm she had when Helen Rule walked in on them, she casually smiled at Irene before taking a bite of her food.

And she looked great, too, in a gray suit with a button-down shirt opened at the neck. Two silver chains peeked through the opening, and her hair was pulled back, revealing diamond studs that sparkled on her earlobes.

"Do you know Maureen Ball? She's some sort of bigwig at the bank?"

Kirby nodded. "Oh, yes. She's amazing. A pioneer, really. One of the first women in the country to serve as a bank president."

"Yes, she's a good person. She was a classmate of mine all through school, and I've always done my banking with her. I was very upset when our local bank got bought out, or merged, or whatever they call it, but I'm really happy they kept her. She's good for the community."

"I agree," Kirby said.

"Do you know Mrs. Ball?" Kirby directed the question toward Sam.

"Yes. I remember getting lollipops from her when I was little."

"I can see that," Kirby said

Suddenly, Sam found another memory in her mind, and she used it to turn the conversation. "Mom, I remember another time with Maureen. You weren't there. It was just me and dad. He went to her for the loan for the Mercedes. And when he signed the papers, she gave him an air freshener for the car. One of those evergreen trees that smells like cinnamon."

"Is that where he got that?" Irene said, and Kirby laughed.

"We still have those." Kirby chuckled.

"I should get back to work, and Samantha, you should, too. Kirby, it was a pleasure to finally meet you," her mother said dismissively, and although Sam would have liked to linger a moment longer, to say good-bye and cement plans for the next day, Irene lingered, too, and Sam felt herself offering Kirby a generic good-bye as she walked back with her mother into the hospital.

"What a nice friend she is, Sam. First, she cooks you dinner, and now she buys you lunch."

"Yes, she's very nice," she replied, swallowing the defensive retort that would have felt wonderful but accomplished nothing.

Irene handed her the wax-paper-wrapped deli sandwich. "Here's your dinner. Unless you have other plans with Kirby?"

"No other plans. I gotta go. See you later."

Sam went back to work, and when Kirby called that evening and asked if Sam needed food, she declined. Obviously, someone had noted Kirby's presence at the hospital. The last thing she needed was more gossip getting back to her mother. Instead of the playful banter she would have enjoyed with Kirby on the patio, Sam talked baseball with the housekeeper and a nurse while she ate her sandwich in the breakroom.

By the next afternoon, Sam couldn't stand the separation a minute longer. After playing tennis with her cousin, she showered and dressed for her date with Kirby and was ready two hours early. She read and channel-surfed, cursing the clock. Finally, she left the house and had absolutely no Friday traffic to deal with.

As Sam sat on the front steps of Kirby's apartment, anxiously watching the approaching cars for a sign of her Jeep, she thought she might ask her for a key. That wasn't too forward, was it, for someone she was sleeping with? They were dating, or something, weren't they? She wished she had some point of reference, some resource to turn to on matters like this. She knew she couldn't, though. The only person in her life who could understand her situation was Teddy, and she wasn't about to talk to Teddy about her ex-girlfriend.

Just then Kirby's car pulled up, and she hopped out, wearing a suit and pumps that made her legs seem miles long. Suddenly Sam forgot about keys and dating and imagined running her fingers from those lovely ankles all the way up.

When Kirby said hello, she had to swallow before she could reply and force her mind to not think about what she'd find at the top of those legs. Not for the first time she marveled that in the not-so-distant past, she'd only scratched her head in wonder when people spoke about the joys of sex.

"We have two options for right now," Sam proposed.

"Go on." Kirby leaned against the rail at the bottom of the stairs.

"You can change, and we'll hit the road, and we'll have lots of time before the game to eat pizza and hang out with my friend Jim."

"Or?" Kirby said as she crossed her arms. The sun lit her from the side, and she tilted her head to avoid it. She was such a vision Sam wanted to fold her in her arms and kiss every inch of her. *Please pick option two.*

"I can help you change, and we'll have less time to hang out with my friend Jim and eat pizza."

Kirby moved her hands up and down in front of her as if weighing the options. "Let's see…Jim or you?" she asked, as she moved her right hand up dramatically in favor of Sam.

"Does it make me a bad friend if I agree with you?" Sam asked as they walked inside.

"Hmm," Kirby said. "Not a bad friend to me…"

An hour later, with Kirby behind the wheel, Sam guided her on the back roads to Old Forge and in through the rear door of the crowded restaurant. As promised, two stools at the corner of the bar were empty, and Sam and Kirby eased into them, ignoring glares from patrons queuing for seats.

Leaning over the bar, Jim hugged them both and didn't even ask their order. Two frozen drinks containing a mixture of juice and alcohol appeared before them a minute later.

"What is it with you Scranton people? You never ask anyone what they want. You just order for them."

Sam covered her smile with her glass and sipped another delicious drink. "Jim's thinking of forgoing medical school and staying here to tend bar."

Kirby looked around and seemed to study the atmosphere of Francesco's. "Seems like a good idea to me. This place is popular."

"Every day except Monday, when they're closed."

A second later, Jim delivered a half tray of pizza. "Nonna has another one in the back for you when you're ready, and one to take home for your mom. Now, Kirby, tell me you adore my drink. Go on. I know it's fabulous." He stood expectantly, with a hand on one hip and the other suspended in midair.

Kirby laughed at Jim's typical flamboyant mannerisms. "What is it?"

"I made this in honor of myself. It's called The Celebration. It's vodka, champagne, cranberry, and a splash of lime. And maybe a few secret ingredients as well. I shake it but don't bake it, and voilà."

He winked, then returned to serving his customers. Sam watched him. He spoke as much with his hands as his words, and he seemed to skate behind the bar as he mixed and poured.

Kirby studied him as well as she ate her pizza, and a minute later he was back with two glasses of water. "More Celebrations?" he asked.

"Long drive," Kirby said as she shook her head.

"I know better than to ask Sam. Coke? Something besides water? More pizza?" he asked as he slid the last two slices onto their plates and removed the empty tray.

"I don't think so," Sam said and looked at Kirby.

"Does it come in a quantity less than six?"

He swatted at the air. "Don't be ridiculous. You'll take the rest home for a midnight snack."

When he walked away, Kirby leaned in close to Sam. "Is he dating anyone?"

Sam thought carefully about her response. Could you out someone who wasn't even out to themselves? Sam decided that wasn't fair. "He's never been on a date in his life. He's married to his textbooks. And this place."

Kirby nodded. "Well, I guess it's paid off. He's going to medical school."

Sam agreed and told Kirby the story about how Jim was allowed to attend college only because he'd gotten a scholarship.

"It's funny, isn't it, how different people have different values and priorities?"

Sam knew exactly what she was talking about. Mr. Burns, who worked for the power company, had been so disappointed when his son turned down a job offer to work with his dad and decided to go to college. Dave had done it virtually on his own, while she'd had nothing but support her entire life. And Sam knew Kirby's experience was much like her own. At The University of Scranton, where Jesuit priests still taught requisite classes in theology and philosophy, Sam had thought long and often about such abstractions.

"We think alike, Kirby. Did you ever realize that?"

"We do. You're pretty easy to be with."

Sam bit her lip. Too easy. Kirby came to mind a million times during the course of Sam's day, and Sam wanted to be with her constantly. Kirby made her think, and smile, and laugh. Kirby made her happy.

Even if she tossed sex out of the equation, there was no comparison to what she felt with Doug. They had clicked, on an intellectual level, and since school had been such a significant part of her life ever since she met him, that had been enough. Kirby was so much more than that. Kirby was like the breath that filled her and brought her to life. She was the color in what had sometimes been a gray world.

Love, Sam thought. That's what this is. The idea was terrifying.

"Ready?" Sam asked, needing a distraction from her thoughts. "We don't want to miss the first pitch."

Jim came out from behind the bar with boxes of pizza. "They're frozen," he whispered, as if confessing a sin. "So they'll keep during the game."

Sam was impressed but not surprised. "Your brain is amazing, my friend." Who else would have thought of that?

"Thanks so much," Kirby said, and Sam could tell she was really touched by Jim's kindness. They hadn't paid a cent for their dinner, and they had extra food to take home.

They kissed and hugged, and a minute later, they were on their way. The drive to the stadium took only a few minutes, but the line of cars to get in was backed up. Finally, they parked, using a pass Kirby's client had given her, and made their way inside.

"These are amazing seats," Sam said after they took their place in the first row.

"Pretty awesome, huh?" Kirby asked as she gazed over the dugout on the first-base side. She wore a button-down shirt and jeans, but Sam wore a Red Barons sweatshirt. They both looked casual, but that didn't keep a number of the players in the home dugout from stopping in front of them to offer autographs. One even tried to give them his phone number, which they both declined. When he walked away, looking dejected, they laughed like children at their private joke.

"Do you think any of these guys are going to make it to the big leagues?" Kirby asked. "You might get to watch them play in Philly."

Sam had thought about that. She'd been a Phillies fan her entire life, and after they'd moved a minor-league team to Scranton four years ago, she'd had the pleasure of watching several players who made their way onto the Philadelphia roster. She knew of some prospects on the current team, as well. "A few. The catcher, Lieberthal, will probably make it." Sam nodded toward the outfield. "The right fielder, Amaro. A pitcher or two will probably get called up when they expand the roster at the end of the season. That will be really cool, if I get there and they tap these guys for the post-season. Better yet, if the Phillies make it to the playoffs and I'm there."

"You're a diehard, huh?"

"It's my favorite sport. How about you? What's your team?"

"Baltimore."

"Have you been to Camden Yards yet?"

"Yes!" Kirby said. "It's a really cool park. Have you been?"

"Not yet."

"Something we can think about doing."

"I'd love it. I'd like to visit every MLB park at some point."

"In your spare time, huh?"

"Really."

They skipped out before the game was over and spent an hour on Kirby's porch, just talking. Sam knew her mother was a nervous wreck about graduation, so she didn't even debate staying over, but she felt so guilty. Torn.

She felt guilty she hadn't invited Kirby to graduation, but her mother wouldn't have handled it well. Irene had developed some sort of weird jealousy about her friendship with Kirby, and Sam had to tread carefully. And Kirby didn't seem to mind. It was Sam who minded.

To make it up to her, she invited Kirby kayaking the next day. She risked taking Kirby to her place so they could get out on the river while the conditions were good. And while Kirby was absolutely perfect in her interaction with Irene—eloquent, polite, sweet—her mom seemed distracted and aloof, and her demeanor made Sam nervous. They didn't stay with her long, and Sam was grateful when they finally left the house.

Kirby followed Sam in Mr. Burns's pickup, and they unloaded the kayaks near the bridge in West Nanticoke, then dropped the truck off at a park near Hunlock Creek. Sam drove them back to the bridge, and they launched downstream side by side, coasting on the gentle current.

"The views from the river are amazing," Sam said. "The mountains, the trees, animals. And it's so peaceful out here. I love it."

Kirby nodded. "I can see why."

Their trip took two hours, most of it spent side by side, as the slow current allowed them to maneuver the kayaks quite easily. They stayed along the west bank, talking about their work and the family trip she was planning for the Fourth of July.

"So every year, my parents rent a house in Ocean City, Maryland. Would you like to come with me? Maybe we can add a trip to Baltimore to see the Os."

Sam liked the ideas, but staying with Kirby's family made her nervous. "Will we sleep together?"

Kirby must have sensed Sam's trepidation, because she didn't even tease her. "Probably, but we'll have to share a room with my sister."

The thought of Kirby's sister made the prospect a bit less scary. "I'd like to meet your family."

"I'd like you to meet them."

Sam shook her head. "I'm sorry about my mom. She doesn't seem herself. She's usually a very nice person."

Kirby shrugged. "It was fine."

"And I'm sorry about tomorrow. I wish you were going to be there."

"I thought of going home, but I decided to go to that party at Kathy and Cheryl's. Would you like to come?"

"That'll probably be more fun than my graduation."

Kirby laughed. "I remember mine, and you're probably right."

She was wrong.

Chapter Sixteen

Her graduation day was cool and overcast, and Sam found herself shivering beneath her gown, wishing the entire time she'd skipped the ceremony, as some people had done. Her mom was there, as well as Dolores and her husband, but her grandmother hadn't felt well enough to brave the cold. Afterward, they had a late lunch at a restaurant in Wilkes-Barre with her grandmother and all four of her cousins, their significant others, and a half-dozen kids. Even though this was her family, the people she loved most, Sam felt like she was crawling out of her skin. All she wanted to do was leave and go to Kirby's, to celebrate with her. It didn't help that she was so close she could have walked to Kirby's apartment from the restaurant. The thought of her so near was a torture of sorts.

Trying to keep her mind off Kirby, Sam thought of other things. Jim and Lori. She'd posed for a picture with them after the ceremony and couldn't wait to see it. They'd hang it in their new apartment. And what else would they have? What kinds of things awaited her discovery in the home of a nonagenarian? Louis had died the day before, and they were set to go clean out his house in a few days. She'd rented a U-Haul and couldn't wait to get behind the wheel.

Then she thought of her eighth-grade graduation, when her life was so much simpler. Excited about going off to high school, Sam hadn't had a care in the world. Her father had been so excited, snapping pictures with his fancy camera. Just a month later, he was dead, and it seemed nothing had been right since then. Sure, she had friends, and she did well in school, and she had an adoring family—yet that tragedy had been hanging over her, coloring every page of her life's story, almost defining her. And because she'd chosen to follow in her father's footsteps and study medicine, she wondered if the trend would continue.

"You seem distracted, Lovey," her mother said halfway through their meal.

"Just thinking about Daddy," she said wistfully. With a simple squeeze of her hand, her mother told her she was as well.

"And I feel like I should be more excited. Happier. It's kind of a letdown."

"It is a formality, right? Some graduates didn't even attend the ceremony. But I'm sure it will sink in later."

Later, it did. After going home to change, Sam escaped to Kirby's, telling her mother she was going out with some friends. That was technically true. Thankfully, her mother didn't ask who, because Sam didn't feel like dodging and weaving. She was tired, and she just wanted to see Kirby.

They went for a walk along the river, chatting some but mostly strolling silently. The day was still chilly, but the weather had turned, the sun was shining, the sky bright. After a while, Sam spoke. "I feel like I should be happier about graduating."

"Maybe you're stressed."

"Record-breaking understatement," Sam said sarcastically, and immediately regretted her remark.

Kirby stopped and looked at her with a troubled expression.

"Sam, I've been attracted to you since the moment we first met. I love being with you. I think you're amazing, and I want to spend this summer with you. I want to see where it goes after that. What I don't want is to make you miserable."

Sam put up a hand. "None of this is your fault. It's mine."

"Maybe you're just not ready to deal with the kinds of things being with me forces you to deal with."

Sam nodded. "That may be true." She reached out and closed the gap between them, briefly squeezing Kirby's hand before letting go. "But that doesn't mean I don't want to try."

"Okay," Kirby said. "I just wanted to be sure."

They stopped and watched the river for a moment. "The other day you told me you have some things on your mind. Anything you want to talk about?"

Kirby shrugged. "I'm just wondering about my future, you know? I stayed here because of Teddy. It was an impulsive decision, but I had the offer at the bank, and it seemed like a good option. But it didn't work out with her, and you're leaving, so it seems sort of stupid to stay in your college town after you've graduated."

"I don't know if it's stupid. If you're happy, it's not. But if you have other opportunities, you should explore them. Has something else come up?"

"No, not really. I have a chance to transfer to the Harrisburg area if I want to. It might be a good move. I've always sort of thought about going to law school, so I'd be in the right place if I decide to do that. My parents talked me into business because it's practical, and I do have a good mind for money. But I'm not sure banking is where I want to be. I'm thinking law."

Sam digested Kirby's words. Wow, had she been myopic, focused on herself. "When do you have to make a decision?"

Kirby shrugged. "Soon."

She was sad to know Kirby might leave Wilkes-Barre, even though it made sense. Sam supposed she'd just counted on Kirby fitting into her little fantasy. Sam would go off to Philadelphia and learn what she had to, then come back and play with Kirby on the occasional weekend and school break. She'd thought about it quite a bit. Knowing her mother, Sam couldn't tell her she was with Kirby, but she'd already figured that out. Sam would drive home on Fridays after school and spend the night with Kirby, then head to her mother's on Saturday. If she spent some of Friday studying, she could tell her mother she'd been hitting the books, without technically lying.

If Kirby wasn't here, though, how would that work? When would they see each other? And as much as that thought troubled Sam, she didn't think it was fair to drop the worry onto Kirby. She'd ponder it for a while, devise a solution, and then present it to her. Because one thing was for certain. As much as she'd planned on a summer fling, Sam didn't want to end things with Kirby just because she was moving away. In fact, Sam anticipated things would only get better when she was out from under her mother's microscope.

"Are you ready to head back? I think I'm getting frostbite." Kirby's teeth were chattering, and Sam wanted to kiss her.

"Wanna race?" Sam said as she sprinted ahead, not slowing until Kirby passed her several hundred yards later. Kirby stopped and allowed Sam to catch up, and they walked the few blocks back to Kirby's apartment, chatting about the weather.

"Is it much warmer in Harrisburg?" Sam asked.

"Yes. I noticed the difference in the weather during softball. It's much colder here in March and April. Probably about ten degrees."

"That's huge," Sam admitted, then told her about her flowerbeds, and her graduation party, and her plan to pick up her new car in a few days.

"Thank you for my flowers," Kirby said when Sam reminded her. "You're amazing."

"It was no trouble. You're always so sweet. Besides, I'm looking forward to having a few burgers on your porch this summer, and I'll have something nice to look at." She paused. "In addition to you."

"Do I ever need to water them?"

"Uh, yeah. The front bed a couple of times a week, 'cause they get a ton of sun. The back less. We'll monitor it, okay?"

Kirby looked frightened and Sam patted her arm. "You can do this, K. They're only flowers."

"Easy for you."

At Kirby's they hung out and watched TV, then cooked burgers on the grill, but it was too chilly to sit outside and eat. After they cleaned up, they cuddled on the couch, and Kirby gave Sam a cute graduation card that made her smile, then presented her with a rectangular box wrapped in light-blue paper. Sam recognized the color at once.

"Kirby, is this from Tiffany?"

Kirby smiled. "A special day deserves a special memento."

Sam pulled the white ribbon and then tore open the paper to find a box in a similar color. Lifting the lid, she found a dark-blue pouch and, within it, a silver pen adorned with a caduceus. She turned it over, examining it. It was beautiful, delicate but heavy enough to feel comfortable in her hand. It was a lovely gift, one that Kirby had obviously put some thought into.

"Kirby, this is great. I love it," Sam said as she began scribbling on the paper.

"Well, as a doctor you're going to be writing a lot. You'll need a nice pen."

"You're right. It's perfect."

Kirby beamed, and Sam kissed her excitedly. "Thank you. You're sweet. Do you know that?" Sam turned back to the paper and drew a heart. Within it, she wrote her initials, then Kirby's, and then the letters TLA.

Handing it to Kirby, she waited anxiously for a response. "Did you ever do this as a kid?" she asked.

But Kirby didn't answer, just studied the paper in silence, until Sam couldn't bear it any longer.

"Sam plus Kirby. True Love Always."

Finally, Kirby looked up and met her gaze. "This is either back to second grade or all the way to graduate school."

Sam swallowed. "It's definitely…" Sam sighed. No more word games. "I love you."

Kirby gently fingered the angle of Sam's jaw, then leaned in for the softest, most sensual kiss Sam had ever had. When they pulled apart, breathless, Kirby mated her forehead to Sam's. "I love you, too."

They spent their evening relaxing in front of the television, the energy between them growing as the movie played on. When they were in bed, beside each other wearing only T-shirts and panties, Sam could no longer will her lust into submission. Instead of their usual heated passion, though, this time the lovemaking was slow, tender, and endless.

"I've never stayed up all night for anything," Sam confessed at five a.m., when they finally both pleaded for sleep. "Even at work, I usually doze off."

Kirby, wrapped around her, kissed her neck. "Another first for me."

"I love you."

"I love you, too." Kirby's words warmed her, melted her, anchored her, and Sam realized she had never felt so happy. They ate leftover pizza as a middle-of-the-night breakfast and drifted off to sleep sharing a pillow, just as the sun was waking the Wyoming Valley. Hours later, they awoke in the same position. It was nearly one o'clock, but Sam was still dragging as they headed to the cookout at Kathy and Cheryl's house. Kirby had planned to go, and Sam didn't want to disappoint her, in spite of her trepidation about coming out. Jim and Teddy were one thing, but near-perfect strangers were something else entirely. Sam still wasn't comfortable, but she trusted Kirby, pulled on jeans and a lightweight sweater, and walked beside her carrying a plate of cupcakes Kirby had whipped up the night before.

"We don't have to do this," Kirby said as they headed toward the river.

"I'm too exhausted for anything else."

"I didn't mean that."

"Really? Did I wear you out?" Sam elbowed her.

"Well, I could be persuaded."

"You know what? I'm tired, but it wouldn't take much to convince me."

Suddenly Kirby stopped. "I'm serious. We don't have to go."

"I'm okay, Kirby."

"You could meet someone you know here."

"But you can't tell me who?"

"That would be outing someone, which is not a cool thing to do."

"I get it. But how bad can it be? It's just someone from softball, right? Not one of my neighbors or anything, is it?"

"Sam, you might not know anyone here. But you might. I'm not sure. I just want you to be prepared for the possibility."

Sam's pulse raced as if she were going on stage before all the world. But why? If she met someone she knew, they'd probably be just as motivated as she was to protect their privacy. "C'mon. I'm starved."

The party was a few blocks away from Kirby's, but Sam could tell they were getting close by the number of cars along the road. Most of the houses on South River Street—mansions, really—had driveways and garages, so few cars were parked on the street. As they approached the party, that changed. Two dozen cars were clustered on both sides of the road, and Sam became nervous as she did the math. Even if every occupant came alone, twenty-four people would be at the party. And if they came in twos…wow. What if some walked?

The number of potential guests climbed, along with Sam's trepidation.

Careful to hide her feelings from Kirby, she gently probed. "So who will be here?"

"Based on prior experience, I'd say a mix of people. Kathy and

Cheryl have tons of friends. Some older women, quite a few their age, and then some our age from Wilkes."

"Mostly women, though?"

"All women. Is that a problem?"

Suddenly Sam stopped. It really wasn't. In fact, it sounded amazing. Who could she possibly meet that would out her? "No."

Their house was brick colonial with large columns supporting the roof and tasteful seasonal furniture adorning the front porch. They walked past it, along a brick driveway to a yard completely enclosed with a tall picket fence. Checking for Phoenix, Kirby carefully opened the door and escorted Sam into another world.

The pool was uncovered, and a few brave souls were splashing around in spite of the sixty-five-degree temperature. "It's heated," Kirby informed her, reading her mind. Others played bocce and horseshoes or beanbags. Some sat, at a half dozen tables scattered around the property.

People looked up and waved, but they didn't stop to talk, simply made their way to the base of the stairs. To one side, multiple coolers were clumped, and a keg of beer sat on ice. On the other, tables were piled high with food, and Kirby placed the cupcakes there.

"Hungry?" she asked.

"Famished," Sam admitted. The five a.m. pizza had worn off.

They both prepared plates, then grabbed beers from the keg and found a place at a table of people Kirby knew from softball. Sam always drank beer at parties. She hated it, but it was the best way she knew to keep people from offering her a drink, since the one she had was always full. Warm, but full.

Sam sat beside Kirby, and the table of eight introduced themselves. Sam engaged while she nibbled on the food, trying to be sociable while attempting to satisfy her growling stomach. When they found out she was a Scranton grad, they asked a bunch of questions about who she knew at school. When she told them she played in the Hillside Park league, they asked follow-ups about the people on the teams there.

Everyone was friendly and welcoming, and Sam felt at home. They had almost finished eating when their hostesses came over and managed to squeeze onto either side of the bench seat. "Great to see you, Sam," they said, and offered well wishes on her graduation. Phoenix greeted her but then sat at the end of the table, scouting for food. In a little while, a group of people who'd been playing bocce quit, and some of the ladies went to play, leaving a smaller, more intimate group.

Sam felt more relaxed as they talked about major-league baseball and the Phillies' chances for the season. Their conversation was interrupted as two women approached the table.

"Hi, everyone. May we join you?" one asked.

Sam looked up and felt like her blood pressure had dropped a hundred points as she met the eyes of Dr. Julie Wilde. The smile she offered Sam did nothing to quell Sam's nerves.

"Hi, Sam. Nice to see you. This is my partner, Amanda," she said, nodding to a woman who was taking a seat across from Sam. Then she continued. "Sam is one of the students who works in the ER. She's heading off to medical school in the fall."

"August," Sam said, clearing her throat.

"Amanda is a radiologist in Scranton, so if you have any questions about what that's like, feel free to ask."

Sam nodded as she fought to regain her composure. "Thank you," she said.

"Are you thinking of the ER, Sam?" Amanda asked as she nodded toward Julie. "Julie thinks you're a natural."

The comment buoyed Sam. Dr. Julie Wilde, her hero, had spoken about her? Sam had loved the letter of recommendation Julie had written for her and had kept a copy, but she'd always figured that was just what Julie had to say. Did she really mean all those nice things? Apparently, she had. "I do think I'd like to practice in the ER. What made you choose radiology?" Sam asked.

Amanda laughed. "I'm just the opposite of you two. I don't like blood. In fact, I fainted my first time in the OR."

Sam listened as Amanda told that story, concentrating only partly on the words and more on her breathing. Julie Wilde was gay, and she'd just come out to her. Wow. Why hadn't Kirby told her this? Talk about a shocker.

Sam wasn't sure what to say to her, but she was saved from making further conversation by their hosts, who welcomed the newcomers. Then Amanda looked past Sam and addressed Kirby.

"I haven't seen you since that New Year's party. How's the banking business, Kirby? Are you still thinking of law school?" Amanda asked, startling Sam. They knew each other? More than casually? Sam had only found out about Kirby's law-school plans the day before, and Amanda had known for six months? Wow. This was weird.

Kirby shrugged. "Business is good. I'm considering a transfer. Maybe law school in a year or two. But for now, if you need a commercial loan, I'm your girl."

Amanda wiped her mouth as she shook her head. "Fortunately, we're both humble employees, which makes our lives simple. No worries about managing a practice. We just show up and do our jobs."

If Sam hadn't been so shocked, she would have commented about what an amazing job Julie did.

Instead, Julie quizzed her. "Who do you know here, Sam?" she asked between bites. The question was innocent, just an attempt at conversation, but Sam found it unnerving.

"Kirby. We're on the same softball team."

Julie nodded, but what was that look in her eyes? Understanding? Suspicion? Fortunately, she kept whatever she was thinking to herself, then reached behind Sam and tapped Kirby on the shoulder. "Hi, Kirby."

"Hi, Doc," Kirby replied, and as she did, she leaned back, placing a very uncomfortable hand on the small of Sam's back.

Sam wished she hadn't finished her food, because she wanted to stuff something in her mouth so she wouldn't have to speak. What a great idea! "I'm going to get some dessert," Sam said to no one in particular.

After tossing her plate in the trash, she browsed the dessert offerings, her head spinning. She settled on a brownie, just to justify her trip to the dessert table.

"Kirby's a nice girl," Julie said as she stood beside her, also checking out the prospects.

Taking a deep breath, Sam replied. "I just met her a few weeks ago."

"Well, I can vouch for her. I've known her for years."

"Good to know," Sam said, feeling as awkward as she'd ever felt in her life.

"How's work?" she asked, trying to steer the conversation. While she never had trouble talking to Julie in the ER, she was at a loss for words now.

"Holiday-weekend crazy."

"What shift?"

"Days. Friday, Saturday, and Sunday."

"At least it wasn't the overnight," Sam said with a smile. "I bet that would have been wild on the holiday weekend."

Julie smiled. "Good point. And by the way, congratulations!"

Sam nodded. "Thanks. It still hasn't sunk in. I think I'm still shocked that I actually did it."

"I never had a doubt! And how's your mom? She must be so proud of you."

Sam swallowed the bile that rose in her throat at the mention of her mom's name. What if Julie mentioned that they'd seen each other? "She is. And she's doing okay. Umm, but I would appreciate it if you didn't mention that we ran into each other today."

Julie's eyes flew open wide. "Of course not," she said sympathetically.

Back at the picnic table, everyone talked, some people coming and going as they socialized or played bocce or horseshoes. Sam forced herself to interact, but it was a strain. The party had been a bad idea, and she shouldn't have come. Instead of enjoying the day, and her time with Kirby, she worried over Julie Wilde and how this meeting would affect their relationship.

Understanding that Sam wanted to keep a low profile, Kirby didn't try to introduce her to everyone at the party, but that didn't stop people from seeking her out. They left an hour after they ate, with excuses of another commitment.

Relieved to be out of that situation, Sam said nothing for a minute as they walked back to Kirby's place. Yet she thought about nothing else. How could Kirby have taken her there, knowing Julie would show up? At least she could have warned Sam or, better yet, asked if she still wanted to go knowing they'd likely run into each other. The more she thought about it, the angrier she became.

Finally, she couldn't control her emotions any longer, and she stopped walking. Kirby stopped, too, and turned around to face her. "What's wrong?"

"How could you put me in that situation with Julie Wilde? You know I know her. I've mentioned her multiple times."

"I told you this might happen."

"Not…this. I thought I might meet someone from softball. Not Julie Wilde!"

Kirby looked perplexed.

"She's my mentor, Kirby. She knows my mom!"

"She's not going to say anything. She's not out, Sam. And she's not going to out you."

"But what if I don't want her to know about us? I told you, I'm still trying to figure it all out."

"And you also told me you wanted to come to a party and meet some of my friends."

That was true. Sam had said that. But she'd only said that because she thought it would make Kirby happy. She didn't really want to go, and she certainly didn't want to run into someone she so revered.

"Urgh!" Sam exclaimed. She felt so angry. So frustrated. "Why do you always have to be so rational? Can't you understand why this would rattle me a little?"

"No, actually, I don't."

Sam started walking again, and Kirby fell in step beside her, but neither of them spoke.

When they reached Kirby's apartment, Sam sat on the couch, leaned back, and closed her eyes. She felt Kirby beside her, and when she opened them, Kirby was studying her, her expression pained.

"I don't know what to say to you, Sam. This is a hard position to be in. For both of us."

Sam wanted to retort, to tell Kirby she had no idea, but instead, she remained silent. Her parents had always taught her to try to look at things from other people's perspective, and Sam tried to do that now. It was difficult, though. Why couldn't Kirby just tell people to bug off? It was none of their business. Why couldn't she just give Sam time to figure out what she felt and how to deal with that? Why did she have to be forced from the closet just because Kirby was so comfortably out?

"I think I should go home, Kirby. I'm tired."

Kirby looked sad, but she didn't argue. "Okay."

CHAPTER SEVENTEEN

It turned out that no one except Jim wanted any of Louis's belongings, and Jim, Lori, and Sam were alone the next day as they walked room to room throughout the house, appraising everything to determine what they should take and what they should leave for the yard sale. With Louis barely dead, Sam initially felt a little uneasy going through his things, but in his typical fashion, Jim was lighthearted about the situation and made them laugh. He told stories about Louis and Gracie, and Sam felt grateful to learn a little about the people who were giving them such a gift as they started out for the first time on their own.

Jim's brother Frankie and his cousins told him they'd help lift stuff and load the truck when they were ready, but the future roommates tried to do much of the work on their own. They disassembled the beds, unloaded drawers, wrapped glasses and dishes, and packed dozens of boxes of kitchen and bathroom supplies before it was even time for lunch. They took a sandwich break at Francesco's, and Lori had to leave for her afternoon shift in the ER, so Sam and Jim went back to work, and it was mid-afternoon before they finished.

Sam hadn't thought to bring anything to drink and had been relying on Louis's tap water throughout the day. "Do you think Uncle Louis has anything to drink around here besides water?" She was hoping for a Coke, or a Snapple, but when she looked at Jim, she knew he had something else in mind.

Jim's eyes sparkled as he rubbed his hands together. "I just happened to find a few bottles of booze. Let me see what I can come up with."

Sam wasn't really in the mood for alcohol, but she'd at least taste whatever he created.

Using a can of frozen orange juice and a few shots of his uncle's liquor, Jim whipped up a drink in their newly inherited blender. "This is great," she said as she tried Jim's latest work of genius, deciding perhaps she was in the mood for a drink after all.

They sat on Louis's porch glider looking out at a decaying garden and overgrown lawn, and her mood turned pensive again. She had known Jim all through college. They'd been fast and wonderful friends, and she'd never heard him even mention dating a girl. He was effeminate and flamboyant, and Sam would have bet the entire contents of Louis's house that Jim was gay. Yet he never spoke of his sexual preference, and she'd never asked. It hadn't seemed important. Now, with her own sexuality playing so prominent a role in her mind, she decided it was time.

"Have you ever thought you might be gay?"

He turned to her and playfully slapped her arm. "Samantha! You know homosexuality is a big, big sin!"

"That doesn't answer my question," she said softly.

Pushing the glider with his feet, Jim sipped the drink. "I read this article about sexuality. It says there's a spectrum of gayness. Some people are one hundred percent gay, and some are one hundred percent straight. Most people are somewhere in the middle."

Turning, she met his eyes. "You mean bi?"

Shaking his head, he took another sip. "Not necessarily. Maybe more flexible. So if you met a certain woman you really clicked with, you might develop sexual feelings for her, even though you're not really gay."

Sam leaned back into the glider. Could that be what was happening with her? Was that why she hadn't really been aware of her feelings? Because other than that brief little attraction in high school, she hadn't been crushing on any girls until Kirby came along. Maybe she wasn't gay but just had a connection to one incredible woman.

"Interesting idea," he said when she didn't respond.

"It is." Then, before she could overthink it, she decided to tell him. "I think I might be gay, Jim."

Suddenly, the glider stopped gliding, and she felt him staring at her. Turning her head, she laughed at his dramatic expression: wide-open eyes, arched brows, jaw dropped.

"Samantha! I am *shocked*. This is so unlike you. You're too Catholic to be gay. And too conservative."

"I don't think it has anything to do with that."

"Does this have anything to do with Kirby?" he asked, his tone softer.

"Yes."

"And you're attracted to her?"

"Yes."

He sighed dramatically. "Oh, Sam. This is so not what I expected to talk about today. What a crisis!"

"Hmm. I guess you could call it that." Sam was all over the place with this situation, ricocheting from emotionally high to low, to anxious to angry, elated and defeated, sometimes all within a few hours. If that wasn't crisis criteria, she was hard-pressed to say what was.

"I knew something was up when I saw you two together at the bar."

"Really?" Sam was surprised.

He nodded.

"Why? I mean, what makes you think that?" Sam was curious but concerned, too. The last thing she wanted was to telegraph her feelings.

Jim seemed to think about his response, and Sam sipped her drink as she gave him time. "Well, first of all, you seemed really happy. I've known you for four years, and you're a pretty serious person. You're not necessarily sad, but I'd say you're reserved. Cautious. The other night with Kirby you seemed to be flying high."

That was true. It had been a nice few days leading up to their pizza, and they'd had fabulous sex just before, so Sam really had been feeling high when they saw Jim that night. "What else?"

"Your body language?" he said. "I mean, you sat in a booth next to Lori and you interacted, but it was a totally benign interaction. Neutral. You listened and laughed and engaged, but it was just what friends do. With Kirby, you were just so *into* her. You leaned in to hear her, looked at her when she talked, touched her. You couldn't get enough of her."

Sam thought back to that night and didn't remember anything unusual. She and Kirby were just their normal selves. But was that too much?

"Hmm. I never really noticed that," she admitted.

"Oh, yeah. It's there."

Sam was quiet as she mulled over his observations. Truthfully, she was horrified, imagining everyone who had seen her with Kirby and wondered what was going on.

Placing his hand on hers, Jim leaned a little closer. "You're one of the best friends I've ever had, and if you're gay, I'll still love you. But before you make any dramatic, life-altering decisions, promise me you'll think about this, about what it means for you. What it means for your future. Being gay can't be easy. You'd alienate yourself from your family and some of your friends. I just can't imagine that would be a fun life."

"But if it's who I am, is it really a choice?" She turned to look at him, and as usual, his face was expressive. Focused.

"I think it is. If you're gay, you're not a hundred percent. You're maybe fifty-fifty. That means you can choose to love a man as easily as a woman. You just have to find the right man. Think of the things you like about Kirby and look for that in a guy. And honestly, why would you want to make life any harder than it already is by choosing a woman?"

"Hmmm," Sam said again, trying to accept what he was saying. She might be fifty-fifty, but right now she felt one hundred percent into Kirby.

"Okay. I'll humor you and say maybe you are gay. Not the tiniest little bit of straight in you. Right now, does it really matter? In three months, you'll be up to your eyeballs in the most intense, demanding curriculum you could ever imagine. Gross anatomy, dissecting a freaking cadaver, Sam! Biochemistry. Histology. Microbiology. It's going to be insane. You're going to wake up every morning and go to school for nine hours. Ten, if you count the traffic. You're going to get home at five in the afternoon and have a little dinner, maybe do some aerobics or lift weights at the gym to keep in shape, and then spend three or four hours studying. Every night. You'll have a little free time on the weekends, but not much. You might come home then, to visit your family or do something fun with me and Lori. But you won't have much time for relaxing. It's going to be a grind. If you happen to be with someone like Doug, who's also studying like crazy, maybe you could have a relationship. But anyone else? I just don't think it's possible."

On this point, Jim's argument was a good one. In a few months, she'd be too busy to be gay. She'd thought of seeing Kirby when she came home, but now that Kirby was thinking of moving, that probably wouldn't happen. So what did she have to worry about? And maybe in a few years, when she wasn't so busy anymore, she'd be better equipped to handle her feelings. She'd already thought of all this, but hearing it come from Jim made it more believable.

"You're pretty smart, you know that?" she said, resting her head on his shoulder. He put his arm around her and pulled her close.

"Can I tell you a little secret? Actually, it's a big secret, because no one knows. And it's kind of crazy."

Sam swiveled in the glider so she faced him. "You can tell me anything."

"I once thought I might be gay. I had an attraction to this boy in high school. We were both in the school musical together. All those rehearsals, you know? But I knew that wasn't who I want to be, and I decided that I just had to bury those feelings. And I did. Look at me now? A successful heterosexual."

Sam laughed. "Successful? You've never even dated a girl!"

"That's true, but it's only because I'm so busy. Between school and the bar, when would I ever have time to date? And I'm in the same situation you are, Sam. Once medical school starts, I'll be too busy to even think of dating, for at least a few years. Four years of school, then three or four of residency, and maybe a fellowship at the end for good measure. I probably won't have time to date for ten years."

That was another thing she'd thought of. After this summer, she would have eight years to figure this out. Until then, she was just going to try to enjoy Kirby. If Kirby was okay with that. The way she'd left the night before, she wasn't sure Kirby ever wanted to see her again. Although Kirby had been reasonable, she'd also told Sam how juvenile it was to hide the truth. She'd looked sad as she'd spoken, and Sam knew she'd hurt her. She wanted nothing more than to stop at Kirby's on the way home and apologize, but would it make a difference? Nothing had changed in the past twenty-four hours. Probably nothing would.

"What then, Jim? Will you marry a woman? Or do you think maybe you're fifty-fifty, too?"

"Sam, I'm not a fortune-teller. I can't predict the future. If I meet a nice woman, maybe I'll get married. Or I might date a man, just to see what it's like." He sighed. "The problem is, there are so many vultures out there. If I could only meet someone like you."

"We are pretty perfect together, aren't we?"

"Let's make a pact, Sam. If we're both still single when we're thirty, let's get married. We love each other, and we make each other laugh, and we get along really well. What more could we ask for?"

A few weeks ago, Sam would have agreed. But now that she'd discovered more—so much more—with Kirby, she didn't know how she'd settle for less. But Jim was right, about so many things. She needed to take her time to think about this, not make a rash decision. She needed to concentrate on studying, on becoming the physician she'd always dreamed she'd be. And then, one day, when she was in the place she wanted to be in her career...then she'd think about dating. Maybe it would be a man. Probably, it would be a woman. Maybe it would be both. Who knew? But if she was still single when she turned thirty, maybe marrying Jim wasn't such a bad idea.

"You've got yourself a deal," she said. They shook on it.

"What's going on?" a booming voice asked.

Sam looked up to see Jim's brother Frankie standing at the foot of the porch stairs.

"Oh, Frankie!" he squealed. "I have great news! Sam and I are engaged."

Sam looked to the heavens and rolled her eyes. Nothing was ever easy.

Chapter Eighteen

Halfway into her trip home, as Sam was approaching the Wilkes-Barre exit off Interstate 81, she decided to make a stop. It was late, and Kirby would be home from work. Practice had been canceled, so unless she had other plans, Sam might catch her at her apartment. She didn't want to let the bad feelings between them fester any longer.

Sam wasn't sure if her conversation with Jim had helped her, but he had made some good points. It didn't matter who she dated—men, women, or both—she would be too busy for them once classes began in the fall. Kirby understood that and didn't expect a long-term commitment. Why couldn't Sam just enjoy this relationship and stop worrying? When August came—this August, or next August, or one sometime after that—she'd figure it all out.

Behind the wheel of the truck Sam felt powerful, up high and able to see over the tops of cars. It wasn't until she reached Kirby's narrow street that she considered the issue of parking, and she ended up blocks away, beside a church. Keying the lock, she said a silent prayer that no one hijacked the truck and all of Uncle Louis's treasures.

After knocking on Kirby's door, Sam turned around and looked at the traffic on South Franklin Street, nervous about seeing Kirby after the troubling exchange they'd shared the day before. Her angst dissipated the moment she heard Kirby's voice behind her. "What a nice surprise," she said sweetly, and Sam melted. She hadn't come here for sex, just to see Kirby, to talk to her. Not to apologize, because she didn't feel she'd done anything wrong, but to let Kirby know she cared and that even if they didn't see eye to eye on this one issue, it didn't mean Sam cared any less for her.

During her walk from the truck, she'd rehearsed what she'd say, but now that she was here with Kirby, Sam's words escaped her. All she could think of was folding herself into Kirby's arms and feeling her warmth, the softness of her breasts and the hardness of her muscles, of kissing her mouth and her neck and her belly and a dozen other places, too.

"I came here to tell you I'm sorry we left things the way we did yesterday. I'm crazy about you, Kirby. I love you, and I can't stand that we're out of sorts. I came here to talk, but now that I'm here, all I want to do is rip your clothes off."

Kirby slowly turned her head from side to side, surveying the street. "Not here. You'd better come inside." Grabbing Sam's hand, she pulled her through the door and then into her arms. Their kiss was fiery, and seconds later they were in a tangle on Kirby's bed. Once again, their lovemaking was frenetic, and once again Sam marveled at it all. That she felt such desire. That said desire was for a woman. That the skill with which said woman satisfied that desire was so incredible.

"Wow," Sam said as she rested her head on Kirby's shoulder a while later. "This just keeps getting better and better."

"It is pretty amazing."

"I can't believe I can go from fretting about us to coming in a span of like two minutes."

"I think it was more like two seconds," Kirby joked.

"Don't brag. Is it always amazing with women?"

Kirby eyed her suspiciously, then shook her head. "No. Just with me."

Sam slapped her hand playfully. "C'mon. Don't tease me."

"I think women get each other, so that makes it better. But I've never slept with a guy, so I can't compare."

"You've never been curious?" Sam told Kirby about her conversation with Jim.

"I think I'm a hard-liner. No men for me. Ever. But what do you think? Are you gay, Sam? Or do you just have a crush on me?"

"Well, this is some crush! But I don't know. After our first kiss, I was convinced I must be gay. But I have to consider the possibility that it's just you. After all, I was at a party yesterday with one or two other women, and I hardly noticed them." Sam winked to let Kirby know she was teasing.

"Hardly?" Kirby asked as she made a face.

Sam traced the angle of Kirby's jaw with her finger. "Even though I feel like I don't have to label who I am or what I feel, the scientific part of my brain is longing to clarify this dilemma. Define it. Understand it, and myself."

"I was thinking maybe we're going too fast and your head is spinning."

The implication and what it meant alarmed Sam. Did Kirby want to stop seeing her? Sam sighed and asked her.

"No. I'm just wondering if you need some time to figure things out." Kirby rolled onto her side, so they were nearly nose to nose.

Sam smiled and kissed her softly. "You're sweet. I feel like you really care about me, and that means a lot to me."

"I do care."

Sam nodded. "After Lori left today, Jim and I talked about so many things. Sexuality, as I mentioned. Life. Our futures. He reminded me of something I'd managed to forget. I guess I've been sort of distracted by your body…" Sam kissed Kirby's breast. "And maybe I lost focus a little. But I'm leaving in just a couple of months, and I'm going to be so busy when I get to Philly I won't have time for a relationship. So maybe I shouldn't worry about what all this means. Maybe I should just enjoy this time we have together, and then we'll see what happens in the fall."

"So you'd like to have a summer fling and go our separate ways?" Kirby tilted her head, studying Sam.

Sam swallowed. That was not what she wanted. She never wanted to stop seeing Kirby. Even if she had to drive to Harrisburg, she'd do it. The truth was, she had no idea how much weekend time she'd have free to see Kirby. To see anyone. "Not necessarily, but maybe. Does that bother you?"

Kirby closed her eyes and looked really content. "No. Yes. I don't know how to answer that question."

"Just tell me what you're feeling."

"Sam, I know you're leaving. You have to do your thing. I know our future is uncertain. I mean, I'll miss you when you're gone. But I'm probably not going to stick around Wilkes-Barre anyway."

Sam knew Kirby was thinking of moving; they'd had that discussion. But hadn't Kirby considered the possibility that they would see each other, even if she was in Harrisburg? And then another thought occurred to her—what if Kirby didn't want to keep seeing her? Sam had been considering this relationship from her own perspective, thinking of her own future. What had Kirby envisioned for them? What if Kirby had just been thinking of Sam as a little fling? As ironic as that possibility was, it still stung. Worse yet, what if some other girl was waiting for Kirby in Harrisburg? Considering her own future plans, did Sam have the right to ask?

Taking a deep breath, she pondered all her possible responses and decided that her gut feeling, what she'd known all along, and what Jim had echoed to her earlier, was the right thing. Her future was calling her, and she had to stay focused on it. "I hope you'll give me your number when you move. Just in case I'm ever in Harrisburg." Her tone was dry, hinting at sarcasm.

"Likewise, Big City Girl," Kirby said with half a smile on her face.

And with that smile they reached a truce. Each of them had a big future ahead of her, and even though they loved each other, they had a lot of work to do on themselves.

"I do love you," Sam whispered.

"Me, too." Kirby looked like she wanted to say something more, and Sam watched as she seemed to search for the words.

"Have you ever seen a psychologist?"

"As a patient?"

Kirby nodded, and Sam did, too. "For about a year, after my dad died."

"Why did you stop?"

"She said I was healed," Sam said softly as she bit her lip, remembering that awful time in her life.

"What do you think?" Kirby asked gently.

"I don't think I'll ever be healed." Sam met her eyes, and Kirby pulled her close, burying her face in Sam's hair. After a minute, she pulled back and wiped the tears from Sam's eyes.

"I've been reading about it. What it's like to lose a parent when you're so young."

Sam was shocked and wasn't sure if she should be offended. Was Kirby suddenly a psychoanalyst? Before she could say something, though, Kirby spoke again.

"You're remarkably well adjusted, Sam. So many kids who go through what you did end up with drug and alcohol problems. They flunk out of school. Run away. You're pretty amazing."

"I don't feel amazing, Kirby. I just did what I had to do to survive. I kept putting one foot in front of the other. And before I knew it, the scenery was a little different, and I was doing okay, so I just kept doing it."

"So, you just worked out all your grief, huh?"

Sam shrugged. It was a fitting descriptor.

"It seems like you have a lot of friends. But do you ever feel like you have problems getting close to people?"

"Are you asking if my friends are fake friends?"

"I think of Teddy, and I wonder what scars she has. She doesn't let anyone get too close. Yet she's one of your best friends. So…"

"You wonder if we're really friends?"

"What you guys talk about."

Sam thought for a moment, and as she did, she really felt the weight of Kirby's words. She and Teddy were so superficial. They did things together, but their conversation the day they'd talked about Kirby was probably the deepest they'd ever had.

"That's a good point, K. And this may sound awful, but that's why I like her. Because everything else is so serious. School—and my pre-med kind of friends—are serious. Don't get me wrong, Lori and Jim are a lot of fun, but they're on a mission, too. The fun happens when it can, when we have a break in the crazy routine. With Teddy, fun is the routine. I can relax with her. It's mindless."

"That's why I liked her, too."

Then Sam thought of her other friends, of the deep conversations they had about religion and science and philosophy. Sometimes politics, but mostly deeper things. "Lori and Jim are my soul mates."

"Really?"

"We're all really the same. We come from conservative, middle-class families. Lori's mom and my mom speak Ukrainian when they're together. What are the odds of that? God is a big factor in all of our lives—we all graduated from Catholic high schools and a Jesuit university. We have the same priorities and the same values."

"What would they say about this?"

"I was wondering the same thing. I…" Sam hesitated, but then she figured it didn't much matter what she said about Jim. Kirby was cool. "I suspect Jim is gay. But—if he is, he's not any more ready to come out than I am. Today was the first time we've ever talked about it. Maybe that's a start for both of us."

"It sounds like you had some kind of day."

Sam was happy to change the subject as she described packing up Louis's house and bringing what they'd chosen home.

"Wait a minute! You mean to tell me you drove a truck, like a U-Haul, by yourself, in South Wilkes-Barre?"

Sam was insulted. "Do you doubt my abilities?"

Kirby shook her head. "No. But I admire your balls."

Sam kissed her. "I think one reason you like me is because I don't have any balls."

Kirby shook her head. "Gross. I can't even think about that. But I want to see this truck. Where is it?"

Sam rolled over. "I have to go anyway. I have about thirty cousins coming to my house at eight tonight to unload it."

After they dressed and kissed again, they walked side by side back to the church. "I think you need a union card to drive a big truck, Sam. You have to be a Teamster."

"If the medical-school thing doesn't work out, I have a skill. Because really, what else can I do with a biology degree?"

"There you go. What other skills do you have? Can you do plumbing?"

"I probably could, if I read about it. I kind of liked electrical work in physics class. Circuits and such. But I also know a guy who got electrocuted, so that sort of freaks me out."

"Yeah. Electrical is kind of scary. What about painting? Can you paint?"

"I love to. And wallpaper. Anything artistic."

They arrived at the church, and to Sam's relief, the truck was exactly where she'd left it. Unlocking the big padlock on the back, she and Kirby worked to give the door a strong push, and it opened, revealing the neatly stacked contents of Uncle Louis's house. The truck was nearly full, and Kirby gazed in wonder at the boxes and furniture before turning to Sam. "You did all this in one day?"

Sam nodded proudly. "With a lot of help from half of Old Forge."

"You really are amazing. Do you realize that?"

Sam looked at her, surprised by her serious expression. "Really?"
Kirby nodded.

"Really."

"I just did what I had to do. Do you want a ride? I can drop you off at your door."

Kirby laughed. "Of course!"

They secured the locks and climbed in the cab, Sam eased the truck onto the road, and a few blocks later, she pulled up before Kirby's apartment.

"Call me later. I can't wait to hear about you backing this thing up into your driveway."

Shit! "Oh, no. I didn't think about backing up."

"You'll be fine. Just make sure that Mercedes is far, far, away."

Sam blew her a kiss and headed home, driving carefully on the two-lane roads, then stopped the truck on the street in front of the house. One of her cousins could back it into the driveway for the unloading. After opening the garage, Sam pulled the Mercedes out and onto the street, then surveyed the empty space. Hopefully it would hold the truck's contents, but she wasn't sure. She went into the house to find her mom and elicit her opinion.

"That's a big truck, Sam. I can't believe you drove that yourself!"

Sam chuckled. "That's what Kirby said. But it was this one or a really small one, so I figured bigger was better. And I was right, because that thing is almost filled. Wanna see?"

"Yes, of course." They walked toward the street with Brandy running circles around Sam, and she unlocked the back so her mother could look before holding out her arms for the dog.

"What do you think? Will this all fit in my side of the garage, or should I move your car out, too?"

Irene pursed her lips and walked around the side of the truck. "It's never going to fit. You'd better move mine."

As they walked back toward the house, Irene continued. "That was a lot of work. Did Kirby take the day off to help out?"

Sam looked at her, confused. "Kirby? No, it was just me and Jim most of the day. Lori was only there in the morning. We spent the whole day packing boxes and organizing everything. Then his brother and some other guys came and did the heavy lifting."

"So when did you see Kirby?" her mom asked.

Sam tried to keep her cool. "Oh, I had to give her something, so I met up with her at a church parking lot, and she saw the truck."

"What did you have to give her?"

An orgasm, Sam thought. Fuck! "What did I have to give her?"

"Yes? What was so important that you drove this truck through the streets of Wilkes-Barre?"

"Money. I had to give her money."

Irene's eyebrow shot up. "You're lending her money?"

Sam shook her head. "No, no. She loaned some to me. I just had to pay it back."

Irene stopped and stared at Sam. "I have a feeling you're not being completely honest with me, Samantha."

"Mom, why would I lie?"

"That's a very good question."

Sam was saved from further inquiry when Dolores arrived with a car full of movers. Her cousin, two in-laws, and a fiancé all spilled out of the car, and they immediately got to work. They moved Irene's car, and after backing up the truck, two of the guys climbed up, and the others stayed down and caught the boxes and pieces of furniture they passed down. Sam and her mother and aunt carried the light boxes, making neat piles in the back of the garage.

They'd just about finished when Irene turned to Sam. "Lovey, can you get me a chair? I need to sit down."

Sam looked at her mom, literally watched the color drain from her face, saw the life fade from her eyes as her mother collapsed to the garage floor. "Choch, call the ambulance," Sam directed. "Use the kitchen phone. The number's on the base on an orange sticker."

Breathless, Sam knelt beside her mom, who'd been fortunate enough to fall into some of the newly stacked boxes. They'd toppled over but broke her fall. Sam and her cousin eased Irene to her back, so she could breathe, and Sam's ER training kicked in. She listened for breathing and, to her great relief, felt the gentle puff of air against her cheek as she watched her mom's chest slowly rise. Placing two fingers on her neck, she felt a strong pulse, but more important, her mother began to move beneath her hand.

Her eyelids fluttered, seemingly too heavy to open, and Sam softly called to her. "Mom, it's okay. You're okay. You just fainted. Choch called the ambulance, and we're going to take you to the hospital."

Irene nodded but didn't argue, and Sam took that to be a very poor sign. If her mother was willing to go by ambulance to the ER, something was wrong. Hell, she'd passed out. That was clearly wrong.

Within minutes the ambulance arrived, and during that time, Irene's strength returned. They didn't let her sit up, but she seemed to breathe okay, and she answered all the attendant's questions appropriately. Sam and Dolores drove together to the hospital, and the cousins went home in Dolores's car. They promised to return the U-Haul and retrieve Sam's Toyota from the rental place, as well.

It was a stressful ride to the hospital, with Sam wondering every second if her mother was still alive. Dolores prayed the rosary in the seat beside her, Sam chanting right along with her.

At the ER, Sam didn't even wait to be told where her mother was. She just marched directly to the cardiac room and found her mother there, surrounded by the ambulance people and the ER workers. To her great relief, Julie Wilde was bent over her mother's chest, a stethoscope in her hand as she listened to Irene's heart and lungs

Everyone seemed relaxed, except her mother, who still looked pale and weak. Wires were attached at every conceivable piece of skin, two IVs were running, and her heartbeat blipped in real time on the EKG monitor. Sam's knees wobbled, and she leaned against the wall as she took it all in.

Get it together! She scolded herself. She would do her mother no good if she fell apart now. Keeping her wits about her was more important than ever. She tuned in to the questions Julie was asking as she felt pulses and prodded and poked. No, she had no pain. She'd been tired lately, and a little winded. This was the first time she'd passed out.

"Reenie, have you always had this loud heart murmur?" Julie asked when she finished examining her.

"I've had a murmur since I was a little girl," she replied. "But no one ever told me it was loud."

"Oh, it's loud. And it radiates into your neck. I think it's your aortic valve. And," she paused and looked pointedly at Sam, "if I'm right, you're going to need valve surgery."

Sam swallowed hard, and Irene closed her eyes as she digested Julie's words. "Okay. What do you do now, an echo?"

Julie grinned. "Nurses are the worst patients! I suppose you want me to get an echo in the ER so I can send you home. You have to work in the morning."

Irene closed her eyes, and Sam thought she was going to pass out again. She seemed drugged. "Exactly."

"I'm not getting an echo tonight. But I'm getting labs and an EKG, a chest X-ray, and you're getting admitted. Who's your favorite cardiologist, cuz you've earned the right to a consult."

They bantered and bickered as Sam stood helplessly and watched in disbelief, feeling as if she herself might pass out. All the lights in the room seemed to swirl, the noises blended and blurred, and she felt heavy as she finally sat into a chair that someone offered.

Her mom. Her rock. Her everything. What if she died? What would Sam do? She'd really be alone in the world. Sure, she'd have her grandmother, and Dolores, and her cousins, but that wasn't the same. What if her mom couldn't work anymore? She was only sixty. Could she collect her retirement that early? Would she have enough money to keep up their house? Irene often joked she'd go bankrupt if she had to hire a gardener to tend their two acres of pristine grass and flowerbeds. But she had taxes and a phone bill, cable and electricity. The mortgage was paid off, but it still wasn't inexpensive to run a house.

Why did this have to happen now, just when Sam was getting ready to leave home? A summer before, Sam would have been able to spend a year nursing her mom back to health without it affecting her much. With only two months on the calendar before she was destined to move away for medical school, would Irene have enough time to recover before Sam left? Maybe she would have to postpone her studies for a year.

A hand pressed firmly against her knee, and Sam opened her eyes to see Julie's concerned expression. "She's doing fine, Sam. She's really stable. I'm ordering everything in the book just to be sure, but I really think she has aortic stenosis, which is not going to come up on any of these tests."

"What's that?"

"I suspect your mom had rheumatic fever as a child. She's the right age for that. The germ caused damage to her heart valve, and it grew worse over time, so now it's not opening and closing correctly. She probably doesn't notice it much because it came on gradually, but if she does some heavy labor like tonight…"

Sam frowned as she remembered her mom carrying boxes, then falling on top of them.

"Hey, this isn't your fault. And maybe it's better that it happened now, rather than after you'd left for medical school. You were right there to help her."

"How do we treat it? Does it have to be surgery?" Open-heart surgery sounded so scary, and her mother looked so helpless.

Julie put a hand on her shoulder and said nothing for a moment, just rubbed gently as Sam watched her mother sleeping. After a few deep breaths, Sam regrouped and felt her strength return. Whatever this was, her mom would fight it, and she'd be right there beside her, helping in every way she could.

"We're getting ahead of ourselves. First, we need an ultrasound of the heart to check the valve."

"And you think it's the valve?"

"The murmur is suggestive, along with the passing out. If that's what it is, then most likely it means surgery. A new heart valve."

"Shit," Sam said. "It sounds pretty bad. Who decides this? The cardiologist?"

"Yeah, and a heart surgeon. But that's tomorrow. Tonight, she's going to rest, and we'll monitor her and deal with any problems that arise."

"Thank you for taking such good care of her."

"Sam, of course. You're one of us. She's one of us."

Sam tried to smile but couldn't quite get there. "Is there anyone else you can call? A friend perhaps?" Julie looked pointedly at her, but Sam could only shake her head. Kirby, whose very existence on the planet seemed to irk Irene, was the last person she needed at the hospital.

With a squeeze of Sam's shoulder and a wave to Dolores, Julie left the room.

"They do this all the time, Lovey," her mom said as she opened her eyes. "It's pretty standard these days. But I *am* exhausted. You should go home. I'm just going to sleep."

"I don't think I could sleep at home, Mom. I'd rather stay here."

"Well, I'm going to go," Dolores said, and she stood next to her sister and said something in Ukrainian that made Irene smile.

"Do you want to take my car?" Sam asked.

"No, no. It's okay. Nancy's on her way. I'll just wait for her outside so she doesn't have to try to find parking. I'll see you both tomorrow."

When Dolores left, Sam pulled her chair closer to her mom's bedside.

"This certainly puts a new twist on my summer plans."

Sam laughed as she fought tears. "I'll say." Sam looked at her. "Did you know something was wrong?"

Irene shrugged. "Yes, of course. But I made excuses. Stress, work, my age."

"I guess you're lucky you got a warning. With Dad…"

Irene turned her head and looked at Sam, her eyes filled with sadness. "Yes. He didn't have a chance. At least he didn't have a second chance."

"But you do, Mom. Julie says you're going to be okay."

Irene nodded but ignored her comment. "Your father loved you unconditionally, Samantha. This thing with Kirby—he wouldn't have cared."

Sam just stared for a moment, too stunned to figure out a reply. She wasn't sure what shocked her more—that her mother knew, or that she was bold enough to say something. "Mom, it's not what you think," she said, as her brain scrambled for a way out of the situation. Truthfully, she didn't have the strength to be clever or to deny the truth.

"What is it, then? I may be old, and apparently frail, but I'm not stupid, Sam. You've been prancing around like a puppy for weeks. Ever since you met her. You are *enthralled.*"

"We're just good friends." Sam closed her eyes, preparing for whatever came next. Her wait was short.

"I'm not him. I'm not as kind or as understanding. I don't approve of this sort of thing. It's unnatural. It's a sin. And it breaks my heart to know what you'd be throwing away if you pursue a relationship with that…girl."

Sam couldn't deal with this right now, and her mother shouldn't be, either. "Mom, you need to rest. We shouldn't be talking about this while you're in the hospital."

"Why? You think I'm not worrying about it, just because we don't speak of it?"

Sam sighed. Had worrying about her put Irene into that hospital bed?

Irene wouldn't let up. With a voice so quiet Sam had to strain to hear, Irene spoke her mind. "Well, I am. I'm worried about you. I'm worried about your future, not to mention your soul."

Sam tried to laugh it off. "Mom, it's nothing, really."

"Nothing? Oh, I don't believe that," Irene said softly as she closed her eyes. "I was in love once, too."

"I'm not in love with her," Sam protested.

"Oh, Lovey. Please don't disrespect me any more by lying."

Sam, always quick to respond in crisis, was at a loss. Burying her face in her hands, she sat back in the chair. Why was this happening?

"Have you slept with her?"

"Mom!"

"It's a legitimate question."

"Why would you think that?"

"Well, for one—I'm your mother. I know you, very well, in fact. Two, Suzanne told me her suspicions about this girl. She used to be very cozy with Teddy, and Suzanne had to put a stop to it."

Sam didn't respond. What could she possibly say?

"I guess that answers my question."

"Mom, don't do this." Sam met her mom's eyes, pleaded with her own.

"Lovey, listen to me. Right now, I'm very sick, and I could die. If I do, you're going to have to make your way in the world without anyone else to guide you. I hope that everything Daddy and I taught you sticks. Kindness. Compassion. Responsibility. And morality. This is wrong, Sam. You have to promise me you're going to end this…affair. For me. I can't bear it." Her last words were just a murmur, as if her speech had sucked all the life from her.

Irene closed her eyes, and as Sam had done so frequently since her father's death, she simply watched her mother breathe. After a few minutes she realized she'd fallen asleep.

Sam looked at her mom, so pale and frail in the bed, surrounded by life-support equipment, more scared than she'd ever been in her life.

She should have seen this coming. But even if she had, what could she have done differently? By the time Irene was tuned in to her relationship with Kirby, it was too late to pull back and play it safe. Sam supposed the only thing she could have done was pretend Kirby didn't exist. If she had never mentioned that name, Irene might have had suspicions, but they would have been of a totally different nature. Something like drugs, or a boyfriend. Those things, Sam could have handled. This wasn't so easy.

In fact, it was impossible. Exactly what she feared when she told Kirby she wasn't ready to come out to friends. Why she'd been so uncomfortable about seeing Julie Wilde at the party. She knew her mother, and she knew the risks. She'd gambled, and she'd lost. Now she'd have to pay.

Sobbing, Sam leaned forward and covered her face with her hands. It took a minute for her to get her emotions under control, but when she wiped her eyes on her sleeve and opened them, nothing had changed.

Sam leaned back into the chair, and sighed, defeated. "I promise, Mom," she whispered.

CHAPTER NINETEEN

Present Day

When blinking didn't clear her vision, Sam squinted, and as she peered across the room, Kirby was still there, sitting at a conference table at the Saxton Pavilion. "I'm sorry. I'm looking for Harry Johnson," she said as she turned to leave.

But Kirby's voice caught her, pulled her back. "Harry's sick. I'm filling in for him."

Sam looked at Kirby, still as beautiful, with all those papers spread out on the table. "You're an attorney?"

"Yes. *Your* attorney, apparently. If you're Dr. Samantha Brooks."

Kirby was her attorney. Wow. The words echoed in her head as Sam walked slowly into the room, placed her briefcase on a chair across from Kirby, and stood for a moment behind a conference-table chair, using its large bulk to shield her from her own emotions and its strength to keep her upright. "I am." In spite of her shock, Sam smiled. "You made it to law school," she said softly.

For a moment they studied each other, and Sam realized that Kirby still had the ability to mesmerize her. Over the years she'd often wondered if she'd imagined that power Kirby had, because she'd never experienced anything like it again. As time passed and the sharp edges of her memory were blunted, she rationalized that it really wasn't as amazing as she remembered it.

Now she knew she'd been lying to herself. Kirby still had the same intoxicating effect on her. Taking a breath, Sam wiped her palms on her pants and willed herself to be calm. Sam was older now, not the inexperienced college student who'd experimented with the first woman who'd hit on her. Yes, Kirby looked the same, but Sam was a much different woman than she'd been then.

"I did," Kirby said, matter-of-factly. "Can you take a seat? I'd like to get started."

"Wow. Hi," Sam said with little chuckle. "Sorry. This is…a surprise, to say the least." Sam was glad for the chair to support her because she was really off kilter.

Kirby nodded and puckered her lips. "I'll say."

Pulling the chair out, Sam seated herself across from Kirby and fumbled with her briefcase as she set it before her on the table.

"How are you? You look…really great," Sam commented as she searched for something, although she wasn't sure quite what she needed. A portfolio and a pen seemed reasonable, so she took them to the table and then rested her sweaty palms in her lap.

Kirby gave a half nod. "You do, too."

Suddenly, Sam couldn't stop talking. "No, you really do. You're the only fifty-year-old woman I know who looks thinner than she did in college."

"Don't remind me. But the truth is, I was too heavy then."

"I thought you were perfect." Sam sighed, as she thought of how amazing Kirby's body had been. She had been sculpted like a statue, her body built in the weight room as she prepared to be the best shortstop she could be. Kirby's comment drew her back.

"Well, you look great, too," Kirby said, but unlike Sam, who was staring like a star-struck teenager, Kirby was now shuffling papers, preparing to steer the conversation to the matter that brought them together. Sure enough, before Sam could say another word, ask about the life she'd been living, Kirby met her eyes again and spoke.

"I am an attorney representing the insurance company. The attorney who was supposed to be here today had an emergency, and it looks like I'll be in charge of this case for the duration." She paused, allowing the words to set in. "Are you entirely comfortable with that change?"

Shocked by the question, Sam thought for a moment. If Kirby was her attorney, she'd have to work pretty closely with her. And based on her initial reaction to seeing her, that might prove difficult. For Kirby as well. She had a job to do. Would her own professionalism be compromised by lingering anger or resentment for how callously Sam had ended their relationship?

Sam thought for another second, remembering the girl she'd known. Her looks didn't hurt, but more important, Kirby had been efficient, and organized, and so very intelligent. Sweet, and kind. Sam bet she was fabulous at her job. Kirby had always exuded confidence, and Sam saw it now. She owned this conference room.

"The Kirby I once knew was an amazing woman. I suspect she's great at her job, so I would feel very comfortable with her—with you—representing me. Are you okay with this? You didn't know it was me, did you?" If Kirby had been surprised to see her when she'd walked into the room, she hid it well. Her facial expression hadn't changed at all, and her posture was perfect. Erect, professional. Even the way she held her pen, with her wrist slightly cocked, seemed practiced.

"No clue," Kirby said. "In fact, I must apologize. I was at the beach all day yesterday, and I left my phone at my parents' condo. I didn't get the message about Harry until very late, and by the time I got home last night, I didn't have much time to prepare. I was hoping to use our hour together today to go over some basics of the case, clear up any questions, and then we'll arrange another meeting to review your testimony. The deposition is scheduled for six weeks from now, so we don't have much time."

"I'm sure it'll be fine. I don't think we have much to prepare. But you feel comfortable with this? With me?"

"Absolutely," Kirby said, her gaze cold, steely.

"Okay. I guess that's settled," Sam said, wishing she could be so calm.

"Are you nervous?"

Sam shrugged, not willing to admit it. "Should I be?"

"No. Have you ever been involved in a lawsuit before?"

"No," Sam said with a shake of her head.

"Lucky for you. I'll go through the entire process with you, so you'll know what to expect. I don't like surprises. Okay?"

Sam nodded, and Kirby pressed on. "I'm going to give you all the documents you need to review. I'm sure someone already gave you a copy of the hospital record." Kirby went on to produce another file and pushed it across the table to Sam. "Destroy whatever you have. You don't need it. This file is now your Bible. Everything you need to know for this deposition is in this folder. Protect the patient's privacy, please. That means lock this in your filing cabinet, or your closet, or wherever a curious eye can't see it."

"Okay." Sam nodded as she tried to take it all in. Truthfully, she was still spinning from seeing Kirby. Actually comprehending her words was a bit much to expect.

"Do you remember anything about this case?"

"Actually, I do."

Kirby's arched brow conveyed a message of disbelief. "It was a long time ago."

"The events were memorable."

"Okay. I don't need to hear about them today. We'll go over everything at the next meeting. Today is about getting you prepared. Does that sound okay?"

Not really, but Kirby was the expert. "Yes."

"I need a few things from you. First, your resume."

Sam shook her head. "Kirby, I've had the same job for twenty years. I don't think I've updated my resume since residency."

Frowning, she glared at Sam. "Well, it's time, then. If we don't give it to the opposing counsel, they'll wonder why. They'll think you didn't complete your residency or never graduated from medical school." Kirby paused. "You did, by the way, didn't you?"

Sam shot her a scowl to match her own. "Finish school and residency? Yes, I did."

Kirby smirked back. "Okay. Just checking. Please get that to me as soon as you can. Next, I need you to refrain from discussing the case with anyone, especially the other defendants. Namely," Kirby referred to her paperwork, "Dr. Kimberly Perkins and Dr. Oscar Klinger."

"Okay, sure," Sam said, thinking Kirby was being a bit paranoid.

Kirby must have detected her attitude. "Seriously, Sam. You seem to be the least culpable party here, which is most likely why you haven't been named. But one of these two could throw you under the bus to save themselves. You have nothing to gain from talking to them, and a whole lot to lose."

Sam sighed, relieved. It was nice to hear from the expert that she wasn't culpable. Or, at least, she was the least culpable. "You really think so? I won't be sued?"

"They can do what they want, but Pennsylvania requires a plaintiff to have an expert opinion supporting the claim of malpractice. I imagine they don't have that at this point. Let's not give them any reason to dig further."

Sam digested that good news.

"You did a commendable job with this patient, Sam. Both times you saw him you advocated for him, and it seems the pediatrician really missed an opportunity to do that on the first ER visit. I'm sure that's why she's being named. But it's not a slam-dunk case against her, either. The parents signed him out against your advice, and thankfully, you documented everything quite thoroughly."

"The radiologist?" Sam asked.

"Yeah. That's a tough one. It's not easy to defend misreading a CT can."

Sam understood that Kirby probably couldn't talk much about the other physicians, aside from what Sam already knew, so she didn't press her.

"Well, in his defense, I didn't see the abscess on the initial CT either. It was small."

"You remember quite a bit," Kirby said as she sat back and studied Sam.

"It was an unusual case. But the way it played out was really memorable. I think there really was…" Sam stopped herself. She was about to tell Kirby she thought an angel had intervened, but she didn't want Kirby to think she was crazy.

"What?" Kirby pressed her, but Sam was reluctant to speak her mind.

"Nothing. I just remember seeing the CT scan and not spotting the abscess."

Kirby nodded. "That brings us to my next request. You have an electronic fingerprint, Sam. If this case progresses, the plaintiff's attorney will be looking for little things like that. Under no circumstance, no matter how tempting it might be, should you look at this patient's chart on the hospital computer system. Not even a little peek. Because the first thing they will ask you is why, and no matter how you answer, they will twist it to make you look bad."

Sam had to confess she'd been tempted to go back into the chart after Julie had told her the news about the lawsuit. She now said a silent prayer of thanks that she'd been able to resist the urge. "Good thing,"

Kirby said when she told her, and it was the first time Kirby smiled since Sam walked into the room.

Suddenly, the opening bars of "Bohemian Rhapsody" began playing from within Sam's briefcase. "Kirby, excuse me. I need to take that. It's my son." Pulling the phone from her bag, Sam slid her finger across the screen and answered. "Hey, what's up?" She looked away, toward the window, where sunlight seeped through the slats of the blinds.

"I just found out we need money for new lifeguard uniforms. We have to take it to the meeting today," Charlie informed her.

"There's money in the drawer."

"We won't have time to go home after school and make it back in time for the meeting. Can you drop it off at school?" His voice was pleading.

"How much?" Sam pursed her lips as she prepared for battle.

"Probably a lot. Can you just give me a check?"

Sam closed her eyes. "Charlie, I am not giving you a blank check. What are we talking here? Bathing suit, T-shirt, hoodie? A hundred bucks, tops."

"We should have two, so we don't have to do laundry every day."

"You made three thousand dollars last summer. You are not going to spend three hundred of it on uniforms. If you don't feel like doing laundry, wear it dirty. Or wear last year's."

He sighed. "Fine. Will you drop the money off?"

"I'll leave it in your car."

"Thanks, Mom."

"You're welcome. Love you."

"Love you, too."

As Sam hung up the phone, she found Kirby laughing. "Adventures in parenting, huh?"

Shaking her head, Sam sighed. "Shit. You have no idea."

Kirby nodded. "Actually, I do," she said, and Sam seemed to detect Kirby softening just a little. She'd been totally professional during their meeting, but suddenly, she became human again, and Sam was pleasantly surprised.

"You have kids?" Sam asked as she leaned forward just a bit.

Smiling, Kirby seemed to relax as she replied. "Two."

"How wonderful!" Sam said softly, truly meaning it.

"How about you?" Kirby questioned. "Did you get all five of them?"

Sam shook her head. "No, just two. Boys. And that's about all I can handle. How about you? Boys, girls, one of each?"

"One of each," she said, and Sam didn't have a hard time imagining her with kids. She had always been so patient and sweet, although lately, what Sam found she needed when it came to her children was more of an iron fist.

"How old?"

"Kaitlyn is nineteen and just finished her first year at Penn State. Kyle is eighteen and about to graduate from high school."

Sam smiled. "My boys are twins. They're graduating in a couple of weeks. And one of them is heading to Penn State."

"Great school," she said. "My ex, their other mother, is an alum, so both kids wanted to go there. How can I argue? She got a great education, and she's done well in the world."

"I agree. I'm a little worried because it's just such a big campus, but he's got a good head on his shoulders, and he'll do okay. Plus, he knows a whole bunch of kids there. That makes it easier."

"Absolutely. Where's the other guy going?"

Sam beamed with pride. "Scranton."

Kirby smiled back. "Ah, let me guess. Pre-med."

"One out of two isn't bad."

"Pictures?" Kirby asked, and Sam immediately began scrolling through her phone.

Holding her phone to her chest, Sam looked at Kirby. "Do you want me to start with baby pictures? Or something more recent?"

Kirby chuckled. "Don't forget, I have two kids as well. We could be here all night."

"Fair enough. How about graduation pictures?" Sam asked as she handed Kirby her phone.

"This is Danny, my future doctor."

"He looks like you."

"Yes, quite a bit. Tall and thin, too, just like I was at eighteen. If you scroll, you'll find Charlie."

Kirby swiped her finger across the screen, and the next image popped into view. "So who's this one's mom?" she asked.

"Right? They're total opposites."

"What's Charlie's plan, if not medicine?"

"Right now, he's thinking game-show host. If that doesn't work out, he'd consider taking the job as commissioner of the NFL."

"It's good to have options," Kirby said with puckered lips as she handed the phone back and began scrolling through hers.

After handing it to Sam, she sat back in the chair. "This is yesterday, at my parents' beach house."

Sam looked at two tall, dark-haired kids. "Wow, Kirby. What gorgeous kids. They both look like you." Sam wasn't sure why, but when Kirby told her she had kids, she'd assumed Kirby adopted them. It was difficult to imagine her pregnant, but looking at the picture, she definitely saw a biological connection.

"Thanks. They're very much like me, too. Serious, but able to have fun once in a while."

Sam couldn't help but think back to some of those fun times, and she flushed. To cover her reaction, she asked a question. "Was it hard to let Kaitlyn go?"

"You have no idea," she said, then paused. "Or actually, I guess you do. It's tough. Really, the hardest thing ever."

"Even Scranton seems too far away," Sam admitted.

"If it helps, you can track them constantly. They're never without their cell phones."

"Yes. I do that now. What are their future plans?" Sam asked as she leaned back in her chair.

"Kait wants to go to law school and save the world, just like her other mother. Kyle just wants to be filthy rich. I'd don't think he's figured out how just yet."

"Are you still close with your ex?"

Kirby shrugged. "We're civil, because of them, but..."

Sam was sympathetic. "I'm sorry, Kirby. That sounds rough."

Waving a dismissive hand, she shook her head. "It's fine. We've been split for a few years, so it's all good now."

"How did your kids handle that?"

Kirby seemed to weigh her answer, or perhaps whether to answer the question at all. "I'm sorry," Sam said after a moment. "It's not my business."

Holding up a hand, Kirby halted Sam's protest. "It's okay. They were great about it. They're pretty open-minded kids, and I think they saw that we weren't happy anymore. I don't think they were surprised by the news when we told them we were splitting up."

"And you're both in Harrisburg?"

"Essentially. The suburbs. She's only ten minutes from me, so it's easy on the kids."

They were quiet for a moment, and Sam debated if she should say anything more. They'd shared a great deal of personal information, so what was one more detail? "Doug and I live in adjacent houses. It makes it much easier."

Kirby's eyes opened wide at the information. "You're divorced?"

Sam rolled her eyes. "I'm Catholic, Kirby. I can't get divorced. We're separated."

Kirby's face returned to that unreadable expression. "Is this something recent?"

"Uh, like seventeen years."

Kirby bit her lip, and Sam could see the laughter in her eyes. "You've been separated for seventeen years and haven't gotten a divorce?"

"It's complicated," Sam said, but it really wasn't. Their separation was amicable, and neither she nor Doug had ever pushed it past that. Sam kept the house, which had once been owned by her mom's neighbors, Helen and Nick Rule, and Doug moved out. In truth, Sam had just been so relieved to be free, to have her sons and her life to herself, that she didn't need or ask for anything else. And her mother, who'd still been alive then, had of course encouraged her to just let it be. And so months had become years, and when her mom died a decade later, Doug moved into her mom's house, and they shared the parenting of their sons and barbequed together in the backyard, and went back to their own houses at night.

"Life tends to be," Kirby said, and Sam felt she somehow understood.

They were quiet for a moment, and then Kirby reached into her portfolio and pulled out a business card. Picking up her pen, she flipped the card over and wrote something on it. When she spoke again, her tone was softer than it had been. "Here are my office phone and my email, and my cell number's on the back. Do you have your schedule, so we can set up our next meeting?"

Sam frowned. "I'm leaving in a couple of weeks for vacation. Can we wait until I get back?"

Kirby looked at her calendar. "What day is that?"

Sam told her.

"Yikes," she said. "That's cutting it close."

"You said I don't have anything to worry about."

Shaking her head, Kirby frowned. "That doesn't mean we don't have to prepare."

"I'll come in the day I get home."

The lawyer was back. "You'll have to. Can we touch base by phone?"

Sam shrugged. She truly wasn't sure. "I don't know what kind of service I'll have. We're going out West, national-park hopping."

Kirby's eyebrow shot up. "Okay, then. Let me see if I can pull my thoughts together in the next few days, and I'll email you. Hopefully, we won't have any issues."

"Will you call me?"

"I can. Or email."

Sam liked the idea of talking to Kirby, but she shared both contacts.

"Okay. I guess we're done," Kirby said with a sigh. Leaning back in her chair, she tilted her head and studied Sam. "It was really nice to see you again, Sam. Not ideal circumstances, but still nice. And I'm incredibly jealous about your trip. What parks are you going to?"

Sam told her the plans.

"I'm so jealous."

Sam put on a blank face. "I hear it's not that amazing."

"I've been there. It is."

They spent a few more minutes talking about Sam's trip before they said their good-byes.

They both stood, and Kirby offered her hand across the table.

"Thank you," Sam said. "I feel good about this. I'm really happy it's you that's representing me. I'm in good hands."

"See you in a few weeks," Kirby said as Sam walked out the door.

Measuring her breaths, Sam walked slowly and deliberately to the car, waiting until she was seated behind the wheel of the Benz before she took out her phone.

"Holy fuck. You will not believe what just happened to me."

"Your best friend was nominated for a great award, and you're calling to congratulate him?" Jim said with a bounce in his voice that told her he wasn't angry about her recent silence.

"No, not that. Can you stop playing with lab rats for a minute and talk, or does the future of the world depend on whatever experiment you're doing right now?"

He sighed dramatically. "I guess I can take a break. What's going on?"

"Jim, I'm getting sued. Well, deposed anyway. That's why I haven't called—I've been preoccupied."

"I'm sorry, Sam. That has to be a scary feeling."

Sam sighed at the mental suffering she'd done for the past week. As hard as she'd tried, she'd found it difficult to think of anything besides this meeting. "It truly is. And it's just started. This morning, I had to meet with my attorney to go over the case."

"How'd it go?"

"Jim, Kirby is my attorney."

Jim was silent, and then he exploded. "Shut up! Kirby—the Kirby? From college?"

"She's the one." Sam sighed again.

"Oh, Samantha. That's awful. You did her dirty. Can you switch lawyers?"

He was as dramatic as always, and Sam just listened as he went on. "She has to drop off this case. It's unethical, or possibly even illegal. You cannot have your entire professional future depending on someone you practically left at the altar. She must hate you."

"We dated for about three days. And she actually seemed very professional." Sam told him the story of how she'd reconnected with Kirby at the Saxton Pavilion.

Jim sounded skeptical. "Never trust a former lover."

"You sound so experienced."

"The stories I could tell you, Sam. Uh!"

Sam couldn't help laughing. "It was strange, Jim. Like I'd just seen her yesterday. Don't get me wrong. It was awkward for a few minutes, but then, once we started talking, we just clicked. Again."

"Is she still drop-dead gorgeous?"

Sam didn't hesitate. "Uh-huh."

"Is this going to be a problem? You'll have to work pretty closely with her. I remember when I was sued, I had months and months of meetings, and testimony, and it just never ended."

"I don't think it'll be a problem. I'm a big girl."

"That's what I'm afraid of. You know what it's all about now, and if you're thinking of hot lesbian sex with your attorney, you may be too distracted to defend yourself."

Sam tried not to laugh. "That's not going to happen," she said, although she wasn't sure. After all these years, she still thought of Kirby, and that was before seeing her again. Now…Sam wasn't positive she could steer the direction of her thoughts.

"You *are* human."

"Jim, I need a little help here. You're not helping."

"I'm sorry, Sam. Was it bad? Seeing her?"

Sam suddenly re-experienced the emotions of a lifetime ago and cleared her throat. "It brought back some bad memories. That was a hard time in my life, Jim. Stressful. And I think I took it out on her. But I've spent my entire life avoiding my feelings. I just focused on work or other things. Seeing her today was hard. I was in love with her. And not only did I ditch her when things got difficult, but I really did a job on my own heart, too. And now I suddenly feel like shit all over again."

"Don't kick yourself too much. Hard is an understatement for what you were dealing with. Maybe your relationship with Kirby would have flourished under different circumstances, and maybe it was just a fling that would have fizzled no matter what happened. But you couldn't worry about it back then. That was another time. It was hard to be gay. Plus, you had to take care of your mom, and you did. She lived another twenty years, Sam. She got to see you become a doctor. She had the chance to be a grandmother." He paused, and Sam didn't reply. "You did what you had to, and it was the right thing. But maybe now you need a little closure."

"What does that mean?"

"Maybe you need to apologize. I mean, I know you told her your mom was sick, but I'm not sure she really understood what that meant to you. What your *mom* meant to you. So maybe you should tell her."

Jim was wrong, but he might be right, too. Sam had no question Kirby knew exactly what Sam was dealing with when her mom was sick. Kirby had just understood her and was so damn perceptive and intelligent. It was probably why she'd done what Sam asked of her and stayed away. Yet, maybe telling Kirby how sorry she was would at least make Sam feel better.

Choosing the right course of action seemed no easier now than it had back then, and she told Jim so.

"You'll figure it out, Sam. You're a good person."

"You'd say that no matter what, wouldn't you?"

"You know me too well!" He laughed. "Remember when we said we'd get married if we were still single at thirty?"

"I do."

"Thirty seems so long ago, doesn't it?" he asked.

"It is a long time ago. I think we're the same people, though, right? We haven't changed much, except for you. You're an award-winning cancer researcher. What's this all about?"

Jim told Sam he'd won an award for his work on flow cytometry in diagnosing leukemia, and it would be presented in Las Vegas, and Sam was invited. She immediately put the date into her calendar, and they promised to catch up soon.

CHAPTER TWENTY

Sam's head was still spinning a few hours later when she arrived at the hospital. After changing into scrubs, Sam donned her white lab coat and headed into the ER. A few people greeted her as she walked toward the fishbowl, the glass-enclosed central office area where the providers worked during their shifts. Julie looked up with an expression of concern as she entered.

"How'd it go?"

The last thing Sam wanted was to tell Julie she'd seen Kirby, but how could she not? Within a few days, she was sure Julie would have some sort of communication from Kirby, so she might as well tell her now and get it over with.

"I'm glad you're sitting," she said.

"What happened?"

"You will never in a million years guess the name of the attorney representing me."

Julie pursed her lips. "Tell me."

"Kirby Fielding."

Julie's eyes flew open. "Kirby? Holy shit, Sam. How'd that go?"

"Much better than it probably should have. Kirby always was a class act." Sam nodded. "She still is."

"I never really knew what happened between the two of you. But I suspect it didn't end well."

Sam sighed. "I just...wasn't ready. I was overwhelmed by everything that was happening in my life, and I needed to concentrate on medical school. I didn't need any distractions. And Kirby was definitely a distraction."

"No distraction now, though?" she asked as she eyed Sam suspiciously.

Sam had spent the intervening hours between the meeting and her ER shift thinking of little else. In the end, she trusted Kirby to work hard to defend her, and that was all that mattered. "How could I not be distracted? But Kirby is a pro, and it'll be fine." Sam truly believed that.

Julie was silent, then nodded. "Room four is a traumatic bleed, awake with normal vitals, waiting on neurosurgery. All the paperwork is done. Room five...I'm not sure. My gut is telling me to admit this one. Indigestion and back pain. Normal EKG. I'm waiting on labs— cardiac and GI. I'd appreciate your opinion on her, but she's going to be a sign-out."

"How old?"

"Fifty."

Sam cringed. Definitely old enough to get into heart trouble, she thought as she studied the computer screen that told her a little about each of the ten patients currently in the ER. In addition to the two Julie had mentioned, three others were discharged or admitted, the PA was seeing three, and only two were left for Sam to treat.

"It looks manageable," she observed. "Let me see the indigestion now."

"There's an overdose, too. He's stable. I saved him for you."

Sam nodded. She'd spearheaded the hospital warm-handoff program, wrote the policies herself, and worked with the county DA and other community leaders in trying to reduce overdose deaths. She never minded picking up those cases.

Sam spoke with the woman with indigestion and examined her, agreeing with Julie. No matter what the labs showed, she wasn't taking a chance with that patient. She'd admit her and let the hospitalist come down to the ER and battle it out if they didn't like it. After checking on the labs, which were still pending, Sam knocked on the door of the patient who'd overdosed on heroin and stepped into the room.

"What's going on?" Sam asked after introducing herself.

"I guess I got some bad dope. Probably fentanyl."

Sam nodded. That was a good bet. Fentanyl was found in the blood of most overdose patients, because it was much more powerful than heroin, and cheaper. Dealers were mixing the two drugs in random combinations, and patients didn't know what they were getting and often took too much.

After examining him, Sam pulled up a chair next to his bed. "So, Anthony, talk to me. How many times have you OD'd?"

He puffed out his cheeks and slowly blew all the air from his lungs. "I don't know. Maybe seven? I'm losing count," he said with a mirthless laugh. "The first time was with my mom's boyfriend. He didn't make it."

"And that was?"

"When I was fourteen."

Sam cringed. At fourteen, her boys had their noses in books and spent their free time at the library, just like she had. But Sam supposed Anthony was just mimicking his parent, too. "Even cats have only nine lives. You're running out." She tried to keep her tone light, non-threatening.

"Don't I know it, Doc."

"How many times have you been to rehab?" she asked gently.

"A bunch. I do good, you know, for a little while. Then I see somebody from the old days, or something happens, and I feel like—what's the point?"

"Did you ever try Suboxone?"

"Off the street, when I couldn't get dope."

"How'd you feel?"

"It didn't get me high. Just okay."

"So do you want to get high, or do you just want to stay alive?"

"That's the thing. I like getting high. And I definitely don't like getting dope-sick. But sometimes I just don't think there's a point to being alive anymore." The emptiness in his voice rattled Sam. He was only a few months older than her twins. How could her sons, growing up just a few miles away, have such different realities from this young man? Not that they didn't deserve to have good parents—but didn't this boy, too? What had he done to deserve his horrific social situation? At times like this she found her faith challenged and was at a loss as to what she could do for him.

"I'm glad you're planning to talk to the recovery specialist. He might be able to help you figure some things out. Can I do anything for you right now to make you feel a little better while you're waiting? I have a secret stash of ice cream in the back."

"Chocolate?"

Sam winked at him. "Of course," she said, and his grin matched her own.

It took her only a minute to reach the physicians' lounge and get the ice-cream cup, and another to return to the ER. When she arrived at Anthony's room, he was gone. Sam blew out a loud breath and said a prayer to St. Jude, the Patron Saint of Lost Causes, that he didn't come back dead.

A few moments later she was in the fishbowl again, where her phone beeped, letting her know she'd missed a text. It was from Teddy. *How'd the thingy go today? Call me after work. I'll be up.*

Sam chuckled. She was going through one of the most stressful ordeals of her life, but leave it to Teddy to call it a *thingy*. Sam would call her, as she often did on her way home. Since Teddy had taken over in marketing at the family car dealership, she didn't usually begin her day until ten or so and was usually still awake at midnight, when Sam finished work. Talking to Teddy was always refreshing and helped Sam unwind after her shift. She texted a thumbs-up, then sent a text to both her sons, asking them to let her know when they were home from their meeting. Then she ate the ice cream.

Usually her job didn't feel like work. It was fun. She helped people, saw and did exciting things, and the time flew by. This shift was no different, and Sam was surprised when her relief greeted her at eleven that night, and a few minutes later she was out the door. Thanks to a remote log-in system, she could complete her charts from home the next morning, after she'd gotten the boys off to school. Or, if she wanted to, she'd come in early for her next shift and finish them then. One of the other things she loved most about her job was the pay. She was compensated well for her work, and the money allowed her to live a great life and work only part-time. It was her solution to burn-out and work-life balance.

"What's up?" Teddy asked her when she called her a few minutes later.

"You won't even believe it."

"What? Did you lose your lawsuit?"

"No. I just met with my lawyer today. My lawyer, Kirby Fielding."

"Shut the fuck up."

"Right?"

"Is she still hot?"

Sam smiled. Good old Teddy. "She's fifty, just like us."

"That's a good thing. I don't know if you could concentrate if she was still hot."

Sam didn't tell her just how hot Kirby still was because, really, what did it matter?

"How'd you end up with her?"

Sam told her the story, and at the end, Teddy whistled. "This seems like rotten luck."

Sam told her she thought it would be fine.

"I hope so. Listen, I need to ask you something. It's the Wilkes Athletics Golf Tournament this Friday, and I need a fourth. We had to fire someone in the auto-body department, so we're down one. The business is a sponsor, so there's no cost to you. You can buy the mulligans, though."

"What time?"

Teddy gave her the details, but Sam didn't even have to consult her calendar. Since she worked only twenty hours a week, it was easy to keep track of her schedule. "I'll count you in."

"Sounds like a plan," Sam replied, and then they chatted for a few minutes more before Sam pulled into the driveway.

Quietly, she made her way into the house and into the master suite, where she threw her clothes into the hamper and showered. When she was in her jammies, she walked across the hall to the boys' rooms and peeked in. Either they were sleeping or faking it well, but either way, they were safe. In the kitchen, she poured herself half a glass of wine and then grabbed the same book she hadn't been able to concentrate on earlier and walked out to her sunroom.

It was peaceful out here—quiet, decorated in soothing shades of green—and Sam could look out at the moon and stars. The only house she could see was her parents', where her estranged husband now lived.

Doug's lights were on, and she knew he'd be up late answering emails and reading whatever journal had been delivered with the day's mail. When she saw him next, probably at dinner tomorrow, he'd fill her in on what she should read and what wasn't worth her time. Although he'd specialized in surgery and critical care, many of the topics in his professional literature crossed over into emergency medicine, and Sam still enjoyed their conversations. As a young man, if Doug had been interested in accounting or the arts or anything other than medicine, it never would have worked between them, even for the short time Sam had tried. But she supposed it was just meant to be.

She often wondered if she'd ruined him when she left him, when she just couldn't fake it anymore and admitted she really was gay. Sam had told him about Kirby when he'd asked her out again, in medical school, and Doug had been able to convince her that it was completely normal for young women to experiment with other women. And because she'd wanted to believe that theory, Sam had allowed herself to be convinced. Being with him, though, after Kirby, was almost torture, and he was smart enough to know it.

After all these years, though, Sam still didn't understand why he still wanted her. Jim had suggested that Doug was gay, too, but Sam didn't really think so. He was almost disconnected from the world, and since autism and its many variants had become so prevalent, Sam suspected Doug might have just a touch of it in his genes. It was a mystery, and Sam wondered why she still tried to figure things out, when she knew there were sometimes simply no answers. He was happy, she was happy, the boys were thriving, and the hows and the whys were just not that important.

As she sipped her wine, her thoughts shifted from Doug to Kirby. Where was she now—had she stayed in Kingston because she had work to do here, or headed back to Harrisburg? She hadn't thought to ask. Was she with someone, in a serious relationship, or like Sam, did she find involvement difficult with her family commitments?

In the early days after she'd left Doug, Sam didn't even think of dating. Of course, as a mother of one-year-old twins, she didn't think of much. Her life was one loop of activity. Eat, sleep, work, feed babies, change diapers, wash laundry. Repeat. When they were three, Sam started dating a friend of Teddy, a teacher named Wendy who shared many of Sam's passions. Yet even though they had fun together, and great sex, Sam found it a chore to carve out time for herself when that meant being away from her sons, and the relationship failed.

When the boys started kindergarten, Sam began dating a Realtor, which worked out well. Her name was Olivia, and she didn't mind seeing Sam in the mornings after the boys went off to school. It was a perfect arrangement for a few years, until Olivia had a job opportunity with her company and moved to Florida. They'd tried the long-distance thing for a while, but ultimately, Liv had met another woman, and that was that.

It had gone on like that for years, with semi-serious relationships scheduled around her life as a physician and mother, and Sam had been content. With her boys getting ready to leave for college, she wondered at the cosmic meaning of meeting Kirby again. Was it fate? Time for a change in her life, time to finally give herself the gift of someone to truly care for her, as Kirby once had? Was Kirby that one? Did they have a chance, after all the time that passed, or would it end badly, again?

Sam supposed she was getting ahead of herself, but when it came to Kirby, she'd never been very rational.

Wow, had she looked amazing. Sam knew gray hairs were woven through her blond strands, saw the wrinkles creeping into the corners of her eyes, felt the extra pounds around the middle—but Kirby seemed to defy the laws of aging. Perhaps it was her darker skin, or maybe just blessed genetics, but whatever it was, the years had been kind to her.

A yawn escaped, and Sam decided to call it a night.

As usual, she was up early and had breakfast ready when Charlie plopped down in his favorite kitchen chair after swiping three pieces of French toast from the warmer. "Thanks for the money," he said as he poured fruit over the top.

"Is there change?" she asked over the top of her coffee mug.

"It's in the drawer," he mumbled while he chewed.

"What's your day look like?" she asked.

"Nothing notable. How about you?"

"I'm going to go play nine this morning. Eighteen, if I'm playing well. Teddy asked me to be her fourth in a tournament on Friday, and I don't want to embarrass myself."

As he ate, he scrolled through his phone. "Nice weather for golf. High of eighty. No chance of rain."

"Does it hold out all week?"

He gave her the forecast. "Rain Friday, with thunderstorms."

Sam closed her eyes. Fun times.

In the clubhouse at the Wyoming Valley Country Club, Sam met up with two ladies from her league and joined them for her round. She'd been out to play a dozen times already, but never more than nine holes. She didn't like to push herself early in the season. Her boys hated golf, but when they were out of school, she'd drag them out, and she'd hook up with Teddy, who was also a member of the club, and get in a few rounds a week. For now, though, she was happy to swing the club.

"Your game looks good, Sam, for someone who doesn't play over the winter," one of the ladies commented. Sam wasn't sure if that was a compliment about her game or a criticism of her lifestyle, so she ignored the remark. "I'm in a tournament Friday."

"Oh, these tournaments! They're always closing the course, and I'm getting tired of it."

Sam shrugged. Doing just that brought in a ton of revenue to the club and helped keep her expenses down. It required a little planning on her part, but she didn't mind. She enjoyed the break in cost. After her round, she left her clubs with the pro, who promised to have new grips on them by the next day, and headed toward home.

Her first stop was Dundee Gardens, where she bought plants. She still landscaped the beds at Doug's house, plus her own, and her parents' graves. Her boys didn't enjoy gardening like she did, but they didn't mind doing the heavy work for her. Sam dug holes and bedded the plants, but the boys mulched and raked and hauled away the detritus when she finished. After ordering a truck of mulch for delivery, Sam stopped at Weis Market and picked up the food she'd need for grilling. She'd texted Doug, and as she'd expected, he wanted to share dinner with her and the boys.

They were home when she arrived, and after kissing them both, she started dinner. At six, they all walked across the yard to Doug's, and Sam turned on the grill while they carried all the food inside. Charlie emerged with plates and a pitcher of tea, and then Doug came out and went to work. He told her about his most recent meeting, and the journal articles she should read, and the plans the medical school was making for training students to treat opioid-addicted patients. The boys joined in, and Sam found it interesting that Charlie knew so much medicine, yet wanted to be the next Alex Trebek. Danny was so far ahead of the game Sam knew he'd do well. Like her, he worked in the ER, in the same job she'd had when she was his age. Danny had been there since the day he turned sixteen.

The boys cleared the table and began throwing a Frisbee while Sam and Doug talked. "I didn't want to ask in front of the boys, but how'd the deposition go?"

She told him about Kirby, and he didn't seem shocked.

"I think you have unfinished business with her, Sam."

"Hmm. It's an interesting thought."

"Think about it. She's your gold standard."

Sam couldn't help laughing at his ability to cut to the heart of the matter. "It was a long time ago."

"And think about this. You believe in angels, and fate, and craziness like that. Your mom got sick, and that caused you to lose Kirby. Now your lawyer got sick, and it brought you back to her."

Sam hadn't thought of that, but it was an interesting observation. Kind of like Tara's grandmother, the almost-nun.

"If the circumstances were different, if your mom weren't sick and you weren't so scared, and vulnerable, and Catholic...you wouldn't have ended things. Maybe the universe is trying to make things right."

"I can't go backward."

"Who says it would be backward? You're just meeting her farther along the same road. She's not the same person she was then, either. You've both changed, but truthfully, Sam—how much do any of us change? We might be older and grayer, with more sophisticated palates and polished opinions, but who we are is the same. You clicked with her once, and I'd bet you still do."

Sam considered what he'd said. Through the years, she'd thought about Kirby from time to time, wondering what she'd done with her life, always feeling guilty about the way things had ended between them. No matter what, Jim was right. She owed her an apology. And maybe they could be friends again.

Sometimes, Sam had trouble remembering what she'd even liked about Kirby, and she sometimes thought she'd imagined it all. Their connection was intangible, which made it so much more difficult to explain, even to herself. If they'd been softball buddies, or lab partners, or something else, Sam could think of that commonality and understand their link. But it wasn't—it was just a feeling, a joy and understanding, a link to another person that made Sam feel so alive. That Kirby could kiss her and melt her, and take her flying through the stratosphere as they made love—those were just bonuses.

They'd known each other for only a few short weeks. They'd met on a Tuesday, during softball tryouts. Four weeks later, also on a Tuesday, her mom had collapsed. The next day, Sam had ended it with

Kirby. Thirty days after Kirby had knocked her off her feet, Sam had said good-bye.

How much could she have really known her in that short time? It was such a tiny stretch of days in the course of her life. Sam had been on the earth nearly six hundred months, and Kirby had walked beside her for just one of them.

Yet it had been one of the best months. Her children were amazing, but with them, she was "Mom." She couldn't argue that her best moments as Sam had been in that thirty days with Kirby.

CHAPTER TWENTY-ONE

I'm too old to play golf in the rain, Sam thought as she pulled her SUV into the parking lot at the club on Friday morning and looked out at the fog-shrouded course. A line of evergreens between fairways was clipped by the mist, and even though the sky was quiet now, the forecast wasn't promising. As she walked toward the bag drop, she ran into a few people she knew and chatted about the weather, then found her clubs on one of the carts and drove to the practice area.

Protected by a waterproof jacket and pants, Sam started with a few putts, then chipped a dozen balls before pulling out her driver. As she approached the practice tee, she looked up and saw a ball soaring down the range, where it struck the flagpole a hundred yards away.

"Nice shot!" Sam said as she turned to congratulate the golfer who'd hit it.

Kirby. Sam swallowed as her heartbeat pulsed in her throat. "I should have known you'd be here." Sam spoke her thoughts aloud.

Kirby rested her club in front of her and leaned into it. "Why is that?" She looked so damn sexy, with her hair pulled up and her dark eyes peeking out from under the brim of a baseball cap.

Sam walked slowly toward her, their eyes locked, and she mimicked Kirby's pose. If she were smart, she'd make a joke right now. Laugh it off. Yet she couldn't think of a single retort that wouldn't sound lame. She opted for the truth. "You've been on my mind."

"Yeah," Kirby said, a soft smile lifting the corners of her sensual mouth.

Sam looked away. "I've tried very hard to not think of you for the last half of my lifetime, and now I find it impossible not to."

"Why do you think that is?"

Once again Sam looked at her. "I think it's just you, K. I've been disciplined in every aspect of my life, except when it came to you. With you, I just threw out the rulebook and let loose."

Kirby tilted her head. "Was that so bad, Sam?"

Before she could reply, a noise behind Kirby drew their attention. "Mom, are you ready?"

Sam recognized Kyle from his photo even before Kirby made the introduction.

His eyes flew open wide, and Sam had no doubt Kirby had told her son at least a little about their past. His reply confirmed her suspicions. "Oh, so *you're* the doctor. It's nice to meet you."

"Your mom tells me you're heading to Penn State in the fall," Sam told Kyle as a young woman appeared beside him. "What am I missing?" she asked the group.

After introducing her daughter, Kaitlyn, Kirby told them about Charlie's plans for college. "I'd love to meet him," Kyle told Sam. "Is he here?"

She grimaced. "No, unfortunately. We still have another week of school, so he's in class."

Kyle looked to Kirby. "Can we get together tomorrow, Mom? We don't have any plans, do we?"

Sam had to manually close her jaw as Kaitlyn added her opinion. "Yeah. That's a great idea. Maybe we can have breakfast together before we head home."

In all the times they'd been together, Sam had never seen Kirby speechless, until this moment, when she seemed to choke while formulating a response. Sam was about to rescue her with an excuse when, finally, she uttered a reply. "We'll talk about it later."

Ignoring his mother, Kyle turned to Sam. "That's code for *no*. It makes her seem more reasonable than an outright refusal would, so you're going to have to work on her, Dr. Brooks."

Did Sam want to work on her? Or should she let it go? She had to admit that the idea of seeing Kirby again was appealing. Especially with her kids in tow. That seemed much safer than seeing her alone. "My sons have their first day of work tomorrow, here—at the club pool. They have to be here at eleven. How would nine thirty work?

Breakfast at my house?" That would give them an hour to eat and talk before Danny and Charlie left for work. Enough time to get to know each other a little bit, but not so much to make it awkward if they all hated each other. That was hard to imagine, since Kirby's children seemed so nice.

"Hmm," Kirby replied.

Sam looked at Kyle. "There's a pretty cool mountain behind my house, and I hear you like to hike, so maybe that'll help persuade her."

"Hmm," Kirby murmured again. "Go on."

Sam laughed. "Stookey's?"

"For breakfast?"

"We're grown-ups. We can make the rules."

"Nine thirty, you say?" Kirby asked, and when Sam nodded, she turned to her kids. "Are you sure you want to get up that early? It's a chance to sleep late."

"We'll never sleep late at the hotel. It'll be too noisy. Let's do breakfast," Kaitlyn said.

"Okay." Kirby finally agreed, but even after all these years, Sam could tell she was hesitant.

"I'm going to hit a few balls, and I'll see you guys later, okay?" she said, knowing she'd try to catch Kirby after the tournament and give her a chance to back out of the breakfast invitation.

"See ya," Kaitlyn said.

"Bye," Kyle chimed in, and Kirby just waved. Sam thought she saw her taking a deep breath first. Or maybe Sam just imagined that's what she would have done.

Teddy found her a few minutes later as she was walking off the range. "Kirby's here," Sam said in greeting.

Teddy squinted at her and screwed up her mouth. "I know. I'm really sorry, Sam. I had no idea. I've played in this golf tournament for like twenty frickin' years, and I swear, she's never been here before."

Sam had been pondering the situation while swinging the club, and she remembered Kirby mentioning someone from Wilkes at the law firm whose space she was borrowing. "Maybe she's playing with someone else. She's with her kids, but I didn't ask who her fourth was."

"Wait…Kirby has kids, too? Is everyone a breeder now?"

"Fortunately, you're here to represent the holdouts."

"Yes, thankfully, I am. Are you ready? I think we're actually going to get this round of golf in."

Teddy was right. Although the mist barely cleared, the rain held off, and they finished the round. Sam looked for Kirby in the clubhouse and found her chatting with some women Sam recognized but had never formally met. Kirby introduced them, and after a moment, they excused themselves, leaving Sam alone with Kirby.

"How'd you hit 'em?" she asked.

"Okay. How about you?" She sipped from a tall glass of something that looked like Coke.

"Okay. I played with Teddy."

"I figured you would. I mean, why else would you be supporting Wilkes Athletics?"

"This is actually the first time I've played in this tournament. Teddy usually invites people from work, but this year one of them couldn't play. I was a sub."

"The ringer?" Kirby grinned.

"Hardly. Teddy says you don't usually participate. What made you decide to play this year?" Sam was curious about Kirby's sudden reappearance in Wilkes-Barre.

"Honestly? You."

"Me? But I told you, I've never played before."

"The first time I got that flyer for the tournament, I saw that Teddy was a sponsor. And that was enough to keep me away," Kirby explained.

Sam chuckled. "She doesn't hate you, Kirby."

"Despise. Is that a better word?"

"I think she was just hurt that you broke up with her, and she didn't know how to deal with her feelings. But she's grown up in the past twenty-something years and is an amazing person. I bet she'd love to talk to you and relive some of those old softball memories."

Kirby rolled her eyes.

"Should I invite her to breakfast?"

"Sam, I'm sorry about that. All I did was mention that I ran into you, and that we dated once, and my kids' imaginations ran amok. You *do not* have to cook us breakfast."

"I'd like to. But you seemed uncomfortable about the idea, so I actually sought you out so I could give you a chance to cancel. You can tell your kids I had a schedule conflict or something."

"You actually want to cook us breakfast?"

"Well…it's not you. I kind of like your kids."

Kirby swallowed a smile as she nodded. "I get that. I've been hearing that for twenty years. Somewhere along the line I ceased being Kirby and became their mom."

Sam felt the same way, but it shocked her to hear that Kirby suffered from a similar identity issue. "I'm really worried about what'll become of me when my kids leave for college."

Kirby's eyes found hers, and her response was a sigh. "I hear you."

Sam reached across the space between them and held Kirby's forearm. "We're tough old girls, K. We'll figure it out."

Kirby looked down at her forearm, then to Sam's hand, and when Sam tried to pull it away, she grabbed it, held onto it.

"Can I have bacon with my pancakes?"

"Do you still eat like a horse?"

"I'm blessed with a great metabolism," she admitted.

"Lucky you."

"What are you talking about? You still look great."

"That's because I eat rabbit food and exercise, not because of my genetic privilege."

"Whatever the reasons, they're working for you."

Sam felt herself blushing as if this was the first time someone had complimented her. Or was it flirting? Sam didn't think so. This wasn't the flirtatious Kirby she'd known, but a more poised, confident—if that was even possible—and mature version of that young woman she'd loved.

Sam swallowed. "So, breakfast?"

"Yes, okay. But please don't go to any trouble."

"No worries. Do you remember how to get there?"

She nodded.

"One house past my mom's old house. It's a bungalow, gray with stone pillars and a big front porch. Red door. Detached garage on the side."

"I'll find it."

"Then I'll see you tomorrow."

"Don't forget the bacon," Kirby said with a wink, and Sam walked away smiling.

After dinner, she called her boys, who were heading out for the evening, and then drove in the opposite direction of home as she dialed.

"Hi, Doc. How's everything?"

"It's all good, Frankie. How about with you?"

"I'm plannin' my trip to Vegas, baby. How about you? You gonna come out and cheer on my brother? That's somethin', gettin' an award for cancer research, huh?"

"Indeed it is. He's a brilliant doctor," Sam said with pride.

"Well, hey, I'm gonna' have to catch up with you in Vegas, 'cuz it's busy as usual on a Friday night. Whattaya need? Coupla pizzas for those strapping young boys?"

"I feel like such a jerk. I guess the only time I call you is when I need a pizza, huh?"

"Ah, but when I call you, you always come through. Who else has their own personal ER doc on speed dial?"

"And the way you and your staff swing kitchen knives, it's a good thing. You'd be out of business if you claimed all those stitches on your worker's comp."

Frankie laughed, but it was true. After Jim's parents died, staffing the restaurant had been quite a battle, with the workers cycling through every season. The rookies made frequent mistakes with the knives, and Frankie always called her when something happened. She'd usually meet him in the ER and sew everyone back together in exchange for a pizza and a few meatballs or stuffed shells—whatever was on the menu at Francesco's.

"Yeah, yeah. You sound like my wife. But anyway, I'm gettin' busy here. Tell me what you need."

"I think two par-baked pizzas should do it, if it's not too much trouble."

"I made meatballs today. I'll get you some of those, too."

"See you in half an hour."

Sam figured the pizza would be a nice gift for Kirby, who'd loved it when Jim had served them all those years ago. Back in town, she stopped at Stookey's before heading home. "Hi, Lillie," Sam greeted the teenager behind the counter when she walked in. "I'm just picking up a quart of frozen barbeque."

Stookey's had begun packaging their product to go, and Sam figured that would be another special treat for Kirby and her family to take home.

"Don't make too much of this, Samantha," she told herself aloud as she climbed back into her car. "It's just breakfast. With kids. No big deal."

At home she showered, then retreated to the sunroom with her dog and a book, which she didn't put down until she heard her sons. They spent ten minutes telling her about the party they'd been at, and then she told them about the breakfast plans.

"Cool," Charlie replied when he heard about meeting Kirby and her kids. "Maybe we'll be able to do orientation together or something."

And even though Danny had no motivation to get up a little early to meet them, he was equally enthusiastic. Sam kissed them both good night, and they promised not to stay up too late. Sure enough, she heard them heading to their rooms just a few minutes later.

It was difficult to clear her mind, and Sam couldn't help but think of seeing Kirby in the morning. Kirby was the only one who'd ever caused her to lose sleep, and even now, she still could. Sam thought of what she'd wear, and wondered how Kirby would be dressed, and how she'd wear her hair, and if she'd wear that baseball hat again. She always did rock a hat, and Sam smiled just thinking of it. She drifted off to sleep with that image in her mind.

Sam was up at eight and pulled her hair into a messy bun, then slipped on a pair of stretchy jeans and a faded old sweatshirt from Rehoboth Beach. After putting an entire pound of bacon into the pan to fry, she made her coffee and walked to the curb for the newspaper, reading the highlights while the bacon cooked. At nine she woke the boys, and five minutes later she was trying her best not to pace the floors to pass the time. After driving herself mad for another few minutes, she grabbed her book and headed to the front-porch swing, where she mostly gazed into the distance as she wondered if Kirby would show up.

Kirby had her cell-phone number, right? Surely she'd call if her family's plans had changed, wouldn't she? She was a class act, not the kind to stand her up, wasn't she? Sam glanced at her watch. It was twenty after nine. Should she call to confirm the plans?

And then, just when she thought she couldn't bear the wait a moment longer, a white Jeep pulled into her driveway, and Kirby waved to her from the passenger seat. She stood and waited at the top of the stairs for the trio to make their way from the car. Kirby got there first.

"What a lovely place," she said as she gazed at the landscaping. "You're still a gardener, huh?"

"Yeah. It's mindless work, and very gratifying. Good morning," she said to Sam's kids. "How are you guys today?"

"Great." Kyle took the lead. "We did a little shopping last night, so I'm ready for summer."

"The mall's sort of dead, huh?" Kirby asked.

Sam frowned as she nodded. "Sadly, it is."

"We ended up at Montage," she said.

"Come on in." Sam beckoned them up the steps and into the house. "That's a good place to shop."

"Mom took us for Valley Forge pizza," Kyle said as he bounded up the stairs.

Sam laughed. *Valley Forge, Old Forge, what's the difference?* "Really? Which restaurant?"

"Francesco's, of course," Kirby replied. "We saw Jim's brother Frankie."

"Did you remember him?"

"Sort of. I introduced myself and told him I'd been there with you once before, and he pulled out this laminated article about Jim winning some sort of award. He's like a proud papa."

"It's a pretty prestigious award. Did Frankie tell you I was there last night?"

"He did. I wondered if we might be having pizza for breakfast again."

Kirby wore her blank lawyer face, but Sam felt a blush explode across her own, and she turned to lead them into her house, hoping Kirby wouldn't notice. She and Kirby had had Francesco's pizza for breakfast in the early morning after they'd spent the night of her graduation making love. Kirby had given her the Tiffany pen, and Sam had told her she loved her. Sam sighed. It was the shortest love affair in history. Two days later Sam broke up with her.

"I still have the pen," she said a moment later when she regained her composure.

"Get out!"

Sam nodded as Charlie came up behind her. "Hey," he said.

Smiling, Sam introduced them all, and just as she finished, Danny appeared, and she did it all over again. They retreated to the kitchen, and then the four kids made their way to the sunroom while Sam and Kirby stayed back. "I threw a pizza in the freezer for you. So you could take it home."

"Really?" Kirby's smile stretched across her face.

"Yep. And I got you Stookey's to go, too." Sam told her how the restaurant had started selling takeout, then about Jim as she warmed up the griddle.

"Would you like coffee or tea?" Sam asked, remembering the night Kirby brought her coffee and doughnuts at work.

Kirby's smile told her she remembered, too. "I've graduated to coffee."

Sam put a cup in the Keurig and pressed the button.

"That's amazing about Jim. It sounds like he's done great things with his career."

"He has. He truly has."

"Did he ever come out?"

For a moment, Sam debated whether to out Jim, but it wasn't such a big deal now as it'd been back then. And even then, it was pretty obvious to anyone in the know. And this was Kirby, after all. "Yeah, he did. He's married to a very successful oral surgeon named Alberto."

"That's great. It looks like he could have made his fortune selling pizza in Old Forge, but he's saving the world, which is good, too."

"You know, when he comes home, he still tends bar. It's like his therapy. I go and hang out with him, he makes me specialty drinks, and I have to Uber home."

Kirby didn't flinch. "Uber's useful under such circumstances."

While they talked, Sam mixed the pancake batter and then drizzled a drop onto the griddle to test the temperature. When it sizzled, she poured eight pancakes, then loaded a tray with drinks, fruit, and condiments for Kirby to carry to the sunroom. A moment later she delivered the first stack of pancakes, and when the second was cooked to a golden hue, she joined everyone.

"Mom, guess where these guys are going when they leave?" Charlie asked.

"Work?" Sam asked.

"No. The beach. Why is it we're all working on the holiday weekend, and they're going to the beach?"

"Penance," Sam answered as she plopped a raspberry into her mouth.

"What kind of doctor are you?" Kaitlyn asked.

"ER. Hence the holiday weekend."

"That kind of sucks, but at the same time, it sounds cool," she said.

"That's a great description. I have a fun job, but weekends and holidays are tough."

"Don't forget overnight shifts," Danny added.

"Do you work every weekend?" Kyle asked. "Or do you think you could come to the beach some time?"

"Just one weekend a month. And a couple of holidays a year. But I don't know about the beach. We have a big trip planned already, so I don't think we can do another vacation this summer."

"You could stay with us. It'd be free."

Sam swallowed her smile as she watched Kirby shoot Kyle a stern look, which he ignored.

"We have plenty of room. My grandparents' condo has four bedrooms."

"That sounds wonderful, and I promise to talk to your mom about it when we get back from our trip."

"Where are you going?" Kaitlyn asked.

Charlie filled them in.

"Whoa! Yosemite!" Kyle said, and the conversation turned as they began talking about the upcoming vacation.

Sam and Kirby were mostly observers to the interplay between their children, but Sam also noted Kaitlyn checking her out. While she hadn't clued her sons in about Kirby, Kyle and Kaitlyn definitely understood that something significant had once happened between her and their mom. And while Kyle was trying to light a fire between them, Kaitlyn was more reserved, holding back her energy and collecting evidence before she rendered an opinion on the matter. Even with their opposite approaches, Sam liked them both for their obvious love for their mom.

And then, to her surprise, her sons melted her heart. "Our mom is amazing. She plans the best vacations," Charlie said.

"And then, when we get home," Danny added, "she makes us photo books."

Kirby smiled. "I love photo books."

"Me, too," Kaitlyn added.

They talked until the boys reluctantly left for work, and Sam walked them all to their respective cars, lagging back with Kirby as their children led the way to the front of the house.

"I'd say breakfast was a great success," Sam observed.

"Yes. Thank you so much for having us over. We should do it again, but I'll cook next time."

"Sounds good to me."

"Maybe at the beach."

Sam turned and their eyes met, and she saw happiness on Kirby's face, instead of the mask she'd so often worn when they were together. "Let's get through this legal business."

"Call me, or text me, or email me. Something."

"It's a crazy world, isn't it?" Sam asked.

"It's a lot easier than it used to be," Kirby said, and Sam knew she wasn't talking about methods of communication.

"Yes, it is."

CHAPTER TWENTY-TWO

Sam looked in the mirror and frowned. Her two weeks on vacation had been wonderful, but now that she was back home, she had a million things to do. Laundry. Gardening. Work. And this stupid deposition for the non-lawsuit.

She'd worked on her resume and emailed it to Kirby before the trip, and they'd set up a date to meet again and go over details and to stage a mock deposition. And then she'd sent a text to make sure Kirby approved of her resume. It was perfect, she told Sam, and she included a picture of her kids at the beach along with the message. And then Sam sent a picture of her boys at the Grand Canyon. And back and forth it went, at first once a day or so, and then a few times a day, until they were practically pen pals via text.

Now she was home, and despite jet lag, and all the other things she had to do, she was meeting with Kirby today. The real thing was in two weeks, so they couldn't put it off until later.

Their last business meeting had been very casual, and Sam was tempted to dress that way, but another part of her wanted to look really good. They were taping this, after all. And Kirby would be there.

Sam wasn't sure why that mattered, but it did, and she'd spent the last several weeks oscillating between visions of Kirby her lawyer and Kirby the mom, and memories of her former lover. She was almost giddy at times when she thought of her, so much so that Charlie and Danny commented on her good mood. It brought back something her mom had said years earlier, about how Sam had pranced around like a puppy.

Back then, Sam had been oblivious, unaware of how she'd been broadcasting her feelings. Now, she understood, even if her sons didn't. Seeing Kirby again, having the chance to talk with her, to meet her children, had Sam flying high. She had no idea if Kirby felt the same way, but something told her that she did.

In a little while, she'd be seeing her again, and perhaps she'd have a chance to find out.

Thirty minutes later, dressed in a skirt that accented her legs and a bold floral button-down shirt, Sam arrived at the Saxton Pavilion. As she had been on the prior occasion, Kirby was waiting for her.

"Welcome home," Kirby said.

Sam rolled her eyes. "I hate coming home. There's so much work to do." She groaned.

"We have to work, right? To pay for the vacations."

"I suppose so."

"Did your boys have fun? Bonding with their mom?"

It *had* been fun, and they *had* bonded. It was therapeutic. Sam had always been a hands-on mom, coaching T-ball and volunteering for PTA activities, chauffeuring the swim team and helping with school projects, so the separation from her sons as they grew more independent had crushed her. This trip had been healing, and they'd all be okay when they left home for good. Separate, but still strong. "Yeah. It was just what we needed."

Kirby looked at her in a way that said she understood, and the attention made Sam a little uncomfortable. "How are your kids?"

Kirby beamed. "Great. They're at the beach for the summer, hanging out with my parents."

"How does that work?" Sam asked, curious.

"What do you mean?" Kirby looked confused.

"When do you see them?"

"Oh. Well, my parents created a kind of dorm at their condo. They have bunk beds in every room, so it sleeps like twenty. People are always coming and going. I try to take Fridays off, or at least Friday afternoon, so I see them on the weekend. And sometimes, they get tired of their cousins and come home for a few days. Sometimes their other mom goes there to see them, or they come home for a few days to see her."

"Do they work?"

"No," she said, and then seemed to feel the need to explain. "I didn't work when I was their age, and I turned out okay. Besides, they'll be employed for the rest of their lives. Why rush it?"

It was a strange concept for Sam, who'd been working since she was sixteen. Even during med school, when she came home, she filled in shifts for the other techs in the ER. Yet she understood Kirby's point of view, and she supposed there was no right or wrong way to raise kids. "I get it. I'd probably spend the summer at the beach if my grandparents had a beach house."

"Back to your trip. Did you hike Half Dome?"

Sam frowned as she thought of Yosemite's most iconic peak. "No. I just didn't trust that the boys were experienced enough. Plus...do you know you have to win a lottery just for the opportunity to hike there? It's crazy. And then there's me. I don't know if I could have done it. That's a fourteen-hour day."

Kirby sighed. "Being almost fifty sucks, Sam. But if it makes you feel any better, my family didn't do it either. Our kids were too young. Do you have more pictures?"

Sam laughed. "That depends. Are you charging me by the hour?"

Kirby looked thoughtful. "I actually don't know the answer. But if I am, I'll give you the friends-and-family discount."

Sam looked at her phone, then back at Kirby. "Can we use your laptop? The pictures will be better."

Kirby pushed it toward Sam, and she logged into her Shutterfly account, then pulled up the photo book she'd been working on. Sitting beside Kirby, she pressed Play on the slide show.

"Wait a minute, hold on, pause this," Kirby demanded when the cover came up.

Without question, Sam paused the slide show.

"Sam, you drove an RV?" she asked, in obvious wonder as she pointed to the picture of her sitting behind the wheel of the motor home, leaning out the window, her sons standing below her.

"I did."

"Cross country?"

Shaking her head, Sam clarified the situation. "No, we flew to Las Vegas, because it's a direct flight, and rented it there. We camped."

Kirby looked at her, and Sam knew what she was thinking. They'd always had that connection. "You know about my backup plan as a trucker," she said softly. That had been their last time together. The last time they made love, before Sam's world fell apart. The next day she'd met Kirby at the park and ended their fledgling relationship.

"You're amazing," Kirby said, shaking her head.

Sam's face heated. "Anyway, may I continue?"

"You may, but I would like the authority to press that button and stop the slide show whenever I have questions."

"As long as you're not charging by the hour, authority granted."

Even though she could have, Kirby didn't stop the show. She simply watched and commented as the pictures changed before her. The boys relaxing in the club chairs in the RV, sitting by a fire, hiking, swimming. Mountains, trees, waterfalls, wildlife. From Las Vegas to the Grand Canyon to Sequoia to Yosemite. One hundred pages and almost three hundred pictures later, the show ended, and Kirby turned to her, admiration in her eyes.

"Can I ask you a question?"

"Sure."

"Where do you get your courage?"

"Whatta ya mean?"

Pursing her lips, Kirby seemed to struggle to form her words. "You just tackle things, Sam. You want something, and you figure out how to get it done."

The words hit her seemingly at the exact moment they hit Kirby, and they stared at each other. Kirby had to feel the same punch Sam did, based on her expression. "Most of the time," Sam said quietly.

"I didn't mean anything—"

"No, it's good. I understand perfectly."

They stared at each other for a moment. "Shall we get to work?" Kirby finally suggested.

"If we must," Sam sighed, the energy draining from her.

Laughing, Kirby moved around the table and sat so she was facing Sam. "Okay. I'm going to behave as I anticipate the other side's lawyer will. I'm not going to be a jerk, but I may bore you into a state of relaxation where you let down your guard and say something really incriminating. So, no matter how mundane my questions—or his or her questions—may seem, don't relax. Nothing is innocent in this situation. Does that make sense?"

"Perfect sense."

Kirby gave a slight nod. "Let's start with your resume."

Handing Sam a copy of the document she'd only just recently created, she reviewed Sam's credentials. "I see you did your residency at Newark Beth-Israel Medical Center. That was an emergency-medicine residency, correct?"

"Yes."

"So you have no formal training in pediatrics. Is that correct?"

"That is incorrect. Emergency medicine includes pediatrics. During my residency, I spent six months in the pediatric emergency department and an additional month in the peds ICU."

"I see. Thank you for clarifying that point. Is there any additional training in neurology, or neurosurgery, or infectious diseases that isn't mentioned on your resume?"

Sam thought back to her training almost twenty years ago. "I did spend a month on the neurology service. It was an elective."

"Okay, Doctor, thank you. On that neurology elective, how many cases of subdural empyema did you see?"

Sam suddenly felt defensive. "Subdural empyema is extremely rare, and most physicians will practice for a lifetime without ever seeing a case."

"Thank you for clarifying that point. Can you please answer the question? How many cases did you see prior to this one?"

"None," she said, unable to keep the impatience out of her voice.

Kirby leaned back in her chair and held up her hands. "Relax, Sam. Whatever you do, don't show the other attorney that he's getting to you. Keep your answers short. Less is better. Stick to facts. If you don't know an answer, simply say 'I don't know.' If you don't remember, say, 'I don't recall.' You could answer that question with either of those responses or a simple 'none.'"

Sam took a breath and reminded herself that this was just practice. Kirby was on her side. Kirby was trying to help her.

They continued the questions and answers, with better success. Sam practiced what she'd always taught her boys when they were in difficult situations. Take a breath and count to three before answering. The results were better. Kirby questioned her for an hour, asking about general protocols and specifics regarding the case. Sam used the responses Kirby had instructed her to use whenever she could and referred to the chart frequently.

After Kirby finished, she stood, poured a glass of ice water for

Sam, and handed it to her, then flipped on the light box on the wall, where a CT scan was hanging. Sam stood and took her place beside Kirby. They both leaned in for a closer look, and Sam suddenly became aware of Kirby's presence beside her. Shifting slightly, she forced herself to focus on the images.

"Can you spot it?" Sam asked.

"I have no idea how to read a CT scan. But a radiologist I consulted pointed it out to me."

"Don't tell me," Sam said. Even though she'd seen the images years earlier, and knew what she was looking for, she couldn't find the abscess.

"Uncle," Sam said, and Kirby pointed it out to her.

"That *is* small," she said, feeling humbled. So easy to miss. So fine a line between the right and wrong diagnosis, between life and death.

"Well, it wasn't small when he reached Philadelphia. You got him there just in time."

Sam absentmindedly fingered the angel dangling from her earlobe and said a prayer of thanks.

"So I have three problems with the chart," Kirby admitted as they returned to the conference table and sat, this time side by side.

"What?" Sam asked, alarmed.

"First, there's no electronic record of you looking at this CT scan when the patient was in the ER."

Sam bit her lip. After a moment, she shook her head. "I remember this case well, because the circumstances were so unusual. But I can't say if I saw the CT then or not. I do remember looking at it later and thinking it was amazing that the radiologist picked it up at all."

"Well, since there's no proof you ever saw it, on the first visit or the second, how should you answer the question?"

Sam thought about that for a moment, too. "What was the question?"

Kirby replied instantly. "Did you review the CT scan and relay those findings to the patient's parents?"

"I'm not qualified to read CT scans. I rely on the radiologist's interpretation to develop my diagnosis and treatment plan. And then I share them with the patient and family."

A big smile spread across Kirby's face. "Excellent, Sam. Or you can just say, 'I don't recall.'"

Sam beamed, relieved she was handling the interrogation so well and happy for Kirby's praise.

"So can you explain to me why your electronic fingerprint is on the CT scan images two weeks later?"

"What?" Sam asked. "I looked at it. I told you that. I think it was when I talked to his pediatrician after his surgery."

"The X-ray log shows that you looked at this film fifteen days after it was taken. What possible reason could you have for going into the chart to look at the images then?" Kirby's tone was just a little brisk, just enough to irritate Sam.

"I…" Sam paused as she scrambled for an answer. "I don't recall why I did that."

Kirby nodded. "Perfect. Because it doesn't really matter, but someone's going to ask you about it."

"I think that's why."

"But you're not sure. So your answer is…"

"I don't recall," Sam said calmly.

"Exactly," Kirby exclaimed.

"Got it."

"Okay, that's two problems addressed. The third is bigger."

"Okay," Sam said and turned, bracing herself for something catastrophic.

"The hospital keeps records of all outgoing phone calls. You have great documentation of everything in the record, including your conversation with the pediatrician. But there's no phone record that you ever called her. No call was placed to her office, her home, or her cell phone during the time frame this patient was in the ER."

"Oh, this is easy," Sam said as she breathed a sigh of relief and explained about Tyler's mother calling the pediatrician on her personal cell phone.

"You're kidding me. They're friends?"

"Apparently not any longer." Sam didn't even try to hide the sarcasm.

"I guess not."

"It is possible the plaintiff's attorney will challenge you on this, but very unlikely. There is no way to prove anything, either way, and as I see it, you had no reason to lie when you saw this boy the first time. He was really rather stable then. Fortunately, you finished his note within minutes of his leaving the ER, so it seems logical that you didn't fabricate a phone call to the pediatrician."

"Fabricate? You've got to be kidding."

"Oh, Sam, I wish I were. People do all kinds of crazy things to cover their asses when things go wrong, including falsifying medical records."

"But you don't think it'll be a problem for me?"

"This one question—this is one of the few times where you should elaborate. Discuss how unusual this was, and how you remember it precisely because it was out of the ordinary for the patient's mother to call their pediatrician on the cell phone. Does that make sense?"

"Perfect."

"Ready to go before the camera?"

"Yes," Sam said, but she actually wanted to leave that office. This process was exhausting. "Can we take a break? Maybe five minutes for some fresh air?"

Kirby nodded. "That sounds like a great idea. Mind if I join you?"

"Not at all."

They walked toward the exit, the same way she'd come in, chatting about the weather. Both had jobs that kept them inside, but with Sam having to work her share of evenings and overnight shifts, she had some days off. Kirby told Sam she worked during the day, so she liked to take her lunch on the bench outside her Harrisburg office building, just to get some vitamin D.

"This is nerve-racking, Kirby," Sam said after a moment. She'd practiced yoga and meditation for years, and had the ability to focus her mind and to push negative energy aside, but she was struggling with this deposition. She felt powerless.

"I can imagine. And there's nothing I can say to help, except that you need to hang in there. It'll be over soon."

"You really think this will be it? They won't sue me?"

"You won't know for sure until he turns twenty. He can still file a lawsuit until then. But it doesn't make sense that they'd sue you separately, at a later date. If they don't name you after your deposition, they're not going to name you at all. That's why this is so important. We have one chance to get it right."

Sam sighed. She'd have to worry about this for another year and a half.

Kirby stopped and looked at Sam. "I know you're worrying. But just remember how much you did for this boy. You saved his life. If you get sued, even if you lose, you know that. There is a young man—the same age as our sons—who most definitely wouldn't be alive today if you hadn't done exactly what you did thirteen years ago."

Sam wished Kirby's reassurance made her feel better, but it didn't. Yes, she knew she'd done everything right, but it was still nerve-racking to be in this position. "C'mon. Let's find that sunshine."

When they reached the sidewalk, Sam kept walking. "I want to show you something."

As soon as they'd passed the bulk of cars in the lot, Kirby stopped. "Wow, Sam. You still have it!"

"I do. I've been driving this car for more than thirty years."

Kirby walked around it, and Sam used the remote to open the doors.

"Classic-car plate, huh? Kirby said as she sat in the passenger seat and stroked the wooden dash. "This is real wood, isn't it, Sam?"

"I think it is. I haven't had to replace it. Yet. So I'm not sure."

"Good cars run forever, if you take care of them." She looked at Sam. "I'm not surprised you kept it."

"Since college, it's never really been my go-to car. I just bring her out on sunny days. But yeah...how could I get rid of her? My only dilemma is which son gets it when I die. They share a car now, so maybe I'll leave it to both of them."

"Remember I told you about my grandfather's Corvette? He still has it! But anyway, he told me about a guy who was buried in his 'Vette. You could be buried in your Benz."

Sam shook her head. "Wait a minute. Your grandfather's still alive?"

"Yeah. He's ninety," Kirby said as she sat back into the seat and turned to face Sam with a big grin.

"Tell me he doesn't actually drive the 'Vette."

"No, but he sits in it."

"You have great genes, Kirby."

"I do."

"I want to be cremated," Sam confessed.

"Makes things easier, doesn't it?"

Sam leaned back, too, and they both closed their eyes. The day was warm, and even with the car doors open, Sam quickly grew hot. Still, she was hesitant to move. It was peaceful in the car, and more bullshit awaited her back in Kirby's office. She'd sit in the car and sweat all afternoon if she could, rather than go inside.

"I'm glad we found each other again, Sam," Kirby said.

"We were good friends," Sam said, overwhelmed with relief that Kirby felt the same way.

"We were. And I'm sweating in my nicest suit. Let's go back in." Her tone was dry, and Sam sensed Kirby was deliberately trying to keep things light.

Sam locked the car, and they began walking, but she stopped to check out Kirby's suit. "It is a nice suit. Do you still hate dressing up, or have you gotten used to it?"

"I hate it with all my heart."

"Maybe we should wear sweats next time."

"Next time, a dozen lawyers will be in the room, and we'll be videotaping it. You should definitely not wear sweats."

"I love that I wear scrubs to work. It makes life so easy. I get up, pull on jeans and a shirt, slip into my flip-flops, and off I go."

"I hate you."

"Do you work full-time?"

"What? Full-time? Yes, of course. Remember—I get no sun." Kirby paused and turned to look at her. "What, wait. You work part-time?"

Sam nodded. "I decided long ago that I was going to live modestly and spend time with my kids. Now that they don't choose to spend any time with me, I have some extra to do the things I enjoy."

"Oh, yeah? Like what?"

"I work in my garden, and as you can probably tell, that takes a fair amount of my time. I still hike. Sometimes I kayak, but not as much as I used to. The ER doctor in me is always looking out for danger, and the river can be dangerous. I love to golf, but I'm not very good at it. They tell me I still have a softball swing."

"Once I started playing golf, I got hooked. I stopped playing softball."

"Me, too." Sam didn't mention that after she'd started medical school, she'd stopped playing softball because the sport reminded her too much of Kirby. "I guess you crush the ball, huh? You won the longest-drive prize."

"I do have power. I just wish I could putt a little better."

When they arrived back at Kirby's office, Sam used the restroom, and Kirby poured her a cold glass of water.

"Ready?" Kirby asked as she handed Sam the glass, suddenly all business again.

"Yeah."

"Okay. A few things. I know you're angry about being deposed. I mean, how can you not be? You did your job, took care of your patient, and now you're here. But think about this—who's in a worse position? You, who's having a bad day, or this boy, who has chronic headaches and seizures? Even if that's no one's fault, there's still an eighteen-year-old boy—the same age as our sons—who has these terrible problems. Invoke your internal Mama Bear and have empathy. That will show you care, which is huge. Huge. Control your anger, and keep your calm. Look professional, because if you do, that lawyer is not going to want to tangle with you."

Sam looked at Kirby with admiration, saw the professional she'd become, and was proud of her. Happy, too, that she'd done so well for herself in the world. And apparently, she was really a better person than Sam gave her credit for, because she showed absolutely no animosity toward Sam. Sam, with her perfect Catholic upbringing, who had to try so hard to forgive and forget when she was slighted, was shamed.

"You are such a good person, K."

Kirby blushed and cleared her throat. "Okay, so ditch the anger. Speak slowly and clearly. Look at the questioner, not the camera. If you need a sip of water, take it. We're going to do this for a few minutes, just until you get comfortable, and then we'll wrap it up. Okay? You ready?"

Sam nodded, and Kirby called in the camera crew and every other lawyer from the office, as well as a few secretaries and janitors. Hoping to prepare Sam for what the actual deposition would be like, Kirby filled every seat at the long conference table and had extras standing in the corners for added intimidation.

They began, with a large, bearded attorney questioning her. Sam remembered the rules and followed them, surprised when after only a few questions and answers, Kirby thanked everyone for their help and told Sam they were finished for the day.

"That was easy," Sam said.

"You're very good, Sam. First of all, I sense that you're confident. You did a good job with this patient, and you know that, and it helps. Second of all, you have a natural poise that helps tremendously. You're authentic. The opposing lawyer will see you and just say 'no way.' They're not going to pursue this."

"I hope not."

Kirby patted her on the back. "I'll see you in two weeks."

CHAPTER TWENTY-THREE

On the day of the deposition, Sam felt unbelievably calm. The ER schedule was already set, so she had to work, but the evening-shift doctor came in early so Sam could get to the Saxton Pavilion by three o'clock. After signing out her cases, she changed into her most serious suit, a chic blue Brooks Brothers pinstriped jacket and skirt, coupled with a vivid teal-colored shell.

The only jitters she felt had to do with seeing Kirby again. Without the excuse of vacation photos, Sam hadn't had a reason to reach out to her, and the line of communication between them seemed to be broken. Sam didn't know what it meant, and that worried her more than the damn deposition.

Kirby met her in the lobby of the same office where they'd met twice before and patted her shoulder. "You've got this," she said as they walked down the hallway together.

Suddenly Sam wanted to hug her, to pull her into the nearest closet and wrap her arms around Kirby, suck some of her strength and energy to help her through this. And maybe just to feel her, to feel that connection she was missing.

In spite of the preparation, Sam was still shocked as they entered the conference room. Just about every seat was occupied, with men and women in suits sitting behind laptops and briefcases and files stuffed with paper. None of them seemed to notice her arrival. A camera was set up on a tripod, and a woman wearing a headset stood behind it, preoccupied by her cell phone. The CT scan hung on the darkened X-ray light box, and a cart with pitchers of ice water and disposable cups stood off to the side.

Wanting to look like she had some control, Sam walked to the cart and casually poured herself a glass of ice water, then poured another for Kirby. Then she had a seat, beside Kirby, and squeezed the tissue in her hand, drying her palms.

Kirby leaned in to whisper in her ear and the intimacy caused Sam to shiver. "Remember. *I don't recall* for anything you don't remember or think you shouldn't answer. Ask to talk to me if you have a question. Refer to the medical record if you need to. Now I'm going to let him sit for a minute, and you just think about Yosemite, and then we'll get started."

After the minute, Kirby, addressing no one in particular, cleared her throat. "It's after three. I'd like to get started."

Instantly, the laptops fell quiet, and the phones shut down as every eye in the room turned to her. A man, petite and clean shaven and probably not more than thirty years old, stood from the seat across from her and offered his hand. After introducing himself as the plaintiff's *lead* attorney, they began.

Sam raised her right hand and pledged to be truthful, and then he started with his questions. After he finished dissecting her resume, he progressed to the chart, and Sam had a better appreciation for just how well Kirby had prepared her. They were at it for an hour before there was a curve ball, a question about the boy's medical record. "Were you aware that the child was already taking an antibiotic when he came to the ER?"

After referring to the chart, where Sam noted the antibiotic, she told him she was. "So you were aware that the child had seen the pediatrician the day before?"

Again Sam looked at the chart and saw that reference. "Yes."

"Did you look into the electronic record, which was available to you, to review the pediatrician's exam findings from the day before?"

Sam could find no documentation in the chart that she'd reviewed the pediatrician's note. "I don't recall."

"Well, luckily, the computer log has a better memory," he said with a broad smile. "No one, including you, entered that note, on either of his trips to the ER. Now, Doctor, with a child who you thought was so sick, shouldn't you have read his chart a little more carefully?"

Sam might have been put off by his demeanor, or the surprise question, but she wasn't. Confident that she'd followed protocol, provided good care, and done her very best, she answered quite calmly. "I review old records when I need to. In this case, I didn't need to. What I needed was a spinal tap, which the parents refused. I needed to admit him, which the parents also refused."

"So, you felt the patient needed testing, and the parents didn't understand the importance of that testing and made an error in judgment. Isn't there a protocol in place for such situations? Couldn't you have taken that child into protective custody and contacted Children and Youth Services?"

Sam took a deep breath, and in spite of her nerves, her answer was clear. Just as she and Kirby had rehearsed. "To my knowledge, there is no such protocol. In my twenty years of experience, I've never seen that happen. I think I would have needed another physician to agree with my plan. And since the pediatrician, who knew the child well, was against admission, I don't feel I had grounds to do that."

He didn't look surprised by her answer, or disappointed. He was as good, or as well prepared, as Kirby. He moved on. The questions became easier, because they'd rehearsed, and it seemed to her that he almost gave up. He'd gone at her with fastballs, and when he realized Sam wasn't going to strike out, that she wasn't intimidated, and that she'd been well prepared, he realized he wasn't going to win this fight. It became a formality at that point, and a little after five o'clock, he suddenly looked up and announced that he had no further questions.

Sam was shocked. "That's it?"

It was Kirby who responded. "That's it! You did it."

Sam took her bag, and Kirby walked her down the hallway. At the end, they stopped, and Sam looked into Kirby's eyes. "Thank you," she said.

"I think we're done, Sam. You nailed that, and I don't think there's any way they're going after you. Congratulations."

"Thanks." Sam felt such relief, her legs almost felt weak.

"Do you have plans tonight?" Kirby hesitated for a second. "We could get dinner, to celebrate."

Sam felt an altogether different sense of relief. Deep down, she'd been waiting for Kirby to ask her that question since their first meeting. Ever since they saw each other, for the second first time, Sam had felt the energy of their connection coursing through her. Her answer required no thought. "I'd love to."

"What's good around here?"

"Rustic Kitchen, at the casino."

"Small world. That's where I'm staying. Half an hour?"

Sam felt the weight of the day—of all the days since she'd walked into Julie's office and learned about her deposition—ease from her shoulders. If it weren't Kirby, and she wasn't facing the possibility of Kirby leaving forever, Sam would have gone home and curled up with a good book. And now, as she began to relax, she might actually read it. It was Kirby, though, and the thought of never seeing her again was much worse than Sam's fatigue. She needed a shower, and a change of clothes, and she'd be ready to go. "Actually, could we make it a little later? I'd like to get out of this suit and into something more comfortable."

Kirby sighed. "I'm with you." Glancing at her watch, she puckered her lips. "Six thirty?"

"See you then."

Sam drove home singing to the radio, and after showering and slipping into jeans and a light sweater, she walked into the restaurant right on time. She found Kirby sitting at the bar, watching the sports news.

"Hey," she said, feeling the same joy she always felt when she saw her. She had changed clothes as well and looked relaxed in a Henley and jeans.

Turning, Kirby appraised her. "Hey."

"What are you drinking?" Sam asked.

"Just water. I didn't want to start without you. The table's waiting for us, but they're not crowded, so we can have a drink first, if you'd like."

Sam moaned and plopped onto the barstool. "I'd like."

"Champagne?"

"Nah. They make a wicked pomegranate martini."

Kirby smirked. "You're so girly."

Sam swallowed her retort. *You used to like that.* Her response was much safer. "What do powerful Harrisburg lawyers drink?"

The bartender arrived, and Kirby placed their drink order. "A pomegranate martini, and a Ketel and tonic, with a splash of lime."

"I see," Sam said. "You're all grown up."

"*We're* all grown up." Kirby winked.

"I'm really happy that you asked me for dinner."

"I felt as if we should talk," she said softly.

Sam nodded. "Me, too. I've been waiting half my life to talk to you again." She paused and turned in her stool so she was facing Kirby, and put her hand on Kirby's forearm. "I want to apologize, Kirby."

Tilting her head, Kirby shrugged, and the hint of a frown appeared on her face. "For being straight?"

Sam shook her head and looked into the dark pools of Kirby's amazing eyes. "No. For not being brave enough to be gay. It took me a long time—almost ten years—to realize that I couldn't bury my sexuality. By then, I'd hurt a lot of people I cared about. Doug, who I not only married but had children with. My mom, my friends—because I lied to them and avoided them, so I didn't have to tell them the truth. But mostly, you. I treated you horribly, and I've regretted it for the past twenty-seven years."

Their drinks arrived. "Talk about timing," Kirby said as she sipped her cocktail.

"What, no toast?" Sam asked.

Kirby sipped again, then raised her glass.

"Thank you for today. Thank you for twenty-seven years ago," Sam said softly.

Kirby rested her head on her palm as she leaned into the bar and turned to Sam. "So, let me see if I have this straight. You're not straight?"

"No," Sam said softly.

"You're gay."

"Yes."

"You're sure?"

"One hundred percent."

Kirby raised an eyebrow. "One hundred percent sure, or one hundred percent gay?"

"Stop it," Sam said playfully, but Kirby's response was all business.

"I think it's a fair question."

Sam sighed, and it turned into a chuckle. "Okay, you're right. I am one hundred percent sure that I'm one hundred percent gay." Sam sighed. "Would you like the whole story?"

"I can't wait."

Sam sipped her martini as she tried to frame her thoughts. "Where do I start?" she asked herself out loud. How did you cover half a lifetime over the course of one dinner?

"How about two days after Memorial Day, 1993?"

"Hmm," Sam said. That was the last time they saw each other, and apparently, Kirby remembered the day as well as Sam did. What an awful time, with her mother near death, and extracting that awful promise from her at a time when Sam was so vulnerable. Then the surgery and cardiac rehab afterward. They ended up canceling her graduation party, and Sam almost delayed medical school. In the end, she went to Philly as scheduled, and buried herself in what she did best—studying. Studying helped her deal with her fears about her mom and helped her grieve the self-imposed loss of Kirby. And time, of course, did the rest.

"You know, Kirby, it's still kind of hard to talk about that. Would you mind if I fast-forward a little?"

Kirby nodded and squeezed Sam's hand supportively. "Whatever you want to share. I'm just really happy to be here with you."

"So you know, I moved to Philly for medical school."

"You moved in with Lori and Jim, and all of Uncle Tony's furniture."

"I think it was Uncle Louis, but yes."

"How'd that go?"

"It was difficult, but we made it. We split up after our second year, but we're all still friends. It was my fault. I'm an only child and extremely difficult to live with."

"Good to know, about the living-with-you thing, in case I'm ever homeless or anything. And good that you're still friends."

"I really didn't date in medical school, but in my third year I was working on the pediatrics service, with this really great resident. Click, click, click. I ended up in bed with her, but it was sort of the same situation as with you. I just didn't want to deal with the truth. I finished my month, and off I went. Never saw her again."

"I detect a pattern here."

Sam bit her lip. "Yes. It wasn't like with you…truthfully, I think she was just a player. It was fine. Except…it wasn't, you know? I didn't want to be gay. That was the bottom line. So I just kind of gave in to the heterosexual pressures, and I married Doug. I ran into him at the church picnic, of all places, and we started talking. Doug seemed like a good idea at the time. Right after graduation."

Sam looked at Kirby, whose face was a big blank. "I know it sounds stupid. It was cowardly. I was just overwhelmed, I think. Does that make sense?"

"Yeah. Strangely, it does."

They both sipped and Sam continued. "Residency is everything you imagine it to be. Exhausting. My third year, first month, I was assigned to the trauma service. Two first-years were under my wing—Glen and Tara. Glen came out to me about five seconds after we met, and we had a ball together. Tara and I clicked. I had a huge crush on her, but at the same time, I knew Tara wasn't…right for me, I guess. But she made me think, mostly because I loved the way I felt when I was with her. I was happy. Just like I'd felt with you. And I was definitely not happy with Doug."

"So what happened with Tara?"

Sam shook her head. "Nothing sexual, but she's one of my best friends. I introduced her to one of my classmates, and she ended up marrying him. They live here in the area. She works in the ER with me."

"That's cool. So you're over your crush?"

"Oh, yeah. But I realized there was a pattern to my…feelings? Or crushes. I don't know what to call it. I was just attracted to women, and no matter who I married or what I did, I just finally realized that wasn't going to change."

"So what did you do?"

"I did what I thought was the right thing. I told Doug I'm gay. He pretty much laughed at me and talked me into having a baby."

"You're kidding me."

"Nope," Sam said, and took another sip. It was her life, and even she couldn't believe it. What had she been thinking? "Wow. I'm going to need another martini soon."

"How about we get our table?" Kirby suggested instead.

Sam left money for the tab, and they asked the hostess to seat them. She took them to a corner booth big enough for four, yet they sat intimately close to each other. After she left them, Kirby leaned forward. "Continue," she commanded.

Sam smiled. "Where was I?"

"The baby."

"Ah, yes. He reminded me how much I wanted children and convinced me that if I was gay, I would never have children, and that if I had a child with him, I would be content. My attraction to women would go away because I'd be too busy to be gay. That strategy had worked before, for a while, so I thought I'd try it again. That was my third and final year of residency, and I figured it was good timing. If I got pregnant then, the baby would have been born just as I was finishing in June. As it turned out, it happened in May, and I started my job back here in July, then had my boys in February. I loved them, but I still wasn't happy. Doug and I separated when they were a year old."

"Wow."

"It was really for the best. I was sad, Kirby, but not depressed, because I loved my kids and my job. I just didn't want to pretend I was with Doug. I didn't necessarily want to be out as a lesbian, but I didn't want to pretend to be married, either."

"So, have you ever dated women?" Kirby asked, as if she didn't believe her.

"Yes, of course. Many."

"Many?" Kirby asked, her jaw hanging open.

"Well, probably not as many as you, but yes. I refuse to get too serious. I've never lived with anyone, but I've brought some of my girlfriends around to meet my boys."

"So you're out to your kids."

"Yes. How could I hide that part of me?" That had never been an option for Sam. Her goal was to raise well-rounded, open-minded children, and she had.

"How about your mom? Did you ever come out to her?"

Sam puffed out her cheeks and blew out a long breath. "Sort of."

"Sort of?"

Sam told her about the conversation she had with her mom when she was thinking about divorcing Doug. "Then, when the boys were about ten, I was dating a teacher, a friend of Teddy. Teddy is my own private dating app. I really liked this woman, and we'd been together about six months, and I wanted to go away with her. So I talked to my mom. And before I could actually say the words and tell her the truth about my relationship with Yvonne, she stopped me. 'There are some things better left unsaid,'" she told me. "And that was that."

"So she knew."

"Yes. And she knew about you, Kirby. I never told her. She just knew."

Kirby sighed. "Moms know, right?"

"Of course we do." Sam picked up her menu. "We should order. I'm famished." She placed a hand across her forehead. "Or maybe drunk."

They spent a minute talking about the menu, and then their server checked on them and took their orders. They both declined another martini and instead accepted her offer of water.

"It's a remarkable story, Sam. Thanks for sharing it with me."

"I don't know how remarkable it is. I regret a lot of things, you know? But ultimately, if I hadn't done the stupid things I did, I wouldn't have my sons. So I suppose I wouldn't have done anything differently at all."

"You're right. In the end, we're where we're supposed to be."

Suddenly her recent conversation with Doug came to mind. "Would you be betraying a confidence if you tell me what happened to Harry Johnson?"

Kirby looked perplexed at the seemingly unrelated comment and was quiet for a moment before she answered. "Something with his heart valve. He needed surgery."

Sam laughed. "How about that?"

"About what?"

"K, my mom's heart valve tore us apart. And good ole Harry's brought us back together."

Kirby stared at her for a moment. "I guess we're meant to meet again, Sam."

"I think so," she said softly as she sat back to just stare. It was like the bears on the mountain, another sign.

"Is he doing okay?"

"He's great. Retiring, so he can enjoy life a little."

"So it worked out for everyone, then." Sam was happy to know that. Her mother had lived twenty years after her surgery, and nineteen of them were good ones.

"It did. So, you're still friends with Teddy?" Kirby asked.

"Since ninth grade."

"Did she ever finish college?"

Sam pursed her lips. "She did. And she worked for one of the hospitals for a while before she was invited back to the family business."

"She looked good. Is she married?"

"Interested?"

Kirby's eyes grew darker. "Not in Teddy."

Sam shrugged. "Well, you really should make amends. She's grown up, and she's a good person."

Kirby nodded. "I hear you. I've been thinking about it since you said something at the golf outing. We'll see. I just don't know what the point is."

"Fair enough," Sam said as she sipped her water. "Tell me about you. I know you moved back to Harrisburg—Teddy told me she was at your going-away party. You have kids, and you're a lawyer. What else?"

Kirby nodded. "That about sums it up."

Sam gave her a stern look, and she continued.

"The bank had an opening, so I transferred. Applied to law school and got in the next year. I met a wonderful woman, and we moved in together, had the kids after we graduated. She works for a nonprofit, and I worked in malpractice defense. After fifteen years together, we decided to go our separate ways. Just like you...I really never left home."

"We've traveled all over but love to crash at my parents' beach house. I tried to be a hands-on mom. I coached Kait's softball team and Kyle's T-ball, taught them both to golf. I've served as housekeeper, taxi driver, and chef until just recently. Now I feel kind of lonely—after going full speed for twenty years, no one needs me anymore."

"I've felt the same way. We're pretty pathetic," Sam said as she turned to Kirby. However, Sam had to admit that since seeing Kirby again, and reconnecting with her, the sadness she'd been feeling for months had dissipated.

"Nah. We're just good parents. Are you any different than yours?"

Sam thought of her mom, and of all the great things she could have remembered, she always seemed to come back to that one defining moment. "I would accept my kids no matter what."

"It's so different now. Easier for us, easier for our parents. And don't forget what you just told me, Sam. If you hadn't done things the way you did—because your mother did the things she did—you wouldn't have your sons."

"I know. I thought life would get easier, but it hasn't. I just have different problems to solve. I still need my parents, and I'm almost fifty. I wish they could just give me some advice."

"I talk to my parents all the time. They tell me I'll never figure my kids out."

"Really?" Sam asked, amazed.

"I think teenagers are always on a mission to defy their parents, no matter what era they live in."

"Not me. I was a good kid."

Kirby smirked. "Oh, I seem to remember a little defiance in you."

Sam thought for a moment before replying, but other than her dalliance with Kirby, she'd never done anything off-script. And then, when her mother had asked her to stop seeing Kirby, she had. She'd followed the rules until she just couldn't do it anymore.

"Maybe one or two episodes of defiance."

"When did your mom die?"

"Six years ago."

"That must be hard, being an orphan."

"My mom was eighty, and she was failing. Sometimes, I see a patient who was born the same year she was. Very few of them are happy and healthy. They're in nursing homes or dependent on their children. She wasn't. She lived in her own house until the day she died. How can I be sad about that?"

The server brought their food—half a dozen appetizers they'd agreed upon—and Sam dug into a meatball as her stomach growled. She was famished. They both filled their plates and nibbled as they talked.

"It's good about your mom. I worry so much about my parents."

"Well, you're very lucky, Kirby, that you still have them."

"I know it." Kirby paused, then reached across the table and squeezed Sam's hand. "It's so nice to see you, Sam. You're still as easy to talk to as you were back then."

"I'd like to say I haven't changed much, but I know that's not true."

"You seem to be the same person, if you ask me."

"I guess I am, at heart. I still eat Stookey's."

"I'll never forget the first time you took me there. I was so hungry, and you kept asking me questions, and I didn't want to be rude, so I was taking these little nibbles of the sandwich, while my stomach was growling."

Sam covered her mouth in shame. "How awful! I'm so sorry. I just wanted to know everything about you."

"It seemed like we could have talked forever."

"It seems like we still can."

Kirby looked around the room, leaned back in the booth, and then focused on Sam. She swallowed, then wiped her mouth. "So, you said you've dated many women."

Raising her palms, Sam offered the hint of a smile. "I had making up to do. Think of the years I lost, pretending to be straight."

"No judgment. I was just wondering if you're seeing anyone now."

Sam swallowed. This was more than a casual question, and Sam knew it. The chemistry between them was magical, as it had always been. Kirby had sucked the breath out of her then, and she did now as well, and Sam wanted nothing more than to take her upstairs to her room and spend the rest of the night in Kirby's bed.

How was that possible?

"As it happens, I am not seeing anyone at present."

"Hmm," Kirby said softly. "As it happens, neither am I."

Suddenly, nerves and guilt flooded Sam, and she shifted uncomfortably in her chair. "Kirby, would you really want to see me again? Take that chance, after the way I treated you last time?"

Kirby leaned forward and rested her chin on the bridge made of her interlaced fingers. "You told me you'd thought about me over the years. I thought about you, too. Why we clicked. It was amazing then, and it still is."

Sam studied her. "You're very brave, Kirby."

"You're worth it, Sam. And what I said earlier is true for me as well as you. If we hadn't gone our separate ways back then, we wouldn't be where we are now. And it sounds like it's been an okay trip for both of us."

Sam thought about her wonderful life. Her only regrets had been about the people she hurt. Her mom, who never spoke to Samantha about issues of sex or sexuality, but welcomed every one of her *good friends* into her home for holidays and birthday celebrations. Doug, who was exactly where he wanted to be in life—married to his job but with the benefit of two accomplished sons to distract him on occasion.

Her straight friends—who she avoided for years while she was secretly dating women—had forgiven her years ago. And it appeared that Kirby, who was always so sweet and kind and caring—that she forgave her, too. She had no one left to feel guilty about. Maybe it was time to let the guilt go.

"It has."

"So, since neither one of us is in a relationship, maybe we've met again when we were supposed to. Whatever forces are at work here, ruining heart valves and such, knew this was a better time for us."

Sam thought back to that other meeting. Her attraction to Kirby had been intense—but she hadn't been ready to handle it. Not with all the other things happening in her life. Life had thrown her a curveball in the form of Kirby, and she'd struck out.

"That was definitely *not* the right time—my graduation, planning my move, starting medical school. My mom's illness. My dad's car. I had so much on my mind that dealing with my sexuality was just too much. I was overwhelmed, Kirby, and felt like I might fall apart. The only way I could keep my sanity was to withdraw into my comfort zone—and I was not comfortable with being gay."

"I get it."

"That's a relief, you know? Because I've felt awful about it."

"You shouldn't have."

"I told myself I wasn't *really* in love with you, but I was lying." Sam sighed and, tilting her head as she stared at Kirby, offered her a slow smile.

"I told myself the same thing," Kirby said, reaching across the table to touch just the tips of Sam's fingers. Her own fingers suddenly tingled from that soft touch.

"Really?"

"What could I do? You were so distraught about your mom and this promise you made to her. I couldn't pressure you. I just had to accept the situation. And Teddy filled me in on some details, so I knew you were having a hard time. I wish I could have been there for you, but I suspected that having me there would have been more stressful for you than if I stayed away. So, I stayed away."

Sam sighed. "It was the right thing."

"But very hard."

"Yes, for sure."

"For a while, I thought you would reach out to me. After about a year, I accepted that a relationship with me just wasn't what you needed, and I kind of gave up on it."

Sam felt awful all over again. "I'm sorry."

Kirby held up her hands. "No, no. No reason to apologize again. You never told me to wait it out, or anything like that. You said you needed to focus on your mom, and on school, and didn't have time to date. I guess I was just...hopeful."

Sam wanted to apologize, again, but Kirby stopped her. "We're both okay, right?"

Sam nodded.

"Did you ever google me? Like years later? Just to see if I was still alive?"

"No," Sam admitted. She'd thought about it, though.

"Really? 'Cuz I googled you."

"You probably didn't find me. I changed my name before Google was invented, I think. But I didn't google you. What was the point? I wasn't going to call you."

"So if we hadn't accidentally run into each other..."

"Kirby, I thought you hated me for what I did. I'm not brave enough to take a chance like that, to just call you out of the blue."

"You're very brave, Sam. Anyone who is living their life openly is brave. Are you brave enough to go on a date with me?"

Sam looked at Kirby. Even at fifty, she was still beautiful. And she still had a beautiful heart. "This is a date."

Kirby looked at the table of food and then at Sam. "Good point. Are you brave enough to come back to my room with me?"

Sam gasped at Kirby's boldness, but it was exactly what she wanted. It was what she'd always wanted, but she'd lacked the courage to take it, even when it was offered so freely. Not now. She didn't know how this would work, with them living in separate cities and parenting four children and navigating two careers, but she'd figure it out. They'd figure it out, together.

Smiling, she reached out, took Kirby's hand and squeezed it. "Yeah. I am. One hundred percent."

About the Author

Jaime Maddox is the author of seven novels with Bold Strokes Books and was awarded the Alice B. Lavender Certificate for her debut novel, *Agnes*. She has co-authored a book on bullying with her son, Jamison, and written an unpublished children's book about her kids' uncanny ability to knock out their teeth. A native of Northeastern Pennsylvania, she still lives there with her wife and twin sons. Her best times are spent with them, hanging out, baking cookies, and rebounding baskets in the driveway. When her back allows it, she hits golf balls, and when it doesn't, she does yoga. On her best days, she writes fiction.

Books Available From Bold Strokes Books

16 Steps to Forever by Georgia Beers. Can Brooke Sullivan and Macy Carr find themselves by finding each other? (978-1-63555-762-6)

All I Want for Christmas by Georgia Beers, Maggie Cummings & Fiona Riley. The Christmas season sparks passion and love in these stories by award-winning authors Georgia Beers, Maggie Cummings, and Fiona Riley. (978-1-63555-764-0)

From the Woods by Charlotte Greene. When Fiona goes backpacking in a protected wilderness, the last thing she expects is to be fighting for her life. (978-1-63555-793-0)

Heart of the Storm by Nicole Stiling. For Juliet Mitchell and Sienna Bennett a forbidden attraction definitely isn't worth upending the life they've worked so hard for. Is it? (978-1-63555-789-3)

If You Dare by Sandy Lowe. For Lauren West and Emma Prescott, following their passions is easy. Following their hearts, though? That's almost impossible. (978-1-63555-654-4)

Love Changes Everything by Jaime Maddox. For Samantha Brooks and Kirby Fielding, no matter how careful their plans, love will change everything. (978-1-63555-835-7)

Not This Time by MA Binfield. Flung back into each other's lives, can former bandmates Sophia and Madison have a second chance at romance? (978-1-63555-798-5)

The Found Jar by Jaycie Morrison. Fear keeps Emily Harris trapped in her emotionally vacant life; can she find the courage to let Beck Reynolds guide her toward love? (978-1-63555-825-8)

Aurora by Emma L McGeown. After a traumatic accident, Elena Ricci is stricken with amnesia, leaving her with no recollection of the last eight years, including her wife and son. (978-1-63555-824-1)

Avenging Avery by Sheri Lewis Wohl. Revenge against a vengeful vampire unites Isa Meyer and Jeni Denton, but it's love that heals them. (978-1-63555-622-3)

Bulletproof by Maggie Cummings. For Dylan Prescott and Briana Logan, the complicated NYC criminal justice system doesn't leave room for love, but where the heart is concerned, no one is bulletproof. (978-1-63555-771-8)

Her Lady to Love by Jane Walsh. A shy wallflower joins forces with the most popular woman in Regency London on a quest to catch a husband, only to discover a wild passion for each other that far eclipses their interest for the Marriage Mart. (978-1-63555-809-8)

No Regrets by Joy Argento. For Jodi and Beth, the possibility of losing their future will force them to decide what is really important. (978-1-63555-751-0)

The Holiday Treatment by Elle Spencer. Who doesn't want a gay Christmas movie? Holly Hudson asks herself that question and discovers that happy endings aren't only for the movies. (978-1-63555-660-5)

Too Good to be True by Leigh Hays. Can the promise of love survive the realities of life for Madison and Jen, or is it too good to be true? (978-1-63555-715-2)

Treacherous Seas by Radclyffe. When the choice comes down to the lives of her officers against the promise she made to her wife, Reese Conlon puts everything she cares about on the line. (978-1-63555-778-7)

Two to Tangle by Melissa Brayden. Ryan Jacks has been a player all her life, but the new chef at Tangle Valley Vineyard changes every-thing. If only she wasn't off the menu. (978-1-63555-747-3)

Best Practice by Carsen Taite. When attorney Grace Maldonado agrees to mentor her best friend's little sister, she's prepared to confront Perry's rebellious nature, but she isn't prepared to fall in love. Legal Affairs: one law firm, three best friends, three chances to fall in love. (978-1-63555-361-1)

Home by Kris Bryant. Natalie and Sarah discover that anything is possible when love takes the long way home. (978-1-63555-853-1)